LEADS & LYNXES

TERRA HAVEN CHRONICLES BOOK 1

REBECCA CHASTAIN

For my sister, Sara,
who taught me to identify my dreams,
then go for them with everything I've got.

ACKNOWLEDGMENTS

Reach around yourself and grab your shoulder blades. Squeeze tight. That's the closest I can get to sending you my hug of thanks for picking up this book! It means the world to me that you read my books. I couldn't do this without you!

If you ever write a fantasy novel and also have the opportunity to pick the absolute best lineup for your beta reader team, you can't go wrong with Renea Kania, Sarah Gibson, Diana Blick, Scott Ferguson, and Rebecca Moore. As always, this book was made better thanks to their thoughtful input and gentle criticism. I'd also like to thank Carrie Andrews and Crystal Watanabe, whose astute edits and expert polish on the final draft made this book shine.

Finally, this book would not be in your hands without my husband, Cody. To be clear, he didn't brainstorm, outline, write, edit, or even format the book. He did nothing. *Except* . . . Every time I grumbled, *I know how the series ends, but what is supposed to happen in* THIS *book,* he reassured me I would figure it out. Every time I moaned about scenes I had to delete, he reminded me this was part of my process. And every time I danced around the house after a good day of writing, he celebrated with me.

Cody believed in me, and that is everything.

Constructive Elements

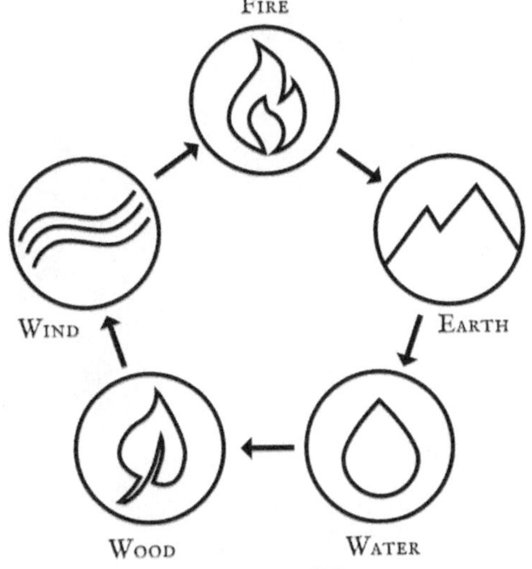

Destructive Elements

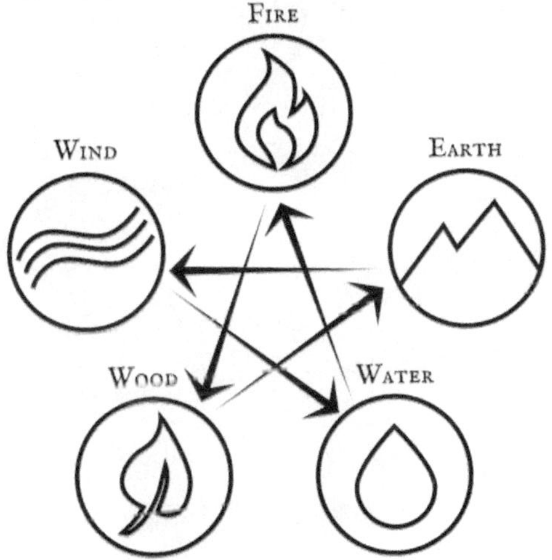

1

———————

I craned to see the everlasting tree through the press of people, a familiar excitement humming through my veins. Any day now, the tree would release its seeds, and I would be one of the thousands of people to receive one. I still couldn't believe my luck. My entire life could be changed by this one event, and anticipation made me jittery. If I could have, I would have jogged, but the crowds confined me to a sedate crawl.

"Coming through," a man bellowed, shoving a floating cart of manure ahead of him.

I shuffled to the edge of the dirt road with the rest of the foot traffic, squeezing past an ox-drawn cart loaded down with what appeared to be half a village's belongings. When an opening appeared between a packhorse and a woman carrying baskets of hooded cockatrices, I darted into it, veering down a narrow alley. Audrey followed close on my heels, one hand latched on to my shirt so we didn't become separated. A fellow journalist with decades of experience, Audrey served as my temporary boss while we were on assignment at the everlasting tree, but she had taken to using me as a guide in the mornings.

"I swear this road didn't exist yesterday," she grumbled. "You would tell me if you were lost, right, Kylie?"

"I know where we are." I envied Audrey's ability to scan any crowd and pluck out the one person with an interesting story, but she had no sense of direction. Or maybe it was Seed Town that made her roam in circles.

Rumors of the everlasting tree's imminent bloom had sparked a migration, and the temporary town had sprung up overnight in the valley below the tree. Every day, the town grew as people flooded in from across the continent for this rare, once-in-a-lifetime experience. If Audrey and I hadn't been here almost two weeks while the town built up around us, I might have found the haphazard dirt roads zigzagging between tents difficult to navigate, too.

"We are headed straight for the marketplace," I assured Audrey. "Or as straight as anything is around here. See, there's Baker Lang's pavilion, and at the next junction will be the blacksmith you drool over, even if he is young enough to be your—"

"Fine. You know where we are. No need to rub it in." She gave me a reproachful glare that would have been more effective if her gaze hadn't drifted up the street. Patting wayward strands of her gray-streaked hair back into its tight braid, she pinned them in place with pinches of air.

I grinned, prepared to tease her more just to watch her blush, but a gaggle of kids thundered past, raising a cloud of dust. I held my breath and settled for poking Audrey in the ribs when her steps lagged in front of the blacksmith's tent.

The delicious aroma of fresh-baked bread hung in the still air, and my mouth watered even though we had already eaten. I considered stopping to purchase a snack from Lang, but the line stretched eleven people deep, and I didn't want to delay. The mayor had been spotted at the marketplace this morning, and if I didn't hustle, she would disappear before I got my chance to interview her.

"Do you think the tree will bloom today?" Audrey asked.

We took turns posing this question to each other every day, and I gave Audrey the same answer she had given me yesterday. "If not today, then tomorrow."

Everlasting trees didn't release seeds yearly. Decades, sometimes centuries, could pass between one everlasting tree's bloom and the next, but some rules of nature could not be denied. The sun chased spring into summer, baking the landscape and drying all the tree's seedpods. Eventually, the heat would burst the seeds open, and everyone gathered would finally get their answers.

I checked the everlasting tree again. Perched atop a slight rise, it dominated the northern horizon of the valley, and its massive canopy could be viewed from anywhere in the town. No other tree in the vicinity—no other tree on this half of the continent—rivaled the everlasting tree in size. Its huge trunk would require fifteen people to circle it, and the top of its highest branches could be seen for miles. Shaped like a cross between an oak tree and a cottonwood, the everlasting tree's branches started over thirty feet in the air and twisted and curled as far outward as they did up. Glossy emerald leaves decorated its limbs, and at the tip of every twig rested a seed—enough for everyone in the town to receive one; enough for everyone on the continent, most likely. My mind boggled at the thought.

"Are you sticking with your question?" Audrey asked. "There's still time to think of something more . . . meaningful."

I rolled my eyes. I didn't want to have this conversation

again. Fortunately, we had reached the hub of the town's commerce, and I could pretend the cacophony of the crowd had drowned out her words.

The marketplace sprawled along the northern boundary of Seed Town, over five hundred feet from the base of the everlasting tree. Even from this distance, the radiant magic of the enormous tree permeated the air, heightening the elements. I collected a modest dose of air, earth, water, wood, and fire and rolled them through my senses for the sheer pleasure of it. In one of my first articles for the *Chronicle*, I had likened being in the tree's presence to being submerged in an aura of purity, every particle of the elements undiluted and invigorating. The description still held true.

I wasn't the only person to savor the clarified elements. Everyone who arrived made the trek to the base of the tree, drawn to its magic, and most people found one reason or another to linger close by—Audrey and myself included. With so many people loitering in the vicinity, it was inevitable that the marketplace would have formed here.

"Didn't you say you were looking for Mayor Valeria Clee?" Audrey asked. "I think that's her holding court at Tess's." She pointed toward a popular tea shop set beneath a temporary awning. A plump woman sat facing the marketplace traffic, her keen eyes taking in the bustle even as she talked with two men standing beside her chair. The knitting needles in her hands never faltered.

"Good eye," I said.

"I'll meet you back at our tent after lunch. We need to get the latest batch of articles off before nightfall."

I nodded, already angling for Tess's. Audrey slipped into the crowd in the opposite direction and disappeared. As the only two representatives from the *Terra Haven Chronicle*, we had been running nonstop since we got here, tracking down story after story for the special editions being published back home. Our mission was to make those who couldn't undertake the pilgrimage feel as if they were part of the experience, too. Among articles about the jovial, expectant atmosphere of the town and various events and happenings, we collected tales from the myriad people who had gathered, hunting for anecdotal, poignant, humorous, or exciting stories to encapsulate the experience. At one point or another, I had talked to everyone in town, or so it seemed. Only one person in a hundred had anything interesting to say, but I was getting better at picking out who those people might be, and my story senses told me a chat with the self-appointed mayor of this pop-up town would make for an excellent article.

I wove through the thickening foot traffic, then paused at the edge of the tea shop's awning, waiting a polite distance from the mayor and the men talking with her, though I openly eavesdropped.

"A burn like you've described needs Faramond," Valeria said, her knitting needles clicking rhythmically. "He's got a special touch with fire wounds."

"Where can we find him?" the shorter man asked.

I thought I recognized his voice and shifted to get a better view of his face. Searching my memory brought up his name: Ian. I had interviewed him my second day here and remembered him because I had included one of his stories in an article. His question for the tree had been about finding his sister, who he had been separated from when they were toddlers. I had been pleased to use the *Chronicle* to expand others' awareness of his search for his sibling, and I hoped having the details of his story printed in the paper along with whatever clue his seed gave him would speed his reunion.

"Faramond is on the west side of town, between the pegasi saddle maker who uses a feathered horseshoe insignia and the Rothfuss clan—there's about twenty of them, and they're all blond, so you can't miss them," Valeria said. "Oh, and stop by Sharri's on your way."

"Who is—" Ian started to ask, but Valeria continued to speak over him.

"Sharri's tent has green and white tassels all over it. Faramond could use some of the milk from her goats. That should help offset the cost of his healing."

I marveled at her memory. I may have spoken with the majority of Seed Town's residents, but I couldn't keep track of everyone's professions, locations, and needs. Valeria made it appear effortless.

"Thank you, Mayor." Ian tipped his hat in respect. When he turned to leave, he caught sight of me and tossed a quick greeting in my direction before hustling off with his friend.

"What can I help you with, child?" Valeria asked, turning her perceptive gaze on me. Up close, she looked vaguely grandmotherly, with her steely gray hair tucked into a loose bun, but few wrinkles marred her mahogany skin, and the eye-popping teal and yellow hues of her floral dress lent her the aura of a younger woman. It was only her eyes, weighted with a lifetime's wisdom, that betrayed her age.

I held up my press badge, which shimmered with the seal of the *Terra Haven Chronicle*. It was one of my most treasured possessions.

"My name is Kylie Grayson. I was hoping to interview you, if you have a moment."

Valeria studied the badge, then my face, her fingers never slowing on her knitting. Finally, she gestured for me to take a seat, even as she said, "I'm sure you can find more interesting people than me to talk to."

"More interesting than the mayor of Seed Town? I doubt it." I formed a recording sphere, weaving the elements together to hold the words of the interview for later reference. Then I pulled up a chair and tugged my notebook from my bag.

"I'm no mayor. No one elected me." Valeria gestured to our surroundings with her knitting needles. "And this is no town. It's a camp."

"Are you sure?" I made a show of looking around. This "camp" was larger than the five nearest towns put together, and its population continued to swell every day. "No matter what term you use for it, it's a lot of people. Any gathering this size needs structure, and you've done a lot to provide it. Everyone here knows that if they need something, you'll know who has it. How did you—"

A child darted through the market to Valeria's side and whispered in her ear. Sweat plastered his black hair to his scalp, and he bounced on his toes while he spoke.

"Some shepherd brought his whole flock?" Valeria asked, leaning back in exaggerated shock. "Those poor sheep must be skin and bones to have walked this far. Put them on the southeast side, but grab Michael and Johanna to take with you. Oh, and let Butcher Theo know."

The boy spun to run off, but Valeria clutched his shirt, holding him in place. "Whoa there. Take a moment to breathe, Will. And drink this." She handed the boy her cup of cooled tea, and he downed it in three gulps. Valeria rooted through a pouch at her waist, then pressed a coin into Will's hand. "Don't forget to eat today."

"Yes, Nana Clee." He scampered off with a grin.

Valeria watched him go with a fond smile before

resuming her knitting. "Will hasn't stopped moving since he came out of the womb. If he could run in his sleep, he would."

Tess brought over a fresh pitcher of sun-warmed hyson tea and refilled Valeria's glass before pouring mine. We both thanked her before she bustled off.

"Do you decide where every new person should set up camp?" I asked, sipping the earthy beverage.

"Oh my, no. That would be a full-time job around here. But some folks need to be prodded into the right place to keep the whole camp organized. Wouldn't it be dreadful to have your tent overrun with sheep? Better to keep them out on the edges where the beasties can mill around without bothering anyone."

"So you're facilitating town planning—excuse me, *camp* planning. You're the person everyone comes to with their problems, and everyone calls you Mayor Valeria, but you still insist you're not the mayor?"

Valeria shrugged. "I've got a lot of common sense, and I know how to run a ranch. This is little different. That doesn't make me mayor, but when you're as bossy as I am— and when you're fortunate enough to have people who let you boss them around—they like to give you a title. It makes everyone feel like they're taking orders from someone important. If they want to call me mayor, who am I to stop them?" Her easy chuckle invited me to join in. I added *radiates charisma* to my notebook.

"What are you writing there?" she asked.

"I'm taking notes. If I can mimic your style, maybe people will let me boss them around, too."

Her head tipped back with laughter. "I like you, Kylie-child."

We chatted for the next twenty minutes, during which

time I learned Valeria ran a training and boarding stable in Pombokom, a small town to the north. She was also the matriarch of an impressive seven children and sixteen grandchildren, all of whom had accompanied her and a herd of horses to the tree. After the horses had been sold the first day she arrived, Valeria had turned her attention to the town.

"I don't do idle well. I can be patient, but I'm not going to waste the time I've got," she explained, and her knitting needles waggled at me for emphasis.

"Are you the mayor of Pombokom, too?" I asked.

"Who has that kind of time? My horses and family keep me plenty busy."

"Something tells me you still run the town."

Valeria's eyes twinkled. "Townsfolk like to drop by to get my opinion now and again." She lifted the blanket and examined it, nodding to herself. A thread of fire element darted through the weave of her blanket, locking on to the earth spelled into the yarn. She manipulated the elements as deftly as she had her knitting needles, finishing the warmth spell with practiced speed before relaxing back with a sigh. "If I stayed here the rest of my days, I'd never grow tired of the way the elements feel this close to the asking tree."

Her use of the colloquialism for the everlasting tree was one I had heard often. Since we all had traveled here to ask the tree a question, it made a certain amount of sense, but I preferred to call it an everlasting tree. It had been standing when the first human walked through this valley, and even if no one else ever returned to ask for a seed, it would outlive the last human to travel the earth.

"Enough with my past. We both know the question you want to ask me, Kylie-girl."

"You don't mind?"

"I'm too old for secrets." Valeria resumed knitting, adding a fancy border to the blanket.

"What are you going to ask the tree?"

In the hundreds of people I had interviewed in Seed Town, I had found shockingly little variety in the questions people hoped the everlasting tree would answer. Most wanted more money, true love, an enhanced social standing, increased magic abilities, or a way to stave off death or illness. A smaller group of people sought to improve others' lives. Few came to the everlasting tree with noble questions and the betterment of society in mind. I couldn't blame them—we each got only one seed, one answer, one chance to voice the question that beat deep in our heart—but I hoped my question would serve the greater good.

Valeria's answer surprised me in its originality.

"A long time ago, I was forced to sell the best horse I'd ever owned and trained. She wasn't anything special to look at, but she had enough heart for three horses, and more brains than a few of my sons-in-law." Valeria quirked an eyebrow at me, inviting me to commiserate. "I loved that mare to the depths of my toes. But my husband broke his leg, and I had children to feed. Selling her got us through the winter, but by the time we were in a position to buy again, I couldn't find her or the horse trader I had sold her to. I searched for years. She's long dead by now, but maybe her spirit lives on in her offspring. I'm hoping the asking tree will tell me where I can find her descendants. People are nice enough, but that horse . . . I've only got so many years left in me, and they would be so much sweeter if I could live them with a horse like her."

"True companions are a blessing," I said, thinking of Quinn. I scanned the sky for my gargoyle companion. He had left on his own story-scouting mission this morning, and I hadn't caught a glimpse of him since. He took his job as my unofficial assistant seriously and had been an enormous help during our weeks in Seed Town. It had been Quinn who landed me interviews with the centaur queens camped at the edge of town, and it had been his friendly face that convinced a ragtag group of orphans to hold still long enough to tell me their collective story. Dahlia, the *Chronicle*'s editor in chief, had been especially pleased with that article.

"I just hope I have time to figure out how to unlock my seed's answer," Valeria said, pulling my attention back to the interview.

"Maybe you'll be one of the lucky ones, and your seed will be easy to interpret. You could get your answer within the year."

The everlasting tree didn't grant wishes, and it didn't give straight answers. It bestowed a single seed in response to a person's question—no matter how simple or complex the question—and it was up to each individual to interpret their seed, take the appropriate actions, and evolve their seed into its ultimate form before it could be planted and the answer attained. Historically, a seed quest could take anywhere from a few days to a few decades to complete. Personally, I wasn't in any rush, but most people were.

"What about you?" Valeria asked. "What question are you taking to the tree?"

"I'd rather not say. It's private." In truth, I didn't want to waylay the interview with a discussion about my question. I had had a hard enough time explaining it to Audrey, a fellow journalist; explaining my question to Valeria would take too long.

The mayor squinted at me. "It's not about a boy or love,

is it? You've got plenty of time ahead of you for that, and men are too easy to come by to waste a question on."

"No, it's not about a boy," I promised with a smile.

"Good. Just look around: You can't crack a whip without hitting a handful of men. Some of them might even qualify as good men. Like this one." Her smile widened, pulling wrinkles across her cheeks and brightening her eyes. For the first time, Valeria's hands stilled in her lap.

I turned, and a jolt of awareness shot through me when I spotted the man Valeria had locked eyes on: Grant Monaghan, Terra Haven's own Federal Pentagon Defense captain and my personal crush.

I had never seen Grant out of uniform before, and the sight of him relaxed and off-duty sent miniature phoenixes darting through my midsection. Worn denim encased his long legs, and his shoulders stretched the limits of a pale-blue, short-sleeve shirt, showing off his tanned forearms and the impressive curve of his biceps. The sun gave his dark hair glossy highlights and twinkled in the premature gray peppered through his sideburns. Yet despite his mellow expression and civilian clothing, he still looked like an FPD man. Every muscle in his body had been honed by the demands of his job, and he moved with a grace and self-awareness only achieved through years of serving as one of the nation's elite warriors.

I drank in the sight of him. Quinn had told me Grant was here, but I hadn't run into him before now—though I had kept an eye out. The last time I had seen Grant, he had been shirtless and battle-worn. He looked fully recovered and as delectable as ever.

His dark eyes landed on me, and my breath constricted in my lungs. I did my best to school my expression to polite surprise. Plenty of women around the marketplace already ogled Grant like moon-eyed fools; I didn't need to feed his ego by letting him know how much the sight of him had flustered me. Besides, I wasn't just a stranger, eager to make the handsome captain's acquaintance. Grant and I had worked together and faced perilous situations together. Obviously he felt a connection to me; otherwise he would have walked past rather than changing course to come over and greet me.

"What can I do for you, Captain?" Valeria asked when he ducked beneath the awning and stopped beside us.

"Nothing in particular." Grant's mouth quirked in a disarming, easy smile full of charm, and my heart flipped in my chest. "I just came over to make sure Ms. Grayson's not pestering you." Then he planted a large palm on the top of my head and rubbed it back and forth, tousling my hair the way he might have a precocious child's.

My whole body stiffened, my greeting dying in my throat.

"She's got a bit of a reputation for sticking her nose in other people's business," Grant said, adding a final pat before retracting his hand.

Fire flared in my cheeks, anger and embarrassment coursing through my veins. I opened my mouth, but indignation clogged my throat.

"She's a journalist; of course she sticks her nose in other people's business," Valeria said.

"It's one way to make a living."

I startled at Seradon's low voice. I had been so fixated on Grant, I hadn't noticed her standing right behind him. Like the captain, she wore casual clothes that didn't disguise her fighter's physique. Amusement crinkled her brown eyes as she surveyed my reaction to being treated and talked about like a favorite dog.

"I prefer an honest living," Grant said.

"Telling the truth is the *definition* of my job," I snapped. Rather than giving in to the impulse to stab Grant's thigh with my pencil, I tugged my fingers through my rumpled hair, smoothing it. I didn't glance up until I had regained control of my expression. I was a representative of the *Terra Haven Chronicle*, and I would be professional.

"And how do you two know each other?" Valeria asked.

"I've covered a handful of their assignments back in Terra Haven." I included Seradon in my explanation. As the earth elemental in Grant's squad, she had played an instrumental part in several of the events I had written about. I didn't mention I had also worked solo alongside Grant on his last mission. We had parted on good terms, too; I would have even said as friends. I didn't understand why he was acting like a complete jerk now, but I wasn't about to hash it out with him in front of the mayor.

Grant hooked his thumbs in his belt loops and gave Valeria another easy, charming smile—the kind he had never directed toward me. "Ms. Grayson is quite the story hound. I can't seem to shake her."

My molars ground together. How many different ways could he make me sound like a wayward puppy chasing his heels?

"Seems to me it was you who came over here." Valeria quirked an eyebrow at Grant.

"Just doing my civic duty."

Be professional. Don't kick him in the shins. Despite my pep talk, icy fury chilled my voice. "If you don't mind, *Captain*, the mayor is a busy woman, and we're in the middle of an interview. I'm sure you have—"

My stomach lurched as a wellspring of magic unfurled

inside me. The elements rushed to my fingertips, waiting to be used.

Quinn was near.

Even after more than half a year in Quinn's company, chasing stories with him and enjoying his friendship, I had yet to grow accustomed to the breathtaking sensation of his magic. Like all gargoyles, Quinn could enhance the elemental powers of others—when he chose—and he never failed to boost my magic whenever he was within range.

I pivoted in my seat, searching the sky through the awning's thin cloth. Grant and Seradon turned at the same time, both squaring off in the same direction. I followed their line of sight and caught a flicker of gold through the fabric. Of course. Quinn must have spotted Grant and Seradon and included them in his boost. Normally I would have thought nothing of it—they were friends and trusted protectors—but with Grant acting like a jerk, I wished Quinn hadn't been so generous.

"Is that your gargoyle, Kylie-girl?" Valeria asked.

"It is." A surge of pride pulled my spine straighter.

Quinn soared over the crowded marketplace, his lion body suspended beneath feathered stone wings. Wavy lines of quartz hair filled out his impressive mane and tufted the tip of his long tail, but delicate curls of dragon scales covered the bulk of his body, and all of him shimmered in iridescent tones of golden citrine. I squinted as the sunlight reflected off his glossy sides, momentarily blinding me. The gargoyle swooped low, back-winging to land near the awning, and Grant raised a quick wall of air to shield us from the spray of dust.

"Kylie!" Quinn cried, but the urgency crinkling his expressive face already had me on my feet. He tossed a look over his shoulder, toward the tree.

My stomach somersaulted. *It's happening.*

I tied off the recording sphere and shoved it into my bag along with my notebook and pencil.

"Thank you for your time, Mayor. Best of luck in finding your horse." I shrugged the strap of my bag over my head so it hung diagonally across my chest, dodged Grant's shield, and sprinted for Quinn.

"It's blooming!" Quinn exclaimed. "The everlasting tree is blooming!"

Excitement licked through the crowd like wildfire, Quinn's cry being repeated around the marketplace. The boisterous exclamations swelled to a feverish roar as people surged toward the everlasting tree. The wooden shutters to Tess's shop wagon slammed closed, and the sturdy woman hustled out the back, pausing only long enough to lock the door. Around the market, other vendors were following suit, and a clamor of wooden doors and windows slapping shut pierced the rising volume of the crowd.

"Come on, Quinn. Let's go!"

I burst into the sunlight and dashed for the nearest street leading to the tree, trusting Quinn to follow in the air. A giddy mob swarmed around me, everyone stampeding in the same direction. I curtailed my stride to avoid kicking the person in front of me, then staggered to the side when a wayward elbow jabbed my ribs. My toe caught on the heel of another person's boot, and my arms windmilled as I struggled to regain my balance.

A large hand clamped down on my wrist, yanking me

upright and to the side of the road. Grant planted himself between me and the flood of people, shielding me. I glared at the subtle cleft in his chin, torn between thanking him for the rescue and stomping on his foot for his earlier comments. If he tried to detain me or slow me down, his toes would suffer. This was *the story*. I needed to be out in front of it, literally, and I wasn't going to stand here debating it.

"Try not to get trampled," he said, not even bothering to look at me before tugging me into a run.

He shoved into the crush, then zigzagged between emptying vendors' wagons and tents, supporting me as much as propelling me until I found my stride. I risked a glance over my shoulder, spotting Seradon close on our heels. She gave me a thumbs-up and a quick shove to prevent me from crashing into the corner of an abandoned table. Behind her, Quinn burst through the mob into the air to chase after us.

When we broke free of the last vestiges of the town, Grant pulled me into a flat-out sprint. His convoluted route through the backside of the market had given us a margin of advantage over the hordes logjammed in the streets, and we surpassed the front edge of the crowd before we reached the grassy slope leading up to the ever-lasting tree. The upper branches of the great tree swayed and snapped, the rustle of the limbs and leaves a siren song to everyone in the valley. The rest of the forest remained motionless, undisturbed by even a hint of a breeze.

The wild grass around the base of the slope lay flattened, trampled by thousands of people who had visited the tree earlier in the week and by people who had spent their days lying beneath the tree's widely spread branches. No one lounged in the tree's shadow now; everyone stood, their attention riveted on the quivering seeds.

A smattering of wood elementals collected around the outer rim of the massive canopy. They held their hands extended toward the sky, and wood element laced with water and air danced from their fingertips, lifting into the branches high above. As we raced past them into the shade of the massive tree, Grant released my hand. I stumbled and righted myself, finding it easier to run unhindered but more difficult to look around.

Quinn swooped beneath the everlasting tree's branches, the shade transforming his sun-drenched glow into a soft lemon yellow. He landed mid-gallop beside us, folding his wings to his sides, his loping stride easily matching our pace.

"There. Marciano and Winnigan," Seradon said, not even sounding winded. She pointed to the far side of the tree at Brandon Marciano, the tallest man I had ever met and the only man I had ever seen who could make Grant appear average size by comparison. His wife, Riley Winnigan, stood tucked under his arm, her willowy frame clad in a loose blue dress that matched her husband's cloth tunic and trousers. Both were part of Grant's FPD squad, Marciano a wood elemental and Winnigan a water elemental, but neither had the fighter's aura the captain and Seradon possessed. Marciano's giant frame might make people hesitate for fear of being crushed, but he looked as if his fastest speed would be a ponderous lumber. Winnigan appeared soft and delicate, especially next to her husband, but I had seen both of them in action, and looks were deceiving. Grant changed course to meet up with them.

I skidded to a stop and dug my camera out of my bag. People flooded out of the city from every alleyway and street, and even more streamed in from forest campsites ringing the tree. They ran with the glee of children at the fair, excitement and hope lighting their faces. I adjusted the focus on my camera and snapped a handful of pictures.

Above me, the tree's canopy seemed to stretch from horizon to horizon like a limb-woven thundercloud, shifting and restless. I pointed the lens upward and snapped several shots, but the tree was too vast to capture properly, and its movements were more likely to blur in photos than show the tree's majesty.

Quinn nosed my hip to get my attention. "Come on, let's join the others."

I glanced around, surprised by how many people had filled the space beneath the tree in the short time I had been standing still.

"Good idea. I'll follow you."

We wove through the thickening crowd, dodging people with faces upturned to behold the mesmerizing dance of the everlasting tree. Technically, it didn't matter where we stood beneath the tree's branches when it bloomed, but I liked the idea of being near people we knew. This was a moment to be shared, and it seemed Quinn felt the same way.

Marciano, Winnigan, and Seradon greeted us as we joined their cluster. I pointedly did not look at Grant. His earlier comments and behavior had been humiliating, and just because he had guided me safely to the tree didn't mean I was ready to forgive him. Or forget his words.

"I'll be right back," I said to Quinn. I double-checked the settings on my camera, then jogged to the edge of the canopy to capture pictures in both directions of the growing ring of wood elementals. Was this something they had planned in advance or a compulsion emanating from the tree, calling them to act? Farther down the curved line, I spotted Marciano's towering form as he linked himself to the elemental chain. I made a mental note to question him —after the everlasting tree finished blooming—and squeezed back through the milling masses to Quinn and the others.

Raquel, the *Chronicle*'s gryphon rider who had flown Audrey and me to Seed Town, had joined our group. She and Seradon were immersed in a quiet discussion, but Raquel tossed me a smile. I hadn't realized she knew Seradon, but it didn't surprise me. Seradon and the whole FPD team worked the most dangerous jobs in and around Terra Haven, and Raquel taxied journalists to those same locations to get the scoop for the *Chronicle*. It stood to reason the two women had met before.

I spun in a tight circle, searching for my next shot, but even standing on tiptoes, I couldn't see beyond the people right in front of me. Jumping wasn't much better. Any picture I took in midair would be too blurry to be useful.

"Want to stand on my back?" Quinn asked.

I considered his offer, surprised to realize I might be able to take him up on it. When I had met Quinn, he had been small enough for me to hold. Now he stood as tall as my hip, and his lion frame was bulky with muscle.

"I won't hurt your wings? Or be too heavy?"

He gave me a look like I had asked if he would like to eat raw meat. "Your shoes are flimsy leather; my feathers are quartz. And you weigh very little."

"In that case, let me up."

I clambered onto his back, resting my feet on either side of his spine below the base of his wings. The vantage point put me head and shoulders above everyone else, providing me a spectacular view of the crowd. A sea of heads bobbed beneath the tree, the dense shadows obscuring the details of their upturned faces. More than twenty feet of air separated the tallest of onlookers—the centaurs and minotaurs—from the lowest of the everlasting tree's branches.

I adjusted my camera's aperture for the gloom and snapped a shot, absently thanking whoever had placed a steadying hand on my hip. Finally I found the right angle to capture the vastness of the tree and the thousands who had come to cluster beneath its branches.

Mine wasn't the only flash illuminating the underside of the tree in blinding strobes. I recognized fellow journalists scattered throughout the crowd, but I couldn't pick out Audrey among them. Keeping in mind my axiom—always having a unique angle to make the *Terra Haven Chronicle* stand out—I concentrated on taking one-of-a-kind photos. Telescoping my camera to its maximum length, I focused on the people who were pressed close to the trunk, their hands resting against the coarse bark. From this distance, I couldn't tell if they manipulated elements, but I thought they might all be wood elementals. Were they assisting the tree like those in the outer ring? Did the tree feel different now than it had before it began blooming? I made a mental note of individual faces. Hopefully I would be able to hunt down at least one of them after the blooming for an interview.

Quinn shifted beneath me, and I wobbled.

"Hey, hold still, please," I said. "I need a few more pictures."

"The view would be a lot better if your butt wasn't in the way," a familiar woman's voice said.

"Mika?" I spun around and would have fallen if Grant hadn't caught me. He wrapped his hands around my waist and lifted me to the ground with impersonal ease. I flushed, realizing it had been his hand stabilizing me while I took pictures—and that my butt had been in *his* face, too. Then

Mika reached for me, and I forgot my embarrassment and pulled my best friend in for a hug before releasing her.

"Mika! What are you doing here?" The last time I had seen her was weeks earlier, when she had been holed up in her apartment, researching a cure for a handful of comatose gargoyles. "How did you get here? Does this mean the sick gargoyles are—"

"Fine. They're fine." Mika laughed.

"Everyone's healthier than ever, thanks to Mika," Oliver said. The carnelian gargoyle twined his Chinese dragon body against Mika's leg, a happy grin splitting his face. Quinn gave Mika an equally adoring gaze before greeting Oliver with a gentle headbutt. The two gargoyles remained with their heads close together, speaking quietly. To look at them—one a dragon, the other a lion; one scarlet red, the other golden—an outsider would never guess they were brothers. Mika watched them both with fondness, but her expression turned sly when she refocused on me.

"I should have known I'd find you with the squad. Or rather, with the captain of the squad."

I shot her a quelling glower and double-checked Grant's expression to make sure he hadn't heard her. He was busy clasping forearms with Marcus Velasquez, the fire elemental of his squad. The two men were cut from the same oversize cloth, both broad chested, muscled, and tall. Even with Velasquez's darker complexion, black hair, and blue eyes, the men could have been mistaken for brothers. Quinn had seemed to think Velasquez had remained in Terra Haven—a fact that piqued my journalistic curiosity. What could have been more important to the fire elemental than the everlasting tree? But with his arrival, the whole squad was on hand.

I waggled my eyebrows at Mika and whispered, "Did you two come together?"

Mika blushed.

My eyebrows darted higher. I had been teasing, but . . . "Like *together* together?"

She tucked her strawberry-blond hair behind an ear, her expression uncharacteristically shy. "Yep."

I silently cheered. I had been rooting for Mika to wake up, realize Velasquez liked her, and do something about it. I thought she had been too absorbed in healing the city's ill gargoyles to pursue romance, though. "How did that—"

I caught sight of the back of Mika's hand, and my words died. She followed my glance and tried to tuck her hand into her pocket, but I caught it before she could. Shiny hexagon scars trailed from her knuckles to her wrist, each geometric shape shimmering a deep amethyst purple.

"What happened?" I demanded.

"I had an accident when I was working with some quartz." Mika shrugged free of my grip and stepped around me. "Quinn, have you grown since I last saw you? I think you're going to be bigger than Oliver."

I gaped at Mika's back. She was a genius with quartz, so much so that she was the only person in Terra Haven with the extraordinary ability to heal living-quartz gargoyles. For her to accidentally scar herself with quartz would be like water setting itself on fire by lapping against the bank of a river.

"Mika . . ."

"Shouldn't you be capturing this?" Mika waved a hand up toward the tree without looking away from Quinn.

I squinted at her, another question on the tip of my tongue, when the tree began to hum. The limber upper branches swayed rhythmically, undulating in a pattern too vast to comprehend from below. A hush ran through the eager mob, giving rise to the susurrus of limbs and leaves, the sound washing back and forth over us, rising and falling in volume. The elements vibrated in tandem with the tree, heightening my anticipation.

A slender tendril of air element snaked from the tree, silvery and insubstantial, eliciting gasps of wonder. Another followed, then another. Each kissed an upraised mouth as people spoke their heartfelt questions to the everlasting tree. Then the tendrils recoiled, disappearing into the dense canopy.

A sliver of air darted from a thick branch above us, dropping to cover Grant's mouth. He stood as if rooted, eyes locked on the tree, the shadows darkening the warm brown of his irises. A rumble of a whisper emanated from his throat, but the tree's elemental conduit muted his words, making it impossible to eavesdrop despite standing within arm's reach.

In my periphery, another strand dipped toward our group. Quinn stretched his neck and uttered his question into it. At his side, Oliver spoke into another air conduit, and Quinn's deep murmurs harmonized with Oliver's chiming tones. I spun in a slow circle, enraptured by the beauty of the tree's distinctive magic. So many lines of air filled the gap between the people and the tree that it looked as if we were underwater, but already they were thinning. The blooming was almost over.

I realized with a jolt that I hadn't yet voiced my question. With my heart beating fast, I mentally ran through my wording one more time to make sure I had it right.

As I opened my mouth, a tendril of air element dove toward it, as if the tree had known the moment I would decide to speak. A gentle feather of air cupped my lips, tugging delicately on my exhale. My question tumbled out.

"Where can I find the story of a lifetime?"

I had always dreamed of changing the world. It was why I had chosen to become a journalist. I couldn't fight bad guys or protect the helpless the way Grant did—I didn't have the physical stamina or elemental strength to be an FPD warrior. I didn't command any special skills I could teach others, and I had no interest in politics. But I did possess unquenchable curiosity, and being a journalist allowed me to channel that thirst for knowledge into a useful outlet. When I wrote an article exposing a horrible event or praising an exemplary action, the newspaper amplified my voice. A single article might positively impact a dozen people's lives, but a huge story—a story of a lifetime—had the potential of helping an entire society. That's what I wanted more than anything else.

The everlasting tree withdrew its air element, carrying my words back toward the trunk, siphoning all my yearning and hope along with it.

My question hadn't been entirely selfless, though. My fledgling career as a journalist had included the coverage of some amazing stories, but most of my success could be attributed to being in the right place at the right time. In other words, I had gotten lucky. Several of those articles had ended up being on the *Chronicle*'s front page—an almost unheard-of achievement for a junior reporter. Even writing the headline-winning story and being sent to cover the everlasting tree had involved a certain amount of luck. This assignment—covering this historic event and being one of two reporters whose articles were featured in daily special editions—was the kind of achievement many would consider a career high point. What if it was? What if the everlasting tree's blooming was the top story of my career? What if everything after this was a letdown and less important? My career could be over before it had truly begun.

Contemplating backsliding into journalistic obscurity knotted cramps in my stomach. I didn't want my first year at the *Chronicle* to be my best year. I didn't want to become a has-been before I even advanced past being a *junior* journalist. I needed to know something bigger existed in my future. I just hoped the seed didn't provide the answer too quickly. Once I had written up the story of a lifetime, I would know without a doubt that my career had peaked and all other stories thereafter would be less important and less grand.

The tree's hum escalated, the energy of everyone's collected questions quivering through the branches until it sounded as if we stood beneath a monstrous beehive. The sonic vibrations tickled my lungs, and I rubbed my breastbone. My other hand massaged a cramp in my neck, but I didn't look down. I couldn't.

The last of the tendrils of air retreated to the tree, and it stilled. I froze, breathless, my ears ringing at the abrupt cessation of sound. Around me, everyone stood like statues, locked in anticipation. I reached for Quinn. He rubbed his cool face against my hand, leaving his cheek resting against my palm.

A faint drone pierced the silence, the sound of a single hummingbird flying through the branches. A seed emerged, pale like sandalwood and the size of a plum pit. It spun through the air on an invisible current, circling the mammoth trunk to land on the outstretched palm of a short woman too far away from me to make out. As one, the crowd took a collective breath and turned back toward the canopy. More seeds fell, three this time—one black, one copper, and one a miniature wooden replica of a temple—none of them the same size. Five more seeds dropped before those found their people. Ten more, then fourteen, then too many to count, until a gentle rain of seeds sprinkled the air. I raised my camera above my head and blindly snapped photographs.

Winnigan lifted her hand, closing her fingers around a seed of clear green glass. An intense yearning circled my stomach like a wriggling puppy, and I let my camera drop, too eager for my own seed to concentrate on anything else. The subtle drone of flying seeds escalated until the hilltop shivered with sound, and still more fell. Above our heads, the air swirled thick with seeds, and though most were barely larger than an acorn and none were larger than a grapefruit, the sheer volume of them reduced visibility to only a few feet. I jumped when a seed whistled past my head, angling for someone behind me. Mika stretched out her cupped hands in time for the seed to tumble into her palms. Another seed, falling as gently as a snowflake, landed on Quinn's nose.

In the churning chaos, a single seed caught my eye. Mottled brown and as large as a hen's egg, the seed trembled with excited energy, and I couldn't look away. Slowly, I raised my hand, and the seed settled in my palm.

3

___

My heart hammered in my chest as I lowered my hand. I could barely feel the weight of the seed. What I had mistaken for dappled coloring as it was falling were actually ridges and hollows bunched across the seed's surface. Two paler concentric circles shimmered around the ridges, the inner circle mirroring the outer except for a divot at the apex of one side.

I spun a simple weave of fire element, and a glowball burst into existence beside my hand. When I twisted the seed in the fiery light, copper and gold glittered in the deep craters of the seed's ridges, filling the inner circle like a mystical eye. The light also revealed traces of gold brushed along the rim of the seed. I flipped it over to verify the pattern repeated on the opposite side. It resembled the ocellus of a peacock feather, only the colors were wrong. Was that a clue?

I rocked the seed on my palm, scrutinizing the metallic shimmers, and it hit me: it looked like a firebird feather.

A thrill of excitement surged from my toes to my scalp,

and I danced in place. A familiar tingle tickled my finger-tips. I had my first clue for the story of a lifetime!

I mentally ran through the extent of my knowledge of firebirds. Their feathers glowed with a magical light, though it wasn't fire, as their name suggested. Like crows, they tended to be attracted to shiny objects, but if I remembered correctly, they were more discerning, preferring refined and expensive metals, especially gold. They also possessed some form of nature-based magic, maybe something that involved a song? I wished I had paid more attention in school when we had learned about firebirds. The only detail I remembered clearly was the teacher warning us to avoid firebirds if we came across them in the wild. They were territorial, violent, and, in rare instances, deadly.

With any luck, chasing down a story about firebirds would not involve getting close enough to be attacked by one. If it did, I would be prepared. The moment we returned to Terra Haven, I was going to learn everything there was to know about firebirds, starting with their known habitats and—

"My seed has a snake on it," Quinn said, his voice timorous.

I dropped to my knees beside the gargoyle, concerned to find him near tears. Mika knelt on his opposite side, and I caught a flash of what looked like a stone seed in her hand before she pocketed it.

Quinn nosed a fist-size seed on the ground in front of him.

"May I?" I asked, reaching for it.

Quinn nodded, his shoulders hunched high enough to touch his small, drooping ears. I plucked the seed from the dirt and held it up to my glowball. Matte black like burnt wood, the seed resembled a thin scaly rope tied into an elaborate knot. I rolled it in my hand until I spied the triangular snake head. Delicate scales outlined its beady eyes and rimmed its unhinged mouth, exposing minute fangs, which were clamped onto its own slender tail, completing the knot. If I didn't know better, I would have thought the snake had been carved rather than grown.

"Wow, this is amazing, Quinn. It's so detailed and specific." I handed the seed to Mika so she could take a closer look, too.

"So specifically a snake," Quinn whined. "I don't want anything to do with snakes."

"If you don't mind me asking, what was your question?" Mika asked.

Quinn's shoulders deflated, and his wings drooped to touch the ground. "I asked: how can I best help Kylie?"

"You did?" I didn't know what to say. I wished Quinn would have told me his question beforehand. I would have talked him out of it. It wasn't right for him to have used his question on me. He should have picked something just for himself.

Quinn peered at me through furrowed brows, picking up on my distress. I wrapped him in an impulsive hug. "I'm flattered, Quinn. You already are so helpful to me. I don't know what I'd do without you."

He leaned into my embrace, and I dropped a hand to the ground before he toppled me. When he sat back, his wings rested tight against his sides, and he didn't look so forlorn.

"But my seed is a snake. I don't know what that means or how it will help you."

"Snakes often symbolize wisdom and cunning," Mika said. "Perhaps you need to learn something new that will help Kylie."

I nodded, having had a similar thought. "You're the most

inquisitive gargoyle I know. You're bound to come across tons of useful information."

Quinn sat straighter. "Do you think so?"

"I do."

"Definitely," Mika agreed.

Oliver pushed closer to sniff Quinn's seed, his own clutched in a paw. "It could be a warning."

"About what?" Quinn asked.

"Not to pursue stories that lead back to you?"

"That's an interesting interpretation," I said.

Mika dropped her backpack between her knees and dug inside, eliciting the familiar *clink* of quartz marbles from its depths. She was never without seed crystals these days, not since she had learned they could be used to heal gargoyle injuries. However, instead of retrieving quartz, she tugged a drawstring pouch to the top of the bag, then freed the string from the pouch. Holding up the braided cloth, she eyed Quinn, then Oliver.

"I don't think I have enough for both of you," she said.

"For what?" Oliver asked.

"You and Quinn don't have convenient pockets, so I thought you might like to carry your seeds on necklaces."

Quinn eyed the snake knot dubiously. "I guess so."

"Do you mind waiting until later for me to make you a necklace?" Mika asked Oliver.

"I think I want you to carry mine." Oliver extended his seed to Mika, and she pocketed it before I spotted more than a glimpse of agate.

After threading the sturdy string through a gap in the snake's twisted body, Mika looped the necklace around Quinn's thick mane and tied it off, using a lick of fire to singe the knot and melt the fabric together for an extra-secure hold. The ebony seed rested against Quinn's chest beneath his chin.

"You look dashing," Mika said, sitting back to admire her handiwork.

"Truly," I agreed. The dark seed contrasted beautifully with Quinn's yellow-gold chest, making the necklace look like a fashion accessory.

Quinn patted the seed with a paw, then shook vigorously, testing the necklace. The seed bounced, but the cord held.

I straightened and brushed dirt from my knees. A thunder of hoofbeats announced the departure of the centaur herd. The rest of the crowd was slower to dissipate, with most people lingering beneath the tree to exclaim over each other's seeds. Of our group, Winnigan had roamed off to be with her husband, but Grant, Seradon, Raquel, and Velasquez stood in a tight circle, admiring each other's seeds.

I squeezed closer to Grant. His seed was smooth, perfectly round, and roughly the same size as mine, though cupped in Grant's large hand, it appeared smaller. Even in the dim light beneath the tree's dense canopy, it shimmered a beautiful pearlescent white streaked with gold. It would have made a gorgeous pendant . . . for someone less masculine.

A bundle of elements blasted across the top of people's heads, slamming to a halt in front of Grant. The cluster of air and fire elements were woven in a pattern reminiscent of a message bubble, but one far more complex. If I wasn't mistaken, it included a visual component. I leaned in, studying the nuanced elemental strands. If I could dissect the pattern, I might be able to reproduce it, though on a much smaller scale.

Grant seized a massive amount of air and dropped a thick, soundproof ward around himself and the message, his barrier falling so close it skimmed against my face. I jerked back and surreptitiously rubbed my nose. When he activated the message, a larger-than-life image of a woman with long gray hair expanded in front of him. Wrinkles etched her sun-darkened cheeks, and worry laced her dark eyes. I recognized her instantly, as would anyone from Terra Haven: Mayor Mary Lowman. I edged closer again. I might not be able to hear what the mayor said, but I might be able to read her lips.

Grant's stern gaze landed on me, and I gave him a wide-eyed look of innocence. He scowled. Water sliced through his ward, adding a subtle distortion that blurred my view of Grant and the message.

"Spoilsport," I muttered, giving Grant a glare he couldn't see.

"Buck up, little reporter," Seradon said, giving my back a friendly pat that nearly knocked me over. "Whatever the mayor has to say, it can't be more important than covering the everlasting tree."

"I'm sure you're right." Choosing to ignore the humor twinkling in the earth elemental's eyes, I turned toward Mika, and my thoughts scattered at the sight of my best friend tucked beneath Velasquez's arm. Mika snuggled up to the tall man, looking at home in his embrace. How much had transpired since I had left Terra Haven?

Since I couldn't pester Mika about her new relationship in front of Velasquez, I followed my journalistic hunch and asked, "What cured the gargoyles?"

Mika's gaze shot to Velasquez's, then down to her toes in an almost comically suspicious manner. She opened her mouth, but Grant interrupted her.

"We're leaving," he announced, popping his ward. The mayor's message capsule dissolved into raw elements.

Seradon pocketed her seed, all teasing gone from her expression. Grant lifted a long arm skyward and flashed a quick hand signal in Marciano and Winnigan's direction. They immediately pushed through the crowd, angling for Seed Town. Grant dropped his arm to point at Velasquez.

"You too."

"What's going on?" I asked, but I was speaking to empty air. Grant wove through the crowd, Seradon on his heels, without a backward glance. My hands balled into fists, and I bounced on my toes, caught between the urge to race after him to demand an answer and maintaining my dignity.

"Are you coming or staying?" Velasquez asked, directing his question to Oliver and Mika.

"Oh. Did he mean us, too?" Mika asked.

"I'm not abandoning you to find your own way home just because the mayor set Grant's ass on fire."

Eyes wide, Mika glanced at me.

"You should go with him. I came on the *Chronicle*'s gryphon. We don't have room for anyone else." I shot Raquel a quick glance, and the gryphon rider shook her head, confirming we couldn't take Mika with us.

"All right." Mika planted a kiss on Quinn's forehead, then pulled me in for a quick hug. "See you back in Terra Haven."

"I'll want details," I whispered before she could pull away. Details about this emergency, about what had happened to Mika and the sick gargoyles, and about her new relationship.

She gave me an enigmatic smile. "Of course you will."

Then Mika, Oliver, and Velasquez jogged off, leaving me alone with Quinn and Raquel.

"It looks like the captain is going to be involved in something newsworthy again," Quinn said, staring wistfully at the departing squad.

"We really should put a tracker on that man." Grant had accused me of doing as much more than once.

"Is that an option?" Raquel asked.

"We haven't figured out how," Quinn said.

I heard my own frustration in his voice. "Not yet," I added. Just because I hadn't been able to invent a tracker that Grant wouldn't be able to detect and destroy immediately didn't mean I would give up.

"I can see how that would be handy," Raquel murmured.

"Strictly for journalistic reasons," I said.

She winked. "Of course."

Grant disappeared into the milling populace, and I gave myself a mental shake. He couldn't have spared two seconds to say good-bye? Or perhaps he had forgotten I was there. How flattering.

If today's interactions had proven anything, it was that my crush on Grant was grossly one-sided. At best, he appeared to think of me as a pesky little sister, if that humiliating head rub had been any indication. He hadn't been shy in the past about sharing his low opinion of reporters, either. Logically, I shouldn't have been attracted to him. The only qualities he had going for him were an impossibly handsome face, an even better body, a job as an elite protector of Terra Haven's citizens, unparalleled elemental powers, and an authoritative demeanor.

Not helping, I scolded myself. *He's also arrogant, thoughtless, overbearing, and oblivious.*

Listing Grant's flaws alleviated my hurt feelings, and I turned my back on Seed Town. I had more important things to do than pine after a man who showed no interest in me.

I spent the next two hours with Quinn by my side, chasing down the wood elementals who had joined the outer ring and several who had been in contact with the trunk during the blooming. Each had a different reason for linking their magic to the tree's—from being caught up in the moment and wanting to join in with their fellow wood elementals to a sensation of rapport with the tree—but all reported the same euphoric elemental experience when the tree had cycled its magic through them.

"It was more purifying than any temple ritual," one woman described, her cheeks glowing rosily. "I feel remade."

By the time I finished interviewing the wood elementals lingering beneath the tree's quiet canopy, most of the crowd had dispersed from the knoll. I meandered back to Seed Town with Quinn, using a fresh message bubble to capture my words as I recited a bare-bones outline of my planned article and my impressions of the wood elementals. Then I anchored the magical bundle in the bottom of my bag to replay for myself later.

I used the rest of the day to chat with anyone I could get to hold still, taking pictures of people's seeds and cataloging their experiences and questions. No more than a handful of individuals had any idea what their seeds meant in relationship to their questions. Some found it frustrating or even infuriating, but most expressed hope and excitement—and an eagerness to get busy evolving their seeds. Since I hadn't yet determined how I would frame my final articles about the everlasting tree, I focused on gathering as much information as possible before everyone left, and my bag bulged with recorded interviews caught in elemental message bubbles.

Seed Town dismantled around me as I worked, everyone

packing up to go home. After weeks of putting their lives on hold to wait for the blooming, it was time to return to normal life. A smattering of airships launched into the sky, disappearing along the horizon. Carts and carriages drawn by horses, donkeys, ceberi, oxen, and alpacas clogged the roads, while free-floating conveyances took more direct routes across the trampled grassy landscape. Gryphons, hippogryphs, and pegasi departed intermittently into the air, their concussive wing beats echoing throughout the valley and stirring up even more dirt into the atmosphere.

Despite my best efforts to stay on task, my thoughts turned frequently to my own seed. How would firebirds play into the story of a lifetime? Would they be an important part or just a stepping stone toward evolving my seed? Despite copious records of seed holders from past bloomings on this and other continents, the transformation process of seeds remained a mystery. Sometimes the actions required to mature a seed had little to nothing to do with the question or the final answer. Other times, every step was a part of the ultimate answer, though typically it was apparent only in retrospect. Having an everlasting seed was like possessing a key to a puzzle without knowing the puzzle's location. Maybe the seed would lead me to a story about firebirds, but it could be that I simply needed a firebird feather—or an entire bird. For all I knew, the seed might require the guano of a firebird to evolve.

I didn't get the chance to return to my tent until night-fall. By then, the semi-orderly town that had contained thousands of people at dawn had been reduced to a chaotic patchwork of pulverized ground and irregularly spaced tents and wagons, all coated in a fresh layer of dust. All semblance of Seed Town's roads had been destroyed in the exodus. A stream of travelers flowed back toward the cities and towns from whence they had come, the lanterns and glowballs illuminating their conveyances looking like a string of fireflies from this distance. I paused to capture a few pictures, not sure if they would turn out, then continued plodding across the churned field.

If not for Bright Fang, Raquel's colossal gryphon, hunkered at our campsite, I would have wandered, lost in the unfamiliar terrain. Where once our tent had sat near the center of town, now it drooped in a secluded gully. Quinn, who had returned earlier in the afternoon to nap in preparation of our return flight home, lay snuggled up to Fang, his normally glossy body covered in grit and almost indistinguishable from the trampled ground.

A similar layer of grime coated me from head to toe, bestowed on me by the dust cloud that had hazed the air all afternoon. The miasma was indicative of the destruction the crowds had inflicted upon the valley, and I had learned in my interviews today that a small group of elementals would remain behind to restore the ravaged landscape and ensure the return of normal flora and fauna to the area. I silently thanked my good fortune to be returning to civilization, where showers were an everyday occurrence and my comfortable bed waited for me.

Quinn lifted his head when he heard my footsteps, then rested his muzzle on his paws again when I indicated I didn't need him. I collected a dose of water and air elements and twisted them together into an air bath spell. The magic responded sluggishly, the elements surprisingly heavy in my fatigue, and the familiar spell took unaccustomed concentration. When I released the elements, they spun through my clothes and against my skin, funneling the majority of the dirt from me into a ring around my feet. It wasn't the same as taking a real bath, but it would have to do.

Dropping to my knees, I ducked under the tent flap and crawled inside. Audrey crouched within, a single lantern illuminating the tiny space as she finished packing her belongings. Raquel's bags already sat in a tidy pile to the right of the tent flap.

"We leave as soon as you're packed," Audrey announced. "Raquel says there's a good tail wind tonight that will increase our speed."

I eyed my bedroll longingly, but instead of flopping on top of it, I forced myself to roll it up. The excitement and frenetic rush for last-minute interviews had sapped my strength, but it was more than that. The tree had bloomed, and once I submitted today's articles, this amazing assignment would be over, and I would go back to normal life. After weeks of anticipation driving me, I felt bereft, with nothing to look forward to except a return to Terra Haven.

There's still my seed and chasing down its story, I reminded myself, but exhaustion numbed my enthusiasm. Instead, I thought about my tiny studio apartment, with my soft bed and minuscule shower, and used the image to keep myself moving.

Audrey knotted her bag closed and crawled to the exit, but she stopped at the threshold. "Did you really ask for the biggest story ever?"

"Basically." I waited for her to roll her eyes or sigh in exasperation at my supposed waste of a question.

Instead, she gave me a shy, curious look. "Can I see your seed?"

I finished securing the ties around my bedding before pulling my seed from my pocket. In the lantern's soft light, it gleamed. Audrey used a finger to rock the seed on my palm without picking it up.

"It looks like a firebird feather," she said, confirming my assumption. "Do you know what it means?"

I shook my head. "What about your seed?"

Audrey retrieved her seed from her brassiere. "I didn't want to lose it," she explained with an embarrassed grimace.

Barely as big as a fingernail, her seed was shaped like a glass teardrop made of pure fire and so realistic I expected it to be hot to the touch instead of merely warm from being up against Audrey's skin. She had come to the everlasting tree to find a cure for her sister's wasting illness. Nothing in the seed gave me a clue about what it might mean or where Audrey might find a cure.

"Does this tell you anything?" I asked.

"Not yet. But it gives me hope." Audrey curled her fingers around the tiny seed and tucked it safely back down her shirt before crawling out. When she reached back inside for her pack, she was frowning thoughtfully.

"You know, I think I saw something about firebirds in an ad recently," she said. "It might have nothing to do with your seed, but you should check it out."

I waited until the tent flap fell closed before diving toward my slender pile of newspapers. Thumbing through the top paper to the ad section, I skimmed the columns for any mention of a firebird. I didn't find any in that paper or in two others, but I finally got lucky in the fourth. My eyes bounced from the word *firebird* back to the top of the ad. It spanned two of the four columns, with plenty of white space to draw the eye.

TIMBER COVE NEEDS YOU, read the headline.

Calling all able-bodied elementals trained in land management and eco-restoration.

Premium pay. Housing available.

The Timber Cove region was devastated by an enormous

wildfire, and now torrential rains threaten to wash away the community. Join the efforts to restore this once-prosperous hub of the logging industry.

The ad listed the skills required and made dubious promises about the suitability of bringing "the whole family to take part in the adventure." I skimmed over the text to the bold print at the bottom that had originally caught my attention.

FIREBIRDS MISSING

A shipment of firebirds slated for the Timber Cove relief effort were last seen outside Sugar Flats.

If you have any information regarding the missing firebirds, contact your local FPD headquarters.

A sizable reward for the birds capped off the ad.

I set the newssheet aside and paged through the rest of the paper, looking for an article mentioning the missing firebirds. Sugar Flats was a wild, mountainous territory east of Terra Haven by over one hundred miles, but more than close enough to warrant a mention in the *Chronicle*. My search turned up nothing, nor did skimming the rest of the papers in my stack. Newspaper delivery to Seed Town had been sporadic, and I had snagged only five editions in the last two weeks. If the missing firebirds had been covered, it must have been in one of the papers I hadn't received.

Frustrated, I reread the ad. Since the firebirds had been part of the original relief effort plan, I had been right in thinking they had nature-based magic, but no matter how many times I reread the sentence, it didn't clarify how the birds had been meant to help. Nor did I gain additional insight into what *missing* entailed. Had the firebirds been stolen? Escaped? Or had they simply fallen off the transport?

Raquel stuck her head into the tent to grab her packs.

"Fang is saddled." She frowned at the open paper on my lap, then at my unpacked bag. "We're all waiting on you."

"I'll be right out." I crumpled the paper and stuffed it into my bag, then piled the other editions on top and crammed my dirty clothes in with them. My fingers fumbled with the buckles as the full import of the missing firebirds sank in. This could be the first step on my quest to evolve my seed.

A shot of adrenaline pierced my fatigue, chased by an anxious, acidic churn in my midsection. As intensely as I desired the seed's answer, I wasn't ready. I had hoped to savor years of journalistic accomplishments before my career peaked. If I found the story of a lifetime now, would I be able to continue working for the paper, knowing I would never achieve similar success again?

4

———

Our deadline drove us home at a punishing pace. We would be delivering the final articles by hand, and we raced the rumors and tales that would flood into the city when our fellow seed recipients returned. Fortunately, we had Fang. Even carrying three passengers and their luggage, the gryphon could fly for hours without needing to land, and she required only short naps between flights.

Soaring gryphonback was an exhilarating if solitary experience. Harnessed one behind the other, with the wind beating against our ears, any attempt at conversation was nearly impossible, but watching the landscape flow past beneath us more than made up for it. Audrey and I used the time to craft our articles, speaking them into message bubbles, then taking turns typing them up on a miniature travel typewriter when we landed. Whereas the rhythmic sway of Fang's body lulled me to sleep more than once, Quinn could rest only during our limited breaks. I kept an eye on him, concerned the pace would be too strenuous for the gargoyle, but he never faltered.

By the time we arrived in Terra Haven two nights later, the last of my articles on the everlasting tree were complete. The glorious weeks of this special assignment were over. However, a quiet sense of pride buoyed my weary body, countering my post-assignment melancholy. I had been part of one of this country's pivotal historical moments, and my words would forever serve as an official record of the event.

As we approached the city, Raquel channeled soft weaves of fire into glass canisters, making them glow a bright amber. She hung the lights off ropes down Fang's sides to illuminate our location and prevent airborne collisions with other aerial nighttime traffic. Glimmers of streetlamps and shining windows gave definition to the sleeping city, and I fancied it looked like a giant quilt of lights crumpled across the gently rolling hills. I soaked in the sight, having missed my hometown more than I had thought.

I spotted several business and private airships navigating the night sky along with a lone pegasus and rider decked out in the distinctive blue and gold of the Pegasus Express mail service. Then Fang banked hard, dropping altitude as we circled the shadowy expanse of Focal Park and swept over Lincoln River before gliding through the business district toward one of the few buildings with the lights still on. I braced my hands against the harness as the gryphon dropped to the top of the *Terra Haven Chronicle*'s roof, landing in the flat space provided specifically for her. Moments later, Quinn flapped to the edge of the roof and collapsed, his sides heaving. Weariness etched his expressive face. Another day at this strenuous pace, and Quinn wouldn't have been able to keep up. I would make sure Mika took a close look at him when we got home, too. If he had strained himself in any way, she would be able to heal him.

I peered south into the darkness, toward our home. It

was conceivable we had beaten Mika and the squad back to Terra Haven, but I doubted it. With five gargoyle-enhanced full-spectrum pentacle-potential elementals propelling their conveyance, and the urgency with which they had left, they could have covered the distance faster than us, especially with their head start. Since I hadn't spotted giant wards quarantining any sections of the city or any magic battles underway, and all parts of the city remained standing, not only had they beaten us home, but also the squad had probably already dealt with whatever problem had rushed them back. Mika would have the details, and I would get them out of her while she checked Quinn.

I half climbed, half fell off Fang, my legs stiff. Bending, I massaged a cramp out of my calf while Raquel unloaded our bags. Audrey shouldered hers and trudged toward the stairwell, tossing us a sleepy farewell. I was slower to follow, needing to first strip my borrowed flight gear and return it to Raquel. The gryphon rider's jacket had been two sizes too big for me, but it had kept me warm during the cold flights. So had the leather helmet, and my hair lay matted against my scalp with sweat despite the cool night. The goggles peeled from my cheeks with audible pops, and I knew from experience I would have red circles outlining my eyes for hours.

Once she was free of our luggage, Fang twisted to nudge Quinn with her enormous beak. Quinn headbutted her back. The gryphon couldn't talk and wasn't half as intelligent as Quinn, but they had formed a friendship nonetheless.

"Good luck with your world-famous story," Raquel said as she stowed my borrowed outfit in one of Fang's saddlebags. "I wonder if your captain knows anything more about those missing firebirds."

"He's not my captain," I said automatically. Raquel had been teasing me about Grant since before we left Terra Haven, having no problem seeing through my feigned indifference toward the FPD's hottest warrior. During the rushed trip back, I had considered sharing my resolve to abolish my infatuation with Captain Nincompoop, but ultimately, I decided it would sound disingenuous. Plus, I hadn't wanted to open the topic for general discussion.

"You should check in with him, just in case." Raquel gave me a saucy wink.

I rolled my eyes and said my good-byes, giving Fang a pat and Raquel a hug.

"Don't get eaten by a firebird," Raquel said, swinging back into her seat atop Fang.

"I'll do my best."

Weariness made my steps clumsy, and I clung to the handrail as I navigated the stairs down to the writer's bullpen. Quinn plodded after me. Dropping my overnight bag by the door, I delivered my film to the darkroom for the night crew to develop, then deposited my articles on the night editor's desk, collapsing into a chair while she read them. If she had questions, I wanted to answer them now rather than risk my articles not making the cut for the morning paper. Quinn sprawled at my feet, his jaw cracking in frequent yawns. To stay awake, I rifled through old editions of the *Chronicle*, searching for a mention of the missing firebirds. I found it in a week-old paper, tucked near the back. The article itself had been reprinted from the *Poughkeepsie Journal*.

ROBBERY OR INTERNAL SABOTAGE?

On Wednesday, two firebirds departed Haverstraw Village aboard a pegasi transport, destined for Timber Cove. Alarms were raised when the pegasi returned to their home stables days later, driverless, and with their harness straps appearing to have been severed by a jagged blade. The Federal Pentagon Defense immediately launched a full-scale interstate investigation.

After days of combing the shipping route, rescue crews discovered the driver unconscious and near death in the middle of the Sugar Flats mountain range, miles off course. The priceless birds and their original air sled transport were not recovered.

The events surrounding the firebirds' disappearance remain a mystery. Could this have been a botched act of sabotage on the part of the driver, the attack of a gang of robbers, or the driver's heroic attempt to save the pegasi's lives during a sled malfunction? The driver, the only person who knows what really happened, remains under around-the-clock healer supervision and has yet to awake from his coma.

When contacted for questioning, Director Evan Herzer of the Bureau of Environmental Management refused to release the name of the shipping company or the driver involved in this costly debacle. "We are conducting a full internal investigation and working closely with the FPD to uncover the culprit," Director Herzer said. "The real victim here is Timber Cove."

The article concluded with a summary of the devastation of Timber Cove but provided no more information about the firebirds. I rubbed my gritty eyes. The article hadn't included any more information than the ad, not even how many firebirds had been in the shipment.

Cultivating uncharitable thoughts about the *Poughkeepsie Journal* staff, I tucked the paper into my bag. After the night editor signed off on my articles, I stood on wobbly legs and stumbled toward Dahlia's door. Quinn fumbled to his feet to follow.

Light glinted around the editor in chief's cracked door, and although I didn't hear any voices inside, I rapped my knuckles against the wooden surface before entering. Belatedly, I checked my appearance. My clothes looked as if they had been slept in, which they had—more than once. I pulled the neck of my shirt away from my body and sniffed. *Pee-yew.*

"Come in," Dahlia said.

I dropped the clumsy bundle of air and water that had refused to form into a basic touch-up spell and pushed the door open. I had looked and smelled worse than this when delivering stories in the past.

Shadows cloaked the spacious office, except for the desk, where a single lantern's light pooled across loose-leaf papers and photographs. Dahlia sat behind her desk, glasses perched on the end of her nose and a pen in hand as she read. With her spiky gray hair and wiry physique, she still appeared fit enough to be a gryphon rider, which was how she had begun her career at the *Chronicle* decades earlier.

"If you're bringing me more coffee, Julian, you read my mind," she said. She jotted a note in the margin of a paper without glancing up.

"Sorry, no coffee," I said.

Dahlia lifted her head to examine me, then Quinn, over the rim of her glasses. A slow smile brightened her face. Setting aside the paper and pen, she removed her glasses and ran a hand through her hair.

"Welcome back. Raquel sent word ahead that you would return tonight. It looks like the trip home was grueling."

"We knew the importance of getting back quickly with our articles."

"Yes, thank you. You and Audrey did a phenomenal job covering the everlasting tree. I'm really proud of you both."

I stood straighter, folding her praise into my memory to relive when I wasn't so exhausted.

"I'm looking forward to hearing the stories that didn't

make it into the paper, but it can wait," Dahlia said. "You two look beat. Take a few days off—you deserve the rest."

"Actually," I said, hesitant to contradict her, "I'd like to pursue a new story."

"Right now?" Her eyebrows arched incredulously.

"In the morning. I got a lead at the tree."

"*At* the tree? Why didn't you pursue it while you were there?"

"Well, it was more of a lead *from* the tree."

Dahlia sat forward. "Explain."

"My question for the tree was where can I find the story of a lifetime."

Her eyes narrowed as she studied me, then she nodded. "You've never been shy about your ambition."

Not sure if that was an expression of censure or approval, I pulled my seed out of my pocket and held it out for Dahlia to examine. "This is my answer." I shifted the seed in my palm, playing the light off the telltale markings shimmering within the seed's ridges. "The seed itself is shaped like the end of a rounded feather, and the interior markings are a ringer for the ocellus of a firebird's tail feather."

"Perhaps." She plucked the seed from my palm, rolling it in the lantern light.

"This means the story of a lifetime, or at least the path to finding it, is linked to firebirds. I looked into it already and discovered the recent disappearance of firebirds destined for Timber Cove. I think I should investigate the event further."

Dahlia shook her head and handed my seed back to me. "That story has already been covered by multiple newspapers. It's a dead end and old news. The birds, their containers, and the gold shipped with them all disappeared over a week ago. The FPD concluded their hunt, and it's just as well; I had a better chance of becoming mayor than they did of finding those birds. Even if the firebirds survived the crash, they're long gone, and if their conveyance was brought down by thieves, the birds were likely killed for the gold."

"Firebirds are valuable. If no one found the birds' bodies, isn't it too soon to call off the search for them?" I clutched the seed in my fist, willing her to agree.

"The last known location of the transport was in the middle of Sugar Flats. There are places in those mountains where civilization has never touched. A full complement of trained shug monkeys could scour those mountains for the rest of their lives and never stumble across the firebirds, and that's only if they're still alive. If they're dead, they would have long since been a scavenger's meal."

"Perhaps a late-night flyover would pinpoint their location." Firebirds' feathers glowed; they would be as easy to spot in a forest as a small campfire.

"It's been tried. Repeatedly." Dahlia waved to cut off my protest before I could voice it. "Kylie, you asked the tree for a major story. That's not the sort of thing to happen at the beginning of a journalist's career."

"I know, but—"

"You have had a promising start and many exciting assignments in your brief time at the *Chronicle*. I'm afraid it might have made you overly . . . optimistic about achieving this groundbreaking story. You have plenty of time ahead of you to chase the story of your dreams."

"Would it hurt for me to spend time double-checking the facts on the missing firebirds?" How could she not see the flaw in her logic? This was the biggest story anyone would ever bring her. She should be behind me one hundred percent. At the very least, she should give me the freedom to confirm I was chasing a dead end, as she claimed.

Dahlia pushed back in her chair and crossed her arms—not a good sign.

"This paper is not going to devote journalistic hours to rehash an old story," she said, her voice as hard as her frown. "Don't make me regret sending you to the everlasting tree. You purported yourself well, but that project is over, and one good field assignment doesn't change the fact that you're a junior reporter. You have to take the assignments handed to you and accept when you're *not* to pursue a story. I need journalists I can depend on, not people who run around chasing whims. Is that clear?"

Cheeks burning, I nodded and turned to leave. Dahlia let me get to the door before she spoke again.

"Kylie, I appreciate your enthusiasm. Make sure you channel it in the right direction. In fact, I think you could benefit from a change of pace. Report to the business desk for an assignment when you come back—after you've gotten some rest."

"Yes, ma'am."

I waited until the door closed behind Quinn before allowing my shoulders to slump in defeat. I wanted to cry. The business desk was one step above the ads department. My chances of working any worthwhile stories had just dropped to nil.

5

Despite our stealthy late-night homecoming, Mika rushed out to greet Quinn when he landed on the second-floor balcony railing, tossing me a wave when she spotted me on the porch steps below. By the time I trudged up the interior stairs of the Victorian, where I rented a top-floor room next to Mika, she had ushered Quinn into her quarters for a full health checkup. I abandoned my bags inside the front door of my apartment, navigated the dark room without the use of a glowball, and crossed the balcony adjoining my room and Mika's. She had left her door open, and I let myself inside.

"How is he?" I asked softly. At two a.m., we were the only souls stirring; everyone else in the neighborhood was asleep, including our sharp-eared landlady, who lived downstairs.

"He has been pushing himself too hard," Mika said, disapproval tinging her tone. She sat on the floor beside Quinn, his wing draped across her lap, seemingly oblivious to the crushing weight of his stone feathers. Intricate quartz-tuned earth element flowed from her into Quinn. The patterns of her magic were too delicate and complicated for me to follow, but the visible loosening of Quinn's posture told me her ministrations were making him feel better.

"We had a deadline," Quinn said.

"The last important deadline we may ever have," I said. Conscious of my dirty clothes, I flopped into Mika's wooden desk chair. If Quinn hadn't been lying in the middle of the room, taking up all the space, I would have sat on the floor. Then again, I might not have been able to get back up, so maybe the chair had been a good choice.

"Oh, come on. The everlasting tree was amazing, but you'll find more great stories." Mika shot me an amused look, then turned her attention back to Quinn.

"Not if Dahlia has her way. She didn't care that my seed is going to lead me to the story of a lifetime."

"Is *that* what you asked for?"

"Yes." I crossed my arms over my chest, waiting for her to voice her disapproval.

"Because the story of a lifetime will bring about the most good?" she asked absently, not glancing up.

"Yes! How did you know?"

"Kylie, you talk about doing that with your stories all the time."

"I do?"

"Mostly when you're trying to convince me to allow you to feature me in the paper." She grimaced, her gaze darting to me, then away. As if she could follow my thoughts, which jumped straight to my unsatisfied curiosity about how she had cured the comatose gargoyles and my suspicion that her story would warrant front-page status in the *Chronicle*, she rushed to ask, "How is Dahlia preventing you from chasing your big story?"

"Look at my seed," I said, drawing it from my pocket and

thrusting it into her line of sight. "It looks like a firebird feather, right? Guess what went missing recently. Firebirds. Only that's 'old news,' according to Dahlia, and she doesn't want me to waste journalistic hours rehashing an old story —her words. Instead, she's got me working for the business section. How am I supposed to follow a story of this magnitude without my editor's support?" I hated the whine in my voice, but I couldn't seem to control it. I shoved the seed back in my pocket with a frustrated punch.

"Did she strictly forbid you from following the seed's clues, or just from following this particular firebird story?" Mika asked.

"I don't know. It felt like both."

"That seems unlikely."

"What are you saying?"

Mika didn't answer immediately, waiting for Quinn to turn himself in the tight quarters so she could examine and heal his other wing. I hadn't realized how nicked and scratched the gargoyle had become until Mika had soothed all the rough spots from his citrine hide. Even his feathers looked glossy in the soft moonlight and dim glowballs.

"Maybe the missing firebirds have nothing to do with the story you're supposed to find," Mika said, finally answering me.

"Dahlia didn't think they did," Quinn said. He lay with his eyes closed, his voice sleepy. "She thought it was too soon in Kylie's career for her to be chasing a story this momentous."

"What if it isn't too soon?" Even I winced at the wail in my tone this time, and Quinn cracked an eyelid to pin me with a chastising look. I ran my hands through my hair, grimacing at its greasy texture. A small part of me that I didn't want to acknowledge had been relieved when Dahlia ordered me to leave the firebird story alone. I wasn't in a rush to have the biggest story of my career completed so soon. But I couldn't squander this opportunity and potentially miss out entirely on the most significant story of my life.

Modulating my voice deeper, I said, "I can't ignore this."

"I don't think you should," Mika said.

"Now I'm confused. What about Dahlia?"

"She forbade you from chasing the old firebird story, but what if you approached it from a different angle?"

"Like what?"

"I don't know. You're the reporter." Mika ran her hands along the underside of Quinn's wing as he stretched it over her lap, pausing to apply her healing magic to several specific locations. "Even if you don't think of a different angle, it sounds to me like she simply didn't want your pursuit of this story to interfere with your assignments. What you do in your own time is up to you."

I opened and closed my mouth like a beached fish. "But—"

I had expected to have the resources of the *Chronicle* behind me as I chased this story. I had even envisioned Dahlia being excited by this amazing opportunity for her paper. If I were being honest, I had expected her to praise my choice of a question and wholeheartedly support me.

"Going after the story on my own will be hard, and it will take more time."

"So?"

"I'll help you," Quinn said.

I leaned forward and stroked his forehead as I contemplated Mika's suggestion. She was right. Half the stories I had written for the paper hadn't been assignments. They had been born out of my intuition, and I had developed and written them independently of anyone's permission. It would have been nice to have Dahlia's support, but I didn't need it.

My lips twisted when I remembered Dahlia's admonishment that she needed dependable journalists, not people who chased whims. The story of a lifetime wasn't a *whim*, and even if I couldn't devote *all* my time to it, that didn't mean I had to devote *none* of my time, either. If I hadn't been so tired, I would have realized it sooner.

"Besides, if you develop the story in your downtime," Mika said, slanting me a sly look, "Dahlia might be so impressed that she promotes you."

"Mika, you're a genius."

She snorted and bent to double-check Quinn's paws. "I'm an entrepreneur who spent years building my business in my free time after I got off work. You do what you have to when you're pursuing your dreams." Satisfied with her final inspection of the gargoyle, Mika stood and ran a loving hand down Quinn's spine. "All better, though you need rest, Quinn. Why don't you join Oliver and Anya?"

She gestured to the roof, where two gargoyle silhouettes lounged at the ridgeline, Oliver's Chinese dragon body twined around a winged panther.

"Thank you, Mika. It's good to be home." Quinn jumped to the railing, then sprang to the rooftop.

I cringed, expecting the railing to squeal in protest to the hundred-pound gargoyle's ascent. When it didn't, I shifted for a better look. Thick boards had been nailed into a crude support for the railing where it was attached to the apartment walls.

"Temporary upgrades," Mika said. "Marcus is coming by later this week to build a sturdier railing for us."

"Oh, it's Marcus now, is it?"

She made a show of yawning. "It's late and I'm beat. Good night." She extinguished the soft lights, plunging the room into shadows.

"Good night? I don't think so. I need answers, Mika Stillwater, and you're not getting any sleep until—" I cut myself off when I realized she was laughing at me.

"You're too easy." She swept a hand toward her bedside lamp, lighting the wick with a pinch of fire element. "How about we catch up over tea?"

I lifted my chin, pretending to be miffed. "I thought you'd never ask. I'll be right back."

Hobbling to my apartment, I opened the windows to air out the musty aroma that had accumulated in the small space during the weeks it had been shut tight. By the time I shucked my shoes and padded in sock-clad feet back to Mika's apartment, she had heated the tea and was waiting for me.

Her floor plan was a mirror image of mine, but whereas I had decorated with colorful pillows and seating for guests, Mika had opted for purely functional decor. We each enjoyed a large bay window overlooking the street, and I had situated my bed beneath it so I could stare up at the stars at night before falling to sleep. Mika chose to cram the largest table she could find into the same space. Its surface currently housed a row of lifelike miniatures of Oliver in various shades of quartz; a stack of books, each spine neatly aligned with the one beneath it; and a jar of clear quartz marbles. The rest of the room was even more Spartan, with a single bed pressed against one wall and a narrow bookcase against the other.

I sat on the floor this time, deciding that if I couldn't muster the energy to get back up, I would sleep there. Mika wouldn't mind. Plus, I would have plenty of space in which to stretch out; the middle of the room used to have a coffee table, but it appeared to have gone missing.

"Did you get robbed?" I asked. At Mika's puzzled frown, I gestured to the wide-open floor.

"Oh. There wasn't enough space in here for Oliver, so I sold the table." Sinking into a cross-legged position in front of me, she handed me a mug of tea.

"I thought you were going to say you are making room for a larger bed. Is that tiny cot even long enough for Velasquez?"

I expected to tease a smile out of her, but she eyed the bed speculatively. "I don't know. I haven't had a chance to get him in it yet."

I laughed at her woeful tone, accidentally splashing hot tea over my fingers. Cursing, I set the mug on the floor and shook off the scalding liquid. "You seriously need to catch me up. On everything."

"There's not much to tell you," she said, knowing full well how much that statement would drive me crazy. "You were the one at the everlasting tree. You should be the one catching me up."

"You can read all about the everlasting tree in the paper. In fact, you should have been following along and already be caught up on the news, since your favorite journalist was doing half the writing. Besides, I think you've been up to more interesting adventures than me." I gave her new scars a pointed look.

Mika curled her hands into fists, tilting them toward the light. I struggled to read her expression. Was that a glint of pride?

"I'm impressed you were able to give yourself such symmetrical, geometric scars." I reached for her hand, and she let me run my finger across the trail of amethyst marks.

If they hadn't been warm, I would have sworn I was touching polished quartz. "They're rather beautiful."

Her green eyes snapped up to meet mine, searching my face. "Do you think so?"

"If you could re-create the 'accident,' I wouldn't be surprised if people asked you to make similar marks on them."

She smiled and shyly admitted, "I think they're pretty, too."

"Could you?"

"Could I what?"

"Re-create the accident."

Her smile died. "No."

"Did it have something to do with healing the sick gargoyles?"

"You can't ask about that, Kylie." Something dark filled her eyes, and when she focused on me this time, the hairs on the backs of my arms rose and a warning tingle fused my spine. "That is a tale meant only for gargoyles."

"Off the record?" The words rasped out of my dry throat, but the weight of her gaze prevented me from taking a sip of tea.

"No."

Her denial—her lack of trust in me—hurt. She saw it, too, and her gaze softened and the darkness receded, freeing me to move again. I gave my shoulders a shake. I hadn't realized Mika could be so intimidating.

"Please, Kylie," she said, and I didn't know if she was asking me to drop it or to forgive her.

I released a pent-up breath. "All right. I won't bring it up again." For whatever reason, keeping the cure a secret was important to Mika, and I would respect that, even if restraining my curiosity made me break out in hives.

"Thank you."

I lasted three seconds before my next question burst out: "What was the reason for the squad's big rush back to the city?"

Mika shuddered. "Murder."

"What?! Where?"

"A body washed up on the banks of the Lincoln River at the Focal Park beach, and the person didn't die of natural causes. That's all I learned from the captain, and we've only been back a day, so I haven't had a chance to talk to Marcus since we parted."

"You've been back a full day?"

Mika nodded.

The squad must have pushed themselves harder than I thought. For one dead body? I rubbed my tingling fingertips against my bent knees, my story senses clamoring. Murders weren't common in Terra Haven, but the city guard should have been more than equipped to deal with one. The FPD was summoned for more dangerous issues. They wouldn't have been rushed back by the mayor for something as simple as a single murder. When I voiced my suspicions, Mika merely shrugged.

"I'm sure they didn't share every detail with me," she said.

"And you didn't ask? With as close as you two seem to be, I bet Velasquez would have shared the whole story with you."

"Maybe. But why would I want to know more details about a murder?"

"Why *wouldn't* you?"

Mika sipped her tea, amusement glinting in her eyes at my exasperation. "Because I like sleeping at night. Besides, it was none of my business."

"Of course it's your business. It's everyone's business if a murderer is loose in our city."

"Thanks for that thought."

Her expression turned mulish, and I could tell she wanted to drop the conversation. Clenching my teeth, I tamped down on my urge to interrogate her further. Obviously, she knew next to nothing, as much as that boggled my mind. If our places had been swapped, I would have spent every hour of the return trip finagling all the details I could out of Grant.

"Maybe I should pay a visit to the captain tomorrow," I mused. If he wouldn't answer my questions about the murder, I would have a legitimate reason for kicking him in his shins.

A *semi*-legitimate reason.

"Didn't you just decide to focus your free time on firebirds? Besides, the murder has already been written about by your favorite person."

I groaned and dropped my head into my hands. "Nathan landed the scoop?"

"Yep."

Of course he had. Like all senior journalists, Nathan received the prominent story assignments. However, he was the only writer on staff who enjoyed using his seniority to impede the advancement of younger reporters, specifically me. He had tried to steal the story that had landed me the opportunity to go to the everlasting tree, and only luck and quick thinking had helped me win out over him. Just thinking about his underhanded tactics made my blood boil. If anyone deserved to be assigned boring business write-ups, it was Nathan, not me.

"Unless you were looking for an excuse to run into

Grant," Mika said. "If so, you could come with me next time I visit their house."

I started to decline but curiosity won out. "*Their* house?"

"The squad lives together in the Copper District. The place is pretty spacious and as nice as you would expect, given its location. It has a big courtyard and, well, that's about all I saw when I was there, but Marcus said Oliver and I are invited over when they finish this investigation. I'm sure no one would have a problem with you coming, too."

I shook my head, mentally wincing at the image of me trailing along on Mika's date in some desperate hope to get Grant to notice me. "No. I don't think that would be . . . a good use of my time."

"Oh?" Mika cocked her head, studying me. "Have you changed your mind about the captain?"

"He has no interest in me. You saw how he forgot I existed after the tree bloomed. What you missed was earlier in the day when he interrupted an interview I was conducting with the mayor to 'save her' from my pestering. His rescue plan included ruffling my hair like a child's." I demonstrated on myself, a flush of embarrassment heating my cheeks at the memory. Mika cringed in sympathy. "My crush on the odious man is officially dead."

"Uh-huh."

"Don't give me that. There are plenty of attractive men in this city. I don't need to pine after the one who treats me like a pesky little sister."

"Uh-huh."

"Besides, I'm going to be too busy to think about him, because I'm going to follow your advice and devote all my free time to tracking down the story of a lifetime."

6

I woke late the next morning and savored the sensation of lying tucked beneath soft blankets and atop my fluffy feather mattress. Best yet, I was clean. Before crawling into bed last night, I had taken a long, luxuriant shower. Watching the light play across the ceiling, I contemplated another shower this morning, just because I could. Seed Town and the everlasting tree had been a marvelous adventure, but the comforts of home couldn't be matched. However, my stomach grumbled, reminding me how long it had been since I had eaten a real meal, and I decided a shower could wait.

After pilfering the communal kitchen for leftovers, I created dozens of rumor scouts to scour the city for any audible mention of firebirds while I ate. An hour later, I made a pilgrimage to the library, returning home with every book that contained a mention of firebirds. The trip exhausted me, and I napped through the afternoon, waking in time to beat the dinner rush at Harvey House. I bought a bubbling-hot potpie to go and ate it in bed while skimming the massive collection of borrowed reference books. Not knowing what to look for made my search tedious. I learned firebirds mated for life, that their guano was especially beneficial to poppies, and that centuries earlier, the native tribespeople had hunted them to the brink of extinction for their feathers. However, several decades ago, laws had been enacted to protect the birds from hunting, so today a firebird faced threats only from rival firebirds, large wildcats, wyverns, and occasionally great horned owls.

I also discovered a lot of wild claims had been made throughout history about the luminescent birds. One book declared firebirds to be more in tune with the magnetic poles than any other avian species, though they were too violent to train as carrier birds like pigeons. Another book touted their supposed good luck, claiming that sighting a firebird in the wild would ensure wealth in one's future. A tattered journal even included a recipe for stewed firebird that would "imbue the diner with abundance." Tribal myths bestowed all manner of import on firebirds, from creation myths, where firebirds crafted the sun from their song and feathers, to morality tales in which the birds played trickster roles, stealing the light and joy from otherwise well-meaning animals.

The most reputable sources all agreed nesting firebirds possessed a unique restorative magic that could counter any devastation the planet or its inhabitants could mete out. The only dispute was the range of a given firebird's magic. Some sources claimed a bird's powers were commensurate with its size, others with its diet, and still others with its age and gender. Depending on which source I trusted, the Timber Cove restoration project would have needed anywhere from two to seven birds.

None of my new knowledge got me any closer to a fresh angle to put on the missing firebirds story, nor did my research spark any insights about what my seed might need to evolve, but I took copious notes anyway. As with any new project, once I put together enough facts, a story idea would emerge.

Quinn slept through the entire day, lying as unmoving as only a gargoyle could. Our rushed trip back from the everlasting tree, as well as the frantic, exhilarating days in Seed Town, had taken a greater toll on both of us than we had realized.

After a night filled with dreams of firebirds, I woke the next morning to a cool breeze that carried the familiar sounds of my neighborhood and an aroma of baking bread. I tugged on a fresh pair of pants and a soft button-up shirt—both blissfully clean, not on their third or fifth day of wear after an elemental scrub—and checked my message bowl. Bundles of rumor scouts filled it to bursting. Having expected only one or two scouts to pick up anything, the sight of the overflowing bowl imbued me with hope.

With a spring in my step, I trotted downstairs to dine with my landlady, Ms. Zuberrie. While devouring oven-warm bread slathered in jam, a vegetable-and-egg frittata, and fresh fruit, I regaled Ms. Zuberrie with tales from the tree, and she caught me up on local gossip. Not much changed in our neighborhood, but she wasn't the kind of woman to let a pruned plant or delivery go unnoticed if it happened on our block. I appreciated her attention to detail —some might call it nosiness—recognizing a kindred spirit in the older woman. By the time I returned to my room, Quinn was waiting for me at the balcony door. I opened it for him, then settled in the center of my bed to give him space to come in.

"Wow! Are those all returned rumor scouts?" Quinn squeezed through the doorway to peer into the glass bowl on my side table. The half-grown gargoyle barely had room to navigate, bumping into my wardrobe and the love seat before he found a place to sit. Maybe Mika was onto something with her extremely minimalist decor, but I was loath to part with the limited furniture I had accumulated. I would rather find a new, larger place to live, one that would fit Quinn and friends. I was pretty sure Mika would be willing to move, too. I made a mental note to broach the subject with her.

"Keep your toes crossed that one of those scouts found something useful for us," I said.

I grinned when Quinn lifted a paw and attempted to cross one toe over another, succeeding only in hooking his claws together.

It had taken me years to perfect the specialized design of a rumor scout. Not only could my scouts detect a specific word or phrase of my choosing, but doing so would also trigger them to record all sound in the vicinity for a short time. Once they were full, the homing portion of the spell activated. I could have tuned the scouts directly to my magical signature, and as each one returned, it would have attached itself to my temple and fed the recorded words directly into my ear. Since I had wanted uninterrupted sleep, I had tuned these to my message bowl, instead.

The scouts were my pride and joy, and they had proved themselves useful beyond measure in pinpointing new leads for me. Even so, they had their limitations: They could only record what they heard; if people were discussing firebirds for hours and my scouts were nowhere nearby, I would never know. They began recording at the sound of my chosen trigger, which meant they often didn't include the word or phrase I selected, just the dialogue that followed it, leaving me to piece together the full statement. They also had a life span limited by the strength of the elements I wove, and even gargoyle enhanced, I couldn't send rumor scouts much more than a mile from my current location. However, the scouts weren't designed to do all the work for me, merely give me a starting place.

Since I didn't want to climb over Quinn, I used a net of air to lift my bag from beside the door and drop it onto the bed next me. I burrowed through the bag, pulling out my journal and a pencil. Then I hooked the top rumor scout with a finger of air and pulled it free of the spelled bowl before activating it. A disembodied woman's voice spilled out to fill the room.

"—are crucial. Without firebirds to assist the forest's regrowth, Timber Cove is going to need people like you and me more than ever. Our work in Focal Park is almost complete. If we left now, we could—"

Her words cut off, the rumor scout having stopped recording them. The elements holding the scout together unraveled and dissipated. I tapped my pencil against the blank page. The woman hadn't revealed anything useful. I triggered the next rumor scout.

"—last time. This time I get to be a phoenix and you're the firebird," a kid's high-pitched voice declared. The child spoke over the background noise of many kids' voices.

"It's my turn to be the phoenix," another kid whined. "I want—"

I slashed a knife of earth through the rumor scout, destroying it. An argument between kids on the playground wouldn't produce a lead.

Quinn stretched, bumping his tail against my desk and knocking several books to the floor as he lay down. I waved away his apology and activated the next rumor scout.

The blare of a scornful voice startled us both. "—about

as bright and half as useful as a firebird, too. Look at the size of him. He'll eat you out of house and home—"

Another fruitless rumor scout. I disbanded the elements and grabbed the next.

"—is a travesty," a self-important masculine voice proclaimed. "One that could have been avoided. Complacency like this is how the taxpayers get ripped off."

I recognized the speaker's voice, as would half the city: Luther Wetherill, one of Terra Haven's wealthiest residents and a prominent businessman—not to mention a full-spectrum pentacle potential. As an FSPP, he could wield massive amounts of all five elements, a skill that naturally boosted him to the top of society's hierarchy. FSPPs often found high-profile jobs, such as working in FPD squads or running global companies, and it tended to give them oversize egos and obnoxious attitudes. Or maybe I was letting my biases color my judgment.

"To be clear, Mr. Wetherill, are you saying the government didn't take the appropriate precautions with the firebirds?" a softer male voice asked.

Wetherill was quick to respond, his answer too polished not to be rehearsed. "The government needs to tighten its regulations. It's people like you and me who foot the bill when disasters like this happen. The government is only as good as—"

The scout fell apart, overburdened by the amount of sound it had captured, but I had gotten the gist. Wetherill owned his own shipping business and seemed to be taking this opportunity to smear his competitors—or to misdirect suspicion. The government had yet to release the name of the shipping company responsible for the firebird transport. Only a few transcontinental shipping companies were large enough to handle such an expensive contract, Wetherill's

Capstone Transportation being one of them. Until the government's investigation concluded, either absolving or indicting the mystery shipping company, rumors would dominate the story.

Chasing down the responsible company would be a logical course of action. Whoever had been in charge would have insider information about the firebirds, their crates, any tracking spells that might have been put on the birds, and any other pertinent information the Bureau of Environmental Management wasn't releasing to the public.

Nevertheless, I hesitated to make a note in my journal. Such an investigation would be difficult. No company would volunteer information to a journalist about their own screw-up. Not unless they felt they could trust that journalist explicitly, the way they would a family member.

Distaste twisted my mouth.

"What is it?" Quinn asked.

"Nothing." *Just thinking about doing something I swore I would never do: use my parents to advance my career.*

My parents were wealthy, influential, and well connected. It would have been easy to use their connections to land a cushy job as a writer for a specialty publication. However, I had been determined to make it on my own, and my parents had respected my decision, even when doing so meant altering my name to hide my lineage. Which was why no one—not my landlady, not Dahlia, not even Mika—knew my true identity. Despite living near poverty for several years, I hadn't once asked my parents for a favor, and I had vowed never to use their connections to further my own goals.

However, I had never had a story lead to their company doorstep, either. As the owners of Airstrong Shipping, one of the nation's largest transport companies, my parents would likely be able to point me toward the party responsible for the firebird shipment. It might even have been Airstrong that had taken on the contract . . .

Guilt sank claws into me. In my preoccupation with the firebirds, I had failed to consider the ramifications of this lost transport. Eventually, the company responsible would come to light and suffer the public backlash. A shipping company traded on its reputation. If they couldn't guarantee the safety of their packages, no one would book their services. My parents' livelihood could be in jeopardy.

"Your face doesn't say *nothing*. You look like you're thinking about a story," Quinn said.

I stilled the pencil I had been absently tapping against my chin and focused on him. "You're right. I'm wondering if we can figure out who shipped the firebirds before it becomes public news."

I shoved aside my unsubstantiated fear for my parents' business. They were savvy and possessed far more experience in their field than I did. If they had anything to do with the missing firebirds, I had to trust they knew how to handle it, just as they would accept I was a professional in my field and knew how to track a story. Contacting the local Airstrong headquarters as *part* of my investigation would not trample my vow of independence. In fact, I didn't even need to talk to my parents, just a representative from their company. I would treat this lead like any other—and with great discretion. The last thing I needed was for someone to connect me to my parents after the years I had worked to build an independent reputation.

"But whoever lost them wouldn't know where the birds are now, would they?" Quinn asked, pulling me out of my ruminations.

"No, but they might give us another clue to keep us

going in the right direction." I jotted *Airstrong* and *Capstone* in my journal. It didn't stop me from hoping one of the remaining rumor scouts would give us a better angle to pursue.

The next six scouts included mentions of firebirds as part of company names; I had never realized how many jewelry companies had adopted the animal's name for their own. Finally, I came across a rumor scout with a recording of people talking, however circumstantially, about the missing firebirds.

"—would be very useful," a man said. He sounded young and enthusiastic. "Think about it: if you had a harnessed firebird, you could use it to sniff out gold."

"If you tried to harness a firebird, it would eat your fingers for lunch," an older male said.

"I had a woman try to harness my firebird once," a new man chimed in, his tone thick with innuendo. I rolled my eyes.

"No one wants to hear about your firebird, George," a woman said.

"Then what about Lunacy?" the young man asked. "I heard if you drink the blood of a creature within the labyrinth, you'll gain that creature's powers."

I should have expected to hear someone trying to connect the missing firebirds with Lunacy Labyrinth. Anytime a new mystery cropped up in or near the city, conspiracy theorists came out of the woodwork to connect it to the distasteful ruins.

Ready to rule this rumor scout useless, I slashed a knife of earth toward it but pulled up short when I heard a familiar sound in the background. Beneath the young man waxing on about gaining the power to light up, and the others teasing him about how that might improve his love life, I caught the chime of a guard station bell.

We were listening to a conversation among on-duty city guards. Interesting. I would have expected guards to detect my rumor scouts before they could make a recording. Either this scout had gotten lucky or my design was more stealthy than I realized. I would have to run some experiments. Later. Too bad these guards hadn't been ranked higher and privy to case details, but I could work with this information.

As the scout dissolved, I wrote *guards* in my notebook. I frequented several taverns popular among off-duty guards, both as a means to form friendships with guards and for information that might lead to stories. I would make the rounds tonight and put out feelers to see if any guards had better intelligence about the missing firebirds. Perhaps I would pick up something more useful than conspiracy theories. I also made a note to monitor local mining companies and precious-metals traders. It was a stretch, but if any one of them reported a sudden increase in revenue, it might lend credit to the young guard's original harnessed-firebird theory.

The next two rumor scouts contained conversations about Timber Cove, a third covered a business transaction conducted at Firebird Investments, and the last deafened us with the strident cry of a merchant hawking a talisman certain to "bring you more fortune than a pet firebird."

Quinn stretched to read my depressingly short list of leads. I tried not to allow the dearth of inspiration to discourage me. I had found big stories on less.

"Why the guards?" Quinn asked.

I explained my reasoning while squeezing around him to survey my wardrobe. My current ensemble would work fine for chasing down the firebird story, but if I wanted to prove to Dahlia that I was taking my new assignment seriously, I needed to look the part of a business writer. Instead of the comfortable shirt I currently wore, I cinched myself into a black leather bustier with gauzy lace straps and paired it with a lightweight jacket. When I examined myself in the mirror, I looked like a businesswoman. Even better, without the jacket, the outfit would be perfect for chatting up the guards tonight.

"Ready?" Quinn asked.

"Just about." I packed my camera, journal, and pencil into my bag, tossed an apple on top, and slung the strap over my shoulder. "All right. Now I'm set."

Quinn maneuvered himself in a tight circle and padded out to the balcony. I followed him.

"What's first?" he asked.

Normally I would have been eager to chase down fresh leads, but the taverns wouldn't get crowded until nightfall, and I wasn't in a hurry to show up at the Airstrong headquarters. More important, I couldn't get Dahlia's disappointed expression out of my thoughts. I wanted to restore her faith in me, and that meant proving I could perform a mundane assignment amicably.

"I'm going to head to the *Chronicle* and get this business job out of the way. It's probably going to be a boring day." Did anything truly interesting ever happen in the business world? "It might be a good day to stay here and rest, if you need it."

Quinn jumped to perch on the railing, his front feet lined up between his rear paws in a position no real lion could have managed. "I feel great. I think I should check in with my sources to see if they've heard anything about the missing firebirds."

By sources, he meant fellow gargoyles. Having taken his

cues from me, Quinn had begun to cultivate a network of contacts he could call upon when we needed information. Most gargoyles maintained semi-stationary roosts around the city, and people tended to forget they were present. More than once, one of Quinn's gargoyle friends had picked up on a rumor my scouts had missed.

"Good thinking," I said.

Quinn smiled and leapt from the railing to glide out into the street before flapping higher. I watched him soar over the closest row of houses, wishing we could trade places.

———

MY BUDDING BAD MOOD LIFTED ON MY WALK AS I REJOICED AT being back among the hubbub of Terra Haven—the ruckus of the thoroughfares crowded with wagons, carts, and riders; the glimpses of colorful birds, pegasi, gryphons, and gargoyles swooping through the skies, their shadows flickering across the sunbaked brick and stone buildings; and the sweet aromas from Neti's bakery on the corner competing with the succulent scents from the meat and sandwich vendors crowding the small park during the morning rush. I rubbed elbows with messengers and shoppers, finely dressed business owners, and ragged laborers on the sidewalk. Best of all, I walked on cobblestones, not dust, and every step didn't threaten to send me into a coughing fit. It was good to be home.

By the time the *Chronicle* came into sight, I had convinced myself that covering a couple boring stories and paying my dues wouldn't be so bad. Then, when the time was right, I would bring the story of a lifetime to Dahlia, and she would be impressed enough to permanently assign me to write features.

I slowed when Quinn sailed over the nearby rooftops and landed beside me, his smooth paws slipping on the cobblestones.

"Burnette hasn't heard anything about firebirds," he announced.

Burnette was a cherubic purple and gold ametrine gargoyle with the body of a bear cub, the head of a hippo, and tiny wings that carried her with surprising speed when she chose to leave the library roof, which wasn't often. Since she overlooked one of the city's most frequented buildings as well as the expansive plaza in front of it, Burnette often had the best tidbits of information. It was disappointing to learn she didn't have any special insights to help us today.

"Everyone is talking about the dead body," Quinn added.

"I'm not surprised," said a voice that made my shoulders hunch. Reluctantly, I turned from Quinn to face senior journalist Nathan Aspell.

If I hadn't been familiar with his personality, I might have considered Nathan attractive. Slender and fit, he maintained a shading of dark stubble that lent strength to his soft jaw, and his dark-framed glasses gave him a bookish countenance I usually found appealing. Since we were well acquainted, however, I noticed how practiced his gesture appeared when he ran his hand through his slicked-back black hair and the smug tightening of his lips when he looked us over.

Nathan hefted a rolled-up carpet, forcing me to step back or be hit. Behind him, the door to the *Chronicle* swept shut. So close. If only I had left the house a minute later, I could have avoided this encounter.

"Hello, Nathan," I said, determined to be professional.

"The whole city is abuzz with talk of the murder," he

said, not acknowledging my greeting. "It's no wonder, since it's the most interesting thing to happen to the city all year."

I suppressed a smile at his absurd statement. The everlasting tree had been the most interesting thing to happen to Terra Haven's residents in the last decade, and if he was excluding the tree's blooming on the technicality of it not happening *in* the city, then the destruction of Focal Park—which I had covered for the paper—outranked a single murder. His self-aggrandizing would have been laughable if it hadn't been so irritating.

"Any new leads?" I asked.

Nathan leaned close, using his marginal greater height to loom as he waggled his finger in my face. "Na-ah-ah. I'm not telling. You get to read about the ongoing investigation in tomorrow's paper."

Clinging to my professionalism, I resisted the urge to make a rude gesture at Nathan's back when he bent to unfurl the carpet. He activated the carpet's built-in flying spell, then sat on the hovering platform. Crossing his arms, he said, "The only thing I can tell you is I'll be working closely with Captain Monaghan today."

His smug smile made my fists clench. Either Nathan had figured out I had a crush on Grant—*past tense,* I silently insisted—or he enjoyed rubbing in that he would be working with important people on a headline story.

Nathan directed the rug several feet down the sidewalk before turning back with a nonchalance that didn't fool me. "I forgot to ask: What was your question for the everlasting tree?"

"It's private," I snapped. No way was I going to tell him I was on the trail of a massive story. If I did, not only would he find an excuse to glue himself to me for the foreseeable future, but he would also steal the story from me the first chance he got.

"Well, way to be back at your post. I heard you got assigned to business. That was smart of Dahlia. You're a young journalist and can use experience in all departments. Business is grounding and will help you fill out your skill set. It's easy to write action-packed stories, but to get readers interested in the humdrum happenings of commerce takes real skill. You'll get there."

The roar of my blood in my ears drowned out everything but my pulse. I yanked open the door to the *Chronicle*, holding it for Quinn to enter, then followed close enough that I clipped his heels. Just before the door shut, I tossed my parting words at Nathan: "If you're lucky, maybe Dahlia will give you one of these tougher assignments one day, too."

I didn't wait to catch his expression. My words were a hollow victory in our petty exchange; Nathan still got to cover the paper's top story today, while I was reporting to the most boring department at the *Chronicle*.

"He's such a jerk," Quinn said. "It's not fair he gets the exciting stories."

I stomped up the stairs, my steps drowning out Quinn's heavy rock tread. "He's been here a long time. And his writing is decent," I forced myself to say. As much as I loathed the senior reporter, Nathan knew how to present facts in an easy-to-consume manner. He didn't go as deep as I would in an investigation, but he met his deadlines. If I had to describe him as a journalist, it would be "not great, but solid." At a newspaper that printed daily editions, being a solid, dependable writer went a long way. Hadn't Dahlia said almost as much to me the other night?

"Still, does he have to be so awful about it?" Quinn asked.

I shrugged, done with defending Nathan.

We swung by the press table to grab the latest edition of the paper and the final special edition of my everlasting tree coverage. I smiled with pleasure to see one of my photos stretched across the front page. It was one I had taken while standing on Quinn's back just before we had all asked our questions. The sun's rays lit the rim of the massive canopy and divided into columns of light and shadows, enhancing the magical moment and highlighting hundreds of eager, upturned faces. Even better, my article and byline flowed beneath the picture.

Take that, Nathan.

I tucked both papers into my bag—today's edition to catch up on local news and the special edition to add to my collection.

Skirting the writers' bullpen, I knocked on the open doorway of Eloise Nazari's small office. The business editor sat behind a cramped desk drowning in newspapers, notes, clipped articles, and photos. On a tiny stand crammed next to the window behind her, a communication bowl overflowed with snarls of elemental messages, and two new bundles of air squeezed through the cracked window to settle precariously atop the others in the time it took Eloise to look up and acknowledge my presence.

"Just a minute, I'll— Oh, Kylie." Eloise waved a slender hand, gesturing for me to enter. Newspaper ink stained her fingertips, and the smudge of pencil lead marred the tip of her chin.

"How can I be of help?" I asked, stepping across the threshold. Quinn took one peek at the claustrophobic interior and lay down against the wall outside the door.

Eloise's thick eyebrows rose, and after a beat, she gave me a decisive nod. "I wasn't sure whether to expect you today or tomorrow. One moment." She set down a type-written draft she had been marking with revisions and stuck her pencil into a loose bun piled atop her head. Humming to herself, she rummaged through a stack of papers on her left, collecting a small pile of notes. "You missed the morning's assignment allocation. I'm afraid all that's left are filler pieces."

I held in a sigh and kept my smile steady. "I'll take whatever you've got."

Eloise treated me to an inscrutable stare. Then she thumbed through the pile of notes, set a few aside, and handed me the rest. Her sharp handwriting detailed names and addresses, one per piece of paper. "When we have extra white space, we cover the openings of new businesses. I need one ready to go by tonight, and four more by the end of the week."

Great. When she said *filler pieces*, she meant it literally.

"What's my word count?" I asked.

"Keep it tight, but we need some flexibility. Give me a hundred-word version and a fifty-word abbreviated version of each."

I managed a jerky nod, speechless. Eloise's word count barely allowed room for company names and addresses. These wouldn't be articles so much as bare-bones listings not much longer than the notes in my hand. Last week, I was writing multiple page-long articles a day for special-edition releases; today I was writing glorified ad copy. If Dahlia had designed this assignment to humble me, it was working.

"It won't be the excitement you're used to," Eloise said,

"but I expect you to treat these articles with the full dedication you would give a feature story."

"Of course," I choked out, wondering if she understood the absurdity of her instructions. How much dedication could I give to fifty words?

The editor graced me with an unexpected grin. "I thought you were going to be hard to work with after your lofty beginnings. I mean, even this morning, nothing on my desk could compete with the everlasting tree, but these assignments"—she flicked her fingers at the pieces of paper I held—"they make even my regular writers moan and complain. Keep up your good attitude, and we're going to get along just fine."

Going to get along? That implied I would be reporting to her for more than today's assignment. How long did Eloise expect me to be working in her department? What had Dahlia said to her? I wracked my brain for a subtle way to ask without contradicting her opinion of me, coming up blank.

"I look forward to your first article," Eloise said, dismissing me.

I trudged from her office. Neither Quinn nor I spoke until we reached the sidewalk.

"Fifty words? How are you supposed to write anything interesting in such a small space?" Quinn asked.

"It'll be challenging." But if this was what Dahlia wanted me to focus on, I would make the most of every word. These would be the best tiny, inconsequential articles the editor in chief or Eloise had ever seen—if they even got printed. I clamped down on a growl and did my best to project optimism. "Let's see where we're headed today. We have a tailor, a custom furniture shop, a new leisure boat rental company, a roof company, and a specialty stable, which, based on the address, will be catering strictly to the wealthy. Any sound interesting to you?"

"Not really."

Normally, I would have striven to accomplish an assignment as quickly as possible, but I couldn't bring myself to rush for filler work. "We have to pick at least one to do today."

"Then we can focus on the firebirds?" Quinn asked.

"Exactly. The sooner we can present Dahlia with a fresh angle on the firebirds, the sooner she'll see we need to be working on more consequential assignments, like evolving my seed." And so long as I turned in my tiny filler article first, Dahlia couldn't accuse me of wasting time chasing whims.

"Do any of those businesses look like they might have information about firebirds?"

"I like the way you think, Quinn." I fanned out the papers, wracking my brain for possible connections a furniture shop or stable might have with firebirds. None came to mind, so I checked their addresses. Maybe one of the businesses would be located near somewhere I already planned to visit.

My gaze snagged on the boat rental's address.

"This one is inside Focal Park, on the same beach where the dead body washed up a few days ago." I waved the paper at Quinn. "Are you thinking what I'm thinking?"

"That their business is going to be affected by the murder?"

"Precisely."

"But what does that have to do with firebirds?"

"Probably nothing, but we might run into a certain FPD squad investigating the murder."

Quinn's eyebrows scrunched together. "Nathan is

already covering that story, and he might be there. Running into him once today was enough."

"I think we'll have to take the risk. If anyone has more information about the missing firebirds, it's the FPD."

Excitement quickened my pulse—because I was following my seed's clue and chasing down a big, potentially life-changing story, of course. It had nothing to do with the possibility of running into a certain FPD captain I had vowed to snub.

Tossing Quinn a grin, I marched down the sidewalk. This day was starting to look up.

7

Since I wasn't a senior journalist with a flying carpet assigned to me, I took the airbus. Quinn rode on top, napping in the sun. People pointed and stared as we passed, and more than one bus passenger hung out the window to gawk at Quinn. Most of the gargoyles in Terra Haven preferred sticking to the skies and their chosen roosts, and they didn't bother with human transportation. The people of Terra Haven weren't used to seeing gargoyles roaming among them, but between Quinn with me and Oliver with Mika, I predicted gargoyle sightings would become blasé to city residents in a few months.

To pass the time, I reviewed my firebird notes, hoping to spark a new idea. I couldn't pin my hopes on the guards having the information I needed. Tracing an influx of precious metals would take time. Tracking down the shipping company remained my best lead, as much as I wished otherwise. When the bus's meandering route skirted the industrial district near the train station, I hopped off, waking Quinn with a soft prod of fire element. He glided to the sidewalk as the bus pulled away.

"Why are we stopping here?" he asked, peering up and down the drab street.

I pointed up toward the enormous Capstone warehouse. "I figured we could check in while we're here." If I played this right, not only would I get the information I wanted, but I also wouldn't have to poke around my parents' business, either.

According to this morning's rumor scout, Luther Wetherill's castigation of the people who lost the firebirds implied it hadn't been his company. However, I tended to trust the word of FSPP business moguls about as much as I trusted the boasts of a drunkard. Their lives of privilege often meant full-spectrum pentacle potentials weren't in touch with their businesses—or as forthright as their employees.

While most of the blocky structures lining the wide thoroughfare had done little more than nail up signs to beautify their storefronts, the Capstone Transportation headquarters gleamed as if prepared to compete with flashy boutique shops. False marble columns clung to the front of the building, graceful molding wrapped the windows and doors, and a tasteful statue of a pegasus sprang from the stone above the door. Hung high against the windowless second floor, steel letters taller than Quinn spelled out CAPSTONE. Even the front door, a heavy mahogany affair, proclaimed the company's wealth.

I grimaced at the ostentatiousness. It was one thing to know most FSPP families possessed unfathomable wealth; it was another to have it flaunted in your face.

Palming my press badge, I held the door open for Quinn. Capstone's lobby reflected the exterior architecture, with marble floors, a mahogany desk, leather chairs, and steel accents trimming everything. When the massive door whisked shut behind us, it cut off the street sounds, giving the sensation of being cocooned inside a hotel lobby rather than in the foyer of a shipping warehouse.

A woman old enough to be my grandmother sat behind the reception desk, but any resemblance to a nurturing figure ended there. Wrapped in a stiff red-and-silver Capstone uniform, she perched on the edge of her chair and glared at us with flat, gray eyes. I couldn't tell if her face had frozen in disapproving lines or if Quinn and I had inspired her censure simply by walking through the front door.

When I strode to the desk, my boots clacked against the polished marble. Quinn's paws rang like hammer blows, creating echoes throughout the cavernous chamber. Ears flattening, he hunched into a slinking gait to minimize the sound.

I waited for the echoes to die down before greeting the dour-faced woman.

"Good morning."

She narrowed her eyes.

All righty, then. "I'm with the *Terra Haven Chronicle* and am interested in interviewing a warehouse manager for an article the paper would like to run." I flashed my badge, "accidentally" covering my name with one finger. It was unlikely she knew who I was, and I wasn't going to give her any hints.

"What is the nature of your article?" she asked. She said *article* the way someone might say *feces*.

"It's a business piece about the best places in the nation to live based on employment. I'm interviewing people from all the top companies." I added a smile to the lie and congratulated myself on coming up with a plausible article idea on the spot. In fact, if I was stuck working under Eloise for a while, I might pitch it to her. It wouldn't hurt for me to gain contacts among Terra Haven's larger and wealthier businesses while biding my time for the firebird story to pan out.

The receptionist's lips thinned. "Wait here."

She pushed away from her desk and marched across the lobby to a side door, her heels pinging against the marble. Quinn and I shared a look when she disappeared, but neither of us spoke. Less than a minute later, she returned, the same put-upon mien of displeasure adorning her features.

"You will need to make an appointment and return another day," she said.

"I don't need much time. Just five minutes."

"We are running a business here. No one can drop their current duties to appease the capricious desires of the *Chronicle.*" She settled on the lip of her chair, then consulted a notebook on her desk.

"When should I come back? This afternoon?"

The receptionist didn't do anything so uncouth as to scoff but instead let her tone convey her disdain when she offered a tentative meeting two and a half weeks in the future with a low-level supervisor.

"That will be too late. My deadline is the end of this week." I pretended to consult my journal; then I spoke to Quinn as if the receptionist couldn't hear me. "We'll have to go with our backup company, Airstrong." I peeked through my lashes to see if mentioning Capstone's largest competitor had gotten a reaction out of the woman. Her scowl hadn't changed.

Holding in a sigh, I strode for the exit, tossing my thanks over my shoulder. With every step, I hoped the receptionist would call out to stop me. She didn't.

"What now?" Quinn asked after the door closed behind us.

"Now we get crafty."

We sauntered down the street until we were out of sight of the Capstone building, then cut between two large warehouses, skirting broken boxes and rotting lumber. The back side of the warehouses nestled up to the tracks, and activity bustled inside the buildings as they loaded or unloaded crates from flatbed railcars. Striding confidently, as if we belonged among the workers, we approached the Capstone loading dock.

Two brown gryphons, both smaller than Fang, hunkered low while sweaty men and women loaded their harnesses with deliveries. Beside them, workers filled the wicker basket of an anchored single-person dirigible with lighter parcels. We slipped past them, across the threshold of the warehouse. The space bustled with a frantic energy, and an unusual number of clients loitered among the staff, monitoring their belongings. With the government leaving it inconclusive whether bandits were striking the transportation lanes or if the unnamed shipping company couldn't be trusted, everyone looked on edge. Capstone's response appeared to be an inflation of their typical number of guards. While I took in the scene, the first gryphon left, loaded down with packages and protection spells, the rider bristling with weapons.

A short black woman with a soft froth of gray hair broke away from the activity when she spotted us. Her gaze flicked to Quinn, then settled on me.

"What do you think you're doing in my warehouse?" she demanded.

I flashed my press badge before she called over a guard. Making a snap decision, I abandoned my made-up story and led with the truth. "I'm investigating the missing firebirds."

"You won't find them here. Capstone has an impeccable reputation because we're honest." She snapped her finger at the nearest guard, and he strode in our direction.

"Was that something you were told by your superiors?" I pressed. "Or do you know for a fact that Capstone didn't ship the firebirds?"

"I know for a fact that I value my job. If I see you uninvited on our premises in the future, I'll have you arrested. Good day."

The guard clamped a hand on my bicep and propelled me through a side exit and all the way to the street, giving me a final shove when he released me. Stumbling, I caught myself before I tripped into traffic. Quinn growled at the guard. Without saying a word, and skirting wide around Quinn, the man stomped back the way we had come.

"So did they or didn't they ship the firebirds?" Quinn asked as we walked away.

"I don't know." Capstone could have been beefing up security as a show of strength for their customers. Or they could have been adding extra guards because they *had* been in charge of the firebirds and knew irrefutably that bandits were striking transports. "What was your impression?"

"They didn't want to talk to us."

"Yeah. That's what I got, too. But were they hiding something or just busy? Either way, we'll need to stop by Airstrong." Just saying the words twisted my stomach in knots. I made a left turn at the next intersection, trudging toward my parents' company. Farther down the street, a dark-haired man on a flying carpet zipped around the corner, making me think of Nathan. As soon as I got this out of the way, we would head to Focal Park and hopefully catch the squad. If we timed it right, we could talk with them after Nathan had departed, too.

"Airstrong is another shipping company, right?" Quinn asked.

"Yep. With our scant leads, I think we might be better off dividing our efforts. Do you want to see if any gargoyles in this area have seen or heard anything that might help?"

I hated deceiving Quinn, but it wasn't the time to dive into my past. Plus, with any luck, I wouldn't need to. Stepping inside Airstrong didn't mean I was stepping back into the role of the Airstrong heiress. Just as it didn't mean I was using my parents' connections to further my own career. This was a routine stop in my investigation, nothing more.

Repeating my reasoning to myself didn't make me feel any better.

"Not a lot of gargoyles roost in this neighborhood. I'll check around."

"Thank you."

All the buildings along the block were four stories high, and Quinn used the length of the street to gain elevation before he disappeared over the nearest rooftop.

Shaking the tension from my hands, I strode up the street and swung into Airstrong's lobby. Whereas Capstone had projected expensive and grandiose, my parents had opted for a more functional aesthetic. Sturdy chairs and a bulky receptionist desk filled the small front office, the rest of the building's square footage dedicated to the warehouse. A single wooden door stood against the rear wall, inset with a tiny window. A spell had rendered the opening opaque from this side, and standard no-trespassing wards barred admittance.

"Good morning." The greeting came from a middle-aged

man with a deep tan and a shocking amount of muscle sitting behind the desk.

"Hello, I was hoping to speak to—"

"Ms. Grayson?" He leaned forward, a grin replacing his professional demeanor. "Charlotte didn't tell me you were dropping by. Just a moment, I'll get her."

My stomach dove to my toes. My mom was *here*? She was supposed to be at the East Coast facility. I waved a frantic hand at the man, my protest stumbling out. "No, wait. There's no need—"

But he had already turned away and formed a sleek air message. He spoke softly into it, then stuffed it into a pipe behind him. The message speared away before I could stop it. I pivoted toward the door, considering dashing out, but it was too late.

Beaming, the muscle-bound receptionist turned back to me. "Your coverage of the everlasting tree was brilliant. I felt like I was there."

"Uh, thank you."

A new message burst from the pipe, and the man gave me an apologetic smile before raising a soundproof ward between us. He listened to the message, then dropped the ward.

"You can head on back. She's in the last office." Using a complicated elemental key, he deactivated the ward on the inner door and waved me inside.

I tossed him a strained smile and ducked through the door, pausing in the shadowed corridor to contemplate my course of action. If I had known my mom was in the city, I wouldn't have come, at least not today. Asking a manager or supervisor about the firebird shipment toed the unwritten line I had drawn for myself; asking my *mother* crossed right over it. But I couldn't leave without talking with her.

After double-checking my coat for wrinkles and stains, I hoisted my bustier higher and fluffed its gauzy straps for maximum modesty. When I realized I was using a rough clump of water and earth element to buff the scuffs from my bag, I made myself stop delaying.

A spacious corridor ran across the back of the warehouse, separated from the inventory by a floor-to-ceiling ward. The elemental sheet shimmered with subtle sparks of electric fire, warning away those not authorized beyond it and blurring the view enough to obscure the shipping labels attached to each crate. *Confidentiality is important to us,* the ward said. It would have been easier to put up a wall instead of a ward, but my mom knew the impact of a good visual, and both the sprawling warehouse stacked with packages and the powerful ward said more for the company's resources and reach than any brochure.

I didn't encounter anyone on my walk, though I could hear the clamor of a well-oiled warehouse through the ward. Every office I passed was immaculately organized but empty, the staff likely busy in the warehouse—especially with my mom on the premises. All the activity buzzed around the enormous loading bay doors at the opposite end of the warehouse, where the day's shipments were being processed.

The door to my mom's office hung open, but she wasn't inside. An assortment of papers lay in a neat grid across the surface of her desk, the contents of each disguised by blatant illusions that blurred the text and made each page appear to be stamped with the Airstrong's winged-A logo. I set my bag down on one of the chairs facing the desk, then walked to the window overlooking the warehouse floor.

A woman approached from the opposite side of the ward. The spell warped her image, but I recognized my mom's posture and stride even before she casually swept aside a section of the powerful ward and stepped through. She wore a suede flying jacket and trim trousers, both an impractical shade of cream that would require industrial-strength spells woven into the fabric to keep them clean. The outfit matched her pale hair, done up today in a tight braid, and it complemented her suntanned skin. With no other color to compete with, her sky-blue eyes seemed all the more captivating.

I had never been able to decide if she had natural charisma or if she understood how to fake it with body language, symbolism, and her masterful blend of empathy and authority. It didn't really matter; either way, she was a force of nature. I had done my best to learn everything I could from her, too, though I eschewed her trademark style. I already shared my mom's white-blond hair, blue eyes, and triangular face structure. I didn't want to look like I was trying to be her twin.

When her bright eyes landed on me, a smile lit her face, and her stride quickened. I made it halfway to the doorway before she barreled inside.

"Darling!"

"Hi, Mom."

"I thought you were still at the everlasting tree, or I would have sent you a message." She enveloped me in a hug, and I breathed in her subtle floral perfume that always made me think of sunshine. Familiar spells brushed against my face, one holding her hair in place and several embedded in her wooden earrings and necklace.

"I got back the night before last," I said, "but I only feel like myself today."

She released me, holding me at arm's length and examining me as if she hadn't seen me in years rather than months. Even though she and my father lived on the East Coast, they traveled frequently for their business and always made time to see me when they were in Terra Haven.

"Was the experience as incredible as you made it sound in your articles?" she asked, drawing me to the plush chairs positioned in front of her desk.

"More so. Why didn't you come?"

"Oh, your father and I had business to attend to. Shipping orders doubled when word of the imminent blooming hit the papers. It's been a whirlwind back at the main office." She glanced at her desk and the work waiting for her. "You should have told me you were going to drop by. I would have made time for you in my schedule."

"I just wanted to say hi. I'm on my way to an assignment."

I held my breath, hoping she wouldn't hear the white lie. Her fingertips drummed on her knee; she was suspicious. Hoping to distract her, I blurted out the first thought that came to mind. "I didn't expect to see you back in Terra Haven so soon."

Her gaze sharpened, and I bit off a sigh. Two minutes in her presence, and I let her get in my head. I should have remained silent.

"How *did* you know I was in town?" she asked.

Not quite meeting her eyes, I weighed the merit of maintaining my bluff against the possibility of missing an important lead for my seed's story.

My mom sat back, her expression tightening.

"Are you here in a professional capacity?" she asked.

I winced. "Sort of."

"This is about the missing firebirds." It wasn't a question.

"Yes, but not for the reason you think. It has to do with the seed I got from the tree."

My mom's shuttered expression eased, and she sat forward in her chair again. "Oh?"

"I wish I had brought it so I could show you." The idea of traipsing around the city with the seed loose in my pocket made me nervous, so I had left it tucked safely in my jewelry box. "It's beautiful, and it has the pattern of a firebird's feather on it. I believe I'm supposed to find the missing firebirds."

"What was your question for the tree?"

I cleared my throat. "Where can I find the story of a lifetime?"

Speaking my question aloud, here, in this office, surrounded by my parents' business and the legacy I had been born into, felt like a betrayal. My parents had expected me to follow in their footsteps and take over their international company when they retired. It had taken me years to convince them that while I possessed the same ambition to make my mark upon the world, I didn't have the same passion for shipping or running a business. I wanted to write. I wanted to hunt down stories that the world didn't know existed and bring awareness to the good and bad events of society.

"Of course that's what you asked," she said softy.

Startled, I met her gaze. I had expected disappointment or frustration at a wasted opportunity, but the compassion in her expression made me wonder if she understood me and my commitment to journalism better than I thought.

She patted my knee, then walked to the window to stare out over the warehouse. When she turned back, a mask of cool professionalism disguised her thoughts.

"You know I cannot show you any favoritism," she said.

"I know."

"I will tell you exactly what I would tell any other

reporter who asked: We pride ourselves on our accurate deliveries. We haven't misplaced a single package since we opened our doors twenty years ago. We also aren't the only shipping company that the government contracts with, Capstone being our main competitor."

"I was just there," I said.

"Really? What did they tell you?"

"That they are an honest company with nothing to hide—right before one of their guards physically escorted me from their premises."

My mom snorted. "That sounds about right."

"And if I asked you about the firebirds, would you have me kicked out, too?"

"Hardly. You can ask me anything you want, but the answer will stay the same: We don't discuss our shipments or our clients. Which, of course, you know."

My heart thundered in my ears. I knew my mom's weaknesses, and if I worded my question correctly, I could guilt her into giving me more information. It would be relatively simple, because she loved me. She wanted me to succeed and be happy. She wanted me to achieve my dreams. All I had to be willing to do was trade on our emotional bond.

I swallowed hard and attempted to smile, and though my lips didn't curve the way I wanted, I managed to inject levity into my tone. "You were the one who taught me I won't get answers to questions I don't ask."

"I did, didn't I?" My mom gave me a rueful smile. "Be careful what you teach your children, darling. Say, do you have your eye on a prospective father for my future grandchildren?"

A hiccup of a laugh escaped me, her abrupt topic change disarming me, as she knew it would. I pretended to think about her question. "I'll tell you, but only if you can confirm how many firebirds went missing."

My mom burst into laughter. "You are a fine reporter, Kylie. I always knew you would be. You have a way with words that's all your own but a tenacity I'm going to blame on your father. Speaking of Owen, he wasn't able to make this trip, but he'll—" An air message blasted from the pipe beside her desk, and she deftly caught it with a flick of earth. "Excuse me." She erected a soundproof ward and listened to it, her expression growing serious. "I'm afraid I'm needed elsewhere," she said after dissolving the message and disbanding the ward. "I'm not staying long on this trip —just sorting out a staffing issue. I'll return when things settle down, and we can spend some time together."

"I'd like that."

I let myself out, feeling a hundred pounds lighter than when I had entered the building, as if I had passed a test. I had come perilously close to choosing my ambition over my relationship with my mom—but I hadn't. I had stuck true to my principles. Closing my eyes, I reaffirmed my promise to myself.

I will never use my position as the daughter of Charlotte and Owen Grayson for personal gain.

Not even for the story of a lifetime? a tiny voice in the back of my head asked.

I stomped on the thought but couldn't crush it completely.

The owner of Lazy Days Boat Rental was more than happy to go over his operating hours, rental prices, and opening-week deals, but he refused to talk about the dead body or the investigation surrounding it.

"Don't mention that *incident* in here," he ordered when I broached the subject. "I spent money I haven't made yet cleaning the taint of it from the elemental eddies on the premises. Now I've got to make this business work or I'm ruined. The sooner you reporters let the story die, the better it will be for everyone. You should be focusing on positive facts—like the fun times people can have paddling around in my boats for reduced rates during our grand opening— and forget all that nastiness."

From the looks of things, everyone had already forgotten. An empty white-sand beach stretched on either side of the rental hut, without even a crime scene ward cordoning off the former location of the corpse. The typical daytime crowds wouldn't return to Focal Park for another few days, when it officially reopened in time for the summer solstice. My press badge had garnered me passage through the barricaded entrance, but once inside, I hadn't seen anyone other than park cleanup crews. If Grant's squad had visited the park recently, I didn't find a single trace of them. I didn't even see Nathan.

"Should you send out rumor scouts to search for Grant?" Quinn asked once we had finished collecting the salient details for my microscopic article and were back outside.

"No, I don't want to risk it." Not for the slim chance the squad had fresh details about the firebirds. So far I had been able to keep my scouts a secret from Grant. If he learned of their existence, I would never be able to get one near him— not without him destroying it. "Maybe the squad is farther upriver."

"And if they're not?"

I shielded my eyes from the sun and squinted against the harsh glare off the bright sand. I didn't want to have to hunt the squad down to ask them about the firebirds. If our encounter looked unintentional, I stood a better chance of coaxing information from them. Above all, I didn't want to give the arrogant captain another reason to get his head inflated about me *pestering* him.

"If we don't find them today, we'll think of something," I assured Quinn. I might have to take Mika up on her offer to tag along for her next visit to Velasquez after all.

Ugh. No. Maybe I could modify a rumor scout to tell me the squad's whereabouts without tipping off Grant.

But before I resorted to desperate measures . . . "Come on. Let's take the long way around the park. Maybe we'll spot them, but if not, we'll head back to the *Chronicle*, turn in this assignment, and see what we can get from the guards."

Focal Park embodied the constructive elemental cycle on a massive scale, dividing the multi-acre pentagon into five pie slices, one per element. Lazy Days lounged at the apex of the water section, a fortuitous location for any proprietor. Farther upriver, the quiet pools and water fountains disappeared into a lush botanical garden and the tree-shaded pathways of the wood section. Following those inviting trails in a clockwise direction led to the air section, where plants gave way to a playground for air elementals filled with sculptures designed to capture, amplify, and showcase the air's natural currents. I had spent countless hours over the last few years sitting among the twisting winds, letting their caresses restore and energize my body. Beyond the air section lay the hotbeds, fire pits, and steam pools of the fire section, then the boulders and pillars of the earth section, before the park wrapped back around to the water section.

As we strode along the rim of the beach, I crafted a handful of small test pentagrams from the five elements. A gentle nudge of air sent them spinning ahead of us, probing for magical imbalances. The violence of a murder would have created residual elemental dissonance, and though Grant's team should have addressed any discordance near the dead body, I didn't want to chance stumbling into eddies of disturbed magic.

I needn't have worried. Quinn and I roamed to the farthest reaches of the water section without catching a trace of perturbed elements or a glimpse of the FPD squad. When the beach butted up against a steep granite cliff, we were forced to turn back.

"I don't think they're in the park," Quinn said. "I don't think anyone is except us."

It certainly felt that way. Copses of ancient oaks and cottonwoods trailing down to the beach blocked the cleanup crews from sight. Lazy Days had disappeared around the bend in the shore. If not for the mansions visible across the river, it would have been easy to believe we were far from civilization. I tilted my face up to the sun, closing my eyes and doing my best to soak in the serenity of the moment. Unfortunately, all I could think about was one infuriating man who wasn't where I needed him to be. What if my seed had a deadline? If I didn't figure out the firebird clue in time, would it become inert? Plenty of people in the past had failed to achieve the necessary evolutions of their seed to receive their answer. Would I be one of them? Would I miss out on finding the story of a lifetime?

I rolled my shoulders, attempting to dispel my tension. "All right. Let's head back to the *Chronicle*."

"Maybe I could—"

The wind shifted, carrying the unforgettable stench of fresh blood, excrement, and decayed meat. I flung a hand toward Quinn, clutching his mane. A vast shadow swept across the beach, silencing the chattering wildlife in the nearby trees. I ducked as an enormous bird-woman dove to land in front of us, her eerie cackle splashing terror through my limbs.

Beldame Zipporah, the most malicious harpy of Terra Haven, had found me.

I yanked earth and fire to me, seizing every last drop of enhancement Quinn offered. Fusing the elements together, I created a crude but functional ward and domed it over us, dropping to my knees to conserve energy even as I anchored it deep in the loose soil. The barrier shielded us from the spray of sand the harpy kicked up as she landed, but not from the putrescence emanating from her filthy body.

An infamous trader of rare and exotic items, Zipporah had cultivated a reputation for being able to get her talons on anything a person needed—for the right price. She was even more notorious for her ruthlessness, and anyone with a drop of common sense avoided her at all costs. Unfortunately, the harpy had been the only person in possession of a singular item Grant and I had needed to save a great many lives not too long ago. In exchange for it, she had accepted a trade of demeaning labor from Grant. I hadn't gotten off so lightly. She had given me a choice between becoming her next meal or owing her a favor of her choosing—no restrictions, no limitations. Like a fool, I had accepted her terms.

While I had been preoccupied with the everlasting tree —first with my assignment, then with the seed—it had been easy to ignore the nagging trepidation of that promise. But Zipporah wouldn't have hunted me down now unless she planned to collect on my debt.

My gaze darted over our secluded surroundings. No one was nearby to help me. I couldn't run fast enough to evade capture, and even contemplating fleeing made dread run hot, then cold through my midsection. If I ran, it would trigger the harpy's predatory instincts, and I would die. I needed to keep control of my fear—and my ward—if I hoped to survive.

Zipporah lifted a foot to scratch her belly, flicking clods of feces against my shield. When she didn't speak, I twisted to meet her cold gaze. The golden eyes of a raptor glared back at me. Though she possessed a human head, it appeared to have been inspired by an eagle's bone structure. Sun-damaged skin stretched tight over a long, pointed nose and angular cheekbones; small ears perched high on the sides of her head; and stubby, oily brown feathers coated her scalp and neck, standing on end in clumps when the breeze shifted.

I braced for an attack. Hunched as I was, Zipporah towered over me. With talons as thick as my thighs and sharp enough to impale me, she wouldn't have to exert much effort to harm me. But she hopped back and stretched, fanning her massive wings and unleashing an unholy scent from her crusty undersides that clogged my throat. Like all harpies, Zipporah delighted in odors that fell on the nauseous end of the spectrum, and she seemed to take pride in wallowing in unhygienic offal.

Quinn crouched, his round ears pinned to his scalp, his snarl exposing sharp lion's teeth, and his wings half flared. His aggressive display should have appeared menacing, but next to the harpy, he merely looked small. He lashed his tail, his thigh muscles bunching as if he were going to launch himself at the harpy.

"Quinn, no!"

I flexed my hold on my ward in case I had to constrain him. He was no match for Zipporah. A low rumble filled the abrupt silence, and the hairs on my arms tried to stand on end when I realized the savage growl emanated from Quinn's rock throat.

Zipporah regarded us where we cowered at her feet, her lipless mouth splitting in a sharp grin. "Good form and a proper greeting, but there's no need for barriers among old friends."

Before I could react, she cleaved my ward in half with a spear of wood element. The backlash of broken magic punched my chest, knocking my breath from my body. My spine bowed, my lungs painfully compressed, but when I finally sucked in a ragged breath, I instantly regretted it. I could taste the harpy's putrescence on the back of my tongue. My stomach roiled and I clamped down on my gag reflex.

Quinn stalked forward, and I snatched a handful of his wing. He could have easily pulled free of my grasp.

Instead, he halted, but his entire body remained tensed to attack.

I scrambled to my feet and squared my shoulders. Standing, I was the same height as the harpy, but she outstripped me in muscle mass, her talons were built-in lethal weapons, and the feathers along the ridges of her wings were razor sharp. Fighting her was out of the question. I scoured my memory for any spells I could use to protect myself. Nothing in my repertoire could compete with Zipporah's elemental strength. I had only my wits to rely on, and they had deserted me.

"Kylie Grayson, you owe me."

I had been expecting her to say as much, but her words still punched fresh terror into my gut.

"What do you want?" The question scraped my dry throat. The last time we had spoken, Zipporah had wanted me as a snack. Even after we struck our bargain, I had barely survived. I dreaded to discover what she would ask of me now.

"It's a small request hardly worthy of your debt," she said.

"In that case, maybe you should wait until you think of something bigger." Fear made me speak without thinking, and I cursed myself.

The harpy stilled, her predaceous eyes devoid of humanity. I forced myself to maintain eye contact.

I had never been so aware of how often I blinked.

"You are unexpectedly brave without your captain," Zipporah said. "That's good, considering where I'm sending you. You might actually live."

"Sending me? That wasn't our deal."

"It wasn't?" Zipporah cocked her head. "As I remember it, you agreed to owe me a debt."

"I said I would answer a question." I tried to sound brave, but I couldn't disguise the quaver in my voice.

"Oh, that's right." She used one of the skeletal claws at the bend of her wing to scratch her featherless, pseudo-human chest, obscenely jiggling the desiccated husk of her right breast. Then, batting her eyes in a mimicry of innocence, she asked, "Kylie Grayson, will you fetch something for me?"

My heart pounded louder. I wanted to protest again, but it was too late: I had walked right into her trap. Ever since our last encounter, I had imagined Zipporah returning to demand a guarded secret from me. It would be some form of costly information, the kind that would force me to break a vow or my own moral code. Somehow, I suspected whatever she wanted me to fetch now would prove infinitely worse.

She let me simmer in my anxiety for another minute before taking my silence as assent. "It's a rock called Chiefmaker."

People didn't give names to rocks; they gave names to gems. Expensive gems imbued with power. The kind kept locked in vaults or under deadly wards in museums. My stomach knotted tighter.

"Why don't you get it yourself?"

"I am. I'm getting you." Her smile held a wealth of menace.

She was being cagey with information, which meant she was hiding something. Knowing Zipporah's reputation, whatever she wasn't telling me was likely deleterious to my health.

"Where is this Chiefmaker? What does it look like? How much time do I have to retrieve it?" If I could buy myself time, I could get help.

The image of Grant looming beside me, protecting me from the harpy, popped into my head. Running to him for help would be a blow to my pride, and I would have to suffer through another of his lectures on my recklessness, but I would be alive.

"You ask too many questions," Zipporah said. "Are you refusing to honor our deal?"

"No, I just—"

Zipporah bent forward, and I caught myself from instinctively retreating. Her breath reeked of rot, and my eyes watered involuntarily.

"Don't forget, Kylie Grayson, there are only two ways for you to pay your debt. You can accept this task or . . ." She snapped her sharp teeth, and I jumped.

I could retrieve the Chiefmaker or I could die. *Choices, choices.*

"Fine, I will get you the Chiefmaker." My stomach dove toward my toes. Hadn't I learned my lessons about making promises to Zipporah, especially ones I didn't know I could keep?

"Kylie, don't do it," Quinn urged.

Without breaking eye contact with the harpy, I said, "I have to. I owe her."

"There must be another way."

Zipporah turned her rapacious glare on Quinn, and my heart fluttered in my throat. I couldn't let her hurt him.

"I'm ready. Tell me where it is," I said, stepping forward. The harpy's gaze snapped back to me.

"No need. I'll show you."

She grabbed for me. I threw myself sideways and slammed a shield in place to deflect her lethal talons. Her claw punctured my barrier as if it were flimsy silk, and the elements imploded, battering me. Disoriented and half blind, I fell to my hands and knees. Zipporah seized me, clamping her claws around my torso. Effortlessly, she lifted me.

The sand slid beneath my feet, the awkward angle preventing me from attaining leverage. Magic slid through my grasp, my connection to the elements numb. Zipporah squeezed one of my arms against my side, trapping it, but I used the other to pound against the harpy's foot. Dried excrement and rotting clumps of carrion speckled with maggots flaked away beneath my assault, but Zipporah appeared unaffected. She constricted her leathery toes, and the crushing force of her talons ground my ribs together and set fire to my confined arm. I struggled harder, only stilling when the tips of her talons pierced my sides.

The harpy took ponderously to the air, and I flopped impotently in her grasp.

"Don't do it, rock brains," Zipporah hissed.

Quinn's golden form flashed across my jostled vision, then abruptly fell away with a sharp cry. My heart leapt to my throat.

"Stay down," the harpy ordered.

The ground spun and jounced as I strained to catch sight of Quinn. Zipporah held him smashed beneath a slab of air. Fury lit his golden eyes bright white, but he appeared unharmed. Then the earth beneath him shifted in a vortex of quicksand, sucking him downward.

"No!" Quinn might be made of stone, but he needed air to breathe. If she buried him, she would kill him.

I resumed my struggles, slicing pathetic blades of earth at Zipporah's trap and hammering my fist against her leg as hard as I could.

The harpy tossed me into the air, then caught me. My neck whiplashed, spiking agony down my spine. My vision tunneled and darkened before fear surged to override the pain. If I lost consciousness in Zipporah's grasp, I was as good as dead. I sucked in a deep lungful of air, and the vile miasma of her underbelly worked better than smelling salts on my senses.

Panic squeezing my heart, I searched the beach for Quinn. We had already cleared the treetops, Zipporah's powerful wing beats lifting us rapidly higher, and I almost didn't see his small lion head protruding from the sand, the rest of his body buried. Trapped but alive. I sobbed with relief.

Zipporah kept climbing, until Quinn's golden head was indistinguishable from the beach's sand and the buildings of Terra Haven shrank to the size of toys. Then even the city disappeared, and I hung helpless in her talons as she carried me far from any hope of rescue.

9

———

Zipporah clutched me tight to her nether region, plastering me against the vile grime crusting her feathers. Each wing beat jolted me in her punishing grip, sparking fresh waves of pounding pain in my head and shooting fiery pulses down my abused neck. I longed for Raquel's flight goggles to protect my eyes from the stinging wind, but they wouldn't have shielded me from the harpy's stench. At least when I stopped straining to hold my head up and let my neck muscles relax, I caught wisps of fresh air.

The high sun flattened the rolling hills far below into a patchwork of dense green trees and pale-yellow meadows, the nominal shadows providing little definition to the land-scape. I searched for roads or familiar landmarks, but I had been so disoriented and distraught when we had left the city, I couldn't tell if we were traveling north or south. The glistening blue ribbon twining through the forest could have been Lincoln or Toypurina River. Either way, it didn't matter. We had traveled far beyond my range for sending messages back to Terra Haven, so even if I figured out my location, I wouldn't be able to tell anyone. My only hope of rescue lay with Quinn.

I prayed he was safe. Zipporah must have surpassed her own range, too, and whatever elemental spell she had used to suck Quinn into the sand would have dissipated by now. Once he climbed free, he could seek out Mika. She would heal any injuries he had sustained. Then they could contact Grant, and he would come to my rescue.

That's where my fantasy fell apart. No one would be able to trace our flight. Even the harpy's noxious scent trail would dissipate within a half hour. Grant and Quinn wouldn't have a clue where to look for me, and by the time they tracked down Zipporah and questioned her, I could be long dead.

Unbidden, my imagination bombarded me with potential lethal scenarios: Zipporah could change her mind about our deal and toss my body against the rocks far below, breaking me and feasting on my mutilated corpse. Or she could tire and accidentally let me slip to my death. Even Grant enhanced by a gargoyle and linked to the rest of his squad wouldn't have been able to create a landing cushion of air thick enough to prevent my death if I fell from this height. Solo, I wouldn't stand a chance.

Surviving this trip was no guarantee of my continued good health, either. Zipporah wouldn't call in my debt for something simple. If retrieving the Chiefmaker were easy, she would have collected it herself. Wherever we were headed would be perilous, and the harpy had dragged me along because she considered me expendable. Maybe the Chiefmaker was in the control of a camp of murderers and thieves. Or it could be hidden in the midst of a militarized zone, where I would be killed on sight. Or it could be lost deep in the den of a wild kludde pack. Or—

Zipporah tucked her wings and dove. My stomach

lurched toward my mouth, and a high-pitched scream tore from my throat as the forest surged toward us. Wind whipped tears from my eyes, blurring my vision. Zipporah squeezed me tighter, her vise grip depriving my next scream of oxygen. Then, as abruptly as she had begun the dive, Zipporah snapped her wings open, and I flopped in her talons as our trajectory evened out.

Blinking my vision clear, I caught sight of our destination, and terror iced my veins.

Acres of gouged limestone canyons twisted in a demented labyrinth indecipherable even from our vantage. The raw terrain festered in the midst of the rolling greenery, its decay oozing into the lush forest, tainting the nearest trees a sickly yellow.

This desecrated land served as a living cautionary tale, one every child learned about no matter if they lived a few hours' ride away in Terra Haven or halfway around the world. The ruins had been created with blood magic, an abhorrent form of magic that stole its power from the blood of sacrificed victims. As corrupt as it was potent, blood magic warped the minds of those who used it and polluted everything it touched. Although the misguided tribes who had embraced blood magic had died out centuries earlier, the taint of their dark magic continued to thrive in their places of worship, as dangerous today as it had been in its heyday.

Of all the blood ruins, Chicomoztoc was the most deadly. A heavy-duty ward had quarantined the toxic canyons for the last century, but a handful of people had managed to break in. Even fewer had escaped with their lives, and none with their sanity, earning the ruins the nickname Lunacy Labyrinth.

All traces of the ward were missing now, leaving the

malignant ruins unmasked and accessible. Zipporah speared straight for them, her intent clear. Panic clawed my brain and I clutched at the harpy's talons, but I couldn't tear my gaze from the labyrinth.

I was looking at my own death.

Sweeping low, Zipporah angled for a slender, flat-topped spire. The labyrinth whisked by beneath us, shadowy gorges and sunbaked plateaus flickering past too fast to track. The harpy banked, then released me. Flailing, I dropped, my yelp of alarm cut short when I slammed into the hard rock. Momentum somersaulted me head over heels, and I scrabbled for purchase, afraid I would catapult off the cliff's edge before I could stop. I jerked to a halt when my bag caught against a lip in the rock, the strap snapping against my throat and chest. Panting, I rolled to my hands and knees. Pain blossomed in my hip and pinged through my kneecaps, but adrenaline drowned it out.

Zipporah perched at the edge of the oblong plateau, the tips of her claws pinching the rock, her wings flapping to steady herself, holding a position somewhere between hovering and landing. Sand and small stinging pebbles pelted my face, and I ducked behind the flap of my jacket.

"When you return the Chiefmaker to me, your debt will be cleared," Zipporah said. She gathered herself to take off.

I surged toward her. "Wait! This is a suicide mission. I can't—"

"Are you refusing to honor your debt?" Her body tensed for a strike; her golden eyes promised death.

I scrambled for a reasonable argument to convince her to return me to Terra Haven. Nothing came to mind, and until inspiration struck, I needed to buy time. Fortunately, I was a journalist. Asking questions was as instinctive as breathing.

"You never told me: What does the Chiefmaker look like?"

"It's a bloodstone. If you need a reminder of what blood looks like, I can show you." She slashed her talons through the air between us.

I stumbled backward, remembering at the last moment the steep drop-off near my heels. My heart beating in my throat, I eased forward.

"How big is it?"

"Smaller than a human kidney." Her tongue flicked out to rim her lips.

Lovely.

"Any idea where it's at?" I flung a hand out to indicate the entirety of the ruins. "This place is huge and literally a labyrinth."

"Find the heart, and you'll find the Chiefmaker. Stop dawdling. I won't wait forever." Zipporah pushed off from the rock, her massive wings pummeling the air to lift her.

"Please! Don't leave me here!"

The heavy downdrafts from her wings spawned a dust storm atop the plateau, forcing me to shield my face behind the flap of my jacket again. The buffet of wind knocked me off balance, and I hunkered down to keep my footing. All too soon, the rhythmic pounding of the harpy's wings faded.

Coughing, I squinted through the dirt cloud. Whirl-winds of dust plowed across the plateau and plummeted into the canyon, disintegrating into a haze of dust on all sides—except one. A gritty dervish hit the edge of the plateau across from me and compressed into a horizontal blade of dirt. Still spinning, it ricocheted off an invisible barrier and shot back across the plateau straight at me. I dove to my stomach. The dirt blade cleaved the air where my head had been moments earlier. A clump of severed white-blond hair drifted to the ground in front of my nose.

Pulse thundering in my ears, I twisted to check every direction. Dust plumed in an impossible fountain on my right, dissipating into a beige fog dozens of feet above me, but no other whirlwinds transformed into murderous blades. Cautiously, I sat up and pulled my knees to my chest.

Zipporah disappeared over the nearest tree-covered ridge without a backward glance.

Tears rolled down my cheeks, instigated by the grit in my eyes and fed by the despair in my heart. Any which way I examined my predicament, I ended up dead. If I accepted Zipporah's task and searched for the stupid rock, I would die. If I refused to do the harpy's bidding and stayed here, I would die—of exposure or starvation or dehydration, or I would go mad and kill myself like everyone else who had ever entered Lunacy. Even if I managed to make it out with my sanity intact, Zipporah would kill me.

My tears turned to sobs, but after several ragged breaths, I forced myself to stop. Heavy breathing drew the foul odors emanating from my clothes and hair deep into my throat, and each inhale tasted as if I had licked the underside of the harpy. The visual chased bile up my esophagus, and I took shallow breaths until the compulsion to vomit passed. Forcing myself to take a step back from my panic, I considered my options: I could wallow in my self-pity, or I could determine a way out of this impossible situation. I liked option B.

Pulling my spine straight, I swiped my damp cheeks with the back of my hands, then tugged my bag upright beside me. I opened it, hoping to find a forgotten treasure that would ensure my survival. My camera came out in pieces, the leather folding that had once protected the camera's innards ripped in half and the interior plates shattered. Blinking away fresh tears, I retrieved the glass shards from the bottom of my bag and set them on the rock next to me, telling myself cameras were replaceable. Expensive, but replaceable.

My journal appeared no worse for the beatings it had taken, having suffered through greater abuse in its lifetime. The two editions of the *Chronicle* I had grabbed this morning lined the bottom of my bag, and amid sparkling fragments of my camera's lens, I found three pencils, a cloth sack containing a handful of almonds, and a bruised apple. I lined up my belongings on the rock beside the broken camera and peered back into the bag. No flying carpet had squirmed its way inside when I wasn't looking, no convenient rope ladders had materialized, and no protective armor lay neatly folded and waiting for me to don it. I tipped my bag over and shook out the pulverized remains of my camera. Several scraps of paper fluttered to the rock—Eloise's assignments in her neat handwriting.

I snorted. In light of my current crisis, these filler pieces seemed even more ludicrous. An article about Lunacy Labyrinth's missing ward would make the front page. However, Dahlia's words resurfaced in my mind: *I need journalists I can depend on, not people who run around chasing whims.*

My humorless laugh turned into a coughing fit that spurred fresh tears. Dahlia couldn't fault me for shirking Eloise's busywork to pursue this story. I had literally been dropped into the middle of it. If I didn't write about my unprecedented access to Lunacy, I wouldn't have to worry about disappointing Dahlia; I would be dead.

My grim humor evaporated. I scanned the horizon, hoping to spot Zipporah. I had never dreamed I would be in a situation desperate enough to hope for rescue from a harpy.

A gyrating bundle of elements shot across the labyrinth, spearing straight for me. I sprang to my feet. The plateau was hardly larger than my studio apartment, and I didn't dare shift far from my current location. Whatever had turned the sand into a blade could do far worse to me. I couldn't predict what other dangerous illusions and booby traps lurked atop the plateau. Since I couldn't run or dodge, I gathered a magical defense, fear making the elements slippery in my grasp.

The attacking bundle skipped and bounced, as if tumbling over invisible obstacles. I readied myself to fling a destructive pentagram when the wild energy slammed to a halt ten feet from me and spilled open, revealing the warped image of a man's face and shoulders crafted out of pure water. Not just any man: Grant Monaghan. Even with his forehead distorted to twice its normal height, his chin squeezed to a point, and his entire face rendered in tones of blue, I recognized the captain.

My pentagram crumbled. Relief washed through me, leaving me trembling. I wasn't alone. If Grant was here, my death wasn't inevitable.

"Wait there." The voice that issued from the elemental projection held Grant's authoritative tone, but it came through high and squeaky, as if his vocals had been pulled through a balloon.

"Where are you?" I wiped my shaking hands down my thighs and glanced around as if I might spot him. I had linked with Grant in the past, and I knew his strength; he could be a lot farther away than I wanted. But he had known right where to send the projection, which meant he had to be close enough to have seen me dumped like a sack of garbage atop this plateau. Was he within the ruins?

"Don't move," Grant ordered, and his squeaky voice plummeted to a gravelly rumble several octaves deeper than his natural tones. "Don't touch anything. Everything could be a trap, and you don't know what is an illusion."

"I already figured that out for myself."

He talked over me, his words fast. "Don't try to use—"

The projection melted into a tight ball of water, then exploded, drenching my face and chest.

Absentmindedly, I swiped the moisture from my face, my thoughts racing. For Grant to have witnessed my arrival, he had to have already been here. Which meant he could have been responsible for the labyrinth's missing ward. No, Zipporah had known the labyrinth would be undefended, or else why would she have chosen today to collect her debt? Following that logic, the missing ward would have been enough to warrant the immediate action of the FPD squad, but my instincts told me something more was going on here. Grant's team had been immersed in the investigation of the murder victim that had washed up on the beach at Focal Park. I mentally reviewed my geography. Lincoln River didn't run through Lunacy, but a tributary that fed into the river did. Had Grant come here looking for a murderer? That's all Lunacy needed to enhance its macabre appeal: a homicidal madman lurking around one of these blind corners, waiting for his next victim.

From the air, the labyrinth had seemed relatively small in the midst of the sprawling forest, but from atop the plateau, the trees at the edge of the desecrated grounds looked smaller than my hands. Lunacy had to be more than a mile across. The limestone cliffs blended together in an undulating expanse, giving only hints of the deep canyons twining between them. Facing the direction of the elemental bundle's origin, I shaded my eyes from the sun's glare and squinted for all I was worth, but I couldn't see any sign of Grant or the rest of his squad.

I crept to the edge of the plateau, testing each step gingerly. The flattened top dropped in a rough cliff to a rocky trench at least four stories below. I wouldn't survive a jump—or fall—from this height. However, the cliff face appeared to have plenty of handholds, and I was a decent rock climber. If I hadn't received Grant's message, I would have had to chance climbing down, even knowing Lunacy would attempt to kill me during the descent.

Instead, I waited.

I hated waiting.

The reek of harpy saturated the air around me, intensifying as the sun heated my dark clothes. I removed my jacket and shook it, refusing to examine the crusty matter coating the back for fear I might identify it—and learn exactly what caked my hair and scalp.

"This is ridiculous." Being submerged in Zipporah's funk made it hard to think, and who knew what sort of permanent damage it was doing to my nostrils.

I stepped away from my bag before drawing water and air into the familiar pattern of an elemental bath. When I had amplified the spell to the fullest extent of my capabilities, I situated it above my head and released it.

Instead of swirling around my body, gently separating grime from my skin and clothing, the elements scoured me, abrading my flesh like sandpaper. I cried out as pain flared across my cheeks and neck. My attempts to disband the spell only intensified it, and it whipped faster around me, tearing into my clothing. Chunks of dried feces and wetter, unidentifiable gore flung across the plateau rather than delicately dropping in a circle around my feet. When the spell tore itself apart, taking the tip of my boots' soles with it, I swayed in place.

The palms of my hands pulsed bright red and blood seeped from abrasions on my knuckles. My lips tasted like bitter iron. I tenderly patted my stinging cheeks, surprised when my fingers didn't come away bloody. Using a shard of my camera's broken lens, I examined myself. I looked sunburned, and blood welled in the cracks in my lips. Light streamed through holes in my coat, the seams frayed as if from years of abuse instead of months. My pants were equally damaged, though my skin beneath them was blessedly untouched. The spell had eradicated every last trace of the harpy from me, and it had removed an additional layer of my flesh, too.

Belatedly, I realized this had been Grant's cut-off warning: Don't try to use the elements. I should have figured it out for myself when the whirlwind spun itself into a dirt blade. Grant's malfunctioning projection had been my second tip-off. The labyrinth's tainted magic could have mutated my spell into something much worse.

I wrapped my arms around myself, cold despite the noonday sun. I couldn't afford to make another thoughtless mistake, because the next one might kill me.

10

If I had ever thought to imagine myself within the corrupted confines of Lunacy Labyrinth, I would never have dreamed I would be bored. Or more accurately, antsy. Patience was not one of my virtues. I admired it in Mika, who could sit for hours to fuss over a single piece of quartz, but I had never mastered it. I wanted to pace, but not knowing if a step too far would mean my death in an invisible trap, I remained seated. Sweltering in the sun now, dabbing trickles of sweat from my tender forehead, did nothing to help my restlessness.

My fingertips tingled, and I drummed them on my legs, irritated by my body's intuitive signal that I was on the precipice of a story. I was miles beyond the tingle of a promising lead. I was sitting in the middle of heretofore inaccessible ruins, witnessing sights not seen by more than a handful of people in the last seven generations. A tingling in my fingertips was an annoyingly redundant reaction to my predicament.

Worse, the more I thought about it, the less I wanted this

story—and not just because I would have given my next five major leads to Nathan if it would have transported me anywhere other than Lunacy. No, I didn't want this story because no one should carry word of the missing ward back to Terra Haven. Not yet. If rabid conspiracy theorists and curious innocent civilians discovered they could enter the famed Chicomoztoc Labyrinth unobstructed, they would flock to the ruins. People would get hurt.

People would die.

The story only became worthy of printing once the ward was restored, and even then, acknowledging the ward had been destroyed in the first place would give rise to speculation on how to bring it back down. This was the kind of story I detested—a sensational piece that did little more than titillate and potentially endanger the public.

But I was here. The ward was down. Lunacy Labyrinth was open to the public for the first time in living history, and I had a front-row seat. I had an obligation to the *Terra Haven Chronicle* and to Dahlia to write this story. Thus, I jotted notes in my journal, defining the color striations in the limestone cliffs—ivory, slate, russet, and cinnamon—the cool powdery scent of undisturbed rock wafting from the canyon, the subtle sinister presence of the ruins' dead creators, and the residual poison of their blood magic. I tried to remain objective, but the words *creepy* and *ghastly* made it into my notes, especially when I contemplated the sacrificial victims murdered to create the labyrinth.

Many early cultures had placed undue importance on blood, typically fixating on the purity of the royal lines, since magic abilities bred true. So long as rulers married the most powerful magic wielders, their children's powers surpassed those of commoners, thus guaranteeing the reigning family remained in power. The custom was so deeply entrenched in most societies that, to this day, FSPP families still practiced arranged marriages to ensure their children were born with the desired elemental strengths.

The natives here, however, had embraced a more cannibalistic logic when it came to the significance of blood. They had reasoned that because special components in human blood enabled each person to use the elements, it meant blood was the true source of magic, not the other way around.

They must have felt the raw power of blood magic confirmed their beliefs. Through ritual murder, when they stole magic directly from their victims' blood, they experienced untold powers. The labyrinth canyons were proof; historians believed they had been carved by magic—wood and earth and blood fused together to hammer through the mountainside. But the natives had paid a steep price for their powers. The few surviving records spoke of an entire population that had grown more paranoid, ethically corrupt, and outright delusional. The Chicomoztoc ruins, one of their crowning achievements and sacred sites, remained a living testament of the mentally unbalanced society, the canyons riddled with inimical illusions and deadly traps.

When my thoughts began to circle the dangers lurking all around me, summoning a lifetime of rumors and horror stories, I set aside my journal. I could make only so many useful observations from my perch, and everything else bordered on unprofessional speculation. Even though I wasn't hungry, I methodically ate the stale almonds I had found in the recesses of my bag, reasoning that I would need my strength for whatever ordeal awaited me. I wished I had something to wash them down with. The apple would have been a better snack to combat the heat, but it had shards of my camera embedded in its skin, so I left it to rot in the sun.

I braided my hair while I skimmed the paper's contents, too fidgety to concentrate on most of the information. Only Nathan's article about the dead body found in Focal Park held my attention. His front-page piece included the victim's name, quotes from the city inspector about the ongoing investigation, and a statement from the mayor to pacify possible panic, but it didn't reveal any new information, specifically anything that might have pointed Grant's squad in the direction of Lunacy.

"I guess I'll have to read about it in tomorrow's paper," I said, then scoffed as I surveyed my surroundings.

When my hair slid free of the braid, the fine strands too squeaky clean to hold the loose shape, I rebraided it into twin plaits that began at my temples and ended in tiny tails at my neck. String torn from the frayed seam of my jacket served as ties.

None of these activities provided a worthwhile distraction from my thoughts, which dwelled on my shortened life expectancy. If Zipporah discovered I survived Lunacy and didn't return with the Chiefmaker—the most likely possibility, since exploring the labyrinth was out of the question— she would kill me or devise an even worse task for me. Since I couldn't imagine her forcing me into a circumstance more dire than Lunacy Labyrinth, I spent a good deal of time envisioning my painful demise at her talons.

Worries for Quinn I shunted to the back of my mind. I could do nothing for him from my present location, and for my sanity, I needed to believe he had not only survived but was also safe at Mika's side.

As the hour oozed past, my impending conversation

with Grant loomed in my thoughts. I had kept my promise to Zipporah a secret from Grant partially out of shame that I had made such an idiotic deal in the first place, and partially because I didn't want to hear his "I told you so." Grant had warned me to stay away from the harpy, but hubris and curiosity had blinded me, and now I might pay with my life. If he had seen Zipporah dump me here, and I had every reason to believe he had, I wouldn't escape explaining my rash bargain to him this time.

Lucky me. Grant's condemnation was just what I needed to cap off this all-time crappy day.

A thunderous crack followed by a deafening avalanche reverberated through the canyons. Dust plumed into the air on my right, a few ridges away. My stomach dropped and I shot to my feet, straining to see through solid rock. Had Grant triggered a trap? Was he injured? Buried?

Dead?

Sharp expletives ripped the air, the female voice familiar: Seradon, the squad's earth elemental. When her words dwindled, the deeper murmurs of additional voices snaked through the canyon; Grant had brought his whole team for this mission. No one sounded alarmed, not even Seradon. Then again, they were FPD warriors; they wouldn't be afraid if they stood in the middle of a dragon's nest during hatching.

I cupped my hands into a funnel around my mouth and shouted, "Everyone all right?"

No one answered. I rocked up onto my toes, then jumped in place, but when I didn't miraculously gain the ability to see through stone, I decided to conserve my energy. Crouching, I loaded my meager belongings into my bag and flung the strap over my neck and shoulder, so it hung diagonally across my chest. Pushing the bag behind me, I adjusted the length of the strap until the pouch rested against my lower back. Gingerly retracing my steps to the edge of the plateau, I peered into the shadowy canyon. The empty, uneven rock floor of the trench stared back at me. Sounds of the squad skittered through the narrow corridor, indistinct and impossible to pinpoint. I settled in to wait.

Minutes later, Seradon rounded the corner to my left, being led by a small animal on a leash. I expected relief, but my stomach constricted with trepidation. The easy part was over; now I had to interact with Lunacy Labyrinth. And Grant.

The captain strode behind Seradon, followed by Velasquez, Marciano, and Winnigan, who walked another leashed animal. Were they dogs? No. The creatures moved too fluidly. Maybe badgers?

"Up here!" I waved to get their attention.

Seradon pulled up short, and everyone in the group turned to look at me.

"Are you injured?" Winnigan asked. Even though she had yelled, her words were faint when they reached me.

"No." I shook my head vigorously. The bruising on my ribs and arm, the cuts on my sides from Zipporah's talons, and the abrasions from my unexpectedly harsh spell didn't count.

Grant gestured to his squad members, his words inaudible. Winnigan and Velasquez retreated to monitor the trail behind them. Seradon urged her animal companion forward, taking lead position at the opposite end of the corridor. Everyone stayed within sight of each other, but they had formed the best defensive configuration the canyon would allow. Grant and Marciano remained beneath me, and even the towering wood elemental looked squat and small from my perch.

"You're going to have to climb down," Grant said, and I had no trouble hearing his battle-trained voice.

As much as I would have preferred to be gently lowered from this height by a platform of air, the way Lunacy had manipulated my simple elemental bath made anything as complicated as solidifying enough air to support one hundred and twenty pounds impracticable.

"What about traps?" I hadn't been able to see the trap that had turned the funnel of dust into a blade. The cliff side could be riddled with murderous cloaked spells.

"We'll be right here," Grant said.

It wasn't an answer. It wasn't even a particularly reassuring statement. It was, however, the most efficient way of telling me I didn't have another choice.

"All right." I dried my palms on my pants. "I can do this." I had climbed cliffs higher than this for fun in school. I had never done it without ropes and elemental safeguards, but it was the same principle. Stick to the cliff. Don't fall.

I wished Grant and Marciano didn't look so small and unhelpful.

"I'm coming down," I announced. On hands and knees, I backed up to the edge of the cliff and extended my leg over the drop-off. I found my first toehold and lay there, my chest resting on the dirt, my fingers clutching the flat surface. I held my position until my breathing evened and my mind cleared of everything but the climb. I couldn't think about where I was or who waited below or what Grant would do when he discovered I had made a promise to Zipporah I couldn't keep.

Cautiously, I felt for another protuberance in the cliff, then another, easing myself over the plateau's edge until I clung to the vertical surface. I didn't look farther down than my next toehold. The drop below didn't matter; staying attached to the cliff face did. Inch by inch, I crawled down into the deadly ruins.

My fingers cramped and fire licked my shoulder muscles before I had descended more than a third of the precipice. I ignored the pain, concentrating on the climb. I would rest my quivering arms when I reached the bottom. Until then, *slow and steady* was my motto. Rushing wouldn't improve my odds of survival.

My foot slipped, jerking me off balance. Rock scraped my cheek. I dug my fingers into a jagged vertical crack, my biceps screaming under the strain. Sweat slid down my temples, plastering strands of hair to my face. Hastily, I wedged my dangling foot into a narrow crevice and rested my weight on it to alleviate the strain on my arms. I tried to wriggle my toes, but they had gone numb. These boots had been designed for walking, not for climbing, and that was before my malfunctioning spell had torn strips of leather from their soles.

Stretching, I selected my next handhold, then swung my left leg toward a nearby divot in the cliff. Tingling swept from my toes to my knee, my overworked muscles protesting. I inched lower with my right hand, then shifted my right leg. Instead of sliding toward the slender ledge I aimed for, my foot dropped as if tugged. I lurched to hold my position and strained to lift my foot, but my leg muscles refused to work. My knee wouldn't bend; my ankle wouldn't pivot. Numbness encased my leg, turning it into deadweight.

"Something's wrong," I gasped. For the first time, I glanced beyond my feet at the men below. Marciano stood directly beneath me and Grant two steps behind him. Both men were still over two and a half stories below me, too far.

"Keep going," Marciano shouted.

"I can't feel my leg. It won't work." I couldn't summon the energy to yell, and I didn't know if he could hear me. My arms quaked under the strain of supporting the majority of my weight, and I fought back tears.

"Did you touch anything?" Marciano asked.

"Other than a cliff in the middle of Lunacy?" Fear and strain turned my voice into a stranger's.

I reached for air element. My arms wouldn't hold out much longer. If I could give my leg a push, I might be able to hook my foot on the narrow ledge near my toe. Determined not to allow Lunacy to use my magic against me this time, I formed a soft cushion of air and prodded my boot with it. My foot didn't so much as twitch. I added more air into the cushion and wrapped it around my foot, pulling it upward. My toes scraped the cliffside. Progress. I fumbled for more air, and my entire dangling leg slapped against the cliff and held, supported by the element. The strain on my arms slackened, and a sob of relief escaped my lungs.

"Release the elements," Grant barked.

"Hang on. I've almost got my foot in place." I layered earth into the cushion of air. If I could raise my foot two inches, I could reach the ledge.

"Release them now!" Authority rang in Grant's voice.

The elements swelled in my grasp, the cushion of earth-laced air ballooning out of control. It flared up my leg and engulfed my body, smashing me into the cliff and driving the oxygen from my lungs. Pinned and suffocating, I lashed out. Yanking wood element to me, I studded it with blades of earth and pierced the heavy elemental balloon. The pressure against me reversed, suctioning me away from the canyon wall. I scrambled for a handhold, but my fingers scraped rough rock, then empty air.

For a moment, I hung suspended on the dispersing elements. Then I dropped. Paralysis engulfed my body. The elements sifted through my grasp, and a blur of beige flashed before my eyes. I couldn't flail. I couldn't scream. I couldn't even breathe. I was going to die, and I could do nothing to prevent it.

11

I slammed into two arms as solid as tree limbs, and oxygen burst into my lungs. Dazed, I stared into Marciano's warm brown eyes and tried to remember how my limbs worked. The giant wood elemental knelt and set me on the ground, supporting me when I would have flopped bonelessly to my back. I had no choice but to hold still as Grant bent over me, filling my vision. His gray uniform strained against the bunched muscles in his arms, and his dark gaze was glacial when it met mine.

"What did you promise her?" he demanded.

"Who?" The dryness of my throat made my voice crack. My eyes watered, and I swallowed hard but didn't blink. I didn't want him to think I was crying. Was it too much to ask that he offer me some water before beginning his interrogation?

"Don't play dumb. You're reckless, impulsive, and naïve, but I never expected you to be this stupid."

Well, as long as he didn't expect me to be this *stupid.*

Grant's hands fisted against his thighs, and his voice

came out a growl. "Are you so hard up for fame that you made a deal with the harpy?"

"I didn't." Pain snapped across my skin, sharp and bright, like a powerful shot of static electricity engulfing my body in a quick flash. The shock barely registered before it disappeared. *What the . . . ?*

"Damn it, Kylie. Tell me the truth. What did you promise her? What possible trade could you have made to convince Zipporah to enter Lunacy and toss you into the middle of our murder investigation?"

He thought I had done this on purpose. He must think me brainless. Anger boiled through my confusion and chased away the last of my near-death daze.

"I told her I had a death wish," I said. Pain nipped my skin, there, then gone. "I told her I couldn't stand to be away from you and your charming personality." Another shock flicked my flesh. "I told her my life was meaningless unless you were telling me how stupid I was." This time, the jolt of pain made me gasp, but I barreled on, riding a rush of fury. "Obviously I traded her my common sense, my self-respect, and my last spare iota of intelligence."

Agony seared my skin, darkening my vision. When it faded, Grant still glowered in my face. His lack of reaction to my obvious pain hurt on an entirely different level.

"Are you through?" Grant asked. The muscles of his square jaw flexed.

"If you let her see the cats, she might drop the sarcasm," Marciano rumbled.

Grant's eyes narrowed, but he straightened and stepped back.

I rolled my shoulders and rubbed the kink in my neck, encouraged when my muscles responded. Sitting forward, I wiggled my toes and bounced my knees, testing my limbs.

Relief swept through me like an elixir. Whatever paralysis had afflicted me during the fall had dissipated.

Marciano shrugged a backpack off his shoulder and dropped it between us. He opened the flap but paused to point before rummaging inside. "Verity and Sooth."

Puzzled, I glanced to the direction he indicated. He had set me down facing Seradon. She monitored the canyon ahead of us, vigilantly scanning for trouble. She wore a backpack similar to Marciano's, hers equally loaded down. At her feet sat a lynx.

The stocky cat possessed dense, silver-brown fur and feet that would have looked less out of place on a mountain lion. At full height, the lynx would have stood no taller than Seradon's knee. Presently, she crouched, glaring at me with pale-yellow eyes, her black-tufted ears pinned to her scalp.

I twisted to confirm Winnigan held the leash of another lynx. Like Seradon's, it wore a soft leather harness and glared at me with equal animosity.

Lynxes were truth seers. No matter the illusion, they could see through it, which explained their presence. The cats would act as early warning detectors, sniffing out Lunacy's hidden traps. They could also sense any verbal lie, and they detested them. The sparking pain had come from the lynxes, their magic punishing me for my spoken untruths.

Flushing hot, I pinned Grant with my glare. He could have warned me.

"That one's Sooth," Marciano said, indicating Seradon's lynx and confirming he had been stating the cats' names, not uttering a strange epithet.

I nodded, taking the moment's reprieve to examine the squad. Along with the lynxes, they had brought an arsenal, the bristle of swords and knives strapped to each member implying they had planned for close-quarters, nonmagical combat. Their standard uniforms had been swapped for thicker, more protective material, too. A maze of silver thread adorned their gray shirts. It formed a constructive pentagram across their chests that fed into a network of elemental clusters spanning their torsos and backs. Their pants had similar markings woven into the material. With unique spells residing in each combination of elemental symbols, the flexible garments could withstand more abuse than the average set of armor. They had come ready to do battle with whatever or whoever had destroyed the ward—and with Lunacy itself.

A dozen questions crowded my tongue, but Marciano waylaid them by handing me a pouch of water. I took a long, quenching drink.

"Thank you, and, uh, thank you for saving my life." I grimaced at my fumbled gratitude.

"You're welcome." Marciano didn't glance up from the small vials he removed from his backpack.

Grant planted himself in front of me again, his arms crossed over his expansive chest. In casual clothing, the man had been impressive. Decked out in full warrior garb, a scowl darkening his rugged features, he embodied *intimidating*. "The truth, Kylie."

I craned my head so I could look him in the eye as I said, "It was Zipporah's decision to bring me here. If I could have prevented it, I would have." No pain licked against my skin this time. *Take that, Mr. High and Mighty.*

Seradon's lynx, Sooth, settled on her haunches, no longer interested in me. Observing the cat gave me an idea. Maybe I could use the lynx's magic for my own purposes.

"Was the murder a human sacrifice? Is blood magic what brought down the ward?" Grant had as much as admitted he and his team were in Lunacy because of the murder. His lack of reaction to my question confirmed it. A ritualistic blood-magic murder hadn't happened in this part of the country for over fifty years. No wonder the mayor had called in the FPD squad, especially if the cannibalistic magic had been responsible for destroying Lunacy's powerful ward.

I pressed for more information. "Is the murderer somewhere in the labyrinth?"

"Why did Zipporah bring you here?"

I crossed my arms, annoyed Grant hadn't bothered to answer my questions but expected me to leap to supply him with information. I wasn't under his command, and I didn't answer to him. I didn't owe him an explanation. Except . . . I gained nothing by withholding the facts. When Zipporah had attacked me on the beach, I would have given anything to have Grant's protection. The encounter had proved that even gargoyle enhanced, I was no match for the harpy. I wouldn't survive being in her debt, not without help.

My anger fizzled to irritation, giving way to the dull, pounding pain of my abused body.

"Lunacy Labyrinth contains an object Zipporah wants. If I get it, it will settle the debt between us."

A spark of tension ran through the squad at my words. No one glanced my direction—or Grant's.

"Debt?" Grant asked, his voice soft.

"From when we helped the dryads."

"You said Zipporah let you go with the promise of a story about her in the *Chronicle*."

"I said I offered her a story." I examined my fingers. Lacerations bloodied the tips of all but my pinkies, and rough scratches abraded my palms. "She didn't accept the trade. She only let me go because I promised I would be in her debt."

Grant's hands fisted, and he spun away from me, cursing under his breath.

"That wasn't smart," Marciano said.

"I know." I wasn't sure if he was referring to making a promise to the harpy or telling Grant, but either way, he was right. I monitored Grant warily in my peripheral vision. I hated how similar my deception now felt to guilt.

"Take off your coat," Marciano said when Grant stalked past us to confer with Winnigan and Velasquez.

I shrugged out of the tattered garment. Goose bumps instantly prickled my bare arms. Cool air eddied along the bottom of the canyon, swirling mounds of dust against the walls. The sun still hung hours above the horizon, but dense shadows along the canyon's floor leached any residual heat from the rocks. I took stock of my wounds. A shallow cut slashed my right bicep, and bruises mottled my left arm from Zipporah's grip. Blood oozed from several scrapes along my legs, where my reckless spell had made tatters out of the material. None of the injuries were as painful as those on my hands, which stung every time I twitched a finger. Considering I had not only been manhandled by a harpy, but I had also fallen almost two stories into Lunacy, it was amazing nothing had been broken.

Marciano dabbed a pungent orange ointment on a cloth and let me treat the wounds I could see; then he cleaned the abrasions on my face. For such a large man, his ministrations were shockingly gentle, and I did my best not to react to the sting of the ointment. Afterward, he dabbed kachina greenthread on my cuts. The salve numbed my wounds before he finished wrapping the tips of my fingers in supple lamb's ear bandages.

"Anything else?" Marciano asked, indicating my torso incased in a leather bustier. It would be impossible to lift it for a casual examination. The only way to check the welfare of my ribs and chest would be to undo the row of buttons along the back.

I stood and prodded my torso with my fingers. My ribs pulsed with the dull ache of bruises, and a sting along my sides indicated I had been scratched. I shrugged. Though the shirt was impractical apparel for a hike or rock climbing, let alone for skulking through Lunacy, the thick fabric had spared me more serious injury from Zipporah's rough treatment.

"Nothing worth stripping for," I said.

Marciano smiled, a quick flash of teeth, before his characteristic somber mien reinstated itself.

"What are you supposed to get for the harpy?" Grant asked, marching up to square off in front of me once more.

"The Chiefmaker." Even standing, I had to look up to meet his gaze. At his blank expression, I added, "It's a rock. She said it was somewhere in the labyrinth."

"Zipporah told you to retrieve a blood-magic relic from Lunacy, and you said yes?"

"I said yes to the option that didn't involve me or Quinn being killed on the spot." I lifted my chin, silently challenging him to chastise me.

"If Kylie can walk, we need to move," Winnigan said, breaking our staring match. "This place isn't getting any friendlier."

She was right. The elements twisted against my skin, prickly and unstable. They hadn't felt like this atop the plateau. I squinted at the sky. A fine, oily film distorted the blue sky. The toxic elements had settled into the canyons, which explained the difficulties I had experienced climbing down the cliff.

"Form up," Grant ordered. "We're going back."

Seradon snapped around. "Back?"

"We don't have time to double back," Winnigan said.

"We can't take a civilian with us." Grant flinched as if pinched, and Sooth hissed at him. Turning his glare on me, as if he expected me to protest, Grant corrected himself: "We *shouldn't* take a civilian with us, especially not this one."

I resented the addendum, but I didn't protest. The FPD squad trained for perilous situations. They had the elemental strength and physical fitness required for survival. I didn't. Arguing to accompany the squad would be foolish, especially since I had already nearly died. I would happily escape Lunacy if given the option, but it wasn't up to me.

"We're going back," Grant said. This time, no one argued.

Marciano finished repacking his medical supplies and stood. Next to Grant, I felt delicate and feminine; next to Marciano, I felt like a child. The towering wood elemental strode to Winnigan's side, and she prompted her lynx, Verity, to lead the way. Velasquez fell in behind Marciano. I followed, with Grant and Seradon bringing up the rear. Grimness etched the expression of every squad member. I felt as if I should apologize. Not only was I delaying their hunt for a murderer, but escorting me also meant they would have to spend extra time in the baneful miasma of Lunacy.

"Did you hear that?" Seradon asked.

Velasquez threw up a hand signal, and the squad came to an immediate, choreographed halt. I stumbled an extra step before pulling up short. Holding my breath, I listened for the mystery noise.

Wind slithered through the canyon, and the rustle of shifting sand stirred near our feet. Soundlessly, Grant and

Seradon pivoted to face our flank, and Seradon unsheathed a slender dagger. The lynx at her feet had been standing relaxed, but she abruptly tensed, crouching to stare at the sky with dilated eyes.

"Ky-LIIIE!"

I swung around, shielding my eyes against the bright sky in time to see Quinn sweep overhead. Sunlight lit his body a blinding lemon-gold. He soared on widespread wings, his head drooped to peer into the labyrinth below him. Then he disappeared beyond the rim of the canyon.

Relief rushed dizzyingly through my body, leaving me light-headed. Quinn was alive! As much as I had tried to convince myself he had survived Zipporah's trap, I hadn't fully believed it until I saw him. Somehow, he had escaped in time to track us. I should have known he wouldn't rest until we were reunited.

I scanned the sliver of sky, hoping to spot him again. When my gaze snagged on the oily film of elements swirling through the canyon, my elation crumpled. From above, the twisted magic hadn't been visible.

I reached for Grant without looking, clutching his forearm. "We can't let him—"

"Kylie!" Quinn burst into view. He cupped his wings and dropped into the canyon, coasting toward us, a grin on his face.

I waved my arms frantically to warn him away. Gargoyles were solid, living stone. Wings alone did not keep them aloft. Their bodies interacted with the elements, giving them buoyancy. Without it—or when blood magic mutated the elements—gravity would act on gargoyles the same as it would any airborne boulder.

"No! Don't come down—"

Quinn hit the top of the tainted elements and plummeted. Panicked, he snapped open his wings. The stone feathers of his left wing clipped the canyon wall, spinning him. Helpless, he tumbled through the air and crashed into the opposite cliff. His momentum bounced him across the vertical surface like a skipped stone, hurtling him straight for us.

"Clear out!" Velasquez bellowed.

Grant seized my arm and yanked me off my feet. I landed running, fleeing Quinn's out-of-control descent. Seradon sprinted with us, the lynx at her feet easily outpacing her. Velasquez, Marciano, Winnigan, and their lynx raced in the opposite direction, disappearing around the bend in the canyon behind us. Relying on Grant to guide me, I ran blindly, unable to tear my eyes from Quinn. Gravity should have ripped him from the sky already, but the mutant magic toyed with him, pitching him mercilessly against the canyons. Quinn somersaulted into a fissure in the canyon wall, the collision as thunderous as an explosion. Wings and paws flailing, he careened into the opposite wall. Behind him, the cliffside crumbled. The sheer rock face fell in slow motion at first, then gained momentum, sliding into the canyon and pulverizing the hard floor. A delayed *boom* of its impact slapped my eardrums.

I whipped around, facing forward and squeezing every last ounce of speed out of my burning thighs, trying to outrun the avalanche. The narrow canyon amplified the deafening concussion, battering my body with an endless pummeling of sound. Quinn blasted into the canyon wall above us, close enough for his passing to whip my hair into my face, yet inaudible beneath the roar of falling rocks. Shards of sandstone pelted my scalp, and I belatedly ducked. Quinn hit the smooth canyon floor far ahead of us, fast as a locomotive, and skidded out of sight.

Please be alive. Please be alive.

A wall of air punched our backs, and dust billowed to fill the canyon. The lynx leapt to run three gravity-free strides along the wall before dropping back to the canyon floor, and Seradon seamlessly followed. My brain was still processing the acrobatic feat when Grant yanked me after them. I flew through the air, legs pumping uselessly. My toes scraped the cliff, but it was Grant's powerful leap that propelled us over the invisible trap. I stumbled when we landed, kept upright once again by Grant's vise grip on my bicep.

The cacophony of the avalanche abated, and we slowed. My lungs burned as if I had sprinted a mile. When Grant released my arm, I bent in half, gasping for air. I used my jacket's lapel as a filter, but the air still tasted like dirt. Coughing, I stumbled after Seradon.

"Hold up," Grant wheezed.

A rough, white-and-citrine scrape skipped down the center of the smooth canyon floor, evidence of Quinn's crash landing stretching out of sight. The fall would have killed a flesh-and-blood creature, and even his tough quartz body couldn't have withstood such a beating without injury. I would never be able to live with myself if Quinn died because of me.

A muted cough issued from deeper within the labyrinth, and my breath gusted out in relief. I rushed forward, but Seradon pulled me up short before I made it two steps.

"Slow down. Anything could be lurking in this mess."

The dust had thickened, reducing visibility to a few feet. I squinted into the gloom, blinking teary eyes and fanning a hand in front of my face. None of it had any effect on the dirty air. I strained to hear Quinn again, but between the ringing in my ears, our coughing, and the sporadic clatter of rocks settling into the canyon behind us, I couldn't determine how close he was. Seradon let Sooth set the pace, and the lynx crept forward in slow, slinking steps. I bounced on my toes, visions of Quinn lying mangled and in pain filling my imagination.

A shadowy figure stumbled through the dust and coalesced into the shape of a winged lion. My heart soared.

"Watch where you step, Quinn," Seradon called. "There are traps everywhere, most of them hidden by illusions."

The last of the avalanche's rumbles subsided, and the dust hanging in the air thinned, giving me a better view of Quinn. He walked with a limp, holding his wings at a peculiar angle. Seradon kept her hand on me, restraining me as we crept behind Sooth. Finally, she gave the all clear, and I burst from behind her, running to Quinn's side.

A sinuous dark shadow twisted from a cleft in the cliff wall, swelling to arch over the canyon floor. I lurched sideways and swallowed a scream. The shadow billowed into a massive ten-foot-tall inky-black cobra, its hood flared wide. Beady onyx eyes as large as my fists fixated on me, and I froze. Behind me, Sooth hissed, then growled deep in her throat. Neither sound distracted the colossal snake. Holding my gaze, the cobra bobbed in a hypnotic figure eight. Its scales rasped against the rock wall, the sound spiking my panic, driving all rational thoughts from my head.

The cobra flicked an obscenely long tongue out to taste the air, exposing fangs worthy of a dragon. Twin drops of poisonous saliva glistened on their hollow tips.

"Don't move," Grant said, his voice low.

The cobra struck. I fell over my own feet leaping away from it. The snake snapped its mouth closed on my bag, snagging its teeth in the burlap. The strap slapped tight across my chest. I jerked to free myself, but the cobra was faster, dragging me several feet across the canyon floor before tearing itself free. It reared high for another strike. I scrambled backward on hands and heels, knowing I would be too slow.

Releasing a mighty roar, Quinn launched himself between me and the cobra. The snake twisted, locking its sights on the gargoyle. Rearing onto his hind legs, Quinn spread his wings wide, shielding me with his body. The cobra struck again, lightning fast. Its teeth slammed into Quinn's quartz chest with an impotent, dull *clink*. Quinn lunged, snapping his jaws around the snake's body just below the flared hood, and the clap of his rock teeth echoed through the canyon. The enormous cobra stiffened; then its body imploded into tiny black flecks. The particles swirled apart on subtle air currents, filtering toward the floor.

Quinn dropped to all fours, his face contorted. He scraped the pad of a paw across his tongue. "Ugh, that was nasty."

Laughter burst from me. I scrambled to hug Quinn but stopped before touching him, my mirth dying. A long, shallow gouge bisected his broad nose, and the delicate dragon scales that covered his body looked as if they had been sandblasted in wide slashes. The tips of his left primary feathers had snapped off, leaving his left wing a foot shorter than the right. More alarming was the gouge of muscle missing from his right wing. When Quinn attempted to fold it against his side, the wound pulsed raw and bright, and a fine trickle of citrine spilled to the ground. The wing sagged to rest on the canyon floor.

I dropped to my knees in front of Quinn. "How can I help?"

"I'm fine," Quinn said bravely. Sooth hissed, and Quinn's eyes flared wide as his whole body convulsed in a fine tremor. When it ended, he shot the lynx a dirty look.

"You're not fine," I said. "You can't even retract your wing."

Grant knelt beside Quinn, laying a gentle hand on the gargoyle's wing. "Hold still. You're going to injure yourself more if you keep moving." He rummaged through his pack, pulling out a wool blanket. Using a knife, he cut it into strips.

"A brace?" Seradon asked.

Grant nodded.

"Here, hold this." She thrust the lynx's leash into my hands, then grabbed the opposite end of the blanket and began hacking off strips.

I slid my hand through the loop in the leash, pushing it up to my elbow. Sooth padded to my side and sat. In my crouched position, she was nearly as tall as my shoulder. Despite being attached to a harness and under my control, when the lynx turned her gaze on me, it held a hint of challenge. Lethal claws tipped her oversize paws, and when she yawned, she revealed impressive ivory fangs. If not for my association with Quinn, I might have been intimidated, but next to the gargoyle, the lynx looked more like a harmless kitten.

I traced my fingers gently across Quinn's forehead. He leaned into my touch, and I petted the wavy lines of his ruff, careful to keep my fingers clear of any scratches or nicks.

"I can't believe you found me." Guilt burned like acid in my midsection. He wouldn't be suffering if not for his loyalty to me. I couldn't tell him I wished he hadn't tracked me down. I wouldn't diminish his bravery by informing him he had made the wrong decision.

"I didn't think I would," Quinn said. "I just kept flying in the direction I had last seen Zipporah. I thought . . . I thought I would save you." His head drooped, his wide mouth downturned.

I put both hands underneath his chin and lifted his head until he looked me in the eye. "You just did, Quinn."

His golden eyes searched mine, and he smiled.

Seradon and Grant knotted together the blanket strips and wound them through Quinn's front legs and over his shoulder. Quinn whimpered when they pulled his wing tight to his side, but once the sling supported its limp weight, he relaxed.

"That's better," he said. When the lynx didn't react, I believed him.

I helped Grant and Seradon affix lamb's-ear bandages over the worst of Quinn's wounds to protect them from the elements, but we couldn't do anything for his pain.

"You're sure greenthread won't work on you?" I asked Quinn for the third time. The salve had done wonders for me, numbing my injuries and muting the pain. Even the lacerations on my fingertips no longer bothered me, and I had removed the lamb's-ear bandages wrapping them when they began hindering my dexterity.

Quinn shook his head. "Plants don't affect me."

"When we get back to Terra Haven, I'm going to see if Mika can create a salve for gargoyles. There has to be something those of us who aren't gargoyle healers can do for your injuries when she's not on hand."

I handed Sooth's leash to Seradon and had just started to rise when my gaze snagged on Quinn's seed. It no longer resembled a knotted snake's nest. If it weren't hanging from the same sturdy string as before, I would have sworn it wasn't even the same seed. The fluid, meticulous ebony knot of a snake biting its own tail had been replaced by a misshapen, vaguely woodlike lump. The muddy brown lines of the seed might have once mimicked a pinecone before it simultaneously inverted and exploded.

"Oh. Wow." I jerked my gaze from the seed when it elicited a bout of dizziness. Had Lunacy warped the evolution of his seed, or was this ugly mess its intended form?

"What?" Quinn asked.

I untied the string's knot and lifted the seed for Quinn to examine. Grant and Seradon pulled their seeds from their pockets. Grant's was unchanged, a beautiful opalescent sphere veined in gold. I hadn't seen Seradon's seed at the tree, but from her reaction, hers hadn't altered, either. She pocketed it again before I caught more than a glimpse of a butterscotch-colored acorn.

"It's . . . hideous." Quinn sounded close to tears. He touched the seed with one citrine claw, as if he was about to push it away from himself.

"I've never seen anything like that," Seradon said, bending closer. Her mouth twisted, and she straightened, looking away from the seed. I couldn't ask her in front of Quinn, but I was pretty sure the seed had the same nauseous effect on her.

"How did this happen?" Quinn asked.

"The cobra," I said. "You asked the tree how you could help me. Your seed looked like a black snake biting its own tail, and you just saved me from a snake bite. Saving my life is a spectacular way to help me."

Quinn nodded glumly. I tied his seed back around his neck, searching for the right words. I yearned to give him a hug, but I was afraid I would hurt him.

"It's peculiar, but we don't know what it means yet. This could be a really important clue that will be invaluable later."

Quinn nodded again and sighed. "I hope it's helpful."

The thing I wanted the most help with was finding the story of a lifetime. Since Quinn's seed had just altered, did that mean I was a step closer to getting my own answer?

Hoping to lighten Quinn's mood, I jokingly asked, "You don't think there might be a firebird in here with us, do you?"

Seradon slapped the end of the leash against her palm. "Well, it's no coincidence the firebird shipment was hijacked just before Lunacy's ward—"

"Seradon." Grant barked her name like a reprimand, and Seradon's mouth clicked shut.

Too late.

"There really are firebirds in Lunacy?" I squeaked. "I might be one step closer to evolving my seed?"

"Your guess is as good as mine." Seradon shrugged dismissively. The lynx licked a paw and cleaned her whiskers, unperturbed.

I glanced around the deadly ruins, a thread of excitement squirming through my dread. Maybe I was right where I was supposed to be after all.

12

Dust trickled from my scalp down my shoulders, tunneling into my bustier. The gritty friction of each inhalation stung my skin, and I dug my fingers beneath the neckline, scooping sweat-slurried dirt out of my top. Flapping the hem of the tight garment only succeeded in unleashing a rain of fine sand into the waist of my pants. Exasperated, I gave up, casting an envious glance at Seradon's uniform. Though dirt matted her short hair and dulled the silver threads in her shirt and pants, it didn't appear to have trapped any of the grit against her skin.

Grant bent in half and ruffled his thick hair, adding a fresh cloud of dust to the air. He slapped the dirt from his shirt and pants but didn't think to wipe away the pale-beige film coating his face and neck. The uniform powder stole the definition from his eyebrows and eyelashes, flattening his features into a stranger's. I swiped my forehead and cheeks, spitting when I got dirt in my mouth. At least I didn't smell like a harpy.

"Let's regroup," Grant said.

Seradon stepped around him, Sooth leading the way.

Grant indicated Quinn and I should follow, and he brought up the rear. I kept a close eye on Quinn. The brace supporting his wing held firm, but he still had a hitch in his stride. I wished I could spare him his pain, but the best I could do was gently stroke my fingers along his forehead and offer him silent encouragement.

"What did you ask the everlasting tree?" Grant asked.

I had been expecting the question, and I saw no reason not to tell him the truth. "I asked it where to find the story of a lifetime."

He made a noise I couldn't interpret, then said, "Let me see your seed."

"You can't. It's at home."

Seradon tossed me an incredulous look.

"It seemed safer." I didn't want to explain that I hadn't thought—and had almost hoped—I wouldn't encounter a firebird this soon. I wasn't sure I could cogently explain my desire to delay attaining my seed's answer.

"So if we come across a firebird in here, you could miss your chance to evolve your seed?" Seradon asked.

My stomach sank. "I guess so."

Would fate be so fickle? What if my seed was like Quinn's, and it required the touch of a firebird before it evolved? I would never live it down if I missed my chance to evolve my seed because I hadn't thought to keep it on my person at all times.

A barricade of boulders filled the passage we had escaped, the mound nearly as high as the fractured canyon walls. Whatever disguised trap we all had jumped over in our panicked flight had been buried, as had our chances of backtracking. After shouting across the rubble to verify Velasquez, Winnigan, and Marciano were alive and unin- jured, Grant and Seradon attempted to climb the unstable stones, but the rocks shifted and slid, threatening to collapse and bury them alive. After the fourth attempt almost crushed Seradon, Grant called a halt to their efforts.

"Continue with the mission," Grant shouted to the separated members of his squad. Irritation burned in his eyes when they landed on me, and I fought against the urge to hunch away from him. I didn't need to be a mind reader to know he cursed my presence. If not for me, the team would never have been divided and the murderer wouldn't have gained another hour's lead on them.

"Everyone, move out."

Seradon shouldered her pack and resumed her place in the lead. I lingered, staring at the only known way out of the cursed labyrinth, now an impassable jumble of limestone. The appropriate emotion in this instance would have been dread or despair. Instead, excitement fizzled in my gut. I couldn't do anything about the obstructed escape route, but I might be able to do something to further my quest for an unparalleled story.

All I had to do was navigate a convoluted maze designed to annihilate trespassers and locate a firebird that may or may not be in the possession of an insane blood-magic murderer.

And survive, of course. Survival was paramount.

My inauspicious checklist dampened the effervescent excitement building in my stomach but couldn't completely stamp it out. Squaring my shoulders, I strode after Seradon, ignoring Grant's scowl.

We retraced our steps to the location of the cobra's attack, then proceeded more cautiously through uncharted labyrinth passageways. I lost all sense of direction almost immediately. The sun had sunk low on the horizon behind the towering trees surrounding the ruins. Without the bright rays splashed across the upper reaches of the canyon, and with the ribbon of sky above us a uniform cobalt, I couldn't determine east from west. The labyrinth itself provided few points of reference, with every corridor composed of variations of the same beige and russet striations and the stone floors uniformly smooth. No handy rock formations denoted passageways; no tall trees served as guideposts. Not even the traps could be relied on as markers, since once they were activated and destroyed, they disappeared, as the cobra had proven. Grant scratched marks into the walls at every intersection, but when we encountered dead ends and were forced to backtrack, those marks had always mysteriously vanished. The best form of navigation we possessed was the sketch of our route Grant made in his notebook. The map gave me hope that we weren't being fooled into traveling repeatedly through the same canyons. However, I couldn't help but wish it showed us where we were going, not where we had been.

"Until you find that story of a lifetime and move on to some new diversion, you need to stop treating this like a game," Grant said, breaking the silence as we trekked down a long empty corridor.

"What?" Where had he gotten the idea I thought this was a game? Or a diversion?

"Look at what real journalists are doing."

"*Real* journalists?" I sputtered.

"Like the guy who talked to us about the murder—that's all he did: question us." Anger seeped into Grant's tone. "He didn't try to insert himself into our investigation, didn't try to follow me around, and he was smart enough to stay clear of Lunacy."

Seriously? He wanted to lecture me on how to do my job?

"If I didn't think it would hurt my hand more than your jaw, I'd give you the punch that comment deserves." A ghost of the lynx's magic pinched my shoulders. I didn't often resort to violence, but being compared to Nathan—and found lacking!—charged my words with the flavor of truth. "And for the last time, I did not 'insert' myself into your investigation. You're here because the ward is down. So am I. Zipporah must have figured out this was her only chance to snag the Chiefmaker, and she plunked me down in here because I'm expendable." Sooth's magic lashed me, and I tripped. Through gritted teeth, I amended, "*To her.* Expendable to her." The pain evaporated, giving free rein to my boiling outrage. "While I'm at it, let's clear up one final thing: I don't want to follow you around."

A whip crack split across my spine, and I shoved my fists into my pockets and locked my jaw to hide my flinch.

Seradon cast a sympathetic glance in my direction. "Grant's gotten into the habit of looking for you wherever we go," she said. "I think he misses you when you're not around."

"Hardly," Grant snapped.

Sooth hissed at him. The captain's face remained stoic, but that had to have hurt. Even my lies hadn't gotten such a large reaction out of the lynx. I picked up my pace, mildly mollified, though the image of Grant expecting to find me trailing along at his heels like a puppy irked my pride.

At the next fork in the labyrinth, Sooth shied away from the right branch. Both routes appeared identical to the naked eye, but the lynx had sensed an untruth. I scanned the walls, inspecting them for shadows that didn't belong. Grant stooped to collect pebbles, then tossed them down the right branch. They clattered harmlessly off the walls, but instead of hitting the canyon floor, they disappeared through it. We all stilled, straining to listen. Several seconds passed before the pebbles hit the bottom of the disguised hole. I studied the canyon floor, searching for the seam between real and illusionary rock. I couldn't find it. Without the lynx, I wouldn't have suspected an illusion existed.

We took the left branch.

"Owing Zipporah is not the sort of problem you can make go away with a wave of your hand," Grant said, as if picking up a paused conversation.

"I never thought it was."

"No one is going to swoop in and save you, princess."

"Clearly." *Princess?* When had I gotten upgraded from "pain-in-the-ass reporter"?

"Why didn't you tell me you were indebted to the harpy?"

"You mean, so you could have told me sooner that you weren't going to 'swoop in and save me'?"

Seradon's cough sounded suspiciously like laughter. I soothed my fingers across Quinn's forehead when I wanted to ball them into a fist. Why was Grant being such a jerk?

"You lied to me," Grant growled.

His menacing tone sent a shiver down my spine, but I rolled my eyes and pretended to be unaffected. "I did not."

Everyone eyed Sooth, but she didn't break her stride, and not even a tingle of her magic prickled my skin. Good, because I hadn't lied; I had omitted a detail and let Grant believe what he wanted to.

"Besides," I said, unable to resist goading Grant, "I wanted to wait to tell you until we were trapped together so you could lecture me about my stupidity. It didn't seem fair to tell you when I could walk away." Sooth hissed, but the sting of her magic was worth it when I caught a glimpse of

Grant's thunderous expression. Seradon shook her head at my foolishness.

The next intersection of the labyrinth was in sight when Sooth planted her feet and refused to advance. No discernible trap lurked in the bland corridor, but as the invisible hole had proved, the blood-magic illusions had lost none of their strength over the centuries. Anything could be lying in wait for us.

"Do we go back, Captain?" Seradon asked.

Grant consulted his sketched map. "We've exhausted every open route. Unless we want to attempt to climb the avalanche again, we either need to go forward here or through one of the other illusions."

"I think this is our best option." It was the first time Quinn had spoken since we had been forced to venture deeper into Lunacy. I had been worried he was in too much pain to talk, but his voice sounded unstrained. A pinch of tension eased from my shoulders.

"Explain," Grant said.

"The other routes we bypassed were single canyons. This one leads to an intersection with five openings. We're more likely to find a path that goes somewhere useful if we go forward here."

"How do you know how many pathways are up ahead?" I asked.

"Did you memorize the labyrinth when you flew over?" Grant asked on top of my question.

"Not all of it, but I remember this part."

Seradon shot me a surprised glance, and I shrugged. I had no idea Quinn possessed such an impressive memory.

"Are you able to keep a map of where we've been in your head?" Grant asked Quinn.

"Can't you?"

Grant squatted and showed Quinn his sketched map. The young gargoyle studied it, then tapped two shaded lines. "These were more curved. If we hadn't run into illusions here and here, we probably would have been able to connect these. This one"—he traced along a sinuous line—"I remember from above, because it looks like Oliver's spine."

Once he pointed it out, I recognized the shape of a Chinese dragon's undulating body, complete with dead-end branches that looked like spikes.

Grant sat back on his heels and made the corrections Quinn had indicated, adding notes to his map. "You are a gargoyle of surprising talents," he said, standing. "Forward it is."

Quinn smiled with just his lips, looking pleased with himself.

Seradon passed Sooth's leash to me. The small cat crept closer to Quinn and sniffed the tip of his bound wing, then his belly, and when she grew bolder, the underside of his chin. When Sooth lifted an oversize paw as if to touch Quinn's muzzle, he released a warning growl. The gargoyle could have easily swallowed the lynx to her shoulders, if he were so inclined, but Sooth appeared unafraid. Giving her whiskers a dismissive twitch, she sat and pretended to be absorbed in cleaning her raised paw. Quinn rolled his eyes.

Grant and Seradon collected pebbles to toss out as bait for the trap. Grant's stones skipped off the rocky floor of the canyon, proving the ground wasn't an illusion. Seradon's stones flew higher, triggering nothing.

"Stay back until I give the all clear," Grant said.

I nodded, apprehension shortening my breath.

Grant and Seradon unsheathed long knives and shifted to either side of the canyon before easing forward. I barely breathed as I watched them, waiting for the nefarious trap to spring.

A ragged, limestone-colored shape separated from the canyon above their heads and dropped soundlessly in front of Seradon. As it straightened, the illusion peeled away, revealing a monster. Naked, vaguely humanoid with a massive triangular bat's head, the creature stood taller than Grant on angular, muscled legs. Coarse black hair matted its slender torso and neck, and scythe-like claws extended from its fingertips. When it raised its fists high and released an ear-piercing shriek, it revealed wicked fangs and leathery bat wings flaring from the undersides of its arms.

A camazotz.

I knew of the vicious, bloodthirsty creatures only by reputation and rumors. It was said their favorite attack strategy was to strike a prey's jugular and bleed them dry. As an added bonus, this one appeared to be rabid, with foaming saliva trailing down its chest and a sheen of red glistening across its irises.

The camazotz crouched, focusing past Grant and Seradon to lock its malevolent gaze upon me, the obvious prey.

"Eyes up front," Seradon barked, waving her arms to get the monster's attention. It spun toward her, lashing out with a long, claw-tipped wing. Seradon jumped aside, leaving an opening for Grant. He surged forward and jabbed the camazotz's chest with his knife. The enormous man-bat nimbly evaded, using its longer reach to slice at Grant's neck. The captain dropped and rolled, avoiding the blow by mere inches. As if they had practiced it, Seradon leapt over Grant and attacked with a flurry of knife strikes, driving the camazotz back two steps before it knocked her aside with a brutal kick to her hip.

Grant sprang to his feet, a knife in each hand, and charged. He struck with almost inhuman speed, his blades flashing in silvery blurs, but the camazotz was just as fast. Slashing with claws and teeth, it fought with animalistic ferocity, unheeding of the cuts Grant opened in its arms and chest. The corridor filled with the sounds of grunts and gnashing teeth and the scrape of feet and wings. I strained to keep track of Grant, marveling at his speed and skill even as I worried it wouldn't be enough.

Seradon stood at the edge of the fight, tensed, ready to leap in. The canyon wasn't wide enough for her and Grant to physically attack in tandem, but that didn't stop her from raining tiny flames down upon the camazotz's chest. The beast shrieked as its hair caught on fire. The sound splintered my eardrums, and I clapped my hands over my ears. Quinn and Sooth cried out in the same tortured octave, their ears flattened to their scalps.

The camazotz slapped out the flames, battering Grant with its wings. He ducked out of range, pivoting low behind the camazotz to hamstring it. Too fast, the camazotz leapt aside, its wings carrying it twice as far as a normal jump. Grant lunged after it. My fingernails dug crescents into my palm when the camazotz twisted midair to rake its claws across Grant's bicep. The captain struck back, his knife slicing deep into the tendon of the camazotz's right wing. The appendage flopped to the monster's side, and its keening wail ricocheted through the canyon, pummeling my eardrums. Flailing, it drove Grant back.

"Heart," Seradon barked. Suiting action to words, she sprinted past Grant and rammed her knife hilt deep into the monster's chest. Momentum carried her beneath the camazotz's retaliatory bite. Grant flowed after her like a shadow, catching the camazotz's arm before its desperate clawing could scratch Seradon. With quick, efficient slashes, he rendered the second wing useless.

The camazotz floundered and toppled. As it hit the ground, it disintegrated into oily black smoke that started at its toes and eroded its way up the camazotz's body. Seradon slumped to brace her fists against her knees, breathing hard. Grant sidestepped away from the smoke and examined his knives. They glinted silver in the shadowy canyon light, untainted by blood despite the recent battle. It wasn't until he sheathed them that I let out a pent-up breath and loosened my death grip on the leash. Flexing my fingers, I encouraged blood back into the cramped digits.

Seradon started to gesture toward me when the camazotz's head detached from its smoking body and floated into the air. As it rose, its pointy black ears lengthened to form wings, and a fresh row of teeth sprouted in its mouth.

"A chonchon? You've got to be kidding me," Seradon exclaimed.

The chonchon pivoted, turning to lock its bloodred eyes on me once again. Icy terror spurted through my veins, and my feet rooted to the canyon floor.

"Sooth, no!"

At Quinn's shout, I tore my gaze from the horrifying head in time to see Sooth charge back into the labyrinth. The gargoyle spun, pouncing on the trailing leash. Sooth slammed against the harness, her momentum carrying her into the air before she crashed to the ground.

The hairs at the nape of my neck stood on end, and I whirled toward the monster. The enormous bat head—the chonchon—sailed high over Seradon and Grant, evading them to spear toward me.

I didn't think. I simply reacted. Seizing every ounce of magic from Quinn's offered boost, I erected an earth shield and slammed it into place in time to deflect the chonchon's snapping jaws. Undeterred, it flung itself at my shield again, a grotesque tongue twice as long as its jaws sliming my magic. The chonchon's rancid breath washed over me, and I gagged. When licking and biting didn't penetrate my barrier, the chonchon circled me, mouth agape, scraping its fangs across my shield. My magic shuddered and bucked, and I cowered behind the fragile elemental ward, wishing I knew offensive spells or even had a blade. Seradon and Grant had to be close. They would save—

My shield imploded. One moment it encased me; the next it crushed me. My knees slammed to the granite. The shield's weight smashed into me, as if the earth in my spell had solidified into rock. I crumpled forward, neck kinked until my forehead pressed against my knees. Pain erupted in my hand. I had braced it beside me when I fell, and my deformed magic pulverized it, pulverized all of me, squeezing me tighter—*tighter.*

I fought the shield, shoving against it with my bones and muscle and elemental strength, but my efforts only seemed to magnify its power. My ribs compressed against my thighs, squeezing my lungs flat, and fiery pain seared my spine. Black spots stabbed my vision.

Quinn's enhancement evaporated, crippling my defensive efforts. I scrambled for more magic, not recognizing the slackening of pressure until I wheezed in a thimbleful of air.

With the trickle of oxygen came a modicum of intelligence, and I surrendered my hold on the elements. The traitorous shield evaporated. I collapsed to my side, then rolled onto my back, sucking in lungsful of air.

The chonchon dove for my exposed throat, jaws agape.

I flung up my forearms in a futile attempt to block its lethal bite. Quinn lunged across the canyon, too far away and too slow. Then Sooth shot out from behind him. She sprang to Quinn's back and launched through the sky to sink her claws into the chonchon's scalp. A flash of silver arrowed through the air, piercing the chonchon's eye. The bat-head creature released a truncated screech, then dissolved into smoke. The knife clattered to the ground beside me. The lynx dropped to my stomach, punching the air from my lungs with her massive paws before shoving off.

Moaning, I curled around my stomach and gasped for air all over again.

Seradon slid to a stop beside me, snatching the lynx's leash from the ground. "That went to splinters fast."

13

"Are you all right?" Grant asked.

I rolled my head to the side, surprised to find him kneeling close enough to touch.

"Never better," I quipped, then cursed when Sooth's magic flayed my skin.

"Is anything broken?" Quinn shoved his nose against mine, making my vision go cross-eyed. Grant tugged him back a few inches, bringing the worried gargoyle into focus.

"I don't think so." I curled my fingers, pleased they each responded with only nominal tenderness. Gingerly, I tested my limbs. I was sore, but flexing didn't elicit any sharp pains. "I'm more resilient than I look."

I tried not to be insulted when Quinn and Grant both checked the lynx for verification. At least only Grant appeared surprised by Sooth's lack of reaction.

"What about you, Quinn?" Lunging after Sooth couldn't have felt good with his injured wing.

"My shoulder hurts, but I'll be fine once Mika patches me up."

What I wouldn't have given to have my best friend and

gargoyle healer with us. I hated the pain that pinched Quinn's expression and my inability to do anything about it.

"At least that little experiment proved my theory," Seradon said. "Small magics are the key."

"What do you mean?" Quinn asked.

"As Kylie so helpfully demonstrated, Lunacy reacts to large amounts of the elements. It took all of three seconds for it to flip her magic against her."

Three seconds? The chonchon's attack felt like it had lasted minutes before my spell imploded.

"However, my tiny flames weren't affected and did exactly what I wanted them to do," Seradon continued. "It's like Lunacy doesn't detect small magics."

In other words, she had possessed the wherewithal to run an elemental test while exchanging blows with the nightmarish camazotz, whereas I had been too busy panicking to think when confronted by the much smaller chonchon.

With a fair amount of groaning, I sat up and took a visual assessment of my battered body. At my current rate of injury acquisition, Lunacy would kill me before sunset.

"Maybe you should keep this on you," Grant said, handing me a jar of greenthread.

"You're such a charmer, Captain." I gasped at fresh flicks of pain and snatched the salve from Grant's palm without meeting his gaze. Someone seriously needed to teach Sooth the difference between lying and sarcasm.

Seradon chuckled. "You lie a lot, Kylie."

"I do not." A ghost of pain raked across my stomach. I shared a squinty-eyed look with the small cat, then turned away to dab numbing salve on my bruised fingers, spreading it around to my fingertips, where several cuts had reopened.

"Here, I'll teach you how to be honest." Seradon

crouched beside me, a teasing grin lighting her face. "We'll start with simple truths and build up. Is your name Kylie Grayson?"

I slid my gaze to Grant. He had stepped away to collect his knife and survey our surroundings.

"I'm not in the mood for games."

"Come on. It'll make this more fun. It might even teach you to be a better journalist. Now, is your real name Kylie Grayson?"

I sighed. "Not really."

"Not really?" Seradon echoed. She frowned at the passive lynx, then at me. "Why aren't you in pain?"

I focused on screwing the lid onto the greenthread jar and didn't meet Seradon's eyes.

"What is your name?" Seradon straightened to tower over me.

I pushed to my feet and hobbled in place as the strained tendons in my thighs protested. My hip popped, and I wiggled my toes within my boots before taking great interest in dusting off my clothes.

"Kylie . . ." Seradon said, her tone softening to a menacing whisper.

"Why does it matter?" I asked. All of the teasing had evaporated from Seradon's body language. I had never really noticed how much taller she was than me, or how threatening she could look. I peeked at Grant; he watched us with an impassive expression.

"Who *are* you?" Seradon demanded.

"I thought you said this was going to be fun."

"She's Harriet Grayson," Grant said.

Shocked, I spun to face him. "How did you know?"

Grant crossed his arms and arched an eyebrow at me, inviting me to form my own conclusion.

"*The* Harriet Grayson? Of the *Airstrong* Graysons?" Seradon blurted. "*That* Harriet?" Her exclamation boomeranged through the canyon: *Harriet-et-et.*

I grimaced, unable to tear my gaze from Grant. He had been so serious, so cold since I had fallen into Lunacy. Even at the everlasting tree, he had treated me with something akin to disdain. Yet before then, he had been exasperated by me, but never outright rude . . .

The answer stampeded to the foreground of my thoughts. Of course. Grant was an FPD captain. He had access to the kind of information and contacts I could only dream of. Maybe his anger wasn't simply because he was saddled with protecting me inside Lunacy or that I was a reporter whose curiosity had entangled me in his operations more than once. Maybe it had to do with discovering I had duped him. He was a Federal Pentagon Defense captain, a man used to being in the know and in control. That I had been able to deceive him must have stung his pride. It wouldn't matter that my deception hadn't been aimed at him and had no bearing on our interactions. Somehow he had learned my true identity and believed it gave him new insight into my personality, conveniently ignoring what he already knew about me so I fit his new, biased conclusions.

"How long have you known?" I asked. At least this explained Grant's earlier comments about me moving on to my "next diversion" after getting the story of a lifetime. As if being a journalist was a hobby I was indulging in until I took over my parents' business.

"Did you get disowned?" Seradon asked.

"I don't understand," Quinn said, his voice small. "What does this mean?"

"It means Kylie—*Harriet*—isn't a real reporter; she's just

playing at one." Grant's fingers twitched against his bicep, and I hoped it meant he had gotten zapped by the lynx.

I planted my hands on my hips and glared at him. Grant had been spewing his anger all over me since I had been dumped in Lunacy. I might have been pleased we were finally getting to the root of it if he hadn't made me so furious.

"I'm not playing at anything," I spat.

"Then why lie about your name?" Quinn asked in that same timorous voice.

Grant's contempt buzzed against my skin, the weight of his unjust condemnation inciting a childish desire to clam up and refuse to explain. However, Quinn's forlorn expression melted my heart. I would have preferred to have had this conversation when he and I were alone, but that was my fault. I could have told him about my past earlier today after meeting with my mom at the Airstrong headquarters or even before then, at my apartment, when I realized this story had set my carefully segregated lives on a collision course. I *should* have told Quinn earlier. He was my partner.

"Kylie is my middle name," I said, squatting to put myself on eye level with the gargoyle. My bruised knees protested, and I planted a hand on the ground to redistribute my weight and ameliorate the pain. "I prefer not to go by Harriet Grayson because that name is closely linked in people's minds to my parents. They have a certain reputation—it's not a bad one, but I don't want to be associated with it. A lot of people focus on how my parents are powerful, at least in certain circles. When I'm Harriet Grayson, people don't see me; they see my parents' daughter."

Quinn tilted his head quizzically. "Isn't that the same thing?"

"Not to some people. To them, I'm a pawn or a tool. I

didn't want that life. I wanted to be a journalist. I wanted to be able to work without people prejudging me." I shot Seradon a pointed look.

"So you picked the least reputable career you could find?" Her tone held a shadow of its former teasing.

I shrugged, seeing no reason to explain my passion for journalism. "I prefer to be Kylie Grayson."

Seradon and Grant both turned to Sooth for confirmation. She sprawled on her side, cleaning her claws, paying no attention to me.

"Let me get this straight," Seradon said. "You prefer to be a no-name reporter rather than be treated as the heiress of the Airstrong empire?"

"I'm not a no-name reporter." My smile turned gloating when Sooth didn't react.

"Of course not. You kept your parents' last name." Derision thickened Grant's voice.

"I kept my middle one, too." I had only wanted anonymity, and being *Kylie* instead of *Harriet* had achieved that. I wasn't going to explain to Grant that I hadn't wanted to throw away my name as if I were ashamed of my parents. I loved them dearly.

I rolled my shoulders and straightened, facing off with Grant. "What are you insinuating?"

Please, Grant, tell me what great crime I have committed.

"You claim to have been sick of the notoriety of being Harriet, but you're so intent on chasing fame that it's nearly gotten you killed, several times here—"

"Not this again. I told you Zipporah—"

"And with the dryads. If you're just a poor little rich girl slumming with us average folks, wishing you were one of us, why are you so intent on getting the front-page stories? Why are you chasing the 'story of a lifetime'?"

Ah. I could either be Harriet Grayson, the heiress, or I could live in mediocrity, never striving for my own accomplishments. I shook my head, through with trying to scale the wall Grant had erected between us.

"Sure, that's all I'm after: fame and glory. I want to see my name splashed in all caps across the front of the *Chronicle*, right *above* the headline." I shuddered under the onslaught of the lynx's biting magic, then shook my arms to release lingering tension and shouldered my bag. "Speaking of my fame, how am I going to get my next big headline if we stand around here talking all day?"

"Sir, this is a political nightmare in the making."

Bitterness welled up my esophagus. Seradon's new attitude exemplified the reason I hid my identity. I wanted to be valued for myself, not for my parents' net worth or influence.

"It's only a problem if we lose her." Grant stared at me while he spoke, his dark eyes evaluating me. "I don't plan on losing her. Do you?"

Seradon raised placating hands. "I'm just saying, consider her parents. You know how irrational people with a bit of power can be."

"Says the full-spectrum earth elemental with an FPD badge," I muttered.

Seradon narrowed her eyes at me, as if trying to decide if she should be insulted. "So what do I call you now? Harriet?"

"Kylie will do." Even if I hadn't hoped Seradon would keep my identity to herself, I wouldn't have preferred Harriet. I had never cared for the name, even in my youth. *Harry* had been a miserable nickname for a juvenile girl, and the runner-up, *Riet*, sounded like something a frog with a speech impediment would say. My dad had gotten away with calling me *Retty*, but I vastly preferred *Kylie*. It fit my personality far better than any version of my first name.

"Still, Harriet *is* your name," Seradon said. "I think I should call you by it."

"Only if I can call you Marabelle."

I had researched all the squad members months earlier, for my first front-page story that had included their heroics. At the time, I hadn't been able to unearth Seradon's first name. The mystery had intrigued me enough to keep digging, especially after I realized no one, not even the members of her squad, used Seradon's first name. Ever. When I chanced upon a city guard who had trained with Seradon years earlier, I had seized upon the opportunity. After plying the woman with many drinks and swearing to secrecy, I had finagled Seradon's first name from her. I had expected something atrocious, but Marabelle was beautiful. However, it suited Seradon about as well as it would have suited Grant.

Seradon's teasing smile vanished. "Kylie it is."

"Thank you."

"If you know what's good for you, you'll never utter that name again, either," Seradon said.

"Why not? It's pretty."

"Kylie . . ." Her gaze promised violence if I pressed the issue, but it was preferable to having her look at me like I had turned into a fragile, poisonous doll.

"Fine. I won't tell anyone if you don't."

"Deal." Seradon slapped her palm against mine to seal our agreement.

"Glad that's settled," Grant said, then spared Sooth a scowl when her magic reacted to his sarcasm.

Ha.

"Seradon, take point. Let's see if we chose the right route."

We fell into our familiar formation, with Seradon and Sooth checking for traps, Grant guarding the rear, and Quinn and me trapped between them. The gargoyle looked introspective, an expression that sat gravely on his nicked face.

"Are you all right?" I asked. "You understand I didn't tell you my real name because it wasn't important, right? I mean, not even Mika knows."

I ignored Grant's cryptic grunt and kept my attention on the gargoyle.

Quinn tilted his head back to meet my gaze. "Really?"

"Really."

I hoped for a smile, but Quinn plodded along quietly. Just when I was going to break the silence, he did.

"I can't fly. I can't enhance you—or my enhancement only makes things worse. I may have helped with the cobra, but I was too slow with the chonchon. You could have died. In here, I'm useless."

I wracked my brain for reassurances, but the closest I came was to confess, "I know exactly how you feel."

———

TWO OF THE PASSAGEWAYS AT THE NEXT INTERSECTION WERE blocked by invisible traps Sooth refused to circumnavigate, and we lost another twenty minutes tracking another two to dead ends, but the fifth passageway eventually spat us out in front of a pitch-black cave carved into the side of a cliff. Seradon halted at the bend in the canyon, where we could survey the opening from a safe vantage. Twilight had crept over the labyrinth, deepening the shadows on the canyon floors. The faint rays of the dwindling sunset did nothing to illuminate the interior of the cavern. The jagged hole gaped like the mouth of a giant beast, its breath seething in irregular gusts along the canyon floor.

My imagination scrambled to conjure fresh horrors lurking out of sight within the cavern, but nothing topped the camazotz-turned-chonchon—except a pack of camazotzs. My palms began to sweat.

"It's about time we found the opening," Seradon said.

"You were expecting a cave?" I asked, pleased when my voice didn't quiver.

"Any labyrinth worth the blood it was carved with has to lead somewhere, right? Hopefully that's a tunnel straight to the heart of Lunacy."

After a nod from Grant, Seradon and Sooth slunk with equal stealth down one side of the canyon. Seradon held her blade unsheathed at her side. An eagerness lit her face, as if she were gleefully anticipating something jumping out of the darkness at her.

It was possible Seradon was a tad insane.

Quinn and I hunkered down at the bend in the canyon, squeezed behind Grant. He had planted himself between us and whatever might spring out of the cave. Wind gusted through the rock corridor, tugging blond tendrils from my braids and whipping them into my mouth. They tasted of dirt, and I impatiently hooked the grubby strands behind my ears. Unfortunately, the reminder of my filthy condition made my scalp itch, and scratching unleashed a trickle of dirt down the nape of my neck.

Seradon tiptoed to the edge of the cavern and peeked inside before drawing back. Sooth skulked at her feet, her whole body tense and focused on the obscured interior. After a second peek, Seradon and the lynx disappeared inside the dark maw. I craned around Grant for a better view, and his impersonal shove rocked me back a step. Holding my breath, I strained to hear any sounds of distress. Grant held himself equally motionless, though he looked coiled to spring into action. Several long, fraught seconds passed before Seradon reemerged unscathed. I sighed with relief, as did Quinn. Grant made no sound, but he relaxed enough to shift his weight from one foot to the other.

"We found our passage," Seradon said when she rejoined us. "From the sounds of the echoes and the small flame I chanced, the tunnel goes deep into the mountain."

"Any sign of people passing this way—ours or whoever opened this place up?" Grant asked.

Seradon shook her head. "There's not enough dust for footprints at the tunnel opening, but maybe we'll get lucky once we're deeper inside."

With the distraction of almost dying twice, I hadn't given much thought to the murderer Grant and Seradon were hunting. I should have been using this time to ferret out more information on their case. One way or another, I would get a story out of this, and near-death experiences and a belligerent, supercilious FPD captain were no excuse for slacking as a journalist.

"What did you mean earlier when you implied there is a connection between Lunacy and the missing firebirds?" I asked Seradon.

"Did I imply that?"

She pretended to be absorbed in the lantern she had removed from her backpack. Using a fingernail's worth of fire element, she lit the wick, then slid the glass shutter closed to protect the flame against a gust of wind. By the time she had her lantern blazing, Grant had a second lantern lit. I hoped one of them would produce a third for me, but neither did.

"How many people are you expecting to find?" I asked, trying a different tack.

"Now's not the time to play journalist," Grant said.

I ground my teeth, refusing to rise to the bait. I wouldn't get any information out of them if I picked a fight with Grant.

"Just do what I say, and you'll be fine," he added.

Surprisingly, Sooth didn't react to his statement, even though none of us had any way of knowing if he spoke the truth. Apparently, the lynx couldn't detect a lie about an event that hadn't yet happened, or maybe she read the truth of Grant's conviction. Either way, he hadn't answered my question.

"How did you know the body found in Terra Haven was killed by blood magic?"

"That style of exsanguination is unmistakable," Seradon said, shrugging her pack into place.

I tried not to react. Thus far, the cause of death had been an educated speculation, but Seradon had just confirmed it.

"You might be able to achieve a full blood-letting if you puncture multiple arteries at once," she continued, "but it would have to be well timed, and the victim's heart would have to already be pumping excessively. I've seen it happen during battle. The husk that washed up had only minor wounds, but no blood left in his body."

I suppressed a shudder, not wanting to give Grant the satisfaction of seeing me regret a question. If Nathan had been more thorough in his investigation, I could have already learned this information from his article. Blaming Nathan made me feel marginally better, even if I knew

Dahlia, the city inspector, and the mayor never would have approved of printing those details in the paper.

Grant shouldered his pack and pinned me with the force of his captain's glare. "From here forward, we move in silence. We don't know what we're walking into, and we don't need to give these lowlifes any advantages."

I opened my mouth to interject a question, but my words died under the weight of his gaze.

"We expect two people, maybe more," he continued. "These men are deranged, which makes them unpredictable and incredibly dangerous. *You* do not engage. *You* stay behind me or Seradon at all times. *You* do exactly as I order you, when I order you. No games. No sarcasm. No questions. Is that clear?"

"So long as you answer all my questions once we're out of here."

"You're in no place to bargain." Grant's tone bordered on a growl.

"I'm not bargaining; I'm laying down the rules."

The muscles in his thick jaw bounced, and something hot flared in his eyes, but Grant turned away without saying anything. Seradon smirked but smoothed her expression when he sliced a glare in her direction. When his gaze landed on Quinn, Grant said, "Same goes for you, too."

"I can't wait to hear about the firebirds," Quinn said, and I had never been more proud.

Grant shook his head and gave me a look that said louder than words, *He gets his impertinence from you.*

I waited until Grant turned away to smile.

We crept toward the tunnel, and Seradon and Sooth padded inside the gaping opening without pausing, but I hesitated at the threshold. I should have felt safe in the company of two combat-trained FPD warriors, but this was Lunacy, and now this was about to be Lunacy *underground*.

What if one of the traps caved in the tunnel on our heads?

Well, then I will be dead.

But what if a trap caved in the tunnel behind us, sealing us inside? We would die of starvation or air deprivation or an attack we never saw coming, because the lanterns wouldn't last forever, and with the elements behaving traitorously, we would be stuck in the dark, and I would never get to see the sun again, and—

Grant tapped me on the shoulder. I turned, expecting to see irritation or impatience etched into his granite expression. Instead, his gaze exuded a gentle intensity, and once we locked eyes, I couldn't look away. He took a deep breath, and I unconsciously mimicked him, realizing only after oxygen entered my hyperventilation-deprived lungs that it had been his intent. I gulped another deep breath, reining in my panic. After the third inhale, I broke our eye contact and took one last look at the navy heavens above us.

Then I turned and entered the dark heart of Lunacy.

14

The tunnel tightened around us, twisting deeper into the earth. Omnipresent darkness smothered the light from Seradon's and Grant's half-shuttered lanterns, and the weak illumination spun shadows across rough-hewn rock walls. The need for silence plucked at my taut nerves. Seradon and Grant padded soundlessly despite their heavy boots. I tried to mimic their grace, but all the bruising my body had taken had caught up with me, and weariness made me clumsier than normal. Too often, my feet scuffed against the uneven rock floor, and more than once my bag scraped against the wall, the crackle echoing in the cramped confines. Even Quinn, with his quartz paws, managed to step quieter than me. I longed to stop and rest, but even without the urgency of hunting down murderers compelling us forward, I would have been unable to relax in Lunacy.

I had hoped heading underground would mean we were done with the labyrinth part of the ruins, but we hadn't been skulking through the tunnel two minutes before we encountered the first intersection. A sickly sweet scent of rotting meat and peonies swirled through the air.

"Poison," Grant whispered. "Don't breathe."

When Sooth indicated the tunnel on the right was safe, we hustled away from the toxic air.

At the next intersection, Sooth once again refused all but one dark corridor. Deep grooves scarred the walls around its entrance, and Seradon slowed to examine them. She shot Grant a look I couldn't interpret before nudging the lynx into the new passage. I traced my fingertips across one chest-high scrape, loosening a trickle of sand. It filtered to the floor, settling into the groove left by a boot heel stamped into the fresh dirt. To my untrained eye, it looked as if a fight had happened here, one where claws or knives had struck the wall. I wanted to ask Grant's opinion, but he silently shooed me after Seradon.

When the path split again, Sooth once more approved only one route as safe. Seradon's hand slid to the knife at her waist.

"I feel like we're being herded," she said, her voice carrying no farther than the four of us.

"Or they are opening the way for us," Grant said.

They being either the blood-magic murderers or the separated part of his team.

I fervently hoped for the latter.

Grant surveyed the seemingly harmless tunnels where the lynx sensed illusions. He didn't state the obvious: none of us wanted to risk triggering a trap if we didn't have to.

"Stay sharp," he said, motioning for Seradon to lead the way again.

The tunnel walls expanded and retracted around us, sometimes dipping so low we had to duck, other times arching out of sight. Neither configuration eased my anxiety.

At least when I was forced to crouch, I could be assured no blood-crazed monsters lurked above me, waiting to pounce. Yet, when the ceiling sank close enough to see—or touch—it only reminded me of how much earth was piled above me, and how easy it would be for the mountain to crush this tiny pocket of space and me with it.

Something heavy thumped deeper inside the mountain, then muffled curses reverberated through the tunnel. We froze as a unit. Seradon turned her lantern's light down to the barest thimble of illumination, and Grant did the same. The murky shadows swallowed us. I reached blindly for Quinn, not taking a breath until my hand rested on his cool mane. The sounds of people continued to filter through the tunnel, the acoustics mutilating their words. My eyes acclimated to the marginal light in time to see Grant give Seradon a hand signal. With a whisper of cloth, she and Sooth disappeared around the corner. Grant laid a hand on my arm to prevent me from following.

I counted the seconds, consciously matching my breaths to Grant's so as not to give in to the urge to hyperventilate. In my mind's eye, Seradon tiptoed up behind a blood-soaked giant twice Marciano's size. He carried a beating heart in his palm and squeezed fresh blood into his mouth—

I slammed the door on my overactive imagination and brought my breathing back under control. My frayed nerves refused to be soothed, and when Seradon popped into sight, I jumped and clapped my hand over my mouth to hold in my startled squeak. She gave me a reassuring squeeze on the arm as she leaned close to speak to Grant.

"Two men," Seradon reported, and I had to strain to hear. "You were right; they are using firebirds for navigation."

My stomach flipped. The firebirds were here. I really was

on track to evolve my seed. Did that mean *this* was part of the story of a lifetime? And what did Seradon mean they were using the birds for navigation? I drew in a breath to ask...and pressed my lips together, breathing out through my nose. I had made Grant a promise to be quiet, and I would keep it, even if I choked on my unspoken questions.

"Threat?" Grant whispered.

"A dagger apiece, and one has a ceremonial knife, but..."

Grant nodded. It took me a second longer to finish Seradon's sentence. The men didn't need physical weapons to be dangerous; as blood-magic users, they wouldn't have the same problems controlling the tainted elements that we did.

"Sir, they were arguing about Kylie's Chiefmaker," Seradon said.

She and Grant glanced at me, and I wanted to protest her calling it *my* Chiefmaker. Instead, I raised my hands in the universal *I don't know* gesture, and they both turned away.

"Whatever it is," Seradon hissed, "I don't want them getting their hands on it."

If attaining the Chiefmaker was these two murderers' goal—if that's what they had sacrificed a person for and the reason they had broken the ward on Lunacy—I couldn't let the harpy have it, either.

I shook my head. I could worry about only one life-threatening problem at a time.

"I recommend we hit them hard and fast," Seradon continued. "Before they reach the heart."

"Agreed," Grant said. He shrugged free of his pack and set it soundlessly against the tunnel wall. Seradon did the same, and I followed suit. Grant extinguished his lantern, and Seradon handed hers to me, along with Sooth's leash. I rubbed my shaking hands down my thighs, unvoiced questions clogging my throat.

Masculine voices bounced off the walls, still garbled, but their tones and increasing volume indicated they were arguing. Great. Just a pair of mentally unbalanced blood-magic murderers getting into a squabble in the underground tunnels of centuries-old ruins. What could go wrong?

Grant tapped my shoulder, snagging my attention and giving me a signal I couldn't fail to understand: *Stay put.*

I swallowed hard and nodded. He narrowed his eyes and repeated the gesture, as if he didn't believe I was intelligent enough to understand the first time—or maybe he didn't believe I would follow his order.

I rolled my eyes and shooed him along. He flashed me a quick grin, and for a split second, I forgot where we were and that I was scared out of my mind and still mad at him. Then he and Seradon eased out of sight, and my fear swelled to fill the darkness once more.

Lingering behind, where I wouldn't get in Seradon's or Grant's way, was the smart course of action, but being unable to watch the confrontation made me jittery. Quinn nudged my hand to get my attention, then tilted his chin in the direction they had disappeared, his unspoken question clear. I nodded. Giving the leash a gentle tug to prompt Sooth, I tiptoed around the bend, hugging tight to the wall. Quinn padded at my side, close enough for me to keep a hand on his neck.

The tunnel opened into a deep cavern with a claustrophobically short ceiling. Pale stalactites hung from above like monstrous fangs, moisture and mineral crystals glistening along their jagged surfaces. Mounds of ivory stalagmite molars dotted the floor, and a jade pool shimmered near the center of the chamber. Multiple shadowy cavities dotted the walls where additional tunnels fed into the cavern.

Two men on the far side of the gloomy room drew my attention. Blood magic or no, Lunacy Labyrinth had not been kind to either of them. The shorter man was pale and wiry, with greasy brown hair that hung limp against his collar. Dried mud and other questionable dark stains coated his pants, and the tatters of his filthy shirt appeared to be held together by sweat and a pair of abused suspenders. The second man's shirt cut low across his leathery chest, revealing grimy muscles slashed with thick scars. An assortment of hawk, turkey, and crow feathers adorned the undersides of his sleeves, as if he had attempted to sew himself wings. A matte-red substance stained his forehead from his hairline to his eyebrows, and two black lines cut through his cheeks from his eyes to his chin. They had probably once been drawn to look like claws, but now sweat and dirt smudged them. His oily black hair had been clawed into a nub of a ponytail, pulling his features tight. I pegged him to be the leader. I also suspected the mystery substance on his forehead was blood.

A metallic-orange light pooled around the men, emanating from the firebirds they held. After the darkness of the tunnel, staring directly at the birds' bright bodies made my eyes water. Squinting, I cataloged details from the corner of my vision until my eyes adjusted. Rough hemp ropes pinched the firebirds' necks against their backs, constricted their feet into useless knots, and crushed their wings against their bodies until they resembled nothing more than pheasant-size lumps of glowing feathers. Only the occasional twitch of their hooded heads confirmed they were alive.

Fury burned beneath my fear. The men treated the firebirds as if they were inanimate objects—specialty lanterns —not living, breathing creatures trapped and in pain. The shorter man swung his firebird by a rope binding, carelessly smashing it against the wall to better illuminate whatever he was studying. The other man bounced his firebird from hand to hand in agitation.

"Death. Death. Everywhere death," muttered the short man. He rubbed sweat from his eyes with a grubby sleeve, his mumbles deteriorating. Abruptly, he whipped his firebird into his companion, eliciting a curse from the feathered man and a muted squawk from the bird. "Not that way, Emmett. Death. That way lies death."

"I told you to call me Eztli Tiacauh."

The brown-haired man scoffed. "You're no chief."

"Not yet."

Even in the unconventional lighting, with eerie shadows dancing across the men as they swung the firebirds back and forth, I could tell something more than a lack of hygiene and compassion afflicted both men. Their limbs jerked mechanically, stuttering when they should have been fluid. Emmett paused often to cant his head, as if listening to voices inaudible to anyone else. The other man stole hateful glances at Emmett, his tongue flicking out to taste the air when Emmett's back was turned.

Oh yes, the use of blood magic had taken its toll on these two.

Seradon and Grant slipped through the irregular formations on the cavern floor, using the shadows for cover. Seradon circled to the left, Grant to the right. Oblivious, the two men scuttled to the next tunnel opening and shoved their firebirds up to the wall. Strange runes flared into existence, made visible by the firebirds' light. I gasped in surprise. This must have been what Seradon had meant earlier when she had said the men were using the birds for navigation.

"Stop breathing on me, Thorpe," Emmett groused, flapping his feathered elbows. "Your mouth smells like the inside of a skunk's ass."

Thorpe snapped his teeth at Emmett but sidestepped to give him more room. Emmett reached to touch the markings on the wall but paused with his head canted, listening to Lunacy. Without warning, he whirled and punched a wall of air into Seradon. The blast flung her toward a sharp stalactite—or would have if Seradon had let it land. Almost too fast to follow, she cleaved his attack in half with a wallop of earth element. Emmett's magic split and dispersed. Then, before Seradon could straighten from her crouch, the cleaver of earth elemental ripped from her control, pivoted, and bludgeoned her. Seradon's head cracked against a stalagmite, and her legs buckled.

The whole sequence of events took less than five seconds. From my position crouched in the shadows, I could see only the toes of Seradon's boots, and they weren't moving. Thorpe belatedly spun, his firebird held high to better see his would-be assailant.

"You can't stop me," Emmett shouted. A flash of silver speared toward his back, and Emmett knocked aside Grant's thrown knife without even looking. His voice rose to a shriek. "No one can stop me!"

Emmett twisted and flung a giant fist of air at Grant. Rather than attempt to deflect or break the spell, Grant crouched, wrapping one arm around a slender stalagmite. I flinched, helpless to do anything but watch as the air slammed him. Wind plastered Grant's uniform to the contours of his flexed chest and thighs, but no strain showed on his face as he used raw, physical strength to maintain his position. Emmett threw another punch of air, then another, pummeling Grant. The madman's attack wasn't particularly strong or creative, but since Grant couldn't respond in kind, it was enough.

Shadows laced Emmett's air magic, hinting at images trapped within the insentient element—dark, disturbing images of death and pain. But no matter how hard I squinted, I couldn't make them out. A chill shivered down my spine. Emmett must have been using blood magic in tandem with the natural element, which was why Lunacy hadn't flipped his attack against him.

Flecks of fire ignited around Emmett, buzzing like bumblebees. A flicker of flame no longer than my fingernail attached itself to one of the feathers draping from Emmett's arms. Another lit upon his scalp. Emmett danced in place, flailing to put out the fires. With his attention diverted, his air punches weakened. Grant braced a foot against the base of the stalagmite he had been clinging to and shoved toward the next closest handhold, muscling through Emmett's sporadic attacks to close the distance between them.

Small magics. Seradon had been brought down by her own warped magic, just as I had nearly been crushed by my shield spell when the chonchon attacked. Grant was fighting the only way Lunacy allowed, using the tiny flames as weapons and a diversionary tactic.

I checked Seradon—or rather, I checked her feet. I willed her to move, to prove she was still alive, but her feet remained motionless.

Thorpe crept closer to her prone body, holding his firebird aloft with one jiggling hand. In the other, fire danced across his fingertips, illuminating the madness in his eyes. When a flurry of flame bees ignited around Thorpe, I almost cheered. For a moment, I thought Seradon was responsible for them, but the added strain on Grant's face confirmed he was behind the magic, not the fallen earth elemental. Thorpe ducked away from the fire, then turned to stare at the fluttering flames, mesmerized. Rather than press the attack and drive Thorpe away from Seradon, the minuscule flames continued to buzz above him in an erratic dance. Confused, I jerked my attention back to Grant.

Doubling his magic had triggered Lunacy's malicious backlash. Even as Grant maintained both sets of tiny flames, heat built around him, warping the air near his body. Sweat plastered his hair to his scalp and ran freely down the thick column of his neck to soak his shirt. Emmett's distracted air punches broke against the elemental heat imprisoning Grant, unable to penetrate past the mutated magic slowly boiling Grant alive.

"Release the elements, you stubborn idiot," I hissed.

The hem of Grant's pants caught fire. Grant bent to slap out the flames, and the fiery bees harassing Emmett shrank to sparks and extinguished.

Grant's complexion darkened from red to purple, and veins bulged in his neck. He wobbled on his feet, his chest rising and falling too fast. Despite Grant having released the fire element, the malicious magic maintained a scorching hold on him, burning through his oxygen and asphyxiating him even as it roasted him.

Lowering his head like a bull about to charge, Grant lurched toward Emmett.

"Die!" Emmett shrieked. He unleashed an anvil of air, crashing it into Grant's side. This time, the elemental cage surrounding Grant shattered, and Emmett's strike flung Grant several feet. A blast of liberated heat whooshed through the cavern, stirring my hair. His expression promising violence, Grant shoved himself to his feet, powering through the buffet of Emmett's air magic to stalk toward the madman, another knife gripped in his fist. If sheer determination could have won this battle, Grant would have already captured Thorpe and Emmett. But deprived of his magic, Grant didn't stand a chance against two blood-magic psychopaths. Not alone.

I slid Sooth's leash to Quinn. "Stay here."

"Be careful," Quinn whispered.

Before I lost my nerve, I sprinted for the nearest bulbous stalagmite and crouched behind it. Shadows darkened this half of the cavern, and I was counting on them to keep me hidden. I would be no use to Grant or Seradon if the murderers discovered me, too.

Channeling the patience of my best friend, Mika, I meticulously crafted three finger-length razors of air. Thorpe was still turning in circles, scanning the grooves in the ceiling for fiery bumblebees. However, any second now, he would remember the helpless woman lying near his feet. I needed to make sure that never happened.

Lining up the tiny blades of air, I shot them across the cavern, curving their trajectory so they jabbed Thorpe from behind. Small, finicky magics were not my forte, and I had no experience in elemental attacks. The closest I had ever come to wielding an element as a weapon had been during my school years when I inflicted air pinches on boys who had irritated me. Even then, I had done so in closer quarters than these. I had also never attempted to draw blood, let alone stab someone with my magic. It didn't surprise me when two of my air razors flew wide. One, however, nicked Thorpe's neck.

The madman shouted and spun in a frantic circle, shooting fireballs into the empty air. My heart in my throat, I darted for the next clump of stalagmites while Thorpe's back was turned, crouching low in the shadows. From my new vantage, I could see Seradon from the shoulders down. I stared at her, unblinking, until I confirmed her chest rose and fell in shallow breaths. She wasn't moving, and I couldn't see how badly her head had been injured, but she wasn't dead.

Hang on, Seradon. I won't let them touch you.

I formed another air razor, focusing my efforts on only one this time. It clipped Thorpe's shoulder, and he slapped the wound as if crushing an insect. If I was going to inflict actual damage, I needed to use more power, but fear of triggering Lunacy's awareness held my hand.

"There's something in here with us," Thorpe said. He jerked left and right, the whites of his eyes glistening as he tried to look everywhere at once. The firebird quivered in his grasp. I jabbed him with another arrowhead of air, and he danced in a flailing circle.

"It's a flaming federal goon, you idiot," Emmett spat. He had erected a shield of air around himself, and rivulets of sweat smeared the dried blood on his forehead, but otherwise he showed no strain from maintaining his assault on Grant.

Emmett had yet to waver from his single-minded, air-based attack. Either he couldn't work the other elements well or his growing insanity prevented him from crafting a more creative attack. Anywhere else, Grant would have easily overpowered him, but inside Lunacy, Emmett's modest magic reigned supreme. Undeterred, Grant harassed him with a nonstop onslaught of flames, shards of earth, and flicks of air. While none came close to touching Emmett, they distracted him—not by much, but enough for Grant to shove through the softer blows and propel himself closer. Inch by inch, Grant closed the gap between them. If he could reach Emmett, maybe he could use his knife to incapacitate the madman. I just needed to buy him time.

"Something *else*," Thorpe said, his words tumbling faster. "Something evil and angry. It's going to eat us alive. Bitebitebite."

I stabbed the nape of Thorpe's neck with another air blade, preying on his fear. He flinched and jumped, swinging the firebird wildly.

"Flee. We need—can't—must fun. Runrun and hide. Hidehidehide." Thorpe scurried to the wall. Runes flared to life across the surface, and he traced them with his fingertips, jostling Emmett.

Emmett cursed and elbowed Thorpe, then turned and swiped a finger through a cut on Thorpe's neck. Fresh blood spurted to the surface, trickling down Thorpe's neck in a glistening red line. Bright energy flared between the men, and Emmett's next wallop of air knocked Grant to his knees.

"Ow!" Thorpe slapped his hand over the wound and glared at Emmett. "What are you doing?"

"Hold still, coward."

I arrowed another air blade at Thorpe, but the shield around Emmett bubbled, blocking my magic without Emmett seeming to be aware of it.

"It's time to realize your higher purpose, Thorpe." Emmett clutched a turquoise-studded hilt at his waist and unsheathed a crude obsidian blade. He slashed at Thorpe's midsection, his jerky movements containing newfound speed and precision. Thorpe jumped aside, using his firebird as a shield. Midstrike, Emmett twisted his knife and severed the leather cord binding the firebird's feet. With another deft flick of the black blade, Emmett cut through the rope binding the firebird's wings.

Thorpe scrambled to contain the firebird, but its wings

snapped open. Light flared bright across the room, throwing the alien landscape into stark relief. Shrieking, the firebird lashed out, launching from Thorpe's chest. Thorpe released a ghastly, keening scream and staggered to the wall. Flapping clumsily into the roof, the firebird twisted to tear at the hood covering its eyes. It slammed into a stalactite and careened to the ground beyond the shallow pool, taking half the room's light with it.

Thorpe toppled over, and Emmett followed him to the ground. Deep bloody gashes flayed Thorpe's stomach open, and Emmett mashed his hand into the wounds. Thorpe's mouth opened and closed without a sound, his complexion white with shock and his eyes staring unseeingly at the ceiling. An astonishingly beautiful golden magic poured from Thorpe to Emmett, infusing Emmett with a glow that burrowed into his skin, darkening as it settled. Emmett tipped his head back, eyes closed, and when they opened, a crazed grin lit his face.

A blur in the periphery of my vision jerked me out of my trance. Grant sprinted for Emmett, a knife in each hand. Two more strides, and Grant would be within range—

A wall of air slammed Grant flat to the ground. Emmett pivoted to face him, rising in spasmodic stages as if his joints were controlled by puppet strings. Despite his questionable coordination, the madman's magic flared with impossible strength, pinning Grant. The captain wouldn't be able to muscle his way out of this hold.

Desperately, I flung daggers of air at Emmett as fast I could form them. One after another, they shattered against his shield. My tiny magic attacks couldn't compete with Emmett's enhanced powers; they didn't even distract him.

Emmett threw his arms wide and cackled. Blood dripped from his hand and stained the feathers dangling from his sleeve. Using two fingers, he slashed gory lines across his cheeks, drawing a grisly smile from the corners of his mouth to his ears. Then he licked blood from his wrist.

Stomach roiling, I searched the cavern for inspiration. What could I possibly do to thwart a psychopath hopped up on blood magic?

Grant strained against the elemental prison, his face beet red and his hands curled into fists, but his body didn't so much as twitch. If he was using the elements in any way to combat Emmett's magic, I couldn't tell. Fresh terror gibbered at the edges of my mind. Grant was the most powerful elemental I had ever encountered, and Emmett's gruesome magic held him single-handedly.

When Emmett finished lapping up Thorpe's blood from his palm, he cocked his head to listen to Lunacy. Nodding to himself, he crafted a massive cleaver out of wood element laced with blood magic. His eyes fixed on the cavern ceiling, he lifted his bound firebird high.

I followed his gaze. A thick stalactite hung suspended above Grant, its pointed tip poised above his chest.

Almost negligently, Emmett swung the elemental blade. It sheared through the base of the stalactite as if cutting through ice instead of hardened rock. The deadly mass dropped.

I wrenched power through Quinn's elemental enhancement and shoved every drop of our combined strength into a single pulse of air. My magic collided with the falling stalactite. It stuttered sideways, tipped, and crashed to the ground beside Grant, shattering. The concussive boom shook the cavern, indistinguishable from the pain exploding inside my skull. I collapsed to all fours, magic slipping from my grasp.

Without my focus to bind the air together, it should have

dissipated. Instead, it reversed course, blasting back toward me. I dove aside. The feral energy shattered the stalagmite I had been hiding behind, then ricocheted to the ceiling and tore through a sheet of stalactites. I threw myself into a second roll as the massive mineral formations crashed to the ground in a deafening cacophony. Slamming against a solid wall of rock, I curled into a ball and cupped my arms over my head.

Terror choked my limited oxygen. A rock punched my thigh, another my kidney. Stinging shards sliced through my coat and jabbed my scalp. I was going to die. The cavern was collapsing, and we were all being buried alive.

Run, Quinn. Run! I silently urged.

I was so intent on anticipating being crushed, I didn't at first notice when the cave-in subsided. It took another minute for the reverberations to die down.

Dazed and disoriented, I cautiously lifted my head, dislodging a handful of rocks. They fell to the cavern floor with muted clacks. Dust choked the air and my ears rang, the high-pitched sound blending with the shrieks of an enraged firebird and the rapid pounding of my pulse. I squinted against the glare of the firebird's feathers when it flashed overhead, its leather hood dangling from one talon. It flew as if under attack, crazed by the deafening rock fall or by its imprisonment underground or by Lunacy itself.

I searched the murky chamber for Grant. Despite how it had sounded, the cavern hadn't collapsed, but it had taken serious damage. Over half the stalactites lay in crumbles across the rocky floor, yet miraculously, Seradon's prone form had been spared. In the shifting light, it took me several more anxious heartbeats to pinpoint Grant. When I found him, my stomach sank.

He hung two feet above the ground, suspended on

hooks of air and blood magic. His fingers curled into white-knuckled fists, but his eyes looked glassy and unfocused. Emmett stood unscathed next to Thorpe's body, his ear cocked to listen to the voices in his head.

If Grant could have attacked, he would have. He needed my help now more than ever. I scrambled for the elements, but my mental muscles refused to form a grip, and the elements slipped like sand through my grasp. Shoving the stalactite aside had overtaxed my elemental abilities. We were both helpless and at the mercy of a madman.

A lion's roar split the air, shaking fresh sand from the ceiling. Emmett glanced around, wild-eyed.

"You can't attack me," he shouted. "I'm the blood chief."

Quinn's responding roar loosened several unstable stalactites, and they crashed to the floor in rapid succession. I clapped my hands over my ears.

"Go away. Go away and leave me alone. I'm Eztli Tiacauh. I'm the blood chief!" Foam frothed in the corners of Emmett's mouth.

With a flick of his magic, Emmett slammed Grant against the cavern wall. Grant's chin slumped to his chest, and he slid to the floor amid a shower of rocks. Giggling, Emmett scrambled across Thorpe's lifeless body, hooked Seradon with a band of air, and fled down the nearest tunnel, holding his trapped firebird in front of him like a lantern and dragging Seradon's limp body behind him. I caught a glimpse of blood smeared across Seradon's temple before Emmett yanked her out of sight.

In my mind, I sprinted after them and tackled Emmett, knocking him out and saving Seradon. In reality, my rubbery legs had lost all coordination, and I struggled to rise from my knees. The freed firebird screeched and flashed through the cavern, chasing Emmett in my place. A torrent of dark magic shot through the dwindling light in the tunnel and exploded against the opening, collapsing it behind Emmett before the firebird reached it. The ground shook, knocking me to my side. When I finally climbed to my feet, rubble blockaded the tunnel opening, nullifying any chance we had of rescuing Seradon.

15

The firebird screeched and raked the wall beside the collapsed tunnel with its claws. Shoving off, it shot back across the cavern. Its eyes—dark pits in a narrow glowing face—locked on to me. Releasing another ear-piercing scream, the firebird swerved through the stalactites, swooping in for the attack.

"Hang on, I'm coming!" Quinn sprinted for me, his speed hampered by his bound wing. Two steps into the cavern, Sooth spotted the firebird, released an eerie, human-like scream, and surged in the opposite direction. The leash snapped taut around Quinn's foreleg, yanking him off balance. He fumbled for his footing, then powered forward, dragging and jerking the lynx along with him. With Sooth impeding his every step and the rubble-strewn cavern forcing him to zigzag, Quinn would never reach me in time.

I spun back to face the firebird. My instincts clamored for me to make an elemental shield. Instead, I dropped into a ball and threw my arms over my head to protect my face. I had seen what the firebird's claws could do to flesh; this was going to hurt.

Quinn roared, and the firebird responded with a stalactite-shaking shriek. Twisting midair, it blasted past me, straight for Quinn. I popped out of my crouch, my warning shout drowned out by the bird's piercing cries. Quinn planted his paws and slid to a stop, hunching to avoid the firebird's razor-sharp talons. The glowing bird overshot him. Clawing the air, it spun and latched on to Quinn's back.

Quinn cringed and went stone still. Sooth froze at the end of the leash, hunkered low in a defensive posture. The firebird battered the air with its wings, then folded them across its back. Clucking softly, it circled on Quinn's spine in tiny steps, its sharp claws clicking harmlessly against Quinn's quartz body. After repeatedly fluffing its feathers, the firebird arranged its long peacock-like tail over Quinn's injured wing, sat, and released a self-important squawk.

I held my breath, afraid to move and break the spell. Sooth had no such reservations. Venting an annoyed yowl, she batted at Quinn with one oversize paw, unleashing her displeasure on the empty air between them. The firebird snaked its head out and hissed at the lynx, its ruffled feathers flaring brighter. Holding his body stiffly, Quinn arched his head and stared down the smaller cat, a warning rumbling in his throat. Grumbling, Sooth backed up as far as the leash allowed and fixed the firebird with her displeased, unblinking glare.

A pained groan emanated from deeper in the cavern. The clatter of displaced rocks followed. I struggled to my feet and peered into the shadows, light-blind from staring at the firebird.

"Quinn, wait here. We'll . . . figure this out." I gestured vaguely to the bird draped across his back. "I need to check on Grant."

My legs still didn't want to work, and I stumbled over

loose rocks and short stalagmites hiding in the deep shadows where the firebird's light didn't reach. When I spotted a soft light glimmering in a hollow, I detoured to investigate. A single firebird feather protruded from the ground, its glow little brighter than a candle flame. I picked it up by the shaft and warily investigated the barbs with the tip of my finger. I had once cut myself on a harpy's feather, and the firebird's metallic-colored plumage looked just as dangerous. However, the individual barbs of the feather were firm without holding an edge, and running my fingernail down them elicited a soft chime.

If only I had my seed with me. I clutched the feather tighter, a kernel of hope stirring within me. Would taking this feather to my seed be enough to evolve it? Or would a more drastic interaction between my seed and firebird be required, like with Quinn's seed and the snake?

My hope morphed to guilt when I realized I was worrying about whether or not I would achieve the pinnacle story of my career while Seradon was in mortal peril and Grant was injured. I wished I could go back to the everlasting tree and reword my question to specify that I wanted the story of a lifetime only so long as no one I cared about was hurt. But the tree didn't work that way. It didn't shape the future; it merely provided waypoint markers and hints. If a person followed the clues down the correct path, the seed evolved and eventually provided an answer to the question. Changing my question wouldn't change Seradon's fate, but I wished it would have. I wished I could do something—anything—to save her.

"Over here." Grant's raspy voice came from the shadows on my right.

Holding the feather in front of me like a tiny torch, I followed the sounds of shifting pebbles. I found Grant leaning against the impact crater his body had left in the cavern wall, dusting dirt and rocks from his clothing.

"Are you injured?" I asked.

"Nothing serious. You?"

"Same."

"Seradon?" He scanned the darkness behind me where Seradon had fallen.

"Gone."

His gaze snapped to me, and I realized he might have misinterpreted my statement. Hastily, I added, "Alive, but Emmett took her and collapsed the tunnel after him."

Fire blazed in Grant's eyes. Without saying anything, he took the feather from me and used its light to search the ground around his feet.

I took a deep breath, then blurted out, "I'm sorry."

"For what?" Grant didn't look up.

"For not stopping Emmett. I should have done better. Done more. I tried to get through his shield, but nothing worked. And then he grabbed Seradon . . ."

Grant swiped his knife from the ground and straightened. I stared blindly at his chest, replaying the memory of Seradon's limp body being carted off. My imagination provided a graphic image of Emmett cutting Seradon open and using her blood to collapse all the tunnels of Lunacy on top of us. Tears welled in my eyes, and I did my best to blink them away.

"I let an evil man abduct Seradon, and I didn't do anything to stop him. I should have—"

Grant cupped a dirty palm over my mouth, silencing me. Exerting gentle pressure on my chin, he tilted my head up until I met his gaze. His eyes held mine, dark and serious, but the harsh lines of his face were softened by the warm light of the firebird's feather.

"This is not your fault," he said. Blood oozed from a gash on his forehead, trickling into his left eyebrow. "I couldn't stop Emmett, either. Neither could Seradon. Rehashing the past isn't going to help us or Seradon. We need to focus on her rescue now. Is that clear?"

I nodded against his palm, and my lips tingled at the gentle friction. Grant dropped his hand and stepped back. Taking a deep breath, I wadded my guilt into a tight ball and shoved it into the corner of my mind. Grant was right; having an emotional breakdown wasn't going to help Seradon. We needed to figure out our next course of action.

"Where's the lynx?" Grant asked.

"With Quinn."

We both turned toward the singular light source at the back of the cavern. From this distance, stalagmites hid most of Quinn's body, but the firebird preening its wings atop him was easily visible.

"Is the firebird perched on Quinn?" Grant asked, incredulous.

"It seems to like him."

"Is that a gargoyle thing?"

I shrugged. Nothing in my research had indicated firebirds were especially fond of gargoyles. Firebirds tended to prefer the wilds of forests, whereas gargoyles resided among dense populations. The two species didn't have reason to intermix often, so perhaps avian enthusiasts had failed to note this discovery.

Grant relinquished the feather to me but took the lead back to Quinn, stopping well clear of the gargoyle and firebird. I hobbled after him, my bruised hip making itself known as my adrenaline tapered off.

"A golden perch," Grant murmured.

"What?"

Grant gestured to Quinn. "It's not that he's a gargoyle; it's his citrine body. I always thought it was the mineral firebirds were attracted to, but maybe they simply have an eye for gold."

Of course. According to the books I had read, the only way to transport a firebird was on a golden perch—and in a cage of some sort, naturally. Without the golden perch, the birds would claw at their container until they broke free or they killed themselves. In the firebird's bronze-orange glow, Quinn looked more golden than ever.

"It sees me as a perch?" Quinn asked, indignation sharpening his words. "Like a tree branch? Or a statue?"

"It's a good thing, too. The firebird would probably claw Kylie and me to shreds if not for you."

The firebird craned its neck to glare at Grant.

"It can't . . ." I dropped my voice to a whisper. "It can't understand us, can it? Like the lynx?"

Grant shook his head. "No more than a chicken could understand us. It recognizes body language and tone, not our actual words. Technically Sooth can't understand us, either. Her magic merely reacts to lies."

I eyed Sooth. She no longer appeared to fear the firebird; instead, she watched it with a predator's hungry gaze. Her stubby tail slashing, she crouched, wiggling her haunches and readying herself to pounce.

Oh no. Firebirds were notoriously fierce, but lynxes were predators with sharp reflexes and wicked claws. This would fast become a bloodbath if Sooth attacked.

"We can't—" I started, but Grant spoke over me.

"I would kill for some water." He winced when the lynx's magic bit his skin. His quick thinking and intentional lie served its purpose, distracting Sooth. She huffed, her ears flicking in Grant's direction. Shifting her weight, Sooth hunched once more in preparation for an attack.

"Let me have her leash, Quinn." I hustled forward, but the firebird's hiss brought me up short. Stretching out a hand, I grabbed for the lynx's harness, but it was still out of reach. The firebird stood, chest puffed, and flared its wings wide.

"Maybe if you release Sooth," I suggested, squinting as agitation increased the luminosity of the firebird's feathers.

"No," Grant countermanded. "We can't take the chance of losing her. Quinn, can you move?"

Quinn took a step backward. He paused while the firebird flapped its wings to catch its balance, then took another step, and another, until he ran out of slack in the leash's line. The firebird bobbed its head and settled itself between Quinn's folded wings.

"All right. Put a rock on Sooth's leash and give us some space," Grant said.

Quinn did as he was instructed, rolling a heavy stone onto the leather leash before slipping his paw free of the loop. He backed up several more steps. I eased forward and retrieved the leash. Feigning disinterest, Sooth sat and groomed her whiskers. The firebird speared malicious glares toward anyone that twitched.

"How long is it going to stay on me?" Quinn asked, an uncharacteristic whine saturating his tone.

"Hopefully until we're out of here," Grant said.

Quinn's head drooped. "It better not poop on me."

"Wait here." Grant circled Quinn, slipping into the shadows of our original tunnel.

Sooth crouched, eyes fixated once more on the firebird. I gave the leash a tug, messing with the cat's balance. She growled at me. Hoping to distract her, I held the firebird feather out for her to sniff.

"You wouldn't want to bite that. I think it would hurt your mouth," I reasoned. A single feather might not be sharp enough to cut, but a mouthful of them would do damage to delicate gums and tongue.

When no pain pinched my skin, I decided Sooth agreed with my assessment. It didn't prevent her from watching the bird hungrily, proving she could measure the truth of my words but not grasp their meaning.

Grant reemerged, carrying our abandoned bags. I flung the strap of mine over my head and reached for Seradon's pack. Grant shifted it out of my reach.

"Let me carry it," I said. It might be heavy, but it made more sense for me to wear her pack than for Grant to be burdened with it. He needed his hands free to face whatever dangers Lunacy threw at us.

Grant set his bag at his feet, then propped Seradon's against it. Crouching, he began to rummage through both bags, removing items and lining them up on the cavern floor.

"What are you doing?" I bounced on my toes and peered toward the collapsed tunnel. Every second we delayed was another second Seradon remained helpless in Emmett's hands.

"Neither of us is going anywhere until we're bandaged. That man could pull blood magic from another person's wound. If you're bleeding, he could use it against you."

"But Seradon—"

"Is a trained FPD elemental."

"Who took a blow to the head. Grant, she was unconscious."

"Seradon's head is a lot harder than it looks. She's an earther through and through."

It occurred to me Grant was downplaying the danger for my sake, and if he thought it would settle my anxiety, he was wrong. "We need to get moving."

"Kylie." Grant enveloped my hand in his, pulling me around to look at him. He knelt on one knee, his face upturned, affording me the rare novelty of staring down at him. "As soon as I'm sure neither of us will make easy victims, we're going to hunt Emmett down. When we catch him, I'll teach him the consequences of messing with a member of my squad."

He should have looked vulnerable in his position, but if I had been the intended recipient of the violence promised in his expression, I would have run and hid. Perversely, seeing his anger helped clear my thoughts.

"What do you need me to do?" I asked.

Grant slapped a familiar jar of greenthread salve in my palm. "Apply this wherever you're bleeding."

I stripped off my abused and tattered jacket and examined my arms. The deep scrape on my right arm had cracked open, as had several cuts on my hands, but the rest of my scratches were still coated with dried salve and a liberal layer of dirt. Fresh nicks dotted my knees and forearms, but the falling stalactites had inflicted more bruises than cuts.

While I slathered salve over new and old wounds, I counted the shadowy tunnel openings. We had seven possible routes out of the cavern, each potentially with an unknown trap primed to kill us.

"Which way should we . . ." My eyes landed on Grant, and my words dried up.

He had removed his shirt and knelt bare chested in front

of me. I had seen this view once before, and it was seared into my memory. However, observing his muscular torso in the warm light of a firebird was a whole new experience, and my thoughts sank in a quicksand of lust. Dried mud and powdery dirt stained his sun-kissed skin and the fine lawn of dark hair spreading like wings across his chest. My gaze dipped to the ridges of his abdomen, which flexed as he twisted to examine his side. *Mmm.*

"We'll start with the tunnel closest to the one Emmett collapsed," Grant said, not looking up.

I clicked my mouth shut and tore my gaze from his body. Had he noticed I hadn't finished my sentence? Had he guessed that the sight of him half nude tied my tongue in knots? I ducked my head so he couldn't see my blush and concentrated on breathing inaudibly.

Grant shifted, turning his back to me. "There are a few I can't reach. Do you mind?"

I peeked through my lashes at his broad back. Despite the grit dusting him, his golden skin shimmered in the firebird's light, every delicious curve of muscle highlighted.

With a fatalistic sigh, I gave up the pretense of squashing my crush on Grant. His recent behavior notwithstanding, he wasn't a total jerk. If he had been, I might have stood a chance of teaching myself to be impervious to him, but he was a captain of an FPD squad, dedicated to making the world a better, safer place. He had a sense of humor, even if it was buried deep. And he came packaged in the body of a fallen god. The best I could hope for was to not make a complete fool of myself.

"Kylie?" Grant glanced at me over his shoulder.

I started and dropped the jar of salve. It clattered up against the heel of his boot. He plucked it from the ground before any of the contents spilled out, and I accepted it back, cheeks flaming. Hastily, I knelt and dabbed greenthread on one of the half dozen shallow cuts marring his back.

"Shouldn't your clothing have done a better job protecting you?" I asked, hoping to distract us both from my embarrassment. With the battle-ready spells woven into the fabric, his uniform should have easily withstood the impact with the cavern wall and protected Grant from injury.

"We removed all spells from our clothing after Velasquez's shirt attempted to strangle him five minutes inside Lunacy."

"Ah." I slathered ointment on an oozing scrape across the top of his shoulder blade, trying not to notice the warmth of his skin or how good he smelled. Hopefully, he couldn't smell me. No elemental bath, not even one that peeled off a layer of skin along with it, could fully remove the foul aroma of a harpy from my garments. Adding dust and fear sweat on top of it hadn't done me any favors. Logically, Grant should smell nearly as bad, but adrenaline seemed to bring out the best in him.

"All—" I cleared my throat. "All done."

Grant turned around, and I busied myself with recapping the jar, concentrating as if it were a difficult task.

"Hold still." Grant cupped the side of my head, and I froze under his unexpected touch. "You're bleeding."

He dabbed salve on my grimy scalp, his touch gentle. With his body arched over me and his arms on either side of my head, his groin aligned squarely in my field of vision. When I realized I was staring at his crotch, I rolled my eyes away, only to become mesmerized by the taut, bare muscles of his stomach. A more genteel woman would have closed her eyes and not ogled a man while he tended her wounds, but I wasn't going to miss this rare opportunity to drink in Grant's perfection from up close.

"That should do it." His soft words stirred wisps of hair across my forehead.

I lifted my head. I expected Grant to stand, but he remained kneeling in front of me. When I tilted my head back farther, his fingers trailed down my temple to my cheek, and I forgot how to breathe.

"Kylie." He looked back and forth between my eyes, his expression grave. "I'm sorry about what I said earlier. I shouldn't have ..."

"Belittled me?" The words popped out before I could stop them.

"Been so quick to judge you."

I should have kept my mouth shut and accepted the apology, but residual anger and hurt prompted me to ask, "Why *did* you? I thought we were ..." It seemed presumptuous to say *friends*, so I let the sentence hang.

"I thought we were, too, but then I found out you lied to me."

I closed my mouth around my reflexive denial. I hadn't lied to him. I simply hadn't confessed to every detail of my past. I suspected I could accuse him of the same.

"I don't enjoy mind games, and I loathe politics," he added.

"And you thought I was playing at both," I said, a spark of understanding giving me insight into his perspective. If I were planning on returning to my parents' business, it would have behooved me to have an FPD warrior to call on for favors, especially one as powerful as Grant. Among the influential people in my parents' world, a person didn't get ahead without leveraging friendships—and cultivating friendships to leverage. That sort of thinking was part of the reason I had chosen a different path for myself. I wanted authentic relationships, not those engendered based on the hopes of future profits.

"It did occur to me," Grant said.

I studied his face, searching for an accusation in his somber expression. He wasn't hiding behind his captain's mask, but I still couldn't decipher his thoughts.

"I don't know how to convince you I have no desire to reclaim my past," I said. I allowed a hint of exasperation to seep into my tone as I added, "But I'm not playing at anything, especially not at being a reporter."

"I'm starting to believe you." His lips quirked in a barely there smile.

"Good."

His gaze dipped to settle on my mouth, and my breath abandoned me again. The light shifted, sparkling through the amber flecks in Grant's hooded brown eyes and high-lighting the contours of his lips. Less than two feet separated us. It would be so easy to lean in and kiss—

"Uh, guys, what's it doing?" Quinn asked.

Grant blinked and looked away. I released a silent, ragged sigh as the giddy bubbles in my stomach deflated. Rolling my shoulders, I strove for an expression that didn't telegraph my crushing disappointment.

"That felt wet," Quinn said, peering over his shoulder at the firebird. "Did it just poop on me? Stupid bird. I'm not a statue. Why can't birds understand the difference between carved rock and gargoyles?"

Quinn pivoted his hind end closer to us, presumably so we could check for the alleged feces. The firebird squawked and flared its wings to maintain its balance. I caught a glimpse of something smooth and shiny beneath the bird.

"Good news: it's not poop," I said.

"It wasn't nothing. I felt something."

"It—um, *she*—laid an egg."

"What?!" Quinn turned in a tight circle, trying to see his own back. The firebird dug her talons into his shoulders, hissed, and pecked Quinn hard on the nose.

"Ow!" Quinn dipped his head to rub his nose with a paw. The firebird performed an awkward shuffle, using her belly to roll the egg back between Quinn's wings. Then she hunkered down over it, hiding the egg from sight.

With the hazards of Lunacy preoccupying me, I had overlooked the importance of one detail of my research: All sources had stated that only *nesting* firebirds exhibited restorative magic. None had specified at what point in the egg's life cycle a firebird's magic kicked in, but offspring had been a key component. The government wouldn't have shipped a pair of firebirds to fire-ravaged Timber Cove unless they had known a baby was on the way. I started to berate myself for not reaching this conclusion sooner but decided to cut myself some slack. A few more pressing issues had consumed my attention.

Quinn gave me a doleful look. "She's not going anywhere now, is she?"

"Um." I glanced to Grant for help. He looked suspiciously like he was trying not to laugh.

"Not until the egg hatches," he confirmed.

"She's bound to poop on me before then. This is so gross." Quinn started to sit. The firebird tilted, sliding down his slick spine. Alarm flared in Quinn's eyes, and he straightened his legs. Squawking her disapproval, the firebird readjusted the egg and settled back atop it. "This is awful. How am I supposed to help if I can't move?"

"You are helping. You're keeping the firebird from attacking us," I said.

"Don't worry." Grant rocked onto his heels and dusted dirt off his knees. "The egg should hatch in a week or two."

"A week or *two*?" Quinn's eyes bulged.

Grant chuckled. "Relax. Once we're out of here, we'll figure something out."

"You promise?"

"The last thing the city needs is a firebird imprinted on a gargoyle imprinted on a journalist."

I rolled my eyes. "I would think you would approve. It might slow us down a little."

"It *would* make you easier to spot coming."

The levity bled from the moment as Grant handed me Seradon's water, rations, and blanket.

"Keep the medical kit, too," Grant said. He tucked two of Seradon's blades into his belt and another into his bag. The shortest knife, he handed to me. I accepted it gingerly and packed it within easy reach on top of the other supplies. Nestling the firebird feather next to it, I closed my bag.

If only I believed having a knife would do me any good against the dangers ahead.

16

We left Seradon's bag at the mouth of the tunnel, marking the way we had come. Grant and I each took a lantern, keeping the wicks turned low to conserve oil as we crossed the cavern. Quinn followed, the bright firebird providing most of the illumination. The hen had settled so she faced forward, looking over Quinn's head, unperturbed by his movements, as if riding a winged quartz lion was a common firebird experience. With his face cast in shadows, I couldn't judge Quinn's expression, but his smooth stride implied he didn't resent the firebird as much as he had complained.

Grant assumed control of Sooth, guiding her to the collapsed tunnel. Rubble spilled from the former opening into the cavern, half burying Thorpe's body. I averted my eyes from his unmoving legs. I didn't mourn the murderer's death, but I felt guilty for being relieved that his gruesome wounds had been covered. After Grant and Sooth verified no hidden traps remained, Grant stood aside while Quinn climbed as close to the wall as possible. The edges of the cavern rose tall and smooth, more closely resembling the walls of a temple than a natural earthen formation. When Quinn and his luminescent passenger neared the former tunnel entrance, the hidden runes lit up.

I crept closer to examine them, stopping several paces from Quinn when the firebird hissed at me. Grant stepped up beside me. I had hoped for easy-to-interpret symbols, or better yet, writing that said "this way is safe." Instead, the hieroglyphs resembled squiggles and blobs, the left side of them torn away and lost among the collapsed tunnel.

"Do you know what any of those mean?" I asked.

Grant shook his head and urged Sooth toward the next tunnel. She regarded the passage warily, her moderate reaction indicating a disguised trap lurked deeper inside the tunnel. Once again, Grant and I stood aside while Quinn approached the opening and the firebird illuminated the runes. None of the hieroglyphs shimmering next to this tunnel matched those beside Emmett's escape route.

We circled the cavern, repeating the process with each dark opening. I marveled that the runes were still legible centuries after they had been written, preserved by the sheltered environment of the cavern, but ultimately they did us no good. None of the hieroglyphs repeated, and none made any sense.

"Did you recognize anything?" I asked.

"Nothing useful. I'm not even sure the symbols make up a language. Even if they did, what is the likelihood that a society of blood-magic-mad people would write anything but gibberish?" He ran a hand through his hair, loosing a trickle of sand down the back of his neck. "I was hoping to be able to match the symbols on the tunnel Emmett chose with another to help us pick the best alternative. Now I think we're just wasting time."

The firebird released a soft, melodic tremolo like that of

a loon. She repeated the sound louder, and the notes echoed back, hollow and faint. Clucking to herself, she fluffed her feathers and adjusted her position on Quinn.

"Why are these markings even here?" I asked. "The original creators of Lunacy didn't have firebirds, did they?"

"The royal family did. They bred and used them to stabilize their society." Grant skirted a large pile of decimated stalactites and tramped back to the base of the collapsed tunnel. "Think about it: a whole civilization of insane, paranoid people using the corrupted powers of blood magic. They would have destroyed themselves and their environment long before they rose to power if not for firebirds repeatedly restoring their surroundings."

The evidence of blood magic's power lay before me, an entire tunnel of granite destroyed by a single man. I tried to envision a whole tribe of people with similar powers, and Grant's explanation made a lot of sense.

"Is this where they kept the firebirds? Is that why these marks are only visible in a firebird's illumination?"

"I think we're seeing another layer of their paranoia. With the writing hidden to everyone but those with a firebird, no one could safely navigate the labyrinth but royalty." Grant turned to contemplate the carved openings on either side of the caved-in tunnel. "These two are the most logical choices, if we can rely on logic inside Lunacy. Sooth didn't react to either in an extreme way, and they're the most likely to parallel the tunnel Emmett took."

I padded to Grant's side, and Quinn trailed close behind me, testing the firebird's tolerance. Already, he had reduced the distance between us by half, and the firebird merely eyed me warily. I silently commended Quinn's foresight. By the time we entered a tunnel, the hen would be acclimated to our presence and not attack. Or so I hoped.

"It looks like we've found our winner," I said, pointing to the tunnel on the left.

"What makes you so sure it's not the one on the right?"

"I hate to trust the reasoning of madmen, but Thorpe said that tunnel lead to death, and Emmett didn't contradict him. I think we should avoid that way, too."

"And if they were guessing?"

"They made it this far. Emmett must understand some of the runes." It wasn't the most reassuring deduction, but it was the best we had.

After a moment's thought, Grant nodded in agreement.

The firebird strung together harmonious, flutelike chirps reminiscent of a wood thrush's song. Rocks stirred and clattered in the shadows of the cavern behind us. I jumped and spun to face the darkness. Grant opened his lantern and let the wick flare bright. A knife glinted in his opposite hand. Squinting, I tried to make out movements in the shadows.

The firebird squawked at Quinn's abrupt turn, then chirped a few more dulcet notes.

"Can you quiet her?" Grant hissed.

"How?" Quinn whispered.

"Rock her?"

Expression dubious, Quinn shifted his weight from side to side, gently sliding the firebird and her egg back and forth across his spine. The hen bobbed as if riding waves and chirped happily to herself.

Grant's lips pinched together in irritation. Minuscule glowballs flickered to life several feet from us, and Grant sent them questing deeper into the cavern, the tiny lights shifting and spinning like fireflies. As hard as I strained, I couldn't see anything lurking among the stalagmites.

The firebird puffed out her chest and sang a series of

complicated trills that would have done a mockingbird proud. A handful of fist-size rocks scraped across the cavern floor, lifting to float toward the ceiling. Pure, untainted air element guided them. I darted a glance at Grant, expecting him to be behind the rocks' animation, but he wasn't even paying attention to them. His eyes the scanned the darkness around the edges of the cavern, checking for hidden enemies. I did the same, finding none.

Quinn continued to rock the firebird, but that didn't stop her from trilling and chirping, her head canted to listen to the echoes as the cavern bounced the sounds back to her. Larger boulders joined the floating rocks, spinning midair into a jumbled clump. Earth and water elements joined with the air, overlapping in a spell so intricate I couldn't distinguish one element from the other. The rocks sorted themselves into a conical column that affixed itself to the ceiling even as dirt and sand streamed from the cavern floor upward, filling in the cracks of the reassembled stalactite. Moisture particles gathered from the air, patching the last of the seams, and when the magic dissipated, a stalactite hung restored from the ceiling as if it had never fallen and shattered.

No human could have interwoven the elements so organically, especially not in Lunacy. Wide-eyed, I turned to gape at the firebird. She fluffed her chest feathers and resettled atop the egg, her eyes half closed in contentment.

"Did she just repair pulverized rock with her voice?" I had expected the firebird's magic to be subtle, instigating changes that would alter the environment over time—the kind of magic that required it to remain in a ravaged location for years to fully restore it. But this had been shockingly fast and thorough, as if the firebird had rewound time, reversing the destruction as if it had never happened.

"That was incredible," Quinn breathed.

"We need to get moving." Grant's firefly lights winked out as he strode past me.

"Hang on," I said. "She's making things better. If we can get her to sing again, maybe she could purify the elements in here." The firebird's magic had cut through the taint of Lunacy when she rebuilt the stalactite. Given a little time, maybe she could cleanse the cavern enough for Grant and me to use the elements without suffering Lunacy's vindictive retribution. "Then we can dig through this and follow Emmett." I gestured toward the collapsed tunnel. "Or better yet, the firebird might fix the tunnel for us."

Grant stopped and turned to face me and Quinn. "Firebirds do not fix things; they restore broken environments to their original condition."

"What's the difference?"

"Most of these tunnels were man-made. What happens if she restores them?"

"It would be as if blood-magic users never defiled this mountain and . . ." I trailed off as the full horror of his words sank in. If the firebird's restorative magic had its way with this mountain, all the man-made routes would be filled back in with tons of rock, sealing us inside.

"We would be killed," Quinn said, finishing my sentence.

"But so would the firebird," I argued. "She wouldn't do that to herself and her chick, would she?"

"Her brain is the size of an almond. I'm fairly certain she can't calculate the consequences of her actions."

"Even so, she couldn't relocate that much rock by herself, could she?" Just how powerful were firebirds? None of the texts I had read had specified their limits.

"I don't plan to find out," Grant said. "Quinn, do your

best to prevent her from making a sound. Both of you, stick close and be careful where you step."

Grant marched toward our chosen tunnel, holding his lantern high. The light illuminated the first few feet of the passage. Like all the other tunnels we had traversed, the rough-hewn walls and ceiling and relatively smooth floor screamed *man-made*. Aside from the cavern itself, every part of the labyrinth had been carved by blood-magic users, which meant all of it could be brought down on top of us by the firebird.

For the first time since learning there were firebirds in Lunacy with me, I questioned whether they were the *correct* firebirds. I couldn't write my big story if I didn't survive to pen it. Unless the tree interpreted "the story of a lifetime" as the story of my lifetime's *end*. I swallowed hard. If I died here, everyone would remember me as the woman who died in Lunacy. It would be my legacy, and the final story of my life.

I stuffed my dark thoughts into a box and slammed the lid shut on them. Succumbing to baseless fears—or even allowing them to fester—would be detrimental to my survival. Lunacy fed on paranoia.

Grant eased into the tunnel, prompting Sooth to walk ahead of him. Quinn followed, and the light in the cavern dimmed as the tunnel encased Quinn and the firebird on his back. Pausing on the threshold, I turned for one last look at the cavern. Lantern light pooled around my feet and the slope of rubble beside me, but it didn't reach far enough to illuminate Thorpe's corpse. How many other bodies lurked among the shadows and tunnels of these deadly ruins?

With a shiver, I turned my back on the oppressive darkness and scurried to catch up with Quinn.

We crept forward in our bubble of light, all of us keyed

to the lynx's mood. As much as I wanted to race ahead to catch up with Emmett—if this tunnel even led to the same location—we were forced to moderate our speed to avoid blundering into any traps.

Maybe Seradon is fine. She could have already regained consciousness and taken out Emmett on her own. I could easily picture the fierce woman overpowering Emmett. The problem was, I could just as easily picture Emmett slitting her throat before she had a chance to fight back.

My nerves jangled between fear and urgency, and I gave myself a neck cramp craning to see into the darkness behind me. Logic suggested any danger would come from ahead of us, but that didn't stop my imagination from hearing a hidden enemy's breath in the rasp of my bag against my jean-clad thigh or the click of a monster's claws in the echoes of Quinn's quartz footsteps.

Sooth growled, and I jumped, jerking to face forward. The small cat shied back, hugging her body against Grant's boot. He halted, bringing our party to a stop.

"Take this," Grant said, thrusting Sooth's leash at Quinn before the firebird had time to react.

Quinn accepted it with his mouth. I stepped forward, an offer to take Sooth from him on the tip of my tongue, but a warning hiss from the firebird made me retract my arm. Instead, I tugged the short knife Grant had given me from my bag and gripped it in one sweaty palm. Quinn gave the leash a yank. Sooth stumbled backward two steps without turning away from the invisible threat. Using the slack in the leash, Quinn transferred the loop from his mouth to a paw, tugging it past the thick pad of his foot until it enclosed his leg like a leather bracelet.

Grant drew his knife. "Get ready."

Squinting past the firebird's glow, I tried to make out the

anomaly that had triggered the lynx's instincts. Darkness ate up the light from Grant's lantern, hiding untold horrors. At first I thought I was letting my imagination get the better of me, but no . . . the passageway really was consuming his light. The lantern's glow ended in a sharp, shadowed edge, as if a black wall and not an open tunnel stood in front of us.

Grant took a short step, stretching the lantern farther forward. The blackness held steady, devouring the light.

Bending, Grant set down his lantern and collected a handful of pebbles. When he straightened, he tossed the rocks into the illusion. The inky shadow swallowed them, but a soft clatter indicated the pebbles struck the tunnel floor out of sight. Whatever barred the way wasn't solid.

The firebird belted out three short, loud chirps, and I almost jumped out of my skin. Sand shifted from the ceiling, raining down on our heads. The shadow oozed toward Grant, absorbing the light. My toes curled inside my boots and tiny hairs on my arms stood on end. Sooth growled low in her throat, and I longed to heed her warning and flee back the way we had come.

Quinn jostled the firebird, cutting off her song. The shadow stilled and the ceiling stabilized. Waddling in place atop the egg, the firebird clucked to herself, then unleashed staccato chirps worthy of a pheasant-size sparrow. She alternated her chirps with velvety tremolos, creating a surprisingly intricate and beautiful melody. The sinister shadow bled across the tunnel.

"Quinn, quiet the bird." Grant retreated a step, monitoring the darkness creeping across the ceiling.

"I'm trying."

Quinn wriggled and bucked. The firebird sank her talons into the muscles at the base of his wings, holding tight. It should have looked amusing, a shimmying gargoyle with a firebird clinging to him, her song warbling with each bounce, but the shadow loomed closer, and fear clogged my throat. Despite Quinn's antics, the firebird's song grew louder, achieving euphonious trills between a metronome of chirps.

"Try harder," Grant ordered.

"I can't. Not without endangering the egg."

For all of Quinn's impressive jostling, the egg barely rocked between his shoulder blades. The gargoyle didn't have it in his nature to endanger another creature, especially not a baby. I agreed with his ethics, but I wasn't ready to die. I darted forward, bracing myself to poke the firebird's back. Allowing her to take out her frustration on me would distract her from singing. I tried not to think about the divot she had pecked out of Quinn's rock nose earlier. Her sharp beak would do a lot worse to me, but being mauled beat being killed by a Lunacy-crafted nightmare.

The shadow tore from the tunnel with a haunting, dry susurrus. Chills swept up my spine, freezing me in place before I reached the firebird. A pale human face emerged from the darkness, floating near the ceiling, its bloodred irises bright against its chalky flesh. The shadow behind it splintered into hundreds of ebony feathers, the mass shifting in a fluid cloud around the disembodied head. Hissing, the creature bared inches-long incisors behind bloodless lips.

Impossible. Vampires were supposed to be extinct. Considered an aberration by primitive civilizations worldwide, they had been ruthlessly hunted and destroyed on every continent centuries ago. Yet, it made fatalistic sense that we would encounter an undead, blood-guzzling ghoul here. If a vampire had survived anywhere, it would be in Lunacy.

The firebird's song swelled, the clear, clean notes reverberating through the tunnel. Shrieking, the vampire lunged for Grant. Clawed hands emerged from the swarm of feathers, lashing bone-white talons at his eyes. Grant ducked, simultaneously striking with his knife. The vampire's feathers parted like a school of fish, evading the blade. Its unattached head overshot Grant, then whipped back with preternatural speed, diving for his exposed neck.

Grant fell in a controlled roll, and when he sprang to his feet, he clutched a knife in each hand. He feigned a strike at the vampire's splayed claws, then pierced through the bulk of the feathers behind the vampire's head. Its nebulous body parted, providing a brief peek at a desiccated gray pouch: the vampire's heart. The monster had no neck to sever, no limbs to cut and bleed out. Its only vulnerability was its shriveled heart.

Grant's deception almost worked, his knife cleaving the air just to the right of the heart. Screeching loud enough to quake pebbles from the ceiling, the vampire jerked sideways, pulling its feathers tight around the tiny target. The stench of putrefied carcass and acrid musk gusted from its back draft—a foul cocktail of harpy nest and rotting mold spores. I clamped my mouth shut, praying the scent wasn't poisonous.

As quick as a whip crack, the vampire reversed course and snapped its lethal fangs on Grant's throat. He leapt aside before the bite connected, and the vampire chased him. Its head led each charge, angling to bite Grant's neck or groin, fixated on his major arteries. Grant deflected a volley of strikes, the scuffle of his feet blending with the eerie rustle of the vampire's feathers. The firebird's bright chirps underscored Grant's grunts, as if the hen was incorporating the fight into her song. Quinn bounced for all he was worth, but none of his antics quieted the firebird.

I couldn't tear my eyes from Grant. He fought in an impressive display of acrobatics, twisting and lunging, driving his blades into the vampire's body again and again, his knives a silver blur among the shadow of feathers. Yet no amount of adroitness could compete with the vampire's elasticity. Each time Grant struck, the vampire evaded, its feathers scattering so Grant's blades cleaved only air. I cried out when the vampire's teeth scraped a gash across Grant's ribs, cutting effortlessly through his thick shirt. Grant's attention jerked in my direction, and the vampire sank its teeth into his forearm. He growled and hacked at the heart. The vampire retreated, only to strike at Grant's neck. I clamped a hand over my mouth, horrified I had distracted Grant, but the blunder woke me from my trance.

I gathered an insignificant amount of fire and tossed sparks into the seething swarm of feathers. A dozen caught fire and burned to ashes in rapid flashes. The reek of smoldering hair permeated the tunnel, coating the back of my throat. Eyes watering, I threw another handful of sparks. This time the vampire whipped to the ceiling, evading my feeble attack. Bloodred irises aligned on me. Releasing a dry, hissing howl, the vampire dove over Quinn and went straight for my throat.

Terror locked my joints. The sounds and scents of the tunnel receded. The vampire's glowing eyes filled my vision, bearing down on me with uncanny speed. I was about to die, and I couldn't do anything to stop it.

A painful flick of air snapped my temple. I flinched. Sound rushed into my ears—the firebird's escalating song, the rustle of the vampire's feathers, and above all else, Grant's booming voice.

"Duck!"

I dropped to a crouch, flinging a hand up instinctively, deflecting the vampire at the last second.

"Don't look it in the eye," Grant barked.

Its gaze. As surly as a basilisk holding a victim frozen, the vampire had spelled me with its gaze. Only Grant's painful elemental jab had saved me.

Then the vampire's feathers swallowed me, their chaotic rustle disorienting me, the stench overpowering my senses. I slashed wildly with my short blade, knocking aside the vampire's head a second time. Claws raked fire down my arm and hip. I stumbled, stabbing and hacking blindly. Sharp pain pierced my neck, and I punched with my empty hand, cracking my knuckles against the vampire's face and knocking it aside.

The feathers parted in time for me to see Grant sprint vertically along the tunnel wall past Quinn and the firebird. He landed in a crouch next to me and drove his knife into the vampire. Behind him, the firebird squawked and flapped her wings, her song dying. The vampire faltered, and Grant's next strike pierced its shriveled heart. With a grating wail, the head collapsed backward into the swarm of feathers. The invisible cohesion holding together the vampire disbanded, and gravity pulled the mass apart. The skull smashed against the floor with a heavy crack followed by the softer pops of finger bones dropping amid the feathers.

Relief turned my knees rubbery, and I staggered to the wall for support. I was alive . . .

For now.

"Kylie, are you all right?" Quinn craned to see over his shoulder past the firebird. The tight corridor prevented him from turning, as did Sooth, who cowered under his belly. At least the firebird had finally quieted.

"I'm—" I caught myself before I said *fine*, sparing myself the painful bite of the lynx's magic. "I gained a few more scratches, but I'll live."

"Grant?"

"Nothing I can't survive."

The vampire's head shifted, and I jerked, cracking an elbow against the rock wall. Grant dropped into a crouch, knives extended. I gasped as the ghoul's flesh decomposed before our eyes. It crumbled from the skull, sifting through the nose slits and down the slick curve of the cranium to mound in chalky piles atop the coal-black feathers. Tiny puffs of disintegrating skin sent tremors through the feathers where the white bones of the vampire's clawed hands had fallen. The jaw, previously gaped wide to accommodate the abomination's mutant incisors, unhinged and fell with a muted crack to the floor. I didn't search too closely for its missing bloodred eyes, afraid I might find them.

I shuddered. Even in death, the vampire gave me the creeps.

Grant scraped his toe through the nearest feather. It crumbled into a fine black powder and smeared across the rocks like ash. When nothing else moved, he straightened and sheathed his knives.

"Have you ever encountered a vampire before?" I asked, straining to keep my voice even.

Grant shook his head. "I didn't think any still existed. Good thinking with the sparks."

I shrugged off his undeserved praise. It shouldn't have taken me so long to act, and I should have done something more useful than flail in panic when the vampire attacked me.

"Ease up." Grant pointed to my side. "You're going to break a finger if you squeeze any tighter."

I glanced down at my hand in surprise: I still clutched the knife in a white-knuckle grip. Letting out a slow breath, I loosened my hand. Blood rushed in a soft tingle to my fingertips. It took me two tries to store the knife back in my bag. I waited until I had retrieved my vial of greenthread and unscrewed it before I examined my new wounds. The three slashes across my forearm burned, but only one bled, and the scrapes on my neck felt shallow. I had been fortunate. If the vampire had managed to latch on to my neck, I wouldn't still be standing. The puncture on my hip worried me the most, and looking at the oozing wound amplified its sting. Gritting my teeth against a fresh throb of pain, I eased the torn fabric of my pants aside and dabbed the salve onto the wound, relaxing when the numbing properties of the greenthread activated. Almost instantly, the oozing wound began to coagulate. So long as I didn't overexert myself, I wouldn't die from blood loss. I was far more likely to die from an infection first. Or from being crushed under tons of rock when the firebird brought the mountain down on top of us. But only if the next trap didn't maul me to death before the firebird's magic took effect.

Lucky me, so many choices for what to worry about.

"Don't give in to it," Grant said.

"Give in to what?"

"This place. Don't let it mess with your head."

I glanced up, shocked he had so easily read my thoughts.

"I feel it, too," he said. "It's in the elements. They're dirty. It adds a layer of . . . bleakness."

"Exactly." It was a relief to know I wasn't the only one affected.

"You're doing really well. You may not have combat training, but what you lack in finesse, you make up for in superior reflexes." He mimed a punch, a faint smile playing at the corners of his lips.

I was pathetically heartened by that slight smile. Protecting me from physical harm was part of Grant's personality and job. Being pleasant wasn't a requirement, as he had proven earlier today. Yet he was making the effort to cheer me up now, treating me almost like a friend. It meant more to me than his apology, and I attempted to rally my spirits.

"Yeah, trying not to die brings out the best in me." My stab at humor fell flat, and pain flared to life in my knuckles at the reminder of punching the vampire's bony face. I flexed my fingers. Several knuckles were swollen and forming dark bruises. With a sigh, I dabbed greenthread on the abrasions. Was it possible to use too much salve? It felt as if more greenthread than clothing covered my body at this point.

Grant tucked the hem of his shirt between his chin and chest to hold it out of the way. Blood ran from deep parallel gashes across his ribs, trickling down the dirt-smeared contours of his stomach to soak into the waistline of his pants. I hissed in sympathy and helped apply patches of salve-slathered lamb's ear leaves to the cuts, binding them with strips of fabric ripped from the remains of the blanket used to make Quinn's sling. A healer was the first stop for all of us if—*when*—we escaped Lunacy.

"Was it my imagination or did the firebird's song make the vampire stronger?" I asked as we repacked our medical supplies.

"It must have. That vampire had been down here, starving, for centuries. It shouldn't have been that fast or strong."

I scowled at the firebird. "Surviving Lunacy isn't hard enough? You have to make it worse?"

She ignored me, twisting to preen her long tail feathers.

Grant grabbed his pack and squeezed past Quinn to take the lead once more. The firebird hissed and flapped her wings, pecking at him. He deflected her sharp beak with his bag, making scolding noises as if the firebird were a recalcitrant puppy, not the creature responsible for nearly getting us killed.

Quinn jerked and moaned, his face contorting.

"What is it?" I asked.

"Nothing." The gargoyle quivered as Sooth's magic nipped him, belying his response. Muttering disapproving meows, Sooth slunk out from beneath Quinn.

"Tell me what's wrong." I rushed forward but pulled up short when the firebird squawked at me. "Did the vampire hurt you?"

"No. It's just . . . she finally did it." Quinn jerked his chin toward the firebird. "She pooped on me."

"Oh." I groped for an appropriate response, but relief tied my tongue.

Quinn hung his head. "I know. I'm sorry. I shouldn't complain. It's just a glob of feces. It's not like it hurts. But it's warm and wet and running down my flank . . ."

"Perhaps if you don't think about it?" I suggested.

Grant grimaced. "And don't describe it in such detail."

"I'll try my best."

Quinn's rope-thick rock tail slashed, and he shot the firebird a dirty look over his shoulder. Clueless, the hen chirped under her breath, waddling in place as she situated the egg beneath her glowing chest again. While she was distracted, Grant reclaimed Sooth's leash.

Once more, we crept forward into the darkness. Tension chipped away at my nerves, but the firebird managed to fall asleep atop Quinn's back. I glared at her bobbing form, envious and resentful. Why couldn't she have been taking a nap when we encountered the vampire?

Eventually, the tunnel came to a fork, neither direction blocked by a trap. Grant took the right branch, letting Sooth set the pace. If this tunnel ran parallel to the one Emmett had taken, it might eventually lead us to the same location. Unfortunately, maintaining any sense of direction was futile. Our route could have been gradually spiraling back on itself, dipping below or slanting above Emmett's tunnel. This entire branch of the labyrinth might lead in circles, going nowhere near the heart. Or Emmett could have already reached the labyrinth's heart and killed—

Nope. Not going there.

After a series of uneventful twists, the passage straightened, stretching before us in a smooth line farther than our light reached. Sooth jerked up short with a yowl. The rest of us froze. Squinting past the firebird's light, I strained to examine the tunnel walls, floor, and ceiling, but I didn't spot anything out of the ordinary—no anomalous shadows, no deadly creatures. Grant must not have seen anything either, because after a long pause, he chanced turning his back on the tunnel. Quietly, as if they had practiced the maneuver more than once, Grant passed Sooth's leash to Quinn, and the gargoyle secured the leather loop around his foreleg. Grant set his lantern at his feet and palmed the largest of his knives. When Quinn indicated he was ready, Grant tossed a handful of pebbles. We all tensed as the rocks scattered across the floor and rolled to a stop. No monsters bubbled from the walls to attack, and the floor appeared to be solid. I allowed myself a shallow breath and rubbed my damp palms down my thighs. After a moment's hesitation, I pulled the knife from my bag.

Grant repeated his experiment, this time bouncing pebbles off the walls. Again, nothing reacted. He double-checked Sooth. She glared at the seemingly harmless passageway, the fur along her spine standing in a stiff ridge.

Drawing a second blade, Grant cast a subtle probe of air element into the tunnel. Dark energy bubbled from the tainted elements saturating the corridor and consumed Grant's delicate sphere. Against the unrelieved black of the tunnel ahead of us, I couldn't make out the elements comprising the latest trap, but it shouldn't have mattered: Grant's tiny magic should have been easily absorbed and dispersed. Instead, Lunacy's foul magic snapped tight around Grant's probe, popping it with a static *crack*. The minuscule spark exploded through the dark energy, forging its composition into raw fire element strung through with unsettling shadows of blood magic.

"That can't be good," I whispered.

A cloud of blue-white flames expanded to halo the elements. They brushed against the tunnel wall, eating through the rock. The flames morphed again, growing diamond-sharp shards of earth element that swelled to encase the flames.

"There's nothing normal left in those elements," Quinn said. "It's more than the blood magic. It's like those elements are diseased."

The violent snarl coasted toward Grant. He retreated, flicking a feather of air against the far side of the fiery bundle. It altered course to consume his magic, and a cascade of micro explosions shot through to the burning heart. The edges of the wild energy expanded to brush the wall again, devouring another chunk of solid granite. Between one breath and the next, the elements doubled in size.

Grant pulsed drops of water behind the deadly snarl. Again, it shifted to devour his magic. The fire should have extinguished Grant's minute water magic while simultaneously being dampened. That was a basic elemental law: water weakened fire. Instead, the wild energy consumed Grant's magic, siphoning the water into its heart, where it formed a crystalline core of ice in the center of the blue-white flames.

"Impossible." The word escaped, unbidden. Ice could not exist inside fire, and yet . . . this was Lunacy, where blood magic reigned supreme and negated the natural order of the elements.

"Maybe the trick is to ignore it," Grant said. He eased to the far side of the tunnel, angling to sneak past the erratic magic. The moment he took a step, the baneful energy drifted toward him. Grant drew up short.

"Nobody move."

Not even Sooth twitched.

Slowly, Grant extended his right hand and waved. The deadly snarl homed in on his moving appendage. Leaving his right arm extended, Grant lifted his left and waved. The elemental bundle redirected its path toward the newest target.

Crap. Somehow the dark magic could sense movement.

Grant backed up a step, and the bundle sped forward, chasing him. Hastily, he distracted it, prodding the far side with a water droplet. The icy core splintered. The wild bundle expanded, brushing the ceiling and raining rock down around itself before contracting back to twice its previous size.

Dread weighted my limbs. Grant couldn't fight his way past the wild energy with his knives. Using small magic against it only made it stronger, and each metamorphosis increased its size in unpredictable ways. If it grew large enough to scrape the ceiling, it would bring the tunnel down on top of us. We would have to retreat—and when we did, it would chase us.

"Turn around slowly and get ready to run," Grant said, obviously coming to the same conclusion.

I pivoted, trying not to move more than absolutely necessary. Quinn eased his head around, his front paws squeaking as they twisted in place. The violent energy bore down on Grant. He faced it head on, unmoving.

My heels hit the rock with twin thumps.

"What are you doing?" I demanded, but I already knew. Grant wasn't planning on running with us. He was going to attempt to hold off the malicious magic all by himself. He was going to sacrifice himself for us.

"There isn't time to explain. You should already be running."

"I'm not leaving you here to die, Grant."

"I don't plan on—" He cut himself off, and I couldn't tell if it was because Sooth would have revealed his lie or because the tainted magic picked up speed. He tossed two more distraction droplets of water behind the wild energy. It barely faltered as it absorbed them.

"Let me help," I said, wracking my brain for an idea. "It feeds on the elements. What if you and I make a chain of elements behind it? It might buy us enough time to escape before it notices."

"Or it will grow so fast we won't be able to outrun it."

"Or it will grow so fast it can't chase us," I countered.

"Anyone ever tell you your optimism is a health hazard?" Grant didn't give me a chance to respond. "Quinn, get ready. Kylie, on my count, line the tiniest pieces of each element up behind the snarl in a destructive sequence. Space them out to make it work to eat them. I'll do the same. Then we run. No more arguing."

"No more arguing," I agreed.

"Ready. Set . . ."

I prepared a delicate line of pearl-size water, air, earth, wood, and fire in my thoughts.

"Now!"

Our twin elemental strings popped into existence behind the wild magic, and Grant jumped backward. Diamond-edged shards of earth speared from the seething energy and shot straight for him, ignoring our small magic. Before I could react, Grant drove splinters of wood into the far side of the bundle. It faltered, then fired shoots of shadowy wood element in all directions. The sweet scent of hyacinths burst into the air as the corrupt elements wobbled drunkenly into the right wall. The mutated magic blasted through the granite in a deafening explosion, ricocheting shrapnel through the tunnel. Grant twisted away from the blast, and I flinched, flinging up my arms to protect my face. The firebird woke with a squawk.

When I lowered my hands, a gaping hole larger than my head had appeared in the wall. Air whistled through the opening, swirling around the violent elements, feeding them. In seconds, the evil energy doubled in size, then tripled. One more expansion and it would fill the width of the tunnel.

Grant had frozen in place, half turned away from the deadly magic, which was now almost close enough to reach out and touch. If he so much as twitched, the bloated bundle would overtake him.

"Kylie." Grim determination etched Grant's profile. "You need to run. Now."

"No. I'm not—"

"I'll be right behind you."

I met Quinn's eyes, seeing my anguish mirrored in his face. We both knew if we moved, the wild magic would kill Grant.

The firebird chirped a trio of confused notes. Then she bellowed a mockingbird's song. I lurched to silence her, expecting to see the deadly energy magnify under the influence of her magic. The firebird shied away, then snaked her beak back toward my fingers, fury glinting in her dark eyes.

"No, let her sing," Grant urged. "Look."

The edges of the malicious energy had unraveled. Flakes of wood and earth element dissipated into the air. It hadn't been much, just a handful of inches shaved off the deadly bundle, but it was a start. I clamped my arms to my sides and willed the firebird to sing again.

She preened her long wing feathers and took time we didn't have to resettle atop her egg. The snarl of terrifying magic grew another foot in diameter, oozing toward Grant. Finally, the firebird sang a melody of cascading notes. The taint of blood magic washed from the leading edge of the violent snarl, freeing the purified elements to unravel and evaporate. More importantly, the gap between Grant and the lethal magic widened.

I breathed shallowly, afraid to move or startle the bird. Quinn stood statue still. The firebird sang a repetitive melody, but the notes themselves didn't seem to matter. It was the magic beneath them that cleansed the elements. As fast as the corrupt magic had expanded, the firebird's song unsnarled it, until the tunnel contained nothing but pure elemental magic.

My heart pounded as if I had been running. I shoved the knife back into my bag and clutched my lantern in both hands to disguise their shaking. Grant released a pent-up breath and rolled his shoulders, turning to face us fully. His eyes sought mine.

"What happened to your promise to obey me?"

I huffed a laugh. "I guess it slipped my mind."

"You could have been killed."

"No, *you* could have been killed. You *would* have been killed if I had followed your instructions." Since Sooth's magic hadn't nipped either of us, we were both right.

"We wouldn't leave you to die," Quinn said.

Grant's scowl softened when he took in the young gargoyle's earnest expression. "Thank you." He met my eyes again. "You too. But don't do it again. You need to trust me, and I need to be able to trust that you're going to do what I say."

I opened my mouth to respond, but the firebird's melody

altered, her excited chirps escalating in volume. A fine tremor ran through the tunnel, loosening sand and small rocks.

"That's enough, Quinn." Grant shielded his eyes and studied the ceiling.

Quinn jostled the firebird, but it was Sooth crawling out from under his stomach that interrupted her song. The hen flared her wings and hissed at the lynx, and Sooth scooted to the end of her leash, glaring murderously at the glowing bird.

The ceiling continued to crumble.

Fresh trepidation quickened my heartbeat. Grant's expression hardened into his stoic captain's mask, but I read his concern in the tightness around his eyes and the firmness of his jaw.

Leaving Sooth in Quinn's control, Grant examined the hole the wild energy had blasted into the wall. He dangled his lantern through the dark opening, then squeezed his head through after it.

"Don't—" I protested too late. Any number of ravenous evil creatures could be lurking on the other side of the wall, waiting to tear Grant's arm from his body and slash his throat. I fumbled to retrieve the knife from my bag again, but Grant was already wriggling free.

"That was foolhardy." Fear and relief sharpened my tone.

"There's another passage here." He quirked an eyebrow at me, apparently amused by my concern. "One where the ceiling isn't in the process of collapsing."

The earth rumbled ominously above me, and I darted aside in time to avoid being clobbered by a rock larger than the firebird's egg. All right. Maybe Grant hadn't been *completely* foolhardy.

"How are we supposed to fit through that tiny hole?" Maybe Sooth could squeeze through, but not the rest of us.

"Are you prepared to be awed by my brilliance?" Grant asked. He reversed his grip on his knife and hammered the hilt against the rim of the opening. Dirt and rock crumbled, doubling the hole's size. He arched an eyebrow at me.

"Smart," I agreed.

"That's why they made me captain."

"Because you smashed your way to the top?"

"Because I possess ingenious problem-solving abilities."

"It doesn't hurt that you back those up with a couple hundred pounds of muscle."

His teeth flashed in a grin as he turned back to hammer the opening wider. Sooth scampered closer to Quinn to avoid the falling rock, then jumped aside when the firebird tried to peck the top of her head. I sidled around Quinn and nabbed Sooth's leash, tugging her a safe distance away. The firebird took loud, vocal exception to my proximity, and the entire tunnel shivered.

"Hush," Quinn soothed, rocking his shoulders. "No one wants to steal your baby."

The firebird squawked her displeasure, neck extended, but the harsh glare of her feathers dimmed, and she settled down.

I urged Sooth farther into the tunnel to give Grant room to work, keeping an eye on the ceiling. How many tons of rock hung above us? It could have been a few feet or a few hundred feet. My sense of depth had gone the way of my sense of direction, but from the coolness in the air, I thought we were deeper than when we first entered this underground maze.

Does it matter? It will only take a well-placed bash on the head by a ten-pound rock to kill me. The rest will just be redundant.

A foreboding series of cracks rang through the tunnel, cutting through Grant's rhythmic pounding. Rocks clattered in the darkness behind us, a sporadic downfall that ramped up into a thunderous deluge. A wall of air and sand blasted into me, knocking me to a knee. I grabbed Sooth and crouched over her, holding my bag protectively above us, all too aware that the flimsy satchel wouldn't provide protection from anything larger than falling pebbles.

More gradually than it had started, the cave-in subsided. I peeked out from under my flimsy shelter. Dust hung thick in the air, reducing visibility, but behind Quinn, I could make out the mounded edge of the rockslide blocking our return route.

Sooth yowled unhappily, pressing herself tighter against my legs. Coughing, I tried to give her a reassuring pet, but my hands shook too badly. I wished I could pull Quinn similarly close. His eyes were round with fear, and his sides quivered beneath the firebird. The hen appeared flummoxed by the whole ordeal. Blinking excessively, she bobbed her head and cast furtive glances in every direction.

Grant hadn't allowed the cave-in to distract him. If anything, he bashed his knife hilt against the edges of the ragged opening with greater speed. I watched his relentless strikes, drawing reassurance from his determination. No matter how slim our odds of survival, Grant would never stop fighting. He would never give up. However, the edges of the too-small opening were chipping away in flakes instead of chunks now. At this rate, we would never escape in time.

A menacing rumble shook the tunnel, rattling loose sharp chunks of stone. Grant cursed, and I thought he had been struck until I saw his knife. The hilt had snapped in half, leaving only a nub for him to work with.

"I can help," Quinn said, nudging Grant aside. He curled the tip of his uninjured wing across his back, shifting the firebird so he could secure the egg in place between his rock feathers. Ignoring the hen's scolding, he reared up and used his massive quartz paws to claw apart the ragged hole. Chunks of rock cracked and tumbled to the tunnel floor. The firebird dug her sharp talons into the base of Quinn's wings, flapping wildly to maintain her balance while furiously pecking the back of his head. Shoulders hunched, Quinn didn't slow his digging. Grant stepped up beside Quinn and used his boots to kick at the loosened edges, his arms raised to shield his face from the buffet of the firebird's wings.

The tunnel ahead of us collapsed in a series of crashes that sounded like a locomotive slamming into the rocks, plowing closer. A scream built in my chest, but I couldn't find the oxygen to fuel it.

I don't want to die!

Black lightning snaked across the ceiling as the next crash drove deep fractures into the slab above us. Hugging Sooth tight, I readied a shield of solid air and prepared to fling it over Grant and Quinn. I couldn't dream of holding the mountain up if it collapsed. I didn't have that kind of strength, and even if I did, Lunacy would never stand for it. The elements would backlash into me, crushing me as surely as the falling rocks. But my shield didn't need to hold long; if I could buy Grant and Quinn a few more seconds, it might be enough for them to escape.

Quinn crashed through the wall, nearly dislodging the firebird when her widespread wings caught on the hole's ragged edges. Grant heaved Quinn's hind end through the opening, lifting the back half of the gargoyle as if he weighed less than a housecat. I leapt to my feet, Sooth in my arms, and Grant boosted me across the debris and into the opposite tunnel. My foot caught in the dangling leash, and I fell. Sooth tried to shove off my chest, but I dug my fingers into her harness, refusing to let her go. Shaking my boot free of the leash, I struggled to stand, urgency making me clumsy. I almost got my footing when Grant slammed into me. One moment, I was falling, the next I was flying as Grant swung me into his arms and sprinted after Quinn deeper into the new tunnel. I clutched Sooth tight, my gaze locked on the passage behind us.

Concussive booms rocked the labyrinth as our former tunnel finished collapsing. An avalanche of rocks and dirt cascaded through the hole in the wall; then the ceiling behind us crumpled, sealing off any chance of backtracking and escaping to the surface.

"Hold up," Grant yelled.

Somehow, Quinn heard him above the deafening rock fall and slowed, but neither of them fully stopped until the cave-in behind us quieted. Struggling not to cough, I peered over Grant's shoulder into the darkness. Loose rubble spilled across the tunnel floor, but shadows and the curve of the passageway hid the bulk of the collapsed section.

Sooth squirmed, mashing my breast with a heavy paw and digging an elbow into my sternum. I winced and grunted. As often as I had fantasized about being swept up in Grant's arms, hugged tight to his solid chest, I had never envisioned it being so uncomfortable—or involving a lynx, being buried under a mountain, or any trace of blood magic.

"I, uh, I think I can stand," I said.

Grant glanced down at me as if surprised to find me still in his arms. His hold abruptly loosened, emphasizing how tight his grip had been. He tilted me, setting my feet on the ground, and I plopped Sooth down beside me. Steadying myself against Grant, I untangled Sooth's leash from my legs. The lynx shook herself vigorously, adding a small cloud of sand to the dust-choked air.

"Quinn, are you all right?" I asked. Dirt gritted between my teeth, and the cough I had been suppressing overtook me. I pressed my jacket's lapel to my mouth to filter the air and dashed tears from my eyes.

"Mostly," Quinn said. His sides heaved, and he favored his front-right paw.

He might have tried to say more, but the firebird buffeted his face with her wings as she repositioned the egg; then she hissed and shrieked at shadows as she settled atop it, her racket loud enough to bore through solid stone. If this was the tunnel Emmett had taken—as I prayed it was—she had just given away our location. I could only hope the tunnels distorted the firebird's cries, or better yet, that Emmett was too far lost to insanity to suspect the firebird might be accompanied by Grant, Quinn, and me.

"At least this tunnel is holding," I groused, eyeing the carved ceiling. Should I be grateful, or had we merely delayed the inevitable? We were trapped underground in a labyrinth designed by madmen, and the firebird's magic could still bring it down on our heads at any moment. We had only one direction we could go. We might never find our way out. These rock walls could be the last thing I ever saw.

Why hadn't I spent more time with my mom this morning? I rarely got to see her, but I had been so intent on my possible story, I had squandered the chance during my visit. I hadn't even left a note for Mika. If I died in here, no one who knew or loved me would know what had happened to me. And Quinn—why did he have to be trapped down here with me? He had endured enough danger and pain already in his short life. I should have told him to stay home. Or maybe I should have told him to stay away from me completely. If associating with me meant endangering his life, I didn't deserve his friendship.

"This is going to make an amazing story."

Grant's voice snapped me out of my spiraling thoughts with a jerk. I refocused on our surroundings—and my white-knuckled grip of his forearm. I could feel the cords of his muscles grinding beneath my fingers, the fabric of his shirt grating against my fingertips. Releasing him, I patted his forearm.

"Sorry," I mumbled, hoping I hadn't left a bruise.

"Don't you think it will?" Grant asked.

"Will what?"

"Make an amazing story."

I glanced around the hazy tunnel. "I guess so."

"What do you mean, you guess? You're the first journalist inside Lunacy in centuries. No one is going to top this scoop."

"It's not a scoop. At best it's a cautionary tale, and an unnecessary one."

Grant's eyes flicked from me to Sooth. The lynx ignored us, contorting her upper body to clean her rump. She had taken being nearly crushed to death with an aplomb I wished I possessed. When Grant's eyes focused on me again, they held cautious suspicion.

"Explain," he said.

"Everyone knows to stay away from Lunacy. It's a death trap." I gestured at both of us, encompassing our torn clothing and the myriad wounds with a sweep of my hand. "Writing up a story detailing all the dangers starts to read like a glamorization. I don't want to be the reporter who glorifies Lunacy. I don't want future kids to dare each other to enter the labyrinth because they want to show off their bravery against a vampire or shadow snake. I don't want blood-magic users hiding within our society to make another attempt to bring down the ward after your team fixes it."

Grant crossed his arms, checking Sooth repeatedly throughout my explanation. "But this is exactly the type of story the *Chronicle* wants."

I shrugged. "It's sensational, but it's ultimately empty. Everyone already knows Lunacy is dangerous."

"It would make the front page."

I narrowed my eyes at him, wondering if we were back to accusations of me being obsessed with fame. However, Grant looked genuinely puzzled, so I tried to explain.

"I don't want front-page stories for the sake of having my articles printed on the front page. I want stories that *deserve* to be there. The kind that serve the readers. I want people to learn about amazing things happening around them or about horrible people brought to justice. The front page should be reserved for what will better our society the most, not what will shock people. Lunacy doesn't make anyone's life better, and everyone already knows that."

Grant's perplexed expression hadn't changed.

"Never mind." I set my bag down and rummaged for my dwindling supply of greenthread salve. Maybe I could better articulate myself if I weren't so tired and beaten up, but we had more pressing issues to worry about than my journalistic philosophy.

When I straightened, my ankle twinged. I rolled it gently, assessing the damage. I had twisted it when I had fallen, but it didn't appear to be seriously injured. A good thing, since carrying me had opened the cuts on Grant's ribs.

"You're bleeding," I said, pointing at patches of fresh blood seeping through his shirt.

Grant studied me a moment longer before glancing down at his ribs. When he lifted his shirt, he revealed a slurry of dirt, sweat, and blood coating his sculpted abdomen. Some of the makeshift bindings had slipped, pulling the lamb's-ear patches with them. I ran my finger lightly across his ribs above the highest cut, lamenting that saving me had inflicted more pain on Grant.

"Thank you," I said softly. Heat radiated from him, warming my chilled fingers. "I wouldn't have survived without you."

"I know."

He spoke with such gentle compassion, it took a moment for his words to sink in. I shot him a frown.

"I believe the appropriate response is 'you're welcome,'" I said.

"Are you sure? You were stating a fact. If I said I have bigger muscles than you, would you say, 'you're welcome'?"

I planted my hands on my hips, flabbergasted—until I saw the mirth crinkling the corners of his eyes. That's right. I had forgotten that brushes with death tickled Grant's funny bone.

"You're lucky our roles weren't reversed," I grumped. "I'm not sure I could have carried you *and* your ego."

"You're welcome."

I chuckled, but my humor quickly faded as we rebandaged his wounds, then checked ourselves over for new scrapes and cuts. I reapplied greenthread to my stinging fingertips and the puncture on my hip. I craved a long hot shower followed by a hearty meal and a trip to a healer. Instead, I had to be satisfied with swishing the dirt from my mouth with the last of my water.

Quinn assured us he could walk without "too much" pain. I detested my inability to help him. I couldn't heal his foot or wing. I couldn't even soothe the gouges the firebird had pecked out of his neck and the back of his skull. I hated this place, and I was beginning to hate the firebird, too. Even if she was the catalyst for evolving my everlasting seed, she wasn't worth it. Nothing was worth putting Quinn or myself through this amount of torture.

"You don't have to write about the challenges we've encountered," Grant said, picking up our abandoned conversation. He dabbed salve on a cut on the back of his hand, not looking at me.

Challenges? I snorted. Only a Federal Pentagon Defense warrior would think of the death traps we had triggered as *challenges.*

"There's more than one way to write a story," Grant prompted.

I studied his face. Pale grit coated his hair and eyebrows, and a heaping of sweat and dirt smudged his skin, but through it all shone an earnestness I had never seen on his face before.

Suspicion circled my grim thoughts, nudging them aside. How many times had Grant complained about my curiosity, especially when it pertained to any events that involved him? He was more likely to insult my profession than praise it. Shouldn't he be happy I wasn't in reporter mode? Why was he trying so hard to get me interested in writing a story now?

The answer came in a flash of insight: hope. He wanted me to maintain hope of getting out of Lunacy.

"I can't write an article about chasing down Emmett, because Nathan is already covering the murder," I said, a perverse impulse making me balk now that Grant was the one pushing for an article.

"I don't see Nathan here."

"No, he was too smart for that."

"Or not as good of a reporter," Quinn chimed in.

"That too," Grant agreed.

"Do you really think I'm the better reporter?" I couldn't hold in the question, not with a lynx present, not even knowing how shallow and juvenile it made me sound.

"Yes," Grant said.

Sooth continue to bathe, not paying attention to our conversation. My chest swelled with pride. Grant thought I was a good reporter.

"I think you're the best," Quinn said.

I smiled at him. "I think you're the best, too." Tapping a finger against my chin, I considered Grant's suggestion. "I might be able to submit an article on the FPD rescuing the abducted firebirds."

Grant wiped a smudge of greenthread off my chin. "That sounds great—"

"No, it won't work. The firebirds were stolen by the murderers, making them part of Nathan's article." Even when he wasn't present, Nathan managed to steal my stories. How did he do it, all without endangering his life? Maybe he was right; maybe I had a lot to learn from him.

What a depressing thought.

"That can't be the only angle you can think of," Grant said. He stowed his jar of medicine in his pack, then slung the bag onto his back.

I shrugged the strap of my bag across my chest. Somewhere in this warren of tunnels, Seradon was being held captive by a blood-magic-crazed man. We didn't have time to waste on chitchat. Reminding myself Grant was once again attempting to rally my spirits, and not wanting him to hesitate on my account, I threw out the first idea I had. "I could write about the firebird hatchling, whenever that happens."

I mentally ran through the potential article. People enjoyed a good baby narrative, especially one with an atypical birth story. Plus, covering the baby firebird might have been exactly what my everlasting seed intended. "Maybe I could do a series of articles on the firebirds, depending on where they get placed to raise the hatchling. I don't think they're going to be transported all the way to the coast now, not with the hen sitting on her egg."

"But we will get her off my back, right?" Quinn whined.

"Of course. How do you feel about being a source for my article? I'll need quotes—ones that don't have anything to do with poop. Maybe you could even write up a firsthand account of your experience."

Quinn's uninjured wing flared with excitement, instigating a flurry of scolding chatter from the firebird. The gargoyle ignored her. "Really? Me?"

"I don't see why not. You have a one-of-a-kind perspective."

Quinn's mouth curved into a broad, toothy smile that lightened my heart.

Grant took Sooth's leash from me, and I thought I detected amusement twinkling in his dark eyes. His emotional manipulation had been blatant, but it had worked—I felt better, and so did Quinn. I considered being affronted but decided I didn't care if he found us humorous. I would take being laughed at over feeling hopeless any day.

Grant took point position once more, but he instructed me to follow behind him this time, while Quinn brought up the rear. I wanted to believe he made the switch because he saw the value in having me at his side, but I suspected he considered me to be the most vulnerable member of our group and decided having me close would make me easier to protect.

"Shouldn't I be in front of Kylie in case she needs my protection?" Quinn asked.

I could justify Grant seeing me as weak, but I struggled not to take offense at Quinn's question. He may have saved me from the shadow cobra, but of the two of us, I should be protecting him. He was younger; he had no magic of his own, not even the small magic Lunacy allowed; and he was handicapped by the firebird and egg on his back.

"It will be easier to pass Sooth to Kylie if I need to," Grant said, which wasn't exactly an answer. "The less we aggravate the firebird, hopefully the less she'll talk and spew her magic."

I thought he was being overly optimistic since the firebird had not stopped chattering since the cave-in had subsided, and no amount of shimmying on Quinn's behalf quieted her.

"Should I . . . ?" I pretended to poke the firebird.

"Not unless something manifests," Grant said.

With Sooth in the lead, Grant marched into the tunnel. I had lost my lantern in the cave-in, so I held Grant's high, using it to brighten the shadows cast by the firebird's glow behind us. Familiar tension tightened my muscles in anticipation of the next "challenge." How did Grant maintain his composure no matter what madness Lunacy concocted? It must have been part of the Federal Pentagon Defense training. If the rest of my journalistic career was going to involve half as many dangers as the first few months had, perhaps I should consider taking some FPD courses myself.

It was Grant who pulled us up short minutes later, not

Sooth. He gestured for silence, and I held my breath. The firebird continue to sing, but between the reverberations of her warbles, I heard the murmur of human voices.

"Wait here," Grant whispered, lumping Quinn and me in the order.

Quinn nodded. I shook my head. Anywhere other than Lunacy, I might have been a liability. But here, where large-scale magic catastrophically misfired, my smaller tricks could come in handy. They had more than once already. I reminded Grant of this through heavy eye contact and a stubborn tilt of my jaw. Grant's nostrils flared in irritation; then he nodded.

We skulked closer to the voices, leaving behind Quinn and the light of the firebird. I shuttered the lantern to all but the smallest trickle of light, just enough to see obstacles in our path and to keep an eye on Sooth's behavior. The small cat walked soundlessly, seeming to understand the need for stealth. Or perhaps that was simply her feline nature. My footsteps wanted to drag. I hated leaving Quinn alone. I felt as if a fragile cable connected me to him, stretching tighter and tighter the farther Grant and I walked. In my imagination, the cable had only so much elasticity before added tension would snap it. If that happened, Lunacy would exploit his vulnerability, and we would never be reunited. It wasn't hard to picture a plethora of scenarios that could tear us apart, starting with the firebird perched on his spine. With her magic capable of collapsing the tunnel on top of Quinn, having her on his back was akin to him carting around explosives—ones rigged to go off at any moment.

Grant wrapped his hand around my wrist, stopping me before I ran into him. He pinched the air with his fingers, and after a pointed glance at the lantern, I correctly interpreted his sign language and closed the lantern shutters completely. Before my eyes had fully adjusted to the darkness, Grant tiptoed forward, pulling me after him. The rising and falling voices crystalized into the ramblings of a single madman: Emmett. A few steps later, the faint outline of the tunnel opening appeared, and we stopped at the edge of the unmistakable heart of the Lunacy Labyrinth.

The huge cavern might have started as a natural earthen pocket, but it had been scraped free of all native mineral formations to make way for religious ornamentations. Huge carvings of broad skeletal faces wearing stone feather headdresses protruded from the cavern walls above a half dozen dark tunnel openings. Higher up along the curved dome of the ceiling, bug-eyed heads of giants glared down at the cavern floor, their insane eyes highlighted by bright white mosaics of crystal and slate. A broad dais dominated in the center of the chamber crowned by a massive stone altar. Twisted rock pillars ringed the altar, each topped with candles and wax drippings older than the city of Terra Haven. A soft glow emanated from deeper in the cavern, but I couldn't tear my gaze from the altar, where Seradon's lifeless figure lay atop the slab of granite.

Were we too late?

Grant shifted, and I jerked, expecting an attack. My gaze darted around the cavern, seeking out Emmett. A maze of animal sculptures littered the floor—wolves, foxes, manticores, jaguars, firebirds, eagles, ceberi, and more. A deep bowl had been carved into the back of each stone idol, and black flakes of ancient blood offerings still lingered inside their hollows. Among all the stone creatures, Emmett was easy to spot, since he had the only light source. He crouched at the base of a half-collapsed ziggurat shrine beyond the dais, digging through the debris, oblivious to our presence.

"Where are you? Where, where, where? I am here to

fulfill our destiny," he babbled, his voice drowning out the faint chirps and trills of the firebird filtering through the tunnel behind us. Rocks clattered and scraped, and Emmett's voice rose to a scream. "I'm the blood king! I'm your master! Where are you?" He whipped his bound firebird aloft, the choppy gesture flopping the bird within its bindings.

The muted glow of the firebird's feathers cast long shadows around the room. When the light outlined Seradon's body, proving her chest rose and fell in shallow breaths, I almost sobbed. Then Emmett dove back into the pile of rocks in front of him, carelessly dropping the firebird to the ground, and the cavern darkened.

Grant released my wrist and made a gesture I couldn't see from my position. I reached for his arm to get him to turn when a flicker of movement against a gloomy tunnel opening across the cavern drew my attention. I strained to make out the shape, but I couldn't discern more than a pale blob.

"No, no, no." Emmett shoved the firebird above his head, propping its bound body atop the shrine. In the brighter glow, I spotted Winnigan's familiar face in the shadows. Stacked behind her were Marciano and Velasquez.

Excitement jolted through me. They were alive!

For the first time since Quinn had crash-landed in the labyrinth, hope blossomed in my chest. Whatever route Winnigan and the others had used to reach the heart, we could retrace it to escape. With everyone back together, we had a real chance of making it out alive.

Grant issued a quick series of hand signals to his squad. Winnigan signaled back, and Grant gave her an exaggerated nod before turning to me. He pointed to my feet and mouthed, *"Stay here."*

I nodded, my head bobbing uncontrollably. I didn't suffer delusions of grandeur. With the others here, my help had become unnecessary, and I was fine with that. More than fine—ecstatic. The sooner Grant and his squad nullified Emmett, the sooner we could grab Seradon and escape Lunacy. I wouldn't do anything to impede them.

Grant looped Sooth's leash around his left wrist and drew a knife in each hand. Keeping an eye on Emmett, who remained bent over the crumbled shrine, Grant tiptoed into the cavern. Across the way, Winnigan, Velasquez, and Marciano emerged from their tunnel. Soundlessly, they fanned out to surround Emmett and cut off his escape. I clutched the lantern handle, my fingernails digging into my palms, my entire body tense enough to spontaneously levitate.

"You shine as bright as the sun, you are my only one," Emmett sang tunelessly, his voice cracking across the notes. "Together we will rise, together they will die." His maniacal giggle climbed in octaves until it turned to a squeal and devolved into curses.

If not for the paranoia of the ancients who had created this macabre temple, the squad's stealthy approach might have worked. But as Grant crept between the dais and a life-size jaguar statue, Sooth yowled a warning, her cry trumpeting through the chamber.

Emmett jerked up, holding the firebird high, his teeth bared. When he spied Grant, he hissed and gathered his magic for a strike.

"Run," I whispered. Emmett's last blood-enhanced attack had flattened Grant. He couldn't muscle his way through whatever Emmett threw at him now.

Instead of taking cover, Grant squared his shoulders, making a larger target of himself—and keeping the madman's attention locked on him. Behind Emmett, the rest of the team edged closer, preparing a strike.

The others were still more than ten feet away when Velasquez's toe brushed against a beetle statue. It imploded into black sand with a resounding crack. Animated by latent blood magic, the grains swirled in a tight vortex, then swarmed across the temple with a drawn-out hiss. The obsidian sand burrowed into the mouth of a giant bug-eyed head. Twin crossbow bolts shot from the carving's eyes. Despite his solid frame, Velasquez jumped aside with surprising agility. The stone arrowheads shattered harmlessly against the cavern floor, but the damage had already been done.

Emmett spun around, his face contorting with rage when he spotted the encroaching FPD squad. "I'll kill you. I'll kill you all!" he screamed.

Winnigan hurled a knife at Emmett's heart, but it bounced off a thick ward. A blood-magic-laced wave of air exploded from Emmett. His magic slammed into all four FPD warriors at the same time. It hurtled Winnigan backward, tossing Verity along with her. Somehow Winnigan managed to catch the lynx before her boots hit the ground, and she dropped into a controlled roll with the cat cradled against her chest. The men all outweighed Winnigan and managed to keep their feet, though their boots slid on the gritty cavern floor.

A flurry of flames, rock shards, and frozen ice blades assaulted Emmett. His ward deflected the small magics as easily as it had the knife.

"You can't touch me. I'm invincible!" Emmett splayed his arms wide, and a fresh wave of magic pulsed from him, this one pierced with jagged spikes of solidified air.

Grant dove behind the altar, pulling Sooth with him.

The lynx landed beside Grant's prone body, her fur standing on end. Emmett's magic blasted into the base of the altar, breaking against the solid stone, but a larger-than-life cockatrice Grant had been standing near seconds earlier exploded. Around the cavern, the other squad members leapt for cover as Emmett's deadly elemental attack decimated centuries-old statues in a series of bone-rattling explosions.

Ignoring the chaos, Emmett ducked out of sight, scrambling once more through the rubble around the shrine. As the last statue shattered, he released a triumphant cry, the sound all but drowned out by the echoes of the demolished stone figures. Straightening, Emmett thrust his fist into the air. The light of the firebird propped atop the altar in front of him shimmered off a bulbous red-and-gold object clutched in his fist. Emmett stared at it with rapt adoration.

"I am the blood king. I am Eztli Tiacauh!" The madman glared around the cavern as if daring anyone to dispute him. When he spotted Marciano surging to his feet, Emmett's eyes widened, and he dropped his arm, clutching the item to his chest. "It's mine! Mineminemine! You can't have it!"

The black taint of blood magic surged through Emmett's ward, darkening it until a solid shadow encased him, obscuring him from sight. A grubby hand shot out of the ward and seized the firebird, yanking it inside the murky veil.

My heart fluttered in my chest as utter blackness consumed the cavern. I cowered against the curve of the tunnel wall, straining to catch a glimpse of Emmett or any of the squad members, but I couldn't see my own hand wave in front of my face. In the oppressive silence, I heard the scuffle of feet and Emmett's wild giggle, the eerie sound dying with a sharp curse. My heartbeat pounded louder, competing with a false ringing in my ears as my brain groped for sound to fill the void.

Tiny sparks of flames ignited throughout the cavern. The faint light transformed every statue into a monster hunched to attack. More candle-size flames sprang into existence, providing better illumination and proving the statues hadn't come to life. Gulping deep breaths, I reined in my terror-fueled imagination.

Then the flames converged on the ruined shrine, and my heart sank. Emmett had escaped.

Hand signals flashed between the team members, and Winnigan trotted silently to collect Velasquez, letting Verity pick a safe path. She and Velasquez then wove through the statues toward Marciano, keeping a vigilant eye on the lynx's behavior. Verity flattened her ears at the base of the shrine, and they veered wide. When they met up with the giant wood elemental, they beelined for the tunnels on the far side of the room. Velasquez and Marciano materialized lanterns and lit them with tiny pulses of fire element. Together, Velasquez and Winnigan examined the floor near each tunnel opening while Marciano stood guard.

Seradon lifted her head. "Did you get him?" she croaked.

Grant climbed the dais steps, a cluster of tiny flames illuminating his path, then Seradon's pale face. She rolled her head away from him to watch the others search for Emmett's trail.

"He got away? I lay down for one little nap, and you all let the bad guy escape?" she rasped.

Grant responded too softly for me to hear. He dropped

his pack next to the altar and tugged out a water bottle for Seradon, looping his arm beneath her shoulders to support her while she drank.

I shoved away from the tunnel wall, feeling foolish cowering in the shadows now that Emmett had departed. After opening the shutter of my lantern to provide a solid beam of light, I trotted through the statues, careful to follow Grant's trail. The pervasive grime of the mutated elements tightened around me the deeper I traipsed into the cavern. I chafed my arms, hoping the friction could scrub clean the slimy sensation of the soiled magic. It didn't.

"I told you to wait over there," Grant said without looking at me.

"Did you mean forever?"

Grant's jaw muscle ticked, but he let the issue drop. He helped Seradon sit up, but she batted his hand aside when he tried to hold the water bottle for her again.

"Did you two make the most of your unchaperoned time?" Seradon wriggled her eyebrows, then winced and lifted a hand to her temple.

"We stayed alive," I said. "It was very romantic."

Seradon snorted, and Grant shot me an unfathomable look. Sooth squinted at me, but her magic didn't react.

"How do you feel?" Grant asked Seradon.

"Like the left side of my head is trying to grow a unicorn horn."

"Did he do anything to you?" Grant scanned Seradon's body with an impersonal eye. Her clothing was in better shape than ours, but she had gained her fair share of nicks and bruises.

"Not that I can tell. He was too busy talking to himself and trying to unearth Kylie's Chiefmaker."

"It's not *my* Chiefmaker," I protested.

Winnigan left Marciano and Velasquez and approached the dais with Verity. Twice, illusions forced her to alter course. Even here, at the heart of their place of worship, the creators' paranoia had driven them to embed enumerable traps among their ceremonial statues. It boggled my mind that anyone would choose to use a form of magic that devolved their brain function to such a degree. No amount of power was worth that sacrifice.

"Did you guys have as much fun as we did?" Winnigan asked.

"Any camazotz-turned-chonchon on your way in?" Grant asked.

Winnigan's eyebrows twitched, and she shook her head.

"What about a vampire?"

"Now you're just trying to make me jealous."

"A vampire?" Seradon asked.

"I think we had more fun," Grant said.

"Wait until Velasquez tells you about the chimera we bumped into. And her mate," Winnigan said, circling the altar to stand beside us. "That was fun."

I decided they both had taken one too many knocks to the head.

Winnigan took my lantern and handed me Verity's leash, nudging me out of the way. Lifting the light high, she examined Seradon's head.

"Watch what you're doing," Seradon said, shielding her eyes from the light. "You're going to set my hair on fire."

"Don't be a baby." Winnigan pushed aside Seradon's hands and peered into her pupils. "Tell me what happened."

"I smashed my head against a rock."

"What did the rock do to deserve that?" Winnigan's slender fingers traced the outline of the goose egg distorting

Seradon's short hair; then she prodded Seradon's cheekbone and jaw. "Anything feel broken?"

"It didn't until you started jabbing it." Seradon winced when magic from two lynxes nipped her for that lie.

"Can you stand?"

"Are you trying to humiliate me in front of Kylie and— Wait, where's Quinn?" Seradon's hand clamped down on my wrist.

"He's safe, back up the tunnel a ways."

"Good. Let's get out of here." Seradon released me and hopped to her feet. Her knees buckled, and Grant caught her before she collapsed.

"Ceto's spawn, Seradon, what are you doing?" Winnigan demanded. "You can't go jumping around after the blow you took to your head. I haven't healed you. I can't heal anything in this splintered sandpit. The elements feel like charred dragon dung."

Winnigan continued to curse Lunacy with a graphic creativity I associated with dockworkers, not delicate-looking water elementals, but Grant and Seradon seemed to expect no less. They even managed to decipher the thwarted healer's instructions mixed in with her colorful rant. With Grant's help, Seradon sat on the steps of the dais and applied a compress chilled by flecks of ice to her temple.

"Should I go get Quinn?" I asked, anxious to have him close again.

"Not yet." Grant's gaze swept the ceiling, and I suspected it was the visible taint of blood-magic pollution he was studying, not the hideous carvings.

"Any injuries I should know about?" Winnigan asked, turning her attention to me and Grant.

"We've about gone through all of our greenthread, but it should do the trick until we're out of here," Grant said.

I nodded. My body ached from so many bruises, cuts, and scrapes I couldn't tell one injury's pangs from the next, but none of my wounds would benefit from Winnigan's curtailed healing abilities.

"Do we retreat or chase him?" Winnigan asked.

"We didn't come down here just to get a few new scars," Grant said. He shouldered his pack and directed his question to the two men. "Which way did he go?"

"Here or here," Velasquez said, pointing at two side-by-side tunnels. Then he indicated a spot several feet from either opening. "All that air he tossed around swept away the dust, so his footprints end there."

"Captain, do we know if that was the Chiefmaker he disappeared with?" Marciano asked.

Everyone turned to me.

"It fit Zipporah's description," I said.

"Anyone have an idea what it does?" Velasquez asked.

Again, they all looked at me. I shrugged.

"Nothing good, I'm sure," Seradon said.

"We can't let him get too far ahead. Let's divide up, two per tunnel," Grant said. "Seradon, you're in no shape to keep up. Kylie, you'll remain here, too."

"Sounds good to me," Seradon said. "Go get that scab picker."

I handed Winnigan the leash for Verity, and she returned my lantern. Then she and Grant threaded the statues and traps before splitting up. Marciano and Winnigan disappeared down the right tunnel, with Verity in the lead. Casting one last glance back toward us, Grant and Velasquez slipped into the second opening. I set my bag beside Seradon but decided I should remain standing in case something malicious crept out of the shadows and attacked. It was probably wishful thinking that I would be able to protect us, but it made me feel better to have a plan, especially after the dim glow of the team's receding lanterns dwindled to black.

"Do you hear birds or did I do more damage to my head than I thought?" Seradon asked.

I spun around, relieved to see a soft glow brightening the tunnel I had exited from. Grant might have been reluctant to invite Quinn—and the firebird he carried—to join us, but I was eager to have my friend where I could see he was safe.

Quinn tiptoed up to the cavern, his stealthy approach negated by the hen's warbling and her brightly glowing feathers. When he peered around the edge of the tunnel and spotted us, his face split in a grin.

"Seradon! You're all right!"

"Mostly," Seradon agreed. "How did you get your hands on that bird?"

"Emmett cut it loose," I said. "It was Thorpe's. That was the other guy's name. He's dead now." I shied away from the memory of Emmett burying his hand in Thorpe's gaping stomach and stealing the other man's blood magic. "The firebird took a liking to Quinn and hasn't left his back since."

"It sees you as a golden perch," Seradon said, making the connection faster than Grant or I had. "That was incredibly lucky."

"If you say so," Quinn groused. "Can I come out?"

I directed Quinn through the maze of sculptures, making sure he steered clear of the jaguar one we knew hid an illusion. Unlike the hen's mate, the firebird atop Quinn shone bright, illuminating the entire cavern in a warm glow reminiscent of a campfire. Seradon and I both surveyed the ceiling and the turbid elements shifting around us.

"This place makes my skin crawl," I said.

"Yep," Seradon agreed.

Quinn stopped at the bottom of the steps, far enough away to appease the firebird. She roosted contentedly upon her egg, singing the same three notes again and again. The shadows pulsed around her, and it took me a moment to recognize what I was seeing: At the end of every third note, the firebird's magic purified the surrounding air, brightening it; and just as fast, the foul magic filling the cavern swooped into the void, negating the purified elements and darkening the pocket of air once more. Blood magic had saturated this chamber for centuries, and the hen was only one small firebird—it would take her days, if not weeks, to purify the labyrinth's heart.

"I didn't get a chance to scout this torture chamber," Seradon said. "Quinn, see if you can't launch the bird. Maybe if she lights up some of those shadowy nooks, we can find a quick way out of here. Or a weapon or two."

"I wish I could," Quinn said. "She refuses to leave her egg."

Seradon had raised the water bottle for a drink, but surprise made her miss her mouth, and she cursed when the liquid dribbled down her chest. Recapping the bottle, she tilted her head as if trying to see through the firebird's feathers. "A baby firebird is incubating on your back?"

Quinn hung his head. "Unfortunately."

"Isn't that a good thing?" Seradon glanced at me, then at the woeful gargoyle. "What am I missing? Are you in pain?"

"No, but . . ."

"She's pooping on him," I said, holding back my smile.

Seradon grimaced. "That would put a damper on the novelty of being a surrogate parent."

Her easy understanding seemed to raise Quinn's spirits, and he stood taller.

"Tell me what happened after I so professionally incapacitated myself," Seradon said.

I winced at the self-flagellation wrapped in her sarcasm. "If we had been anywhere other than Lunacy, that never would have happened. But in a way, your attack worked. It distracted the men and gave Grant a moment to strike."

"Kylie, what are you going on about?"

"I'm just saying that even though you knocked yourself out, it was still helpful."

Seradon burst into laughter. The cavern and all its dirty magic swallowed the sound. "Are you trying to bolster my delicate self-esteem?"

"Well, I don't want you to feel bad ..."

"For making a mistake? Oh, aren't you sweet," Seradon said it with a smile, her voice devoid of the condescension the words might otherwise have implied. She gave my arm a pat. "You're a good friend, Kylie, but I don't feel bad; I'm angry with myself. I knew better than to use normal amounts of the elements, and I deserve the concussion I got. But I learned my lesson, and I won't make that mistake again. Now stop coddling me and tell me what happened."

I marveled at her pragmatism, wishing I could emulate it. My mistakes often haunted me for days, sometimes years long after I had learned from them.

"Out with it," Seradon said, poking my thigh with a finger. "What did I miss? How did Grant take down Emmett's comrade?"

I realized she was asking for more than an update: Seradon was interested in the details of how we had survived so she could learn from our experiences, too. Trying to stick to the facts, I recounted the events she had missed: Grant fighting Emmett and being pummeled; my tiny air blades that did little more than give Thorpe and

Emmett paper cuts; and Emmett freeing the firebird, then using Thorpe's death and blood to enhance his magic, slam Grant into a wall, and escape with Seradon in tow.

"So we're dealing with a blood-magic-enhanced, low-level air elemental with self-esteem issues who lacks combat training."

"You got all that from what I told you?" I asked, astounded. "How?"

"First, if he had combat training, he would have known to finish off a threat," Seradon said, ticking the point off on her finger. "From what you said, he didn't even acknowledge your presence, let alone do anything to prevent you from following him. Maybe I should add chauvinist to the list, if he dismissed you because of your gender." She ticked another finger.

"He did collapse the tunnel after he fled. That was a pretty good deterrent."

Seradon gave me a pointed look. "Obviously not as good as he thought it would be, since you're here. Second, he didn't attack with anything more deadly than blasts of air, which means he's not a formidable elemental. He either doesn't know how to use the other elements or he doesn't have enough experience with them to combine them with blood magic." She ticked off a third finger. "His low self-esteem is common sense. If he had power, he wouldn't have been tempted to use blood magic in the first place. Also, if he had more elemental strength, he wouldn't have needed the blood-magic boost to knock Grant down, not in here where he has the advantage. Finally, he risked everything to get inside this despicable place to dig up the Chiefmaker. Whatever its powers, he thinks it will give him an edge over others. He's a man who has grown up being less than—less powerful, less elementally gifted, less intelligent. He's likely got some pretty twisted revenge fantasies plotted out."

I gaped at her.

"Or so I'm guessing," Seradon added with a shrug. "You learn to recognize the type after you've been doing this job as long as I have. Now tell me about the vampire."

"It was shockingly fast and powerful. And creepy. Its feathers were highly flammable, but that didn't slow it down. Grant thinks that if we hadn't had the firebird with us, it wouldn't have been so strong. I don't get it. Firebirds restore the environment. Why did the hen's magic give the vampire strength?" At the time, I had been too relieved to be alive to give Grant's assessment of the vampire's powers much thought, but now I realized I didn't understand the connection.

Seradon removed the compress and gently probed the knot on her temple as she contemplated the firebird. "Vampires can only exist in places with dry, porous rock and a consistent shadow. They might feed on blood, but they derive most of their mobility from their nesting spot. Somehow they store magic in the pockets of the rock, and when they fly, they draw on that stored magic for cohesion and speed. That's the extent of my vampire lore. If you want a more detailed explanation, you'll have to hunt down a vampire morphologist. My training only covered how to pulverize their nests to starve them of power. Perhaps the firebird's chatter repaired some collapsed pockets in the rock, giving the vampire access to more of its stored magic."

I made a mental note to use Seradon as a source for future articles. She was a fount of knowledge and surprisingly willing to share it, unlike a certain FPD captain.

Wincing, Seradon stopped fussing with her swollen temple. "We haven't seen the full extent of the hen's magic, either," she mused. "If that baby hatches while we're in here, it's going to be . . . problematic."

"That's an understatement," I said, thinking of how close Quinn, Grant, and I had already come to being buried alive.

"At least she was more helpful against the wild energy trap," Quinn said.

"How much did I—" Seradon began, but cut herself off when a melodic whistle echoed from a far tunnel.

I jerked straight, eager for my first glimpse of the returning squad. A golden glow emanated from the tunnel Grant and Velasquez had taken, growing brighter. They had made quick work of capturing Emmett. I had expected nothing less. They were experienced Federal Pentagon Defense warriors; dealing with deranged madmen was commonplace for them.

Seradon grabbed my arm and tugged me down beside her on the dais steps.

"Wha—"

Shaking her head, Seradon raised a finger to her lips. My hopes plummeted. I had assumed the whistle had been a signal from the team, but if it hadn't been them . . .

Emmett sauntered into the cavern, fully visible and unprotected by a ward. He held his bound firebird in his left hand. In his right, he clutched the Chiefmaker, the large red stone filling his fist. Fresh blood dripped from his painted forehead, running down his temples. More darkened his lips and dribbled off his chin.

My heart pounded in my ears. Emmett wasn't cut. The blood wasn't his.

Where was Grant?

Hunkering down on the dais steps next to Seradon, I peered between statues, scrutinizing the tunnel behind Emmett. No light shone from the black opening; no shapes stirred in the shadows. If Grant and Velasquez had encountered Emmett, we would have heard the skirmish. Somehow, the murderer had eluded them.

Seradon reached around me and dimmed the lantern, though it seemed pointless. We remained in a bubble of light cast by the firebird. With her acting as a shining beacon, singing her repetitive soft melody, we would be impossible to miss. Quinn and I shared an anguished look. If he had stayed hidden in the tunnel, would he have been safe? Would Seradon and I have been able to escape Emmett's detection?

Seradon pressed her mouth to my ear, her voice a decibel above a breath. "Wait for my signal, then go left. I'll go right. Use small magic."

I nodded, curling my fists into the strap of my bag. Remembering the knife inside, I reached blindly for it. My finger glanced off the tip, and I bit back a hiss of pain when the sharp blade drew blood. As silently as possible, I slid the knife free and handed it to Seradon. She gave me an approving nod. With shaking mental fingers, I readied a slender blade of air.

Seradon twisted to face Quinn. "Get ready to run," she whispered.

Through the gaps of a ceberi statue's heads, I watched Emmett's knees pivot toward the altar. His tuneless whistles cut off.

"No, no, no! Where did you go, my perfect sacrifice?"

Seradon tensed but didn't give the order. My legs trembled, caught between the urge to charge and flee. When the firebird shrieked in fury, an electric jolt of alarm unbalanced me. Seradon caught my arm before I tumbled down the dais steps. We ducked when the firebird launched from Quinn, her talons grazing the air above our heads. She surged over the altar and dove for Emmett. Stumbling backward, Emmett swung his bound firebird like a cudgel, and the hen shied away with a raucous cry. Belatedly, Emmett flung his other hand into the air as if casting a ward. The Chiefmaker nestled against his palm, the polished bloodstone suspended between five gold chains, each connected to golden rings wedged on Emmett's grimy fingers. In the firebird's metallic luminescence, the enormous stone glistened like fresh, wet blood.

The irate bird dove for a second attack, talons extended. Again, Emmett slung the trussed-up firebird to defend himself, as if forgetting he could use the elements for protection. The hen sank her talons around the rope binding her mate. For a second, I thought she might tug the male away from Emmett, but he jerked the bound firebird to his chest. The hen screamed and snaked her head toward

Emmett. He ducked, finally remembering his powers and knocking her aside with a punch of air. Screeching, the hen righted herself, flapping heavily higher.

Seradon slapped my shoulder. "Now," she hissed.

I sprang to my feet, darting to the top of the dais and around the altar, flinging a slender, deadly air blade at Emmett's throat. Seradon leapt from the dais as if she had never been injured, throwing the knife midair. Emmett didn't bother with a ward. Without looking, he crushed my elemental blade in a wad of solidified, blood-tainted air, then used the same elemental bundle to slap aside Seradon's knife. Trepidation curled into a nauseous snarl in my stomach. Emmett's magic had gotten stronger and more refined since the last time we fought.

The rope around the imprisoned firebird frayed. The bird struggled, his sharp talons tearing through the leather bindings. Emmett yelped and threw the bird. Still bound in a tangle of rope, his wings trapped, the firebird hit the hard cavern floor and rolled out of sight before I could determine if the impact had killed him. Fresh fury infused my fear.

The female firebird vibrated the air with her furious cries, circling near the domed ceiling like an oscillating sun. Below her, shadows spun dizzyingly through the statues. Sand and pebbles rained from the ceiling.

Not again.

Seradon yanked another knife from her boot without slowing, sprinting for Emmett. I jerked my attention back to the madman and chucked air blade after air blade in a futile attempt to distract him, unable to fight back with anything stronger. Emmett batted aside each elemental blade as if swatting flies from the air.

"Kneel," he boomed, raising the Chiefmaker.

Seradon collapsed to her knees, her momentum sliding

her several feet across the rough stone floor. Pressure clamped down on my muscles, bending my legs. My knees slammed to the stone dais. I gasped as much from pain as from shock. No element had touched me, yet somehow he had compelled me. Or rather, the Chiefmaker had.

I planted my hands on the ground and shoved, but my legs wouldn't budge. I could feel my toes, I could even wiggle them, but I couldn't flex my thighs or lift my feet. Using both hands, I grabbed my right thigh and yanked. Nothing happened. My knees might as well have been fused to the rock. Panic surged through me, and my heart banged like a trapped animal inside my rib cage.

I glanced behind me. Quinn hadn't run. He crouched near the steps, hidden from Emmett's sight by the altar. Inexplicably, the Chiefmaker's compulsion hadn't affected him.

"Find Grant," I mouthed.

Quinn mouthed something in return, but I couldn't read his feline lips, and I looked away, afraid if I stared too long, I would draw Emmett's attention to Quinn. For now, the lunatic appeared fixated on the firebird.

"Come to me, pretty birdie," Emmett coaxed, lifting the Chiefmaker toward the ceiling as if offering the firebird a perch.

The shadows receded as the hen swooped overhead, once, twice. On the third pass, I realized it wasn't a trick of the light: The Chiefmaker's inner glow brightened each time the firebird neared. Emmett took deep, intoxicated breaths, closing his eyes in ecstasy. Dread sank heavy claws into my stomach. Emmett and Thorpe hadn't stolen the firebirds just to make navigating the labyrinth easier. No, their end goal had always been the Chiefmaker. Somehow, the firebirds activated or enhanced the Chiefmaker's power.

Seradon sat on her heels, making no effort to escape our invisible bindings. She held her knife against the side of her leg, hidden from Emmett, and her gaze never wavered from the murderer.

The firebird altered her flight path, spinning away from Emmett to circle above the faint light coming from across the chamber, where her mate had landed. Emmett opened his eyes and surveyed us; then he giggled and danced in place. When he stilled, he canted his head, listening to the voices only he heard.

"Yes," he wheezed. "You will both bleed for me. Now."

Pain sparked in my fingertip, then flared through the gash on my hip. Fresh blood dripped from the small cut on my finger. More soaked through my pants. The shimmery, bright energy I had witnessed feed from Thorpe's blood to Emmett now flowed from my wounds to Emmett's hand and into the Chiefmaker. A separate line of shining energy spooled from a cut on Seradon's arm to the Chiefmaker. Emmett's eyes rolled back in his head, and he stopped breathing; then he stumbled forward with a gasp. Blinking the glassiness from his eyes, he gnashed his teeth at Seradon.

Horror kept me fixated on the glowing bloodstone. Emmett had expended no elemental magic; he'd simply ordered it, and the Chiefmaker had taken control of our bodies. This was the coveted magic of the stone—undiluted power over others through control of their lifeblood.

Now would be the perfect time to show up, Grant.

A thunderous clap of stone erupted beside me. For a split second, I thought the altar had cracked. Then Quinn sailed into view, leaping from the tall slab for Emmett. The gargoyle kept his wings clamped to his sides, but his massive paws were splayed wide, and his jaws gaped in a furious roar.

Quinn's citrine body didn't have blood for the Chief-maker to control, but Emmett didn't need to rely on the stone to overpower Quinn. With an effortless gust of blood-magic-drenched air, Emmett batted the gargoyle aside. Quinn cartwheeled helplessly across the tops of statues. With one wing bound to his side and the other locked in place to protect the firebird egg, he could do nothing to save himself. At the last second, he twisted his feet under himself as he landed. His claws scraped the cavern floor, but his momentum slammed him into the wall, crushing his already wounded wing. He crumpled and didn't rise.

A haze of red filmed my vision. "Quinn? Quinn!" I shoved against the ground with all my strength, but I only succeeded in straining my back muscles. Through a blur of tears, I hurled a flurry of air blades at Emmett. I didn't care where I hit him, so long as he hurt. So long as he died.

Emmett crushed my tiny weapons with negligible compresses of air. "Cease attacking me, little girl."

"Never."

His eyes bulged, and an angry red flush flared up his neck and across his hawkish features. When he spoke, his voice dropped to an inhuman growl. "You have to do what I say. I am the blood king. I have the power. You will not harm me." He shook the Chiefmaker at me, his other hand curled in a tight fist.

I formed another blade of air and shot it at Emmett's eye. It flew arrow-straight, but when it was a hand span from its target, I lost control, and the element unraveled. Unde-terred, I shot another. Again, my hold on the elemental weapon evaporated a second before it struck Emmett. My third attempt was equally futile, as was my fourth and my fifth. No matter how hard I concentrated, the moment my attacks closed in on Emmett, the Chiefmaker's compulsion made me spare the madman.

Despair weakened my resolve. Emmett didn't just control my blood through the Chiefmaker; he controlled all of me—my body, my magic, and my free will.

"No one can deny me. No one!" Emmett shouted, spittle flying. He spun, arms wide, addressing the cavern at large. "You will worship me. The whole world will kneel at my feet and obey me. I am the blood king. I am your *god*."

I glanced at Seradon. She wasn't doing anything but observing Emmett through slitted eyes. Fresh blood trickled down her temple and more soaked the knees of her pants, pooling outward. Golden bands of stolen blood magic seeped from her wounds to the Chiefmaker. I expected her to be fighting as hard as I was, but perhaps her head injury prevented her from using the elements, or maybe she had a strategy I couldn't fathom. Either way, I wasn't ready to give up my attack.

Gritting my teeth, I changed tactics, forming flames, ice, and shards of earth element, but none of my minuscule attacks could penetrate Emmett's compulsion, and they all dropped short of touching him. I grabbed pebbles from the cavern floor with tiny scoops of air, but every time I flung them at Emmett, the strength went out of my magic, and the projectiles clattered to the ground.

"No one can stand against me." Emmett spun to lock his fever-bright eyes on me. "Not a little girl like you, and not an FPD captain."

Frost coagulated my veins. No, he couldn't have—

"You're my lucky lady," Emmett said, blowing a kiss to Seradon. "You gave yourself to me, and then you brought me the rest of your team. Now I have you all, a full five, waiting on me." He glanced back toward the tunnels.

Waiting on him. That meant they were alive, right?

Emmett's blissful expression turned vicious when he spun to face Seradon. "Now I'm captain, and you must obey *me*."

The full import of his words sank in, and terror surged up my spine and crested my skull, leaving me light-headed. In the back of my mind, I had merely been keeping Emmett occupied until Grant and his team burst out of the tunnels and charged to our rescue. Instead, they were enslaved just like Seradon and I were. What else had Emmett done to them? How badly were they injured?

Grant won't give up. He will keep fighting. My assurances failed to give me hope. The Chiefmaker's power behaved like nothing I had encountered before. Not even Grant and his highly trained squad knew how to combat it. They would be just as helpless as Seradon and me.

"Maybe I will make you my queen," Emmett said, drawing closer to Seradon. His gaze oozed down her chest, and he leaned close, as if angling for a kiss. "Do you like the taste of blood, my queen?"

Seradon lunged, her knife aimed for Emmett's jugular. He jerked back and screamed, "Stop!"

The Chiefmaker flared with power, and Seradon froze. Cussing, Emmett stomped off, only to circle back. His legs swung choppily, as if his joints were mechanical and the cogs did not properly align. But the closer he got to Seradon, the more his steps smoothed out. He stopped in front of her again and stretched out a finger to poke the flat of the knife. Seradon held it rock steady, unable to do anything else until Emmett released her from his command.

Emmett poked the blade a second time, giggling. He

leaned forward and stretched his neck until the tip of the knife grazed his flesh.

"Is that all you got, sweetie?" he asked.

Seradon's arm quivered as she fought the compulsion. Sweat beaded on her forehead and rolled down her temples to drip off her jaw, but the tip of the knife didn't budge. Emmett cackled.

"Nothing can touch me. I'm invincible."

Fatigue saturated my limbs, and I abandoned my elemental attacks. Blood soaked my pants to my knee, and a small pool formed beneath my fist, dripping from the nick on my finger that should have long since coagulated. My shadow spun around my knees, and when I tipped my head back to check on the firebird, my eyes lost focus and the room darkened. Heart pounding, I dipped my chin to my chest until my vision cleared.

Emmett's mercurial mood snapped, and he stop laughing to snarl at Seradon. "How dare you try to hurt me. Cut your wrist and give me your blood."

Freed from Emmett's earlier order to freeze in place, Seradon slumped forward and planted her empty palm on the ground. Her upper body quivered with the effort to hold it there. In her other hand, the knife twisted, angling back toward her forearm. Then it clattered to the ground.

"That's not possible," Emmett shrieked. "You *must* obey me."

Seradon ignored him, her muscles shaking with strain. Her hand inched toward the knife.

"Hold still. Let me think," Emmett ordered.

Seradon froze, one hand hovering above the blade, but relief flashed in her eyes. I had assumed she had been striving to pick up the knife so she could stab Emmett, but now I realized she had been fighting the compulsion the whole time. Her arm was poised to cut her wrist, just as Emmett had ordered. Only, he hadn't specified which wrist, and she had been clever enough to use Emmett's ambiguity to buy herself time.

If only I could do the same.

Think, Kylie. Be clever.

Emmett had ordered me not to attack him, but what if something else in the room did? Like the lantern. I had left it on the other side of the altar, out of sight. Maybe I could fling it . . . No. Even if I dared wield enough air to lift the lantern, my magic would peter out before it struck Emmett, exactly as it had when I had attempted to fling rocks at him.

There had to be another way. I needed an external attack source, something independent of me or the elements.

I scanned the ceiling, hoping to find a convenient protrusion the temple creators had missed that I could drop on Emmett. Aside from the grotesque heads adorning the dome of the chamber, the ceiling was smooth. I considered and dismissed the white crystal mosaic pieces affixed to the wild eyes of the carving above Emmett. The stone shards were too small. Even if I could eyeball the trajectory so the crystals crashed directly on Emmett's head, using gravity rather than my untrustworthy magic, he would be able to easily deflect them. Whatever fell would need to be larger, bigger than Quinn, who Emmett had so easily tossed aside. If I could shear an entire creepy head off the ceiling, it might be enough to bury him, but Lunacy was more liable to injure me than Emmett if I used elements to chisel into the carving.

The firebird flashed past. She had ignored Emmett since he had flung her mate aside, but perhaps I could instigate her to attack. Firebirds were notoriously violent. She was plenty angry. All I needed was a means of directing her toward Emmett. If Quinn helped . . .

The gargoyle lay in a crumpled heap where he had crashed. Heart heavy, I tore my gaze from his motionless body.

I needed a different strategy.

I clapped my hand to my hip, pressing down on the oozing puncture. Blood slicked my palm and a nauseous wave of pain ran hot, then cold across my skin. The energy feeding from my injury to the Chiefmaker never ceased.

A whimper of despair squeezed my throat. Even if covering the wound *had* cut off Emmett's connection to the magic in my blood, it would only have been a stopgap measure. Emmett continued to draw power from Seradon's blood, and I could do nothing to prevent him from opening another of my cuts. With the Chiefmaker, he could order every single one of my wounds to start bleeding at once, if he wanted. He had all the power. He had—

That was it. Cutting off his access to my blood wasn't the solution. I needed to take away the source of his power.

Barely daring to breathe or hope, I formed a thin air blade, this time aiming it for the slender golden strands connecting the giant bloodstone to the rings on Emmett's fingers. Emmett paced, ranting about the powers he had been promised, his omnipotence, and his irresistibility to all women. I tuned him out. Fatigue weighted my magic, and guiding my delicate slices of air took all my concentration. I made clean cuts through the first two chains, then he about-faced, and my third blade wobbled, grazing his shirt. Hastily, I let the element evaporate, and I couldn't tell if the idea to do so had been mine or the compulsion of Emmett's order to not attack him. Bracing a hand against the ground for balance, I formed another sliver of razor-sharp air and clipped a third golden line. The next two cuts had to be synchronized—

Emmett glanced at me, and I yanked my gaze from the Chiefmaker to his face. He jerked the stone up to examine it, fury burning in his wild eyes when he spotted the broken chains. Clenching his fist around the bloodstone, he snapped his teeth at me, frothy spit dripping from his chin like a rabid animal.

"I will crush you," he bellowed. "Bleed for me. Bleed for your god."

Blood pumped from the puncture on my hip, running hot down my leg. Pain pricked my arms and scalp as scabs tore and blood welled from myriad wounds. A spray of bright energy gushed from me to the bloodstone, and I swayed, my vision darkening.

"You're no god," Seradon said, her derisive tone cutting through Emmett's building rant. "You're an ugly, trivial little man with puny power. You're not worthy of being called the blood king."

"Silence!" Emmett screamed, flinging his hand up, palms spread wide to concentrate the Chiefmaker's power on her. "No one speaks to me like that. No one. Choke on your words."

Seradon gagged, her body held frozen by Emmett's previous command while her face turned a dreadful shade of scarlet.

I grabbed the last of my flagging energy and speared two air blades straight for Emmett's splayed palm. The last of the gold chains snapped. The Chiefmaker dropped.

I toppled sideways, released from Emmett's control. Seradon sucked in a deep breath and leapt for Emmett, knocking him aside as he dove for the stone. I started to stand, but my vision tunneled, and I dropped to all fours.

Scrambling on hands and knees, I crawled across the dais. I could hear Seradon and Emmett fighting, but I didn't take my eyes off the bloodstone. I couldn't let Emmett regain control of the Chiefmaker. If he did, he would kill us all.

Someone's foot kicked the bloodstone, and I lurched to follow it. It bounced off a statue and fetched up against the steps of the dais. Emmett's tattered boot swept through my line of sight. I slammed a shoulder into his thigh and lunged past him, closing my fist around the Chiefmaker.

Energy surged through me, and I sprang to my feet. A tsunami of sickly sweet magic drowned my thoughts and reshaped the world. Emmett and Seradon transformed into two glowing power sources, the blood in their veins singing to me. It would be so easy to manipulate that delicious liquid. All I had to do was open my mouth and utter the words to make them my puppets. Not even Emmett, with his blood magic, could stop me. I was more powerful than him, more powerful than a dozen Emmetts—than a hundred Emmetts. My fear evaporated, taking with it the tension that had knotted my muscles since I had first caught whiff of Zipporah.

Now that I had the Chiefmaker, I never had to be afraid again.

My gaze swept the enormous carvings, all those mosaicked eyes staring, waiting to see what I would do. The first item on my agenda was leaving Lunacy. Nothing would stop me now. Nothing could. I would saunter back to the surface and breathe clean, untainted air. Then I would write a stupendous article about this whole endless day, Lunacy Labyrinth, camazotz and vampires and evil magic, the firebirds, and Thorpe and Emmett. I deserved to take the lead on this story. I had lived through it. I had *survived* it. I would convince Dahlia she was wasting my journalistic talents on filler articles for the business section.

I pictured my future articles printed on the *Chronicle's* front page, the headlines bold and exciting, the prose elegant and bursting with intriguing facts. Dahlia would grant me a position fitting of my skill at the top of the writer's pool. Above Nathan. I wouldn't have to hunt for answers for my stories, either. People would eagerly share what they knew, and if not, one command from me, and they would spill their life stories. Not even Grant would hold out on me. He would leap at every chance to be interviewed by me. He would do whatever I wanted, give me whatever I asked for.

I licked my lips, enchanted by the thought of Grant at my beck and call. He would love me, because I would demand it. I would have all the control in our relationship and never have to doubt where I stood with him again.

All the control.

Blinking rapidly, I stepped back, as if I could distance myself from my own thoughts. I wanted this. I wanted Grant. I wanted recognition from Dahlia and a promotion at the *Chronicle.* I wanted to walk out of this horrid labyrinth and leave all its traps and nastiness behind. So why was I hesitating? Why did I feel like I was battling myself?

Seradon spun in front of me, whipping a roundhouse kick into Emmett's side, and he crashed to his knees. She followed up with a jab to his temple, but her balance wobbled, and she toppled over, her blow glancing off his shoulder. Emmett lashed out with an elbow, striking Seradon in the gut before she regained her balance. I couldn't tell who was winning. It didn't matter. Both potential power sources would be useful to me.

I shook my head, denying the poisonous magic. These

thoughts weren't mine. They were the Chiefmaker, still trying to control me.

Life will be easy and perfect, the Chiefmaker whispered into my mind. *You are untouchable, the most powerful person in all the world.*

Emmett shoved Seradon aside with a battering of elemental magic. She fell against a wolverine statue, sprawling onto her butt. Before she could regain her feet, Emmett charged at me.

"It's mine. Give it to me!"

I backpedaled up the stairs, tripping and fetching up against the altar. The urge to draw upon the Chiefmaker's power flooded through me. I could crush Emmett. One command, and I could end his life.

The image of Emmett's broken body lying before me, his blood splashed across my feet, slammed to the forefront of my thoughts. I felt the exquisite warmth of his blood on my hands, tasted the savory copper on my tongue—

No! That was the Chiefmaker. Not me. I didn't want to kill Emmett, just stop him—and I could. I could forbid him from using blood magic. I could bind him and leave him for the FPD to deal with. That would be a good use of the Chiefmaker's power.

Seradon tripped Emmett, and he sprawled across the steps in an eerie imitation of my vision. This close, I could see flakes of dried blood in his greasy hair and grains of sand plastered to the fresher blood painted across his forehead. Fear sparked anew in my gut when our gazes collided. No humanity remained in his brown eyes, only raw avarice and madness.

The Chiefmaker pulsed in my palm, demanding to be used. I needed it to save myself. I needed it to bring this man to justice—my justice. He had hurt—*killed?*—Quinn. He needed to pay.

I glanced around for Quinn, but the fight had disoriented me, and I couldn't remember where he had fallen. I couldn't concentrate, not with the Chiefmaker pressuring me to use it. It wanted to help me. It wanted to make all my problems disappear.

Shaking my head, I pressed myself into the altar, clamping my lips tight. If I used the Chiefmaker, even once, even for something so righteous as vindicating Quinn, I would be accepting its poison into myself. It would infect me, turning me into a shell of a human, like Emmett.

"Gimme!" Emmett screeched, clawing up the steps.

I flung the bloodstone from me. My world constricted to my small awareness, and relief sang in my veins. The Chiefmaker clattered down the far side of the dais. Emmett tracked it with power-crazed eyes, ignoring me to clamber to the top of the dais. I shoved the stone with a punch of air, rolling it under the feet of the jaguar statue. Emmett dove from the top step after it. He landed on his stomach and swiped a hand beneath the jaguar's legs to seize the bloodstone.

"It's mine. Mine, mine, mine, mine," he chanted. Rocking back and forth, he clutched the bloodstone to his chest, failing to notice the stone jaguar metamorphosing into inky-black powder. It maintained its predatory shape as it swelled in size, its glossy black eyes snapping open to glare at the man who had dared disturb it. Fast as a real cat, it slapped a thick paw down on Emmett's chest, pinning him to the ground. The crazed man screamed as smoky claws sank into his chest. Twisting its head, the jaguar buried its fangs in Emmett's neck, and I flinched at the wet, sucking sound. Emmett's screams devolved to gurgles. I wanted to look away, but I couldn't, afraid to take my eyes from the deadly jaguar. A moment later, Seradon's thrown knife sprouted from Emmett's heart, and he convulsed, then stilled. The bloodstone rolled from his limp palm.

Inky cat eyes lifted to mine, my death promised in their depths. Then the lines of the jaguar hazed, and the intelligence bled from its gaze. An air current ran its fingers through the jaguar's body, distorting it into shapeless powder. I sagged against the altar.

Seradon limped to my side. "Good thinking with the stone," she rasped.

I tore my gaze from Emmett's body and the raw, mutilated mass of his throat.

A ghostly outline of a giant cat stalked through the deep shadows, and my heart lurched in my chest when I recognized the golden eyes glinting in the firebird's erratic light. Gaining speed, Quinn charged, bursting through the smoky remains of the jaguar. Rearing up, he released a furious roar and brought both front paws down on the bloodstone, pulverizing it.

Relief stole the strength from my legs, and I collapsed.

I must have passed out, because when I opened my eyes, Grant was leaning over me. New bruises darkened his jaw, and his mouth was swollen as if he had gotten into a fistfight. Blood oozed from his split lip. He had never looked more handsome: He was alive. Relief sang in my veins. I lifted my fingers to touch his cheek, but memory of the dark desires the Chiefmaker had pulled from my subconscious—to control Grant, to force him to love me— stilled my hand, and I let it drop without touching him. The movement jarred my arm, igniting a chorus of aches. The rest of my body chimed in until the throbbing in my hip drowned out all other pain.

"Can you stand?" Grant asked.

"Yes." I waited for a lynx's magic to expose my lie. When none didn't, I accepted Grant's hand. He pulled me to my feet, and I promptly bent in half to avoid passing out again. Blood loss sucked. An unexpected tightness constricted my hips, and I discovered a bandage cinched across the puncture, stanching the bleeding. How long had I been unconscious? What else had I missed?

I spun around, searching for Quinn.

"Take it easy," Grant said, steadying me by my elbows.

Quinn stood nearby, two firebirds perched atop him, both chattering away. The female roosted over the egg and the male stood between Quinn's drooping ears. Quinn peered anxiously at me through the male's glowing tail feathers. The fact that I had been oblivious to both the light source and the birds' racket told me I wasn't as cognizant as I thought.

"Quinn is fine," Grant said.

Quinn nodded, earning a scolding from the unbalanced male firebird.

"The egg?" I asked.

"It's fine, too. We need to move."

I blinked away the afterimage of the bright firebirds and glanced around, spotting the rest of the FPD squad near a tunnel on the far side of the cavern. The glow of their lanterns revealed torn clothing, bandaged wounds, and a plethora of bruises beneath a thick layer of grime. Marciano's right arm hung in a sling, and Velasquez had lost half his shirt, the remaining fabric singed and the exposed flesh sporting a painful red burn. The team looked as if they had gone up against a dragon and lost.

A bear statue in the center of the chamber burst into black powder with a pop of displaced air. Startled, I stumbled back against Grant's chest. The coalesced blood magic swirled to form enormous claws that slashed five times through the nearby air before dissipating. On the other side of the cavern, a black-smoke boar charged through the statues, its tusks leaving gouges in the solid stone idols it struck before it, too, dissipated.

"It's the firebirds," Grant said, his voice rumbling in my ear. "They're tearing this place apart."

I glanced around, stunned to find the shadowy elemental pollution missing from the air. The firebirds had succeeded in cleansing the dense layers of blood-magic taint from the heart of Lunacy with shocking speed.

"I thought you said the royal family used to bring firebirds down here all the time," I said, attempting to distract myself from the sublime heat radiating from Grant's chest. I longed to curl up against him and take a nap. It wasn't the most lustful thought I had ever entertained about Grant, but it sounded divine in the moment.

"Probably hooded and mute. Let's go."

Grant made sure I was stable on my own two feet; then he shouldered my bag and prompted Sooth to guide us through the maze of statues. Quinn followed. I kept a hand on Grant's arm for balance. I could walk, but my coordination remained sluggish.

When I spotted Emmett's body, I purposefully unfocused my gaze. I didn't need to see his mutilated throat again—the image was seared into my memory. Grant made no move to collect the body, either. Emmett would remain entombed here, in the heart of Lunacy, a fitting end for the megalomaniacal murderer.

My skin crawled when I spotted the glistening shards of the pulverized bloodstone next to him. The Chiefmaker's malignant power had come distressingly close to stripping my morality and turning me into a monster no different than Emmett. Quinn had done the world a favor when he had shattered the stone and its depraved magic.

I considered how furious Zipporah would be when I returned empty-handed, and I almost stooped to pick up the fragments despite my fear of the stone's residual powers. Zipporah never specified the condition the Chiefmaker had to be in when I fetched it. Dumping the shards at her feet and absolving my debt would be immensely satisfying. However, if even a fraction of the bloodstone's power remained active, it would be unconscionable to place it in the talons of the ruthless harpy. I would have to figure out a different way of paying my debt to Zipporah.

Another statue imploded, shooting dark spikes into the far wall, and I jerked my focus to the present moment. I could save worrying about my next encounter with Zipporah until after I had survived escaping Lunacy.

"Pair up," Grant instructed once we reached the others.

Winnigan and Marciano took the lead, Verity poised to precede them. Grant and I lined up behind them, and Seradon and Velasquez fell in behind Quinn, taking Sooth. Despite my fatigue, anticipation bubbled through me. I was beyond ready to see the last of this labyrinth.

"Speed is key," Grant said. "The firebirds are going to trigger traps, but don't engage unless you absolutely have to. The main goal is to escape this mountain before the firebirds collapse it on our heads."

As if to emphasize his point, the ground shook with an ominous rumble, and dirt trickled from the roof of the tunnel ahead of us. Without the tainted elements to purify, the firebirds' magic attacked the next perceived flaw in their surroundings: the man-made tunnels. Given enough time— or very little, considering how quickly they had purified centuries of blood-magic smut from the labyrinth's heart— the firebirds would collapse our escape route.

"Let's go." Winnigan broke into a ground-eating jog, and the rest of us surged after her.

I glanced back to check on Quinn. He ran with a crooked gait, but he looked determined—and absurd. The firebirds were perched atop him like bizarre tandem jockeys, the male crouched low on Quinn's mane, facing forward, his wings arched for balance to counter Quinn's loping bob, and the hen peered around her mate, leaning into the wind. The steady jostling and the novelty of a galloping golden perch did not faze the firebirds; they burst into a new, chipper song, their voices imitating the chirps and trills of sparrows greeting the morning sun. Astonishingly, they appeared to be enjoying themselves.

When I faced forward again, the afterimage of the firebirds blinded me, and I clutched Grant's belt for guidance until my vision cleared. I didn't look back again.

Tremors shook the passageway, and I tripped as the earth shifted beneath my feet. Dirt peppered my scalp and thickened the tunnels with dust. I feared that for the rest of my life, the smell of dust would trigger flashbacks of Lunacy. I also feared that I had already breathed in a pound of silt during the last twelve hours of avalanches and cave-ins, and this final sprint would prove too much for my lungs to process. By the time we reached the first intersection, I ran bent over, a stitch in my side, gasping tortured breaths through my open mouth.

Without slowing, Winnigan consulted her notebook, which contained a map similar to the one Grant had made, and selected the passage to the right. Behind us, the tunnel rumbled, then collapsed. We picked up the pace.

My lungs begged for fresh air, and my legs transformed into twin columns of cinder and pain. Fresh blood matted my pants beneath the bandage around my hip. Judging by the stinging on my forearm and neck, those cuts had reopened, too. I lost track of how many intersections we traversed. Winnigan's route to the heart had been a lot more convoluted than ours, and we ran for what felt like miles. My feet turned to lead, dragging me down, but so long as Grant and Quinn ran with me, I refused to give in to the urge to collapse. If I stopped, they would stop, and then we all would die.

Horrors sprang out of the dark—floating rats with vampiric fangs, winged scorpions with snake heads, shadows with claws, and plants with teeth—all the deadly defenses of the ancients, unleashed from their illusions by the firebirds' song. Some of the monsters were undone by the firebirds' same magic. Others we simply outran, while around us—above us—Lunacy crumbled.

When I thought my legs could carry me no farther, we burst out of the tunnel into the morning light in a cloud of dust and debris. I stumbled, blinded by sunlight and relief. I hadn't been buried alive. The tall canyons blurred in my vision. Clean air rasped hot down my throat, and tears mixed with sweat to drip off my chin. We hadn't escaped yet, but we had made it far enough to see the sky again.

Grant caught me when I my legs gave out, looping his arm beneath mine to support the brunt of my weight. If I had possessed the lung capacity or the energy, I might have protested, but exhaustion had divested me of my pride. Ahead of us, Marciano tripped and staggered against Winnigan. She bolstered him, looping an arm around his waist. None of the squad ran with their usual grace, and our sprint had slowed to a fatigue-drunk stumble. Willpower alone propelled us forward. My awareness narrowed to my feet. Lift, plant. Lift, plant. Keep moving. Escape.

I didn't notice we had stumbled free of the walls of Lunacy until clean, pure elements caressed my senses, boosted by Quinn's enhancement. The sensation was so marvelous that I felt like I could float away on the unsullied magic.

Or be floated away.

Grant supported me on a cushion of air, carrying me

another twenty feet before setting me down beneath the shade of an oak tree. Quinn staggered to the trunk and dropped, managing to keep his spine horizontal even if his heavy landing bounced the firebirds. Gasping for breath, I closed my eyes and dug my fingers into the soil, reassuring myself that we had made it. The ground rumbled and shook as cave-ins continued to tear apart the ruins, but we were safe.

The squad collapsed around me, but they didn't rest. Winnigan linked with Marciano, and she wielded a complex blend of the five elements as she healed Seradon's head. Beside me, Grant linked with Velasquez and crafted a succinct message, summoning healers from Terra Haven. He wrapped it in a coil of air, and the elemental bundle blasted off for the city.

"Send for Mika," I said. "Quinn needs her."

Quinn's head drooped across his front paws, tilting far enough forward to dislodge the male firebird. The bird flapped awkwardly, only partially unfurling his left wing; then he strutted around Quinn to climb atop the gargoyle's haunches. In the daylight, the firebirds' glow appeared muted, lending Quinn's citrine body a warm aura, as if the light radiated from inside him as well as from their feathers. Their golden hue also highlighted the pained furrow of Quinn's brow. He lay stiff, canted away from his bound wing. I yearned to help him, but the most I could do was cleanse the bird poop from his mane and flank with gentle brushes of water and air. When he didn't open his eyes or acknowledge the gesture, I knew his injuries must be worse than he let on.

Velasquez spoke a short message to Mika, including instructions for her to travel using his personal flying carpet.

"I left it in the courtyard. The activation is two parts fire, one part earth. Be safe, little guardian."

His endearment jolted me. In all the excitement, I had forgotten the large fire elemental and my best friend were dating.

Once Velasquez's message was safely on its way, Grant formulated a report to his superiors, requesting another FPD squad be deployed to our location to restore the ward. With nothing to do—nothing I *could* do—I lay flat on my back, admiring the blue sky through the sun-dappled oak leaves. I finally caught my breath, though each inhale scraped like sand down my esophagus, and I had to fight not to cough. I did my best not to think about the rest of my body. Giving it any sort of attention intensified its pain. If I had been shoved through an industrial printing press, then dragged across a desert by a noose around my neck, I didn't think I would have felt any worse. Instead, I concentrated on the most important fact: we had all made it out alive.

Grant sent a final message, this time to the mayor. If she responded promptly to his request, a contingent of city guards would soon arrive to monitor the grounds of Lunacy until the ward could be reinstated.

The rumble of the labyrinth kept me from fully relaxing into the nap my body craved, and after a while, I sat up, biting off a moan when fresh pain stabbed my hip. At some point, Winnigan had finished treating Seradon and pulled Velasquez aside to tend his burns. Only Grant remained next to me and Quinn on this side of the tree.

"Seradon told me what you did," Grant said. "Cutting the chains on the Chiefmaker was smart thinking—and something none of us thought to do."

I shrugged away his praise, uncomfortable with it. My

reasoning hadn't been especially brilliant: I had been desperate and panicking, willing to try anything. I had gotten lucky, too. For all I had known, the Chiefmaker's power could have remained in effect even after Emmett lost contact with it.

"Seradon also said you held the bloodstone," Grant said.

My palms tingled at the memory, and I squeezed my hands together into a single fist. The Chiefmaker's promised power stalked through my thoughts, clawing at my darker desires. I shoved them back out of sight, where they belonged.

"It affected you, didn't it?" he prompted.

"It tried." I leaned forward, peering at my ruined boots without really seeing them. I considered leaving it at that, but when Grant didn't press, I pushed my hair out of my face and studied his expression. Weariness sat heavy on his features, but his eyes were soft and interested. Even exhaustion couldn't suppress my zing of pleasure at being the center of his attention.

"It promised power," I said, keeping my voice low so it carried no farther than the two of us. "When I held it, I could see how blood magic worked. I could see the energy inside Seradon and Emmett and how to control it. I could have commanded them—or anyone—to do anything, and they would have been compelled to obey. It was . . ." I dropped my gaze, then forced myself to meet his eyes again. "It was hard to resist."

Grant arched a brow. "The ability to make anyone do anything I wanted? Yeah, that would be hard to resist."

I forced a feeble smile in response to the teasing in his tone, but I couldn't sustain it. "I don't like what it unearthed in me."

"You mean that you're not a paragon of humanity? Try

not to be shocked, my dear journalist, but most people harbor some dark fantasies."

"I know, I just . . ."

"Thought you might be different?"

I nodded, irritated to discover I was so transparent.

"Trust me, you're different. For starters, you're nothing like what I expected an heiress to be."

"Should I be flattered or insulted?" I asked.

"The entitled wealthy seldom fight alongside the FPD. It was refreshing."

I decided not to point out that most people—wealthy or not—were smart enough not to get themselves into situations that required them to go to battle alongside the FPD.

We sat in silence for a few minutes, listening to the firebirds' melody before I gathered enough courage to ask, "Am I what you expected of a journalist?"

Grant draped his forearms on his raised knees, taking his time answering. "If every reporter was like you, I would have to reformulate my opinion about the whole profession."

This time, smiling required no effort. Grant smiled back before breaking eye contact to focus on something beyond my shoulder.

"Unfortunately, I've met other reporters," he said, his tone losing its warmth. "Speaking of which, your favorite person just arrived."

I followed his line of sight and groaned. "Ugh. Nathan."

The senior journalist coasted above a little-used road atop one of the *Chronicle*'s flying carpets, looking refreshed and clean. His eyes narrowed behind his thick-framed glasses when he spotted me. A lecture brewed in his disapproving expression. I rolled my eyes and turned away, hoping just this once, if I pretended he didn't exist, he would disappear.

My gaze snagged on a small clear ward squatted several yards away next to the road. The elemental dome was embossed with the FPD's insignia, and it encased the stolen firebird shipping containers. The squad must have discovered and quarantined them before entering the labyrinth. Both wooden-slat boxes had been heavily damaged, either when Thorpe and Emmett had stolen the birds or later when they had pried the birds out and bound them in torturous knots. The golden perches that had once been inside were missing, likely lost inside Lunacy.

With the murderers dead, the crates would no longer be necessary evidence in a future trial. Furthermore, between Quinn and the egg nestled on his back, the firebirds were essentially contained, making the crates moot at this point—all except one little detail: the winged A of the Airstrong logo branded into the side of each.

My parents' company had been responsible for shipping the firebirds.

My mom had lied to me.

Releasing a ragged breath, I replayed our conversation. Even though it felt like I had spoken with my mom a lifetime ago, it had been only yesterday, and I recalled her words verbatim. *We haven't misplaced a single package since we opened our doors,* she had promised me.

You misplaced this one, Mom, I silently accused.

She had purposely misled me, and I couldn't fathom why. Perhaps her contract had stipulated she couldn't reveal information about the firebirds. Or maybe she hadn't trusted my motives. Maybe she had thought I would rush off to the *Chronicle* with my exclusive, and I would drag my parents' names through the mud just to see an article printed in the paper.

Except, who shipped the firebirds would have become a non-story the moment I learned Airstrong was responsible. Even before I knew of Emmett, Thorpe, and the connection between Lunacy and firebirds, I would never have doubted my parents' innocence, and I never would have written an article that would have hurt them. My mom's lack of faith in me elicited a dull stab of pain in my chest.

I rubbed my temples, another tidbit of our conversation replaying in my head: My mom had let slip that she had come to Terra Haven to sort out *staffing issues*. Of course she had. The driver of the firebird shipment had been injured too badly to work, and rumors were circulating that he might have been in on the theft. Naturally, the boss had flown in to sort out the matter. How had I missed such an obvious clue?

Nathan floated once around the warded containers before angling for our bedraggled group. So much for my fervent hope that he would spontaneously vanish.

"I'll take care of him," Grant said, rocking to his feet and striding out from under the tree to intercept Nathan. If not for the grit coating Grant and the bandages visible beneath the tears in his bloodstained clothing, no one would have ever suspected he had just survived a night in Lunacy Labyrinth. He carried himself tall, his perfect posture accentuating his wide shoulders. Even exhausted and battered, Grant gave the impression that he could take on an army of lamassu without backup. Next to him, Nathan would never look like anything more than a gangly child.

"Captain Monaghan, it's good to see you safe and, well, not sound, but," Nathan fumbled through his fawning greeting, ending with a lame, "uh, alive."

"Yes, I think so myself," Grant said.

Nathan deactivated the carpet's flying spell and stood, waving a hand in my direction. "What's she doing here?"

"Ms. Grayson is here regarding the firebirds."

"Is that so?" Nathan gave me a squinty-eyed glare.

"Were you sent with a message for her, or are you here following up on the murderers we tracked down?"

Nathan's attention snapped to Grant. "Murderers? More than one person was responsible? Who were they? And what happened to the ward?"

"At this point in time, we are not revealing the murderers' identities. I can tell you that they were blood-magic users and employed an illegal and lethal spell to bring down Lunacy Labyrinth's ward."

"Did they—and you—enter Chicomoztoc?" Nathan asked, using the ruins' formal name, likely because he thought it made him sound smarter.

"My team and I, along with Ms. Grayson, tracked the men inside."

Nathan shot me a vile glare before Grant's words recaptured his attention.

"We were unable to apprehend the murderers, but they will no longer trouble the citizens of Terra Haven . . ."

Grant's voice dipped below the susurrus of the wind through the trees, and I didn't strain to hear the rest of his conversation. I had lived through the events; I didn't need to listen to them rehashed.

Quinn opened his eyes long enough to spread his uninjured wing toward me, bridging the firebird-enforced gap between us. I stroked my fingers down his stone feathers, wishing I could hug him. When he closed his eyes, I let my eyelids drop, too. A tingling burn radiated from my eyeballs. Being awake for twenty-four hours and spending half that time in one dust cloud or another hadn't done my eyes any favors. Keeping them closed helped soothe them. It also blocked out the scowls Nathan cast in my direction while Grant talked, so it was a double win.

The heavy beat of enormous wings jerked my eyes open minutes later. A trio of gryphons touched down, carrying a troop of city guards, and Grant dismissed Nathan to coordinate with the new arrivals. Rather than question the other members of the FPD squad as I would have, Nathan sauntered over to me. He stopped close enough that I had to stretch my neck to look up at him, and knowing him, he had positioned himself purposely.

"I hope this taught you not to steal other people's stories," he said. "It never turns out well."

I gaped at him. "*What?* Do you honestly think I waltzed into Lunacy Labyrinth to follow a lead on *your* story?"

"I think you were assigned piddly fluff pieces, and you decided you'd try to ride my coattails to a better article. I saw you at Capstone's warehouse yesterday, and you spent even more time at Airstrong." He crossed his arms and smirked down at me. "The facts don't lie: you were trying to steal my story."

"You followed me?" Outrage spiked my voice, and several guards' heads turned in our direction, but I didn't care. Dahlia had assigned Nathan the paper's top story, and he had wasted time trailing me? "Why? Did you think I would uncover something you had missed?"

Nathan scoffed, but I detected an infinitesimal flinch first. He really had been following me, hoping I would provide him with a lead. What a lowlife.

"I know you're eager for advancement," Nathan said, condescension dripping from his words, "but stealing other people's stories is not the proper way to get it."

His audacity tongue-tied me. How could he not see the hypocrisy of his accusation? He had literally stolen my last big article before I left for the everlasting tree. He wouldn't have been following me yesterday unless he had planned to steal from me again. It made me question how honestly he had come by his senior journalist title. How many other writers had he nicked stories from? Unfortunately, he had worded his rebuke in such a way that the lynxes didn't even flick an ear in our direction. If I tried to defend myself, or even better, denounced Nathan as a liar and the true story thief, I would only make myself look guilty. Besides, no one but the two of us was paying attention to our conversation now. Arguing with Nathan about his lack of ethics wouldn't change a thing—and it would require energy I didn't have.

I made a mental note to be more vigilant, though. If this slimeball ever thought to trail me again, I wanted to be aware of it.

"It's good I'm not writing about the murderers, then," I said, using my most patronizing tone. "I'm writing about the firebirds."

"The firebirds are part of my story on the murder," Nathan argued. "Captain Monaghan just said as much."

"*Captain Monaghan* doesn't dictate my articles." I planted my hands behind me and leaned back to ease the discomfort in my kinked neck. The reclined position also prevented me from taking a swing at Nathan's groin, which was conveniently within range of my fist.

Winnigan knelt beside me. "Perhaps you two can postpone this argument for a day in which Kylie did not almost die."

Nathan blushed and ducked his head, making a good show of appearing abashed, but as he walked away, he muttered, "We'll see what Dahlia says."

I ground my molars together and glared at his receding backside, imagining it bursting into flames.

"Old lover?" Winnigan asked.

I jerked and checked her placid expression. "Ew, no. He's just an idiot who likes to tell me how to do my job."

"Ah, I've met the type. Lie back."

I glanced around. Marciano's arm still hung in a sling, and Grant's abdomen hadn't been treated.

"Don't give me special treatment just because I'm a civilian. Marciano's arm—"

"Has to wait," Winnigan interrupted. "Mending a broken bone takes a lot of energy and finesse, and I used up my reserves of both on Seradon's thick skull. But I can stop your bleeding, especially with the boost Quinn is giving my powers."

I shot the gargoyle a sharp look. "Are you in any shape to be boosting anyone right now?"

"It's helping distract me. Besides, it feels good to hold clean elements."

Winnigan gave my shoulders a gentle shove. Giving in, I stretched out on the weed-tufted ground, and Quinn retracted his wing to give her room to work. She used a short knife to slice through the makeshift bandage circling my hips, then cut away my pants around the puncture wound. The sharp pangs of pulled scabs transitioned to white-hot agony as her healing spell delved into my flesh. I bit my lip to hold in a scream.

"All done." Winnigan patted my knee and shoved herself to her feet, hobbling away to sit next to Marciano.

The pain took longer to recede. When it abated, I sat up to examine the wound. A shallow gash remained, but the worst of the damage seemed to have been healed. The rest —including the numerous scrapes and cuts scattered across my body—could wait for the more rested hands of a healer. I waved my thanks to Winnigan, and she smiled wanly.

Quinn released a long sigh when I pulled his wingtip back across my lap. I petted his feathers and stared blindly at the bright blue sky, savoring being alive and free of Lunacy. The city guards fanned out around the massive ruins, air messages spinning between them and back to Terra Haven as they coordinated to secure the grounds. Nathan walked among them, gathering facts for his story. If I could have summoned the energy, I might have envied him. He was going to make the front page once again.

Grant returned to sit next to me, close enough for our shoulders to touch. He didn't appear inclined to talk, and I was more than happy to sit in companionable silence.

Quinn quivered, and his head jerked around in alarm. He half folded his wing as if preparing to leap to his feet.

"What is it?" I asked.

"Something just happened. I think it moved."

"What moved?"

Quinn's round eyes glowed with alarm. "The egg."

The male firebird hopped to the ground beside Quinn, craning to see over the gargoyle's bound wing, and his melody altered from desultory chirps to a repetitive four-beat trill. The female scooted backward, revealing the egg. Cocking her head, she examined it with one eye, then the other. After giving it a gentle nudge with her beak, she sat back to sing, this time releasing long, crooning notes that harmonized with her mate's rhythmic trill.

Everyone jumped when the closest plateau inside Lunacy collapsed, crumbling down upon itself in a thunderous avalanche as the towering rock spontaneously pulverized into loamy soil. The next closest plateau imploded before the first had finished falling, disappearing behind billowing plumes of dust. Then the next toppled, as if a series of explosions were demolishing them. The collapsing ruins were deafening, but somehow the firebirds' song lifted over it, providing a musical score for the destruction. A wall of dust billowed outward from the labyrinth, poised to fall over us.

More silt for my lungs, I thought, too astounded by the devastation to be afraid.

Before the dirt cloud reached us, the city guards erected a shield over our group, holding the grit at bay and protecting us from the fallout. I could have cheered.

The egg rocked. The firebirds' song accelerated. Obscured in dust, centuries-old labyrinth plateaus collapsed like toppled dominoes. The devastation seemed far more removed than a mere shield could account for. I could see it. I could hear it. But my magical senses were being bathed in the firebirds' magic, and the sensation overwhelmed all the others. The elements purified around us, crystallizing, as the world sharpened into hyper-clear focus. I cycled through the elements, savoring the cleanliness of each. Only the everlasting tree had felt similar, but the tree's magic had radiated outward from its thick trunk; the firebirds' magic enveloped me and expanded beyond the boundaries of my senses.

Wonder struck, I watched saplings push through the soil where the labyrinth had stood moments earlier, the forest growing in minutes to reclaim the long-tainted land. Wind swirled above the new growth, siphoning dust from the air and settling it around the trees' expanding roots.

This was the awesome power of the firebirds' song. This was the invaluable magic that had been slated for fire-ravaged Timber Cove.

The dirt beneath my hands wriggled, and I squeaked.

Grant leapt to his feet and pulled me up beside him, keeping an arm locked around me as if he thought he might need to lift me. Crisp green grass pushed through the soil, growing inches tall in seconds. The creak and rustle of larger vegetation followed—lilacs, purple needlegrass, poppies, and columbine. They writhed skyward, bursting into flowers and nearly burying Quinn and the firebirds. I breathed deep, inhaling the clean scent of spring and life.

The egg rocked again, and tiny fractures crackled its surface. Then a sharp beak poked through the shell, shattering it. A bedraggled, fleshy baby bird flopped wetly onto Quinn's back. Quinn flexed his working wing muscle, creating a barrier to prevent the hatchling from sliding off his slick spine. The tiny bird shoved itself awkwardly to its rump, lifting a long neck to meet Quinn's eyes as the gargoyle peered over his shoulder.

"Hello, beautiful," Quinn said, his expression smitten.

The firebirds' song softened to gentle tremolos and warbles, both parents singing the same notes in harmony. The air shimmered around their beaks, the elements sharpening to an almost painful, unnatural purity. Again, their song changed, each firebird releasing a long, sustained croon. The notes struck the sharpened elements and compressed them, forming a glossy pea-size pearl at the tip of each of their beaks. When they took a breath, the pearls dropped to the ground.

The firebirds fell out of synchronicity after that, increasing their tempos to materialize pearl after pearl from raw elements and sound, until a rain of opalescence dripped from their beaks. The hen leaned over the hatchling and, without breaking her rhythm, let two pearls fall into the baby's open mouth. It swallowed the pearls whole, then closed its bulbous eyes and nodded off. As if they had been waiting for this signal, the firebirds quieted, settling down to preen their feathers.

I shared a speechless glance with Grant. A pile of pearls lay like hail around Quinn's body, caught in the crook of his wings and clustered around the sleeping hatchling. Bending, I picked up one that had rolled against my boot. It felt as solid and real as an oyster's pearl, but the tiny nutritional capsule was shot through with the same golden light of the firebirds' feather.

Grant tugged his everlasting seed from his pocket and held it next to the pearl in my palm. Though much larger than the pearl, his seed matched its shape, color, and texture. He reached for the pearl, hesitated, then plucked it from my palm and laid it on his hand next to the seed. An intricate swirl of wood and water elements burst from the seed and absorbed the pearl. When the magic receded, the pearl had vanished, and a beige stone twice the original seed's size lay in its place. Porous and shaped like a melted pillar, it resembled a plain hunk of pumice. Grant rolled it in his palm, and the stone's rough surface rasped against his calluses.

"Do you know what it means?" I asked.

The corner of his mouth kicked up in the smallest of smiles. "Maybe." He brushed a lock of hair from my face, gently hooking it behind my ear. His hand lingered against my jaw a moment longer before he dropped it, but he didn't step back. "If I'm right, this is about to get very interesting."

EPILOGUE

"Can you believe this?" I rattled the newspaper at Quinn. He lifted his head and peered over my shoulder. We were lounging on the roof above my apartment, enjoying the last rays of this long day under the open sky. A night trapped underground in Lunacy had left us both reluctant to linger in a confined space, not even inside my familiar, safe apartment, and the rooftop accommodated both of us better, anyway. I rested my head on the roof's peak, my legs bent and feet braced to prevent me from sliding down the shingles. Quinn lay sprawled across the ridge on his stomach, his wings fanned out to expose alarmingly large patches of clear crystal interlaced with his golden citrine, where Mika had mended his torn body.

She had flown up to the ruins at a breakneck speed that Oliver had been hard-pressed to match, arriving shortly after the firebirds had been coaxed from Quinn's back. Oblivious to the rest of us, Mika had flung herself from the still-moving carpet and rushed to Quinn's side. Using her unique magic, she healed his wounds—a task so extensive that she collapsed from fatigue afterward. Fortunately, by then a team of healers had arrived, and they bullied her into accepting their care. I also received my fair share of being bossed around by healers, and all my cuts, scrapes, and bruises had been mended with elemental finesse. The only thing they hadn't been able to repair was my broken camera.

Afterward, despite the hubbub of healers, guards, FPD personnel, city officials, general gawkers, and a flurry of journalists from neighboring cities that had all flocked to the transformed ruins, plus the novelty of a baby firebird only a few feet away, my body succumbed to exhaustion, and I had drifted in and out of consciousness in the shade of the oak tree.

Quinn had spent my nap time assisting the aviculturist. It was her specialized skills—along with a sturdy metal tree covered with gold flakes and a nest of woven golden twigs into which the hatchling had been levitated—that had convinced the firebirds to part with Quinn. However, the firebirds had formed a rapport with my gargoyle, and Quinn alone was able to keep the birds calm and prevent them from attacking anyone who came within ten feet of their baby.

Since most of the firebirds' magic had been expended during the hatching, it no longer made sense to ship the birds to the coast. Instead, the mayor decided to relocate them to Emerald Crown Grove. The grove had recently been devastated by a crazed spriggan, and despite all the recovery efforts the city had made, the acres of ravaged forest were a long way from restored. Though the firebirds' magic would fade as the hatchling matured, in the meantime, it wouldn't go to waste.

The aviculturist wisely requested Quinn's assistance

with the transportation of the birds, and he woke me before they left. I watched enviously as the gargoyle and firebirds departed in the back of an open-air wagon. Quinn sprawled in the ample space around the base of the metallic tree; the hen roosted on the edge of the pearl-filled nest, stuffing her hatchling with the magical seeds; and the male firebird perched atop the tree's upper branches, squawking his displeasure with the whole affair and occasionally flapping his wings aggressively at nothing. The sight made me smile. At some point, someone had healed both birds, and despite the torment they had endured, both would have the chance to live long, healthy lives in the wild. A squadron of guards flanked the wagon, on hand to protect the expensive gold-plated tree as much as its occupants. The city was taking no chances with the firebirds.

A spurt of anxiety had jolted me when the firebirds disappeared from sight. Retrieving my everlasting seed from my apartment before the birds were transported had never been an option, but I couldn't help but worry that my opportunity to evolve my seed might be disappearing along with the birds. All my hopes rested on the feather tucked deep in my bag, but what if it wasn't enough? What if I had already missed my chance? If my seed required the firebirds' hatching song or some combination of the firebirds and Lunacy to evolve, I had no shot at ever recreating the appropriate circumstances to trigger the seed's metamorphosis.

Why hadn't I kept the seed on me?

I had planned on going with Quinn and the firebirds. I hadn't wanted to be parted from Quinn any more than I had wanted to miss out on the final details of the firebirds' relocation for the story I planned to pitch to Dahlia. However, my attempt to walk resulted in me face-planting in the dirt, so it had been Nathan who accompanied my gargoyle and the firebirds—and Nathan who wrote the article for the paper. After his lecture about not stealing other journalists' articles, he not only jumped on my story about the firebirds, but he also rushed back to the *Chronicle* to write it up before I had a chance to return to the city. Apparently even his comment about letting Dahlia determine who could claim the story had been a lie.

Eventually, I regained enough strength to sit in the healers' floating wagon and take the long, slow flight back to Terra Haven with Seradon, Winnigan, and Marciano. Mika and Oliver stayed behind to fly back with Velasquez. The large fire elemental and Mika had fussed over each other and been in quiet conversation since she had recovered from healing Quinn. I tried not to let my envy show.

Grant hadn't been given a reprieve and gave no indications of needing one—or of returning to the city. As soon as the healers finished tending him, he had been inundated by people needing his expertise, and he spent the morning coordinating between city officials, guards, and the relief FPD squad in between fending off independent journalists and corralling busybodies. There hadn't been time to inquire about his question for the everlasting tree, let alone time for a private moment to figure out exactly where we stood with each other. We had come *this* close to kissing in the first cavern before the firebird had interrupted us by laying her egg. Replaying the memory made my stomach flutter, and I was anxious to determine if Grant still felt the same attraction in broad daylight, without a post-battle rush skewing his emotions.

When I settled in the wagon, I chanced a glance in Grant's direction. He stood in deep discussion with a guard, a gryphon rider, and the mayor herself. Dirt streaks dulled his mahogany hair, and dried blood matted his forehead. His official clothing resembled something a ceberi might have used as a chew toy. He had been awake for over twenty-four hours, had battled forbidden magic and monsters thought long extinct, and had survived the collapse of Lunacy. He should have appeared weary. Instead, he radiated strength and virility.

As if he sensed my perusal, Grant glanced up. A familiar zing of awareness shot down my spine when our gazes connected. The wagon shifted beneath me, gliding into motion, but I didn't look away.

Neither did Grant.

From this distance, I couldn't tell if I imagined the smoldering intensity of his gaze or if he was merely squinting. Then he smiled, the fractional curve of his lips hinting at dimples and secretive thoughts, and my stomach somersaulted. The mayor tapped Grant's arm to get his attention, but he didn't look away until several seconds later when a bend in the road broke our visual link. Only then did I realize I had twisted backward in my seat to stare at Grant. My breath gusted out on a loud exhale, and I flushed with embarrassment, but I smiled the whole way to Terra Haven.

By the time I arrived home, I had recovered well enough to walk unaided. I had also built up an appetite that eclipsed even my desire for a shower. After making myself an enormous sandwich, I carried it and the evening edition of the *Terra Haven Chronicle* to the roof. Quinn landed on the ridge next to me as I took my first bite, and he filled me in on the firebirds' relocation while I ate. His account proved far more informative and thorough than Nathan's article about the same thing.

At least the firebird story wasn't the story of a lifetime, I reasoned.

Just a piece of it.

Which Nathan had stolen.

I ground my teeth. If I were being ruthlessly honest with myself, Nathan had been right to take the firebird article. Aside from rescuing the firebirds or surviving the harrowing trip through Lunacy with them, Nathan had been present for all the pertinent events of the story—the hatching, the ancient blood-magic ruins being demolished, the forest regrown with the power of the firebirds' song, and the firebirds' relocation. I had been too weak to follow the story, and I hadn't made it back to the city before the evening deadline. If Nathan had left the story to me, the *Chronicle* would have been a day behind every other regional newspaper in covering the details. He had done what was best for our paper, and a rational part of me approved.

It didn't mean I had to be happy, though. I had unique insights about the firebirds that would have enhanced the article—if Nathan had taken the time to ask me. He hadn't even bothered to get a quote from Quinn, the only gargoyle in history to take part in a firebird hatching. Quinn had been so excited about being interviewed, and my heart hurt for my friend when I realized Nathan had denied him that small honor.

I glared at the front-page headlines, both stories anchored with Nathan's byline. The firebird article had garnered one-fourth of the front-page column space. The other three-fourths were dedicated to details of Lunacy and the murderers.

Nathan had laid out the facts in chronological order, managing to transform the terrifying events into a dry recounting that read like a stale pulp fiction novel: the three criminals' blood-magic-fueled firebird heist; the exsanguination of one of the criminals, the man sacrificed by his own comrades to bring down Lunacy's ward; Thorpe's and Emmett's deaths at the hands of the labyrinth; the baby firebird hatching and the adult birds' magic pulverizing Lunacy; the new ward erected around the former labyrinth; and the planned cleansing of the remaining traces of blood magic from the land. The last would have to wait until the tunnels of Lunacy finished collapsing in hazardous sinkholes.

Unsurprisingly, Nathan skipped all mention of my role in battling the murderers and bringing down Emmett. Being scrubbed from the story was no less than I expected from the duplicitous reporter, but for once, I approved. Grant and his squad deserved the credit. I would have been happy to remain behind the scenes, but Nathan had his own agenda.

"Can you believe this?" I repeated, rage adding a tremor to my hands and rattling the paper.

"What does it say?" Quinn asked, giving up on trying to read over my shoulder.

I resisted the urge to shred the paper into confetti and held it up to the dying light to better see the small print as I read aloud. "'The original shipping crates for the invaluable birds were discovered on the outskirts of Lunacy Labyrinth, proving that Airstrong Shipping was responsible for the abducted firebirds. Airstrong owners Owen and Charlotte Grayson could not be reached for questioning.' Then Nathan included a quote from Airstrong's rival, Luther Wetherill." I gave Wetherill a pompous voice when I read his statement. "'Airstrong Shipping failed to deliver the firebirds as their contract stipulated. That's not the way a trustworthy business operates. Even more curious is how the firebirds were discovered in the possession of the Airstrong heiress.' Nathan doesn't stop there, either. Listen to how he piles on to Wetherill's insinuations: 'The Graysons' daughter, Harriet, has been operating seemingly independent of her parents' business, under the alias Kylie Grayson. However, speculation remains as to how she became involved in the firebird fiasco.'"

The paper crumpled in my fists. "That bastard. 'Operating under the alias'? Could he have chosen more suspicious wording? With the firebirds discovered in my 'possession' and me 'involved in the firebird *fiasco*,' the jerk made me sound like a felon."

The empty plate that had been resting on my stomach skittered down the roof. I caught it with a clutch of air, dropping it safely to the deck below when it would have been more satisfying to smash it.

"He came this close"—I held my thumb and forefinger a hair's width apart—"to open slander. Actually, this might be worse. He implied I was part of some grand cover-up for my parents or that I was in on the theft to begin with. If I attempt to deny anything, it's only going to feed the story."

It galled me to acknowledge Nathan might never have discovered my real identity if I hadn't led him right to my mother. I should have known better than to visit the Airstrong headquarters. I should have found a different way to get information about the firebirds, but I had been in a rush to follow my seed's clue, and now . . .

The despicable paragraph caught my eye again, surging white-hot fury through my veins. "How dare Nathan splash my name across the paper like I'm a fugitive he's unmasked. I have worked long and hard to separate myself from my parents, and in one short line, he destroyed it all." The paper ripped an inch down the middle, and I tore it the rest of the way with a snarl. "I bet Wetherill leapt at the chance to be quoted in this article.

He's my parents' chief competitor. He probably set up the meeting with Nathan, eager to use the *Chronicle* to malign my parents and bolster his own business. This is crass journalism, and I can't believe Dahlia let this go to print." I smoldered at the byline, seeing Nathan's smug smile overlaying his name. "Next time I see that weasel, I'm planting a fist in his face."

"Is it really so bad for people to know who your parents are?" Quinn asked.

I jackknifed up. "Yes! You saw how Grant reacted. When he discovered I was *Harriet* Grayson, he decided I couldn't be serious about being a journalist—and he already knew me. For some reason, people don't think a woman who has wealthy, influential parents can have dreams of her own."

"But Grant knows you're serious now."

"It would take a long time if I had to individually convince every person in Terra Haven of my honest intentions."

Quinn scanned the rooftops visible along the horizon, understanding replacing his confusion.

"Plus, I wanted to know I earned my position at the *Chronicle* based on merit, not because Dahlia wanted to pander to my parents. I don't want to go back to wondering if a person is being friendly to me because they like me or they like my social standing. Living in anonymity these last few years has been a blessing."

It was a lifestyle I planned on reinstating posthaste, too. I would distance myself from anything related to Airstrong or my parents. Actually, avoiding my parents sounded perfect. I needed time to get over the sting of not being trusted by my mom.

"Maybe no one will realize Nathan was talking about you," Quinn said. "There are other people with the last name Grayson, right? Plus, the line was buried in the middle of the article. You always say most people read the beginning and the end, but they often skip the middle."

"Maybe." People in the general public might not recognize me as Kylie Grayson, Airstrong heiress when I approached them for interviews, but my coworkers would know. Hopefully this wouldn't alter their opinions of me. If I laid low for the next few weeks, maybe the whole thing would blow over—

"Oh crap. Mika."

She didn't know, and I didn't want her to find out from the newspaper.

"You're going to tell her?" Quinn asked.

I flopped back onto the roof. "The first chance I get." I hoped she would forgive me for deceiving her.

"What did Nathan say about the Chiefmaker?" Quinn asked.

"Next to nothing." I squinted at the torn pieces of newspaper in the fading light and selected the appropriate tatter. "'In the process of the labyrinth's collapse,'" I read, "'the Chiefmaker, a jewel coveted by the murderers, was destroyed.'" I let the newspaper fall to my lap. "He didn't even get that right."

"I'm sorry."

"About what?" I braced myself on an elbow and rolled toward Quinn to better see his expression. The oranges of the sunset refracted through the crystalline patches mending his mane and the cut across the bridge of his nose, giving him a hint of tiger.

"About breaking the Chiefmaker," he said. "I just reacted. I didn't think."

"Are you kidding? You have terrific instincts. The world

is a better place without that evil bloodstone in it." I patted his paw, but his anxious expression didn't soften.

"What about Beldame Zipporah?"

Dread flipped my stomach's contents. The harpy had given me only two ways to repay my debt: bring her the Chiefmaker or forfeit my life.

"She'll have to extract a different favor from me," I said with false bravery.

Warily, I scanned the sky. The rooftop had always been my chosen getaway when I needed to think, a quiet refuge away from the bustle of the city and the distractions of my apartment. After Quinn and the other gargoyles came to live with us, it became one of my favorite hangouts. Suddenly, however, it felt vulnerable and exposed.

"I think we should go inside," Quinn said.

"Me too. Oh! My seed!" I jumped to my feet, then grabbed Quinn's wing for support when my rubbery legs almost gave out and sent me tumbling down the steep incline. The healers might have treated my injuries, but it would take time, food, and sleep to restore my depleted energy.

"You haven't checked it yet?" Quinn asked.

"I wanted to wait for you."

Quinn grinned. The roof creaked beneath his feet as he stood, and I scooted down the shingles to give him room. Using the railing as a step, I lowered myself to the balcony with greater care than normal, my coordination blunted by fatigue. Quinn waited until I collected my empty plate and stepped inside, out of the way, before he jumped to the balcony and padded through the doorway after me. He stood at the foot of my bed, in the limited clear space available, looking five times larger inside than he had on the roof.

I tossed the crumpled newspaper in the trash bin and strode to my bag. Not for the first time, my thoughts circled around to Grant's seed. It had been triggered by a firebird, and mine resembled a firebird feather. Was that a coincidence, or did our questions overlap? Somehow, I would have to persuade Grant to tell me what he asked the everlasting tree, though I suspected evolving my own seed would prove easier than teasing the information from the recalcitrant captain.

I retrieved the firebird feather from my bag, then lowered the blinds, cloaking my apartment in a deep gloom, with the feather as the only source of light. It shimmered with the radiation of a candle flame, glistening off Quinn's golden body to cast the room in a soft glow.

"Are you ready?" I asked.

Quinn's eyes gleamed with excitement. "Yes."

I hesitated in front of my jewelry box, where I had stored the seed for safekeeping. Anticipation and apprehension bubbled through my bloodstream. This was the moment of truth.

"It will work. It has to," I whispered.

Before I lost my nerve, I plucked the seed from the velvet-lined drawer and set it on the low table in front of Quinn. I placed the feather beside it and jerked my hand back. Having witnessed the dramatic transformations of Quinn's and Grant's seeds, I expected an elemental surge to explode from my seed.

Nothing happened.

I dropped to my knees, a sour rush of bile climbing my throat. Nothing. I had squandered my chance at getting an everlasting tree's answer.

"Is that blue?" Quinn asked. He squinted at the seed, then angled his head in another direction.

I planted my hands on the table and leaned forward. The seed's shape and texture hadn't altered, but the metallic radiance of the firebird feather cast gray and blue shadows in the depths of the seed's folds.

Hope surged through me. I snatched up the seed and held it close for a better examination. The grays and blues vanished, and the seed reverted to an oversize peach pit stamped in brown, copper, and gold with the pattern of a firebird feather's ocellus.

Had we been mistaken?

I nestled the seed next to the glowing feather again. The golden ocellus disappeared and the gray-and-blue pattern reemerged, stronger than before. In unison, Quinn and I leaned closer.

In the feather's rosy glow, the seed appeared to be painted the distinct slate-blue of a storm cloud. Three jagged navy lines slashed across the bottom third of the seed, and pale silvery blue dusted the edges, softening it.

"It still looks like a feather," Quinn said.

"Yes."

"Is that the marking of a thunderbird?"

"Yes." I pressed my hand to my stomach, attempting to soothe the roil of excitement and foreboding souring my half-digested dinner. I had thought firebirds were dangerous and rare, but in comparison to thunderbirds, they seemed like moody parrots. How was I going to get my hands on a thunderbird?

"The other side looks different." Quinn rocked the seed with a claw.

I flipped it over. Airstrong's winged-A logo stared back at me, stamped in navy atop the seed's slate-blue ridges.

I sat back on my heels, stunned.

"I think your parents might be involved in the story of a lifetime," Quinn said.

"I think you might be right," I whispered.

No matter how I twisted the possibilities in my head, I couldn't envision a positive story based around my parents' company that might qualify as the story of a lifetime. Which left only one other option.

"I think my parents are in trouble."

What's next for Kylie and Quinn?

———————————

Turn the page for a sneak peek from
REBECCA CHASTAIN'S
next Terra Haven Chronicles novel.

———————————

HEADLINES & HYDRAS
TERRA HAVEN CHRONICLES BOOK 2

A rapid hammering jerked me awake. I seized a fistful of air element before my bleary vision cleared. *I shouldn't have let my guard down. It's too dangerous—*

The familiar sight of my apartment punctured my panic. I was home. Safe. My escape from Lunacy Labyrinth hadn't been a dream, though the horrors I had witnessed there haunted me in my nightmares.

Breathing deep, I released my magic and fought free of knotted, sweat-damp sheets. Pain flared through my thighs and biceps, and I bit down on a groan. After mending the cuts and scrapes I had received yesterday, the healers had claimed doing more—like soothing away the soreness of strained muscles—would have overtaxed my exhausted body. Allowing those muscles to relax overnight had only invited the stiffness to root deeper.

A fist pounded the balcony door again, hard enough to rattle the whole wall. "Are you awake?" Mika asked, her voice muffled through the door.

"I am now," I grumbled.

Normally I appreciated living on the second floor of a

large Victorian house, renting a room connected to my best friend's by a balcony.

However, my best friend normally didn't wake me at dawn.

Grunting with each step, I hobbled to the door and opened it.

Mika burst into my room, haloed in morning sunshine. I shielded my eyes as I staggered back to my bed, slumping onto the edge. She followed, too fast for my tearing eyes to track. Her long strawberry-blond hair hung loose, still snarled from sleep, and she hadn't bothered to change out of her striped pajamas or put on shoes. Oliver trundled into the room on her heels, his sinuous dragon body casting a red glow across the ceiling as the sun refracted off his glossy carnelian scales. Despite the gargoyle's stubby legs, Oliver's head now cleared my bed, and I hoped he was close to done growing. If he got much bigger, he wouldn't fit in our tiny apartments.

"Is everything all right?" I asked before I spotted a copy of the *Terra Haven Chronicle* clutched in Mika's fist. My heart sank. I scooted back on the bed and drew my feet up in front of me, wishing I could crawl under the covers and avoid this conversation.

"Is this true?" Mika spread the paper open and waved toward the black-and-white print beneath a picture of a fire-bird. "Are you the Airstrong heiress?"

"I . . ." My thoughts scattered when Mika lifted her gaze to mine, the pain of betrayal glistening in unshed tears.

I hadn't wanted Mika to find out about my family like this. I hadn't wanted *anyone* to find out, period. I had chosen to leave behind my parents' world and their upper-crust lifestyle in favor of making my own way. With their blessing, if not their understanding, my parents had freed me from the expectation of assuming responsibility for their international shipping empire and allowed me to pursue my passion as a journalist. Doing so anonymously had been my decision. I had wanted to make sure I succeeded on my own merit, not because someone owed my parents a favor. It had taken years of scraping by before I landed a junior journalist position at the *Terra Haven Chronicle*. Now, just when I was starting to get noticed by the editor in chief, my nemesis, Nathan, had taken it upon himself to out me to the world in his front-page article.

"Your real name isn't even Kylie," Mika said, her voice soft. "It's Harriet, isn't it?"

I flinched. I hated my first name and loathed hearing Mika use it. It had been bad enough to see it printed in the paper. *Grayson daughter Harriet has been operating seemingly independent of her parents' business under the alias Kylie Grayson.* I would never forget the line—nor forgive Nathan for writing it. The article should have focused solely on the recovery of the missing firebirds and the destruction of Lunacy Labyrinth. However, my parents' shipping company, Airstrong, had been the business responsible for the firebirds' transportation. Having the firebirds *discovered in the possession of the Airstrong heiress*—another deplorable quote from the article—had given Nathan the opening he needed to slander me to the world.

Keeping my voice neutral, I said, "Kylie is my preferred name. My full name is Harriet Kylie Grayson."

"You used an alias—"

"Not an *alias*," I said, hating that Mika was quoting Nathan.

The paper crinkled in her fist. "You lied to me about your name."

"I didn't lie—"

"Stop parsing words with me. You lied by omission." Her words landed between us, the vulnerability in her expression cracking and anger seeping out. "You let me believe you were someone you're not. What else have you been lying about?"

"Nothing. I swear." I leaned forward to stand, but she didn't give me enough room. "I wanted to tell you. I just . . ."

"Let me guess. You couldn't find the right time in the last *half decade*." Mika spun away, pacing in the limited space, stepping over Oliver without seeming to notice the gargoyle. Confined by the tight room, she about-faced and bore down on me. I fumbled for the right words to make her understand, but her glare silenced me. Reversing course, she paced away from me again. Oliver hopped onto the love seat and curled his slender tail out of the way, his wide eyes tracking Mika. He reached a paw out to her when she stomped close but withdrew it when she didn't acknowledge him.

Golden light bounced across the walls as Quinn dropped from the roof to fill the doorway, worry etching his feline features. Sunlight slanted across the gargoyle's broad lion shoulders and glinted off his long wings. Quinn's citrine body sported an alarming number of clear quartz patches, testament to all the injuries Mika had healed. Navigating the blood-magic ruins of Lunacy Labyrinth had been harder on Quinn than it had on me, and I resolved not to complain about my own soreness.

Against my will, my gaze dipped to Quinn's everlasting seed. It hung from a cord around his neck, ugly and brown. Thanks to our adventures in Lunacy, it had evolved into its current shape, though maybe *devolved* was more appropriate. The original artistic ebony knot of a snake biting its own tail had transformed into a fist-size mess that resembled a muddy, half-melted, half-exploded pinecone. Staring at it made me woozy. Quinn had used his one question to ask the everlasting tree how he could best help me, which was why I tried not to let on how unnerving I found his seed's new shape. Especially since saving my life had been the catalyst of his seed's evolution, whereas initiating my seed's transformation had nearly killed us both, and its current shape pointed toward even greater danger.

A bundle of elements coasted through the open door, drawing my attention from Quinn's seed. The tight knot of magic curved in the ubiquitous lines of a message sphere, but the magical signature—the texture of structured fire and steady winds underlying the spell—was unmistakably my boss's. Expecting the sphere to settle into my message bowl, I nearly levitated when it dropped to pop in my face. Editor in Chief Dahlia Bearpaw's brusque voice spilled out, as loud as if she were standing in the room with us.

"Ms. Grayson. My office. Now. Don't make me wait."

My stomach flipped. Nothing good could follow that tone.

"Did she know?" Mika asked.

I shook my head.

"So it's not just me." With Quinn filling the balcony doorway, Mika's pacing space had become confined to a few steps, and she stopped to glower at me with her hands on her hips.

"I understand why you're mad," I began.

"Oh really? Please enlighten me, *Harriet*."

My teeth clenched, but I forced them apart. "I should have told you, but honestly . . . it wasn't important."

"It . . . it wasn't important?" she sputtered. Her hands twisted the hem of her shirt, her eyes bright. "Because I'm a commoner and it doesn't matter what I think?"

"That's not it at all," I protested. "Mika, please—"

"What is all this to you?" She swept a hand to indicate the cramped apartment, with its secondhand furniture, faded curtains, overflowing hamper, and claustrophobic bathroom. Or maybe she included the entire low-income neighborhood beyond the curtains in her gesture. "Is this some sort of elitist rite of passage? See how long you can slum it? Now you'll return to your 'peers' and regale them with tales of living among the pitiable poor?"

My explanation withered on my tongue. I shoved to my feet and pointed at Mika. "*This* is the other reason I never said anything! I knew how judgmental you would be."

"I'm the one to blame for your lies? That's rich. Very full spectrum of you. I didn't ask you—"

The house's wards broke, the magic popping against my eardrums as it shattered. Something heavy crashed into the roof, rattling the whole house. I ducked, my hand flinging out to find Mika's.

The rafters creaked and popped. Breath held, I stared at the ceiling, straining to see through solid matter. Mika's fingers clamped a vise around mine. The Victorian's roof had endured extraordinary strain in the last half year from the weight of five growing gargoyles roosting nightly along its ridges, but their movements never made this kind of racket. These steps sounded wider, more scratchy, like a dragon or a—

"Harpy," I whispered, my muscles locking in a wave of terror. The stench of sunbaked feces and carrion oozed into the apartment, confirming my words.

Zipporah had found me.

Quinn whimpered. I jerked my gaze from the ceiling.

"Get inside," I hissed, frantically motioning him forward.

Mika backed up to give Quinn room to squeeze into the

apartment, and I half fell over him in my rush to close the door behind him.

How had Zipporah figured out where I lived? Did she know I didn't have her payment? Was she here to collect anyway? The only item left on the bartering table was my life.

I rubbed sweaty palms down my cotton shorts and glanced around for inspiration—or for an escape. I didn't fool myself into thinking we were safe inside. The bay windows were cloaked by curtains, disguising our movements, but once Zipporah figured out where I was, those panes would be no barrier against her talons.

"What's going on?" Mika whispered.

The answer came from above. "Kylie Grayson, show yourself!"

"Where are Anya, Herbert, and Lydia?" I asked Mika, listing Quinn and Oliver's littermates, who also frequented our rooftop.

"They went to the park before dawn."

"So no one's up there?"

Mika shook her head, and I let out a tight breath.

"Why does a harpy know your name, Kylie? What are you mixed up in?"

I bit my lip, debating if we had time for an explanation. "I made a bad decision and—"

"Little girl, I can smell you inside," Zipporah called. "Come out, or *I'm coming in.*" She screeched the last words loud enough to echo through the neighborhood. If my land-lady hadn't been woken by the house wards breaking, she was awake now—along with everyone else in a three-block radius.

"We can't let her find you," Quinn said.

"I think it's too late for that."

"She hasn't seen you yet." He nosed me toward the apartment's front door, which opened onto the upstairs hallway of the Victorian. In a few steps, I could be downstairs, protected by the bulk of the enormous house instead of one thin layer of rafters and shingles. But as much as I longed to flee, I didn't let him move me.

"Don't make me wait!" Zipporah shouted. "I'm not in a patient mood." Claws raked across the roof, the deafening swipe tearing apart shingles and timber. The pictures on my walls rattled and crashed to the floor. I flinched, eyes darting to the ceiling, expecting to see the harpy's claws puncture the roof. The wood held, but it wouldn't take much additional abuse before Zipporah burst through.

Grabbing Mika's shoulders, I gave her a shake so she would focus on me. "Go. Get downstairs and take Oliver and Quinn with you. Make sure everyone stays inside, even Josephine." I had a horrible vision of our middle-aged landlady rushing up to the roof with a broom and a handful of questionably legal repellent spells, thinking she could chase away a harpy as easily as she did the occasional gang member who thought to cause trouble on our street. Zipporah would flatten her without a second thought.

Mika allowed herself to be pushed a step before she firmed her stance. "What are you going to do? You can't go out there."

I couldn't stay inside either. Zipporah was fully capable of tearing the roof off a house, and even if I was all right with allowing the harpy to destroy my home—my *rented* home—there was nowhere I could hide that she couldn't find me. Running was out of the question, too. She was faster, had an aerial advantage, and could brush aside any spell I cast with depressing ease. But most important, I couldn't allow Zipporah near Mika or the gargoyles. I wouldn't be able to live with myself if they were hurt because of me.

"I'll get Grant," Quinn said.

Zipporah tore into the roof again, ripping a chunk free with an earsplitting screech of shattering boards. A shadow flashed past the drawn curtain; then the lumber hit the cobblestones below with a resounding clap.

"There's no time." I braced myself and eased open the balcony door.

The foul odor of excrement engulfed me, and I wavered. My debt to Zipporah was straightforward: I acquiesced to a favor of her choosing or I died. At the time I made the foolish bargain, my choices had been the same—owe her or die on the spot. I had envisioned all kinds of frightening requests Zipporah might make, but none came close to her horrifying demand that I bring her the Chiefmaker, a deadly, blood-magic artifact last seen inside Lunacy Labyrinth. She had even gone so far as to toss me into the hellacious ruins. Neither of us had expected me to survive. Yet here I was, empty-handed but alive.

How was I going to convince Zipporah not to kill me?

On watery legs, I crept onto the balcony and peered past the roof awning. The harpy filled the sky, her oily wings spread, every glob and crust of filth caking the undersides of her giant bird body intimately visible from this angle. She faced away from me, one clawed foot braced on the roof's peak while the other gouged a hole through the shingles.

I pulled a thick ward of earth and air around myself. The magic came easily, enhanced by Oliver and Quinn. The gargoyles' natural ability to boost the elements in others gave me twice my usual strength, and I added extra layers to my protective ward. It did little to reassure me. Zipporah had proven she could rip through my gargoyle-enhanced wards before, but I couldn't step outside without at least the illusion of protection. I glanced down at my thin cotton pajamas. I might as well be naked for all the protection they would afford, but I didn't dare take the time to change.

Quinn squeezed out onto the balcony behind me, and Oliver and Mika stood inside the threshold. Did they not understand how dangerous Zipporah was?

Stay back, I mouthed. I wouldn't try to stop Quinn—he knew the dangers, and it would take too long to convince him to stay behind—but for once I wished Mika was more of a coward. If she involved herself in this confrontation, she would only get hurt.

Giving Mika one last, stern glare, I vaulted to the balcony railing, then up to the roof above Mika's room. The abrasive shingles bit into my bare feet and scraped my palms. I scrambled for the peak of the roof where my footing would be the most stable, every nerve in my body tensed in anticipation of being skewered. A dog barked several houses over, and I caught glimpses of shocked faces pressed to the windows of the nearby homes as hasty wards flashed into place.

Quinn sprang to the railing, then surged up the roof after me, so close his half-spread wings brushed against my legs. I wanted to order him to fly away for his own safety, but his determined expression stopped me. Instead, I laid a grateful hand atop his shoulders and extended my ward to encompass him.

Mika and Oliver hunkered in the shadows just inside my apartment doorway. Mika mouthed something, but I couldn't read her lips.

Zipporah hopped in a tight circle, shaking the roof as she turned to face me. I bent my knees for balance, hands splayed as if I could hold her at bay by sheer will.

"How disappointing. I thought you might try to run," she said before launching toward me. Torn shingles and ripped boards scattered into the air behind her. Snapping her wings wide, Zipporah closed the distance between us in a single flap, her talons splayed before her. I ducked beneath them, clutching the shingles with my fingertips. Her next flap cupped around me as she back-winged, drowning me in noxious fumes. I struggled to rise, stumbling when she added an elemental enhancement to the buffet of her wings.

Quinn caught me, a sturdy stone wing supporting me until I regained my balance. I glanced over my shoulder. The drop-off to the street two and a half stories below yawned behind Quinn's back foot, one meager misstep away.

Cackling, Zipporah landed, crowding me with her filthy body as she folded her wings loosely against her back. The movement thrust her flaccid human breasts toward me, the skin mottled with sun spots and puckered with permanent gooseflesh above the brown feathers of her abdomen. We were almost matched in height, but she effortlessly loomed.

"Here you are. Alive." Zipporah shoved her face into mine.

I fought against the instinct to retreat. I had nowhere to go. Instead, I squared my shoulders and lifted my chin, attempting to project courage and pretend my knees weren't quivering. Up close, Zipporah's features looked less human than ever. Grime crusted the wrinkles etched in her bald forehead, around her yellow eyes, and down her hollow cheeks. Spindly feathers matted the rounded crown of her leathery head, giving the impression of oily hair, and her nose jutted like a misplaced beak above her lipless mouth.

"Which makes me wonder," she hissed, revealing razor-edged teeth caked with gore, "where is my bloodstone? Where is the Chiefmaker?"

I choked on her exhale, my eyes watering at the olfactory assault.

"I was—" I coughed, struggling for a breath without actually inhaling. "I was unable to find it before the firebirds destroyed the ruins."

That wasn't precisely true, but even if the Chiefmaker hadn't been destroyed, I would never have handed it over to the harpy. The bloodstone had granted the user complete control over anyone with blood running through their veins. I had been helpless against it when it had been used against me, and when I had held it . . . The power the stone had offered would haunt my nightmares for years to come. If someone as immoral as Zipporah had gotten the Chiefmaker in her clutches, she could have wreaked unfathomable devastation.

Zipporah cocked her head left, then right, as if trying to decide if I was telling the truth—or perhaps to decide which piece of me to eat first. "Isn't that unfortunate for you. Or do I have to remind you of the consequence of coming back without my bloodstone?"

Ice crystallized down my spine. "I did my best. In fact"—I summoned the paltry argument I had pieced together last night in anticipation of this confrontation—"I searched as long as I could, until I was forced out when the ruins collapsed. I did everything you instructed."

Zipporah's eyes narrowed, her nostrils flaring and her wings flexing. Quinn's wing dug into my hip as I shrank away from her fury.

Licking my lips, I rushed to get the rest of my words out. "Beldame Zipporah, our deal was that I owed you a favor. You called on that favor when you sent me into

Lunacy Labyrinth. I went; therefore, I am no longer in your debt."

Zipporah's foot shot forward too fast to avoid, her steely talons knocking Quinn aside as if he weighed nothing. The gargoyle tumbled helplessly off the roof. I yelled his name, shoving a brace of air beneath him. It wasn't enough to stop his plummet, but it slowed him. Quinn's wings snapped open, and he flapped heavily to regain altitude. By then, it was too late: Zipporah's claws encased me.

Effortlessly, she crushed my ward. The broken elements snapped back into me. My vision tunneled, pain bowing my body. Zipporah squeezed, grinding my ribs together, robbing me of oxygen. Mika hurled a blade of earth magic at the harpy, but Zipporah shattered it with a negligent slice of wood, then used a punch of air to toss Mika and Oliver deeper into my apartment. A second later, the harpy's magic slammed the door shut and fused it in place.

Zipporah lifted me until I dangled inches above the rooftop. Lungs burning, I clutched her filthy toes, each larger than my thighs, straining to get free. I might as well have tried to straighten an oak's branches with my bare hands.

"Our deal was your life for a debt," Zipporah said. "I see no debt paid, which leaves only your life as payment."

Quinn dove from above, an arrow of golden quartz. Zipporah bludgeoned him with a club of air, and he tumbled into the ruined roof above my apartment.

"Don't hurt him," I wheezed. I would have begged Quinn to stand down if I could have projected my voice that far. Air scraped down my throat in painful rasps, coated in Zipporah's putrescence. Black flecks danced at the edges of my vision. "Give me another chance."

Zipporah tipped me, dangling me higher above the

sloped roof. If she dropped me, I wouldn't have time to catch myself before tumbling to the hard cobblestones far, far below. I stopped struggling and twisted to meet her rapacious gaze. The angle exposed my neck, and her hungry eyes sliced to my visible, pounding pulse.

"Please, one more chance. I won't let you down again," I babbled.

She relaxed her grip. I screamed as I dropped half a foot before she clutched her talons around me again.

"One more chance?" Zipporah unfurled a wing, exposing the bony digits that protruded from the alula like a deformed skeletal hand. Fanning the fingers, she drew a clawed tip through my hair, catching a snarl and cutting through it with a sharp tug. A clump of my pale hair drifted to the rooftop. Dread caused goose bumps to break across my scalp. I trembled helplessly as Zipporah drew the digit down the side of my face, scratching lightly into my jaw, then more heavily down my throat. An involuntary hiss escaped my lips at the white-hot pain that followed in the claw's wake.

"For all I know, you're lying to me about finding the Chiefmaker. I'm not inclined to be lenient."

"I'm not lying to you. I swear the Chiefmaker was destroyed."

"You sound awfully certain for a woman who claims she didn't find the bloodstone." Zipporah's cadaverous fingers squeezed my throat, and I fought not to swallow, afraid I would puncture myself if I did.

"The firebirds," I rasped.

"Yes, the firebirds," Zipporah agreed with a foul sigh that drew bile up the back of my constricted throat.

Sweat trickled down my temple. I wracked my brain for a spell—any spell—that I could use against the harpy.

Quinn and Oliver still boosted my magic, but it was no use. With their help, I might be able to fashion an elemental weapon powerful enough to hurt Zipporah, but I would never be able to complete an attack before she slit my throat.

"Few are stupid enough to disappoint me. No one has lived to do so twice," Zipporah said, stroking her bony claws down my neck again, lighter this time, the scratches chasing shivers down my body. She observed my reaction with unblinking eyes.

In my peripheral vision, Quinn struggled to stand, but Zipporah held him pinned to the mangled roof above my apartment with a sheet of air. She had used the trick on him before, and we both knew he wouldn't be escaping until she let him.

"I can be useful." I hated the words coming out of my mouth as much as I despised my pleading tone, but I had no choice if I wanted to live.

"We'll see about that." Zipporah dropped me.

I plummeted to the roof and slid. The drop-off rushed toward me, and I scrambled for purchase on the steep incline. Fiery pain flared in my hands, knees, and feet, but I managed to claw to a stop with my toes curled into the shingles inches from the edge. Heart pounding, I shoved to my hands and knees, craning my head to look up at Zipporah.

She remained at the peak of the roof, studying me indifferently. Shouts echoed from farther up the street, and Zipporah's head swiveled toward the commotion. Distaste twisted her expression. She hopped to the edge of the roof, shaking the house beneath her. I curled my toes and fingers into the rough shingles, wishing I had a solid handhold.

"I always collect my debts, and yours just got more expensive," she promised. "See you soon, Kylie Grayson."

The gusts of Zipporah's departure rocked me, but it was the full import of her words that caused my arms to collapse. I rolled to my side and stared blindly after the harpy.

One way or another, I had a feeling I wouldn't be free of my debt to her until I was dead.

ABOUT THE AUTHOR

REBECCA CHASTAIN is the *USA Today* bestselling author of the Madison Fox urban fantasy series and the Gargoyle Guardian Chronicles fantasy trilogy, among other works. Inside her novels, you'll find spellbinding adventures packed with supernatural creatures, thrilling action, heart-warming characters (human and otherwise), and more than a little humor. She lives in Northern California with her wonderful husband.

Visit RebeccaChastain.com
for updates, extras, and so much more!

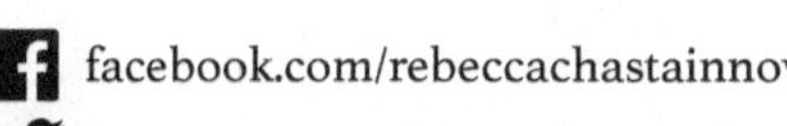
facebook.com/rebeccachastainnovels

twitter.com/Author_Rebecca

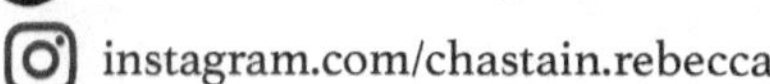
instagram.com/chastain.rebecca